# THE

# INTERPRETER

For Liz,
with best wishes —
Karia Myers
2019.

# THE INTERPRETER

Kazia Myers

Matador
9 Priory Business Park,
Wistow Road, Kibworth Beauchamp,
Leicestershire. LE8 0RX
Tel: 0116 279 2299
Email: books@troubador.co.uk
Web: www.troubador.co.uk/matador
Twitter: @matadorbooks

ISBN 978 1838590 925

British Library Cataloguing in Publication Data.
A catalogue record for this book is available from the British Library.

Printed and bound in Great Britain by 4edge Limited
Typeset in 11pt Adobe Garamond Pro by Troubador Publishing Ltd, Leicester, UK

Matador is an imprint of Troubador Publishing Ltd

*For all of my English and Polish friends*

With my heartfelt thanks and gratitude to

Elizabeth Frost for her constant support and practical help so kindly given throughout the process of creating this book.

Michael Myers and Ola Horbacz for their professional advice on matters that required research.

The Peatling Magna Writers for their patient listening and ever-constructive critique.

# CHAPTER 1

## KRAKOW – May 2005

It may have been minutes, it may have been hours. Time had stopped for Magda. When it was over, he fell away from her, dragged himself off the bed and walked with a sway, his bare feet making sucking noises along the parquet floor. She turned to her side hugging herself, her knees drawn up, her wide-open eyes staring at the wall. Dusky shadows of branches outside her window made ghost-like patterns close to the ceiling. Her brain made no sense of what had just occurred.

With her nerves stretched to breaking point, she picked out the sounds of his staggering movements as he bumped into furniture in their living room. A crash. Then all went deathly quiet. She could picture him sprawled out on the sofa, totally knocked out, as had become a habit of his on drinking nights.

In a flash, her instincts took over. She must save herself. Not a moment to lose. She slid off the bed, dragged the chair and wedged it at an angle against the door. Wood splinters and screws lay scattered on the floor. She must hurry. Frantically, she pulled off her nightdress and wiped herself between the legs. The blood stains sickened her. She stuffed a wad of tissues inside her knickers and pulled them on. She sprayed deodorant all over her body. To kill his smell. She pulled on a T-shirt and wriggled into her jeans. The buttons were stiff, painfully resisting her fingers. Last, the cagoule, and she was ready.

Run. She must run. But first, she must concentrate. She was never going to come back. She must take all her important things.

She pulled open the drawer with her valuable possessions: her passport, her identity and bank cards, her purse, her miniature jewellery box, the oval silver frame with the photograph of her mother. She gathered all the items and dropped them inside her rucksack. Then some underwear and she was ready.

She removed her mobile from the bedside table, switched it off and slipped it inside her pocket. Holding her breath, she loosened the chair from underneath the door handle, and set it aside, careful not to make the slightest scraping noise, then, centimetre by nerve-racking centimetre, she eased the door ajar and listened. All was quiet, apart from the snoring rising from the sofa.

She tiptoed along the edge of the living room towards the entrance hall, picking her feet around the shards of glass littering the floor. She could barely breathe. A sudden break in the rattling in his throat made her heart stop for a terrifying moment. She breathed out and soundlessly slid into the hall. Three long strides to the front door, a twist of her key in the lock and she was out of their flat.

Her quiet, rubber-soled trainers carried her down the stone steps of the communal stairwell to the ground floor. She rushed out of the entrance into the cobbled yard. The freshness of the evening air cooled her hot face. Like a shadow, she ran over the bright rectangles of light thrown from the windows of the upper floors and kept on running through the arched gateway and along the pavement until she reached the tram-stop.

An acute stitch stabbed her groin. She controlled the pain with slow, deep intakes of air.

Best not to draw attention to herself. There were only a few pedestrians about and a fraction of the daytime traffic at this late hour. Two old men stood at the stop, smoking pipes, swaying on their feet and slurring words in their attempted conversation. She stood well away from them and stared into the distance willing the tram to appear.

Did this really happen? A jumble of images. A hammering in her chest. She moved her gaze to the building across the road and began to count feverishly all the windows and doors to take her mind off those horrific thoughts.

Relief swept over her when the tram arrived. Hurriedly she jumped on and keeping her head down, made her way to the back away from everyone. Her armpits were damp and sweat trickled down her back. She caught her reflection in the window as the tram pulled away and was shocked at her appearance. Her long hair, normally held in a tidy plait, was loose and dishevelled. She smoothed down the escaped strands, pushing them behind her ears and peered hard at her ghost-like face, with deep dark shadows for eye-sockets.

The tram's rhythmic sway and the mesmeric gliding by of buildings did nothing to soothe her agitated nerves. The horror of what had just happened assailed her brain with fragments of unbearable clarity. He, breaking down the door, forcing himself on her. She, begging him to stop, crying, appealing to his sense of shame. His hand clamping hard over her mouth, her split lip, the taste of blood. The other pain, far worse. His crushing weight, his beery breath, his sweaty smell. The hair-comb, wedged between her shoulder blades, piercing her skin, piercing…

Magda clasped her hands tight, dug her nails into her skin, stared hard through the window until her eyes stung and watered. Her cut lip throbbed and her shoulders ached with stiffness.

Familiar buildings, streets and crossroads came into view. It would soon be time to alight near the city centre. Where was she to go? Natalia? Not in this state. How would she explain? Even her best friend must never know. Her father? A terrible longing overwhelmed her. If only he did not live so far away. She had texted him earlier, about Aunt Emilia. What would she tell him now? Dominik? Her whole body trembled with anguish at her loss. It was all finished now between Dominik and her. Forever.

In a daze, she stepped off the tram and stood on the pavement. Everything around her was familiar, yet not the same, as if dimmed by the same darkness that had invaded her soul.

She looked down the long Planty Walk, the ground dappled with orange street light filtering through the tree crowns. The walk was deserted except for the last few pedestrians hurrying home. She had nowhere to go. A hotel? Too expensive. Besides, a lonely teenage girl at this hour? Questions could be asked. She could not cope with questions. A youth hostel? Better not. Someone might know her.

The sound of the church bells chiming half past eleven was like a flash of inspiration. She should have thought of it straight away. The nuns!

She hurried down Florianska Street, past the Mariatzki Church and across the Old Square to one of the side streets. The refuge for the homeless run by the Sisters of Mercy was situated in a narrow medieval lane. Her heart thumped when she pressed the bell on the thick oak door. The waiting was torture. But, when the door opened after very long minutes, the nun who greeted her looked kind.

'Prosze Siostry, please, Sister.' Magda steadied her voice, 'I've nowhere to go.'

The nun let her into a dimly lit, sombre-looking hallway, with wood-panelled walls and a stone floor. There was a faint smell of beeswax and frankincense in the air. Strangely soothing.

'What is your name?' the nun asked.

'Magda Zielinska.'

'And how old are you?'

'Eighteen.'

The nun's gaze scrutinised her as Magda licked her swelling lip. Her tone was reassuring.

'A good decision to have come here. You'll be safe with us.'

'Dziekuje. Thank you.' An attack of violent shivering made her grab at the door. The nun slipped her arm underneath Magda's and said, 'Come with me. I'll show you to the dormitory.'

Magda nodded with gratitude, then added urgently, 'I must have a shower first.' The nun gave her another measured look but did not ask any more questions.

Despite her utter exhaustion and the primitive conditions of a communal shower, a square ceramic basin and a yellowed plastic curtain, Magda was infinitely glad of the strong jet of warm water. She soaped herself and scrubbed and rinsed several times, until her skin was raw. The foamy water swirled around her feet and disappeared through the plug hole. All traces of *him* gone.

She stepped out onto the mat and dried herself, weak with relief.

# CHAPTER 2

The gnawing anxiety was persistent. And the shakiness. All those awful images. God, was she to blame in any way? Had she done anything to provoke him? Magda shut her eyes tight and wrung her hands. Her lower lip stung and her tongue pushed automatically against the swelling, hurting it more.

Stay calm. He was not likely to come looking for her, not after what he'd done, yet the tiniest noise or movement in the periphery of her vision made her jumpy. She had imagined him waking up from his stupor, sobering up and suddenly remembering. He'd be paralysed with horror. And then he would have to carry that nightmare with him all day, as he organised his wife's funeral. His side of the family would rally round. There would be questions asked. Bewilderment at her absence. At this very time. Then, perhaps alarm. What would he do?

She shivered and drew her cagoule tight around her, though it was warm in this isolated part of the Public Library, in the Medieval Section. She was so close to the final leap in her escape from him. If only time did not drag so.

She could never have imagined, only yesterday, that her savings, made possible by her father's modest but regular injections of funds into her account, would become so unexpectedly crucial in buying her own safety.

Thinking about her absent father tugged at her heart with gratitude, but more than that with inconsolable regret that they lived so far apart. She had been looking forward to his visit in July. She imagined he'd bring forward his visit now to attend Aunt Emilia's funeral. Only she, Magda, would not be here.

For the hundredth time she ran her hand over her breast pocket to check her coach ticket was safely zipped up. She had been first in at the travel agency, the moment it opened in the morning, and she was ready to leave right now, but there was still the afternoon ahead of her, the long evening and the night at the refuge. At seven tomorrow morning, once she was on that coach, only then she'd be free of the panic. He'd not be able to find her then.

She shuddered and forced herself to think of pleasant things. And good people. Aniela and Bronek in England. As caring as her Aunt Emilia, when she had visited them last summer in Leicester. A longing to see them had overcome her in the middle of her nightmarish night at the refuge, when she could not sleep tormented by her trauma, when every sigh and cry from her distressed colleagues intensified her own pain. By dawn, she had made up her mind.

She had rung them first thing after breakfast. Just a flying visit, she'd said. A student trip? Not exactly. She would explain everything later. She would love to see them. Of course, she'd have to see them. And stay as long as she wanted to. She knew they would say that. Too kind for their own good. There was no time for discussions, but she had already decided to find independent accommodation. She did not wish to be a cuckoo baby in anyone's nest.

But now she needed to concentrate on her task. She had some letters to write. She had bought the writing paper, the envelopes and the stamps, which she spread before her thinking hard for inspiration. It felt relatively safe here, in this enclosed space between the tall dividers, their shelves packed with books. Her desk faced the leaded half-open window which allowed her a glimpse of the view outside.

The sky was clear blue, the trees shimmered in the May sunshine, the birds twittered above the hum of the distant traffic. Everything looked just the same as yesterday. As if nothing had happened. As if her Aunt Emilia was still alive. As if she, Magda, were the same person she had been only yesterday. She was gripped by a grief so strong it was a struggle not to cry out loud. Tears ran down her face. Her Aunt Emilia. Such a beautiful woman. Reduced to skin and bones in her final weeks. Magda had stayed with her at the hospital those last few days, whispering endearments, touching her hollow cheek, stroking her skeletal hand. Was Aunt Emilia aware of any of that? Magda comforted herself with the thought that she had done everything it was possible to do, that she had sent off her dear aunt wrapped in a blanket of love.

He had been there too. Silent and brooding. A stranger. After all the years as her Uncle Zden. She could not bear to think of him now. Not without loathing.

She forced her gaze down onto the writing pad. Dominik. He had been in her thoughts all night in the darkness of the communal dormitory, through the troubled sleep of other women. She had relived every moment of their brief time together the previous afternoon, his warm sympathy, his comforting words, his loving embrace. She'd found several brief text messages from him in the morning. She did not reply to any of them. Dominik. Lost to her forever. What could she say to him, in a few words on a piece of paper? Telling him the truth was unthinkable. Living a lie could never be a basis for their shared future.

The only decent thing to do was to walk away, to give him the chance of finding happiness with someone else. This thought throbbed in her mind, like a feverish pulse bringing on intense headache. She cried silently, dried her eyes and forced herself to write. My dearest Dominik. Her hand would not stop shaking. She put aside the sheet and made a conscious effort to concentrate on the next letter.

This was addressed to her Professor of English at the Faculty of Foreign Languages. She explained with apologies and regret that a serious family situation had necessitated her to go abroad. She would be absent for the rest of the summer term. In her heart she knew she was never coming back.

Next, she checked the text messages from Natalia. There were two: last night's longish one relating to Aunt Emilia, and this morning's brief one:

*Any chance of seeing you?*

Magda yearned with all her heart to tell her best friend everything, but the truth was too terrifying to give it substance with words. Her mind somersaulted back yet again to last night's horror. Bile rose to her throat. She swallowed hard again and again, stilling her shaking body. She was glad there was no one else nearby to watch her behaviour. She wrote,

*My Dearest Natalia,*

*I trust you not to show this letter to anyone. I really mean NOT ANYONE. Uncle Zden is badly affected by Aunt Emilia's death. His behaviour has become intolerable. I must get away. Most probably to my relatives in England. I'll be away for a while, but I'll get in touch as soon as I can. Please be patient with me. Love and hugs, as always.*

*Magda.*

Again, she thought long and hard about Dominik. The truth. Not possible to tell him. Their love was still so fresh and so romantic. He showered her with compliments, amusing her with his ever new-found attributes that she had no idea she possessed. But what he cherished the most, he'd said, was her Catholic upbringing of saving herself for her first love; she'd be wholly, exclusively his.

Not anymore.

Had she been able to tell him, would he believe in her innocence? Would there be doubt in his mind as to her role in bringing this disaster upon herself? She could well imagine the horror and disgust in his eyes.

And the inevitable rejection. He came from a good family, he'd told her enough times. She no longer fitted into that circle.

She started afresh. 'Dear Dominik.'

'My Dearest' would have been like a snake's bite in the circumstances. She made several attempts at the first sentence, but all the painstakingly contrived phrases jumped off the page as distant and cold. And yet, that was how it had to be, if she were to let him go. With sickness in her heart she wrote:

*Dear Dominik,*

*There is no easy way of saying this. Something has happened. I am not well. I'm going away. I'll not come back. I beg you, don't waste time waiting for me. We were not meant to be together. I trust you find happiness with your true love.*

*Magda.*

She was already feeling his heartache. More tears filled her eyes. Where were they coming from? Would they ever stop? Only yesterday she and Dominik had been together, only yesterday. Never could she have imagined then that she was seeing him for the last time.

She tensed all her body to stop herself trembling, clasped her hands tight and shut her eyes. A rustle startled her. For a split second everything died inside her, but then the librarian, in her swishy skirt, passed by Magda's table and looked for spaces on the shelves for the returned books. Magda blew her nose and wiped her face discreetly and stared at the final blank piece of paper, until the librarian walked on.

She did not have to address or sign this final note. He would understand perfectly. She wrote,

*Don't even think of looking for me. If you do, I'll make it public what you did to me!*

As she folded the note and slipped it inside the envelope, she shocked herself with the intensity of her hatred for the man she had loved all her life as her Uncle Zden. She wished he was dead.

# CHAPTER 3

Magda had been allocated a seat at the back of the coach. She scanned the faces of the fellow travellers as they got on and looked for their places. There was no one that she knew and no one appeared to be looking for her. Her neck was stiff with tension. Her lip was sore and felt thick, though the swelling had gone down. She sucked hard on a mint sweet to stop her throat drying. Her mind urged everyone to hurry, so the coach would leave, so her torment would be over.

A middle-aged woman approached the empty seat beside her. She checked her ticket.

'To chyba tu. I think this is mine,' she said to Magda, giving her a greeting nod. She was comfortably plump, her body held in by a white T-shirt, a sky-blue jacket and jeans, all crispy-new, no doubt purchased especially for this journey.

She hauled up her bulging travel bag onto the shelf above, before sitting down with a sigh.

'Nearly didn't make it. My daughter's car wouldn't start. Akurat dzisiaj! Today of all days!'

Magda should say something. Smile. Basic politeness. She couldn't. She nodded, bracing herself against the intolerable slowness of everything around her; stragglers arriving at the last minute, taking ages to settle down, opening their bags, rummaging, putting things back, squeezing their bulky rucksacks into tight spaces above them, struggling, muttering, delaying sitting down. How much longer? Magda's nerves threatened to snap. She sucked harder and harder on the mint sweet. Then, at last, the background music was turned down and the driver began to make his announcements.

She closed her eyes and exhaled deeply at the starting pull of the coach, then its slow sway as it made its way out of the station. She felt weak and limp and suddenly about to release a torrent of tears, held back for so long. She pressed her palm over her mouth.

'Are you not feeling well?' her companion asked with concern.

Magda shook her head and took a moment to reply.

9

'I'm all right, thank you. Just a very late night.'

'Znam to! I know! So much to do, and that before I even started packing!'

The coach was taking the main route north-west out of Krakow. Magda felt as if she were leaving her heart behind. If her eyes had been a camera, she would have taken hundreds of snapshots of her beloved city: the towers, the church spires, the historic buildings, the castle overlooking the river, and further, the leafy suburbs with their pre-war mansions and the sprawling estates with their high-rise blocks. Gradually vast open land came into view, fresh green at this time of the year, the picturesque copses of willows, of the sky-reaching poplars and firs. There was a dream-like feel to everything she viewed and she wondered if she would ever see her beloved country again. Sentiment weighed heavy in her heart, already burdened beyond endurance.

Her companion turned out to be an incessant talker. Strangely, Magda found the woman's chatter a welcome distraction. It cut through her dark thoughts and anxieties. She made an effort to listen and to concentrate on the long-winded account of the woman's family history: names, places, dates, illnesses, fortunes and misfortunes. Her every nod spurred on the woman to more revelations. Around them, against the soft background music, there was just the murmur of other conversations whiling away the journey time.

Magda's weariness at some stage must have overcome her and she must have dozed off, for the next thing she was aware of was someone tapping her shoulder. She opened her eyes and saw her companion's face above hers.

'Our first comfort stop,' the woman informed her.

'Thank you.' Magda straightened her stiff neck slowly, got up from her seat and followed her companion outside.

*

The service station was west of Wroclaw city, some three and a half hours into their journey. The sprawling brick buildings, all new, and their colourful fascias shone vivid in the May sunshine. The forecourt was busy with arriving and departing vehicles. Further, well away from the traffic, there was a picnic area with wooden tables and benches, screened by trees and shrubs. How it all had changed since her childhood, when stops by the roadside were just a small petrol station with a grocery stall.

People were enjoying their refreshments in the open air and it all looked so normal. For the first time since her ordeal, Magda felt safer and inconspicuous in this environment, far away from home.

In the modernised washroom, the waiting queue moved quickly. Magda freshened herself with a splash of water and a spray of deodorant. In the cafeteria, she bought herself a coffee and a ham sandwich, went outside and perched at the end of a bench. He'd never find her now. If only she could shift the weight off her chest. Would it ever go?

Her companion, carrying her take-away breakfast too, appeared in the main entrance, spotted her and came over. They indulged in small talk. Magda nodded and made every effort to keep up with intelligent responses, but harrowing images would not leave her mind.

Magda kept checking her watch nervously, keeping an eye on their allotted half-hour. It dragged, and it was a relief to be back in her seat, the full coach making its way onto the motorway for the next leg of the journey, amidst announcements from the driver's co-pilot.

'We've not introduced ourselves,' the woman remarked and gave her name. Magda hesitated but then she told herself she was safe on this coach among strangers, and her companion was not likely to see her again after they reached their different destinations in England.

'I'm Magda Zielinska.'

'Pleased to meet you.' The woman gave her a friendly nod and in the same breath launched into further descriptions of her family. It was a relief of sorts. She'd most probably not even registered Magda's name.

She informed Magda that she'd been making this trip to England every summer for the last four years. To visit her son. Doing so well, he was, as an electrician. And his wife was a bookkeeper for a haulage firm. They both worked all hours. But now she'd just given birth to their first baby, a boy.

'I'll be staying with them for a while. She wants to go back to work as soon as she can. I know this route with my eyes closed. What about you? Is this your first trip to England? Have you got relatives there?'

Magda was caught unawares by these questions and her first reaction was to hold back. But, as before, when introducing herself, she felt this woman, briefly her travelling companion, posed no threat to her.

'I've relatives in Leicester,' she said. 'I visited them last summer for the first time. This time I'd like to stay longer. Find a job.' This idea had come to her in the long hours she had been waiting for her departure.

Her companion's eyes widened with interest.

'You look so young. Sixteen? What job will you do?'

Magda managed a pale smile. 'I'm eighteen,' she said. 'I'll do any job I can find.'

The woman inclined her head, as if waiting for more information.

'Do you speak English? That's always a help, of course.'

'I hope, I'll manage.' Magda had no wish to go into detailed explanations of how throughout her childhood her father had been sending her books, tapes and videos of the Walt Disney films, how she had learnt all the scripts and dialogues by heart, how she had surprised her teacher of English at school, and later, her university professor with her confident use of this foreign language.

'And your parents?' The woman would not give up. 'They'll miss you, as you will them, no doubt.'

Magda's throat was dry, and her eyes felt gritty. She wished the woman would leave her in peace. But her companion was clearly only trying to be sociable. Magda took a sip of her bottled water, and said, 'I only have a father. He lives in Chicago.'

'In Chicago?' The woman's expression lit up with excitement. 'Forgive me for asking, but why are you here, and not in the States with your father? I'd be over like a shot, if only I had half the chance!'

Despite her wretched state, Magda was amused by her companion's childlike enthusiasm.

'I had my chance,' she said. 'And, even now, I could have it again. But I missed Krakow too much. And my aunt and my friends.'

'You missed Krakow? When you could have lived in Chicago?' The woman's eyes were round with incredulity.

Magda remembered vividly how much she had missed her dear Aunt Emilia. It was like an illness. She had missed her friends too, especially Natalia. Aunt Emilia had been for her the mother that she had lost as a small child, and for her father the sister-in-law, who had given him the much-needed support in his decision to stay on in Chicago until he had secured a good job.

Five years had been a long time in a small child's life to have been separated from her father, so when she went to visit him for the first time when she was nine it was like visiting a stranger and his family. Everything felt alien and overwhelming in this huge city. Her father and his wife were excessively kind to her and she loved her sweet little half-siblings, but she missed home. Her father compromised by visiting her every other summer in Krakow and having her over in Chicago the summers in between.

'So, what's changed your mind now? About leaving home and going abroad to work,' her companion asked.

What changed? If she could laugh, her laughter would have been hysterical. The poor woman would have been frightened out of her wits. Magda replied wearily, 'Transferring to England is different. It's so close. Two hours' flight and I'm home.' This was not going to happen, no matter how homesick she was.

The woman was quiet, as if pondering Magda's words.

'Yes, I suppose this is different,' she conceded. 'Who would have thought it ten years ago? That Europe would shrink like this? And that we, Poles, would travel so freely?'

Magda listened, forgetting her grief for a moment. Unlimited travel. What a blessing that was, and what luck in her present situation.

After a while her companion spoke again.

'And your relatives in England... when did they emigrate?'

At least this was not difficult to talk about and it was a distraction.

'They didn't emigrate. They were refugees after the war, and they stayed.'

'Yes...' the woman sighed, 'so many of them. All over the world. Most families were split up at that dreadful time.' She paused, her forehead furrowed in thought. 'So, did your father decide to stay in Chicago for good?'

Magda offered her companion a mint sweet and took one herself. She was weary and would have been glad not to talk at all. But the alternative was worse. Dark thoughts and tormenting images. She rolled the sweet inside her mouth, took a deep breath and said, 'My parents were born in Poland. They and their parents were the ones from our whole family who didn't get deported either to Russia or to Germany. We had always lived near Krakow. It was Grandma Aniela, my own grandma's sister, who as a small child was taken to Siberia. She just happened to be staying with some relatives at the time and was taken together with them. She survived and ended up in England after the war. She married one of her friends from those days. It's them I'm going to visit now in Leicester.'

The woman nodded.

'It's a blessing to have a family. My family are everything to me. No doubt your relatives will give you a big welcome.'

Magda remembered their kindness last summer. They had said, 'Visit us again. And don't leave it too long.' They did not expect at the time, nor did she, a repeat visit so soon.

She checked her watch. Tomorrow at midday, she'd be with them. The very thought gave her an immense feeling of comfort. To be in a safe place and never to be afraid again. Could that be possible? Could it be possible to erase completely a section of one's past?

She closed her eyes and forced herself to think of Bronek and Aniela's house. It was one in a row of a long terrace, with the front door from the street and the back door looking out onto a long strip of garden, that ended with a tall brick wall and a solid wooden gate, to screen the house from the communal path. She'd be totally protected there from all sides, even if, a preposterous idea, Zden came looking for her.

She'd have to tell them about his drinking problem, but nothing else. Already she was feeling bad about having to deceive them, by leaving out the real reason for her escape from him, but she could not imagine ever disclosing to anyone the horror and the degradation of what he had done to her.

'I feel drowsy too,' she heard her companion say.

Magda did not reply, feigning sleep. Childhood memories filtered through into her mind. Her Uncle Zden had been such a big presence all through her young years. She had loved him. What had brought on this unspeakable behaviour of his? With bewilderment she looked back at the good times they had shared, the holidays in the country, the boating and the swimming on the lakes, the picnics, the coaching sessions with his athletics team, his dreams for her to be a future Olympic star.

It all now seemed like someone else's life. How had it all gone so badly wrong? First Aunt Emilia's illness, then his addiction to drink, then... how could he do that? How could he? With this one most despicable act he had wiped out everything that had been good between them. It had changed everything; her, her present, her future. It had left her imperfect, like someone surviving a horrific accident.

A feeling of irretrievable loss pressed down on her chest. And a deep need for revenge. Would she be able to find peace anywhere, while he was still around? If God was truly just, then He should sort him out.

# CHAPTER 4

Magda was sick with apprehension as she pressed the doorbell. She licked her dry lips, the prickly scab feeling enormous. Bronek Sokolski, her adopted Djadjo, her Grandpa, opened the door. The very sight of him, so unchanged and reassuring, the ruffled hair, the baggy sweater dotted with bits of grass, his relaxed inviting manner, the look of wonder and disbelief playing joyfully on his face, made her heart flip with relief.

'Marta! My dear Marta! Your phone call was such a surprise! And here you are!' He embraced her and held her tight. She melted into his arms, feeling safe in his warm welcome. He smelled of Old Spice and freshly cut grass. He released her and stepped back, looking at her with incredulous wonder, his gaze stopping on the rucksack at her feet.

'Is that all you've got? How did you get here? You should have phoned. I'd have fetched you from the station.'

'No need, Grandpa. I shared a taxi with some people. The coach dropped us off at Leicester Forest East,' she explained with forced breeziness. 'Just a little reminder,' she smiled. Grandpa made it easy to smile. 'I'm Magda, remember? Not Marta. That was my Mum's name.'

He responded with a carefree grin.

'Marta… Magda… you are all the same beautiful girls to me.'

Babcha's, Grandma Aniela's voice called from the kitchen, amidst the sounds of clunking cutlery and plates. 'Is she here, Bronek?'

'Come and see!' he called back, his face lively with anticipation of her pleasure.

Magda picked up her rucksack and followed him down the hall, the walls of the palest green picking up the carpet colour and exhibiting family photographs and Bronek's watercolours of landscapes. It felt like home, just as she remembered it.

Aniela came out of the kitchen, small of stature but prettily plump, her arms extended, her beaming smile welcoming.

'My dear child! So good to see you!' She enveloped Magda in scents of baking, and rose water and fresh shampoo, as her grey curls brushed Magda's cheek. 'Why didn't you let us know earlier of your plans to visit us?'

Magda's oversensitive state picked up the tiniest hint of a rebuke, and all her resolve to appear normal dissolved in an instant as she was convulsed by grief.

'I knew it!' Aniela exclaimed. 'I've had a feeling all along that something must have happened. Magda, come, sit down with us and tell us about it. Lunch can wait for a minute.'

Magda excused herself to visit the bathroom, and after washing her hands and splashing her face she suppressed the urge to cry and joined Aniela and Bronek in the front room, which looked out onto the street. The room was just as she remembered it, proudly kept shining clean with pale green velour armchairs and curtains, and embroidered white runners protecting the dark wood furniture.

She sat down next to Aniela on the settee, with Bronek facing them. He nodded towards the coffee in a dainty china cup that stood steaming on the low oval table.

'Drink this Marta… Magda,' he corrected himself. 'This will do you good.'

Sunshine was streaming through the lace curtain, yet Magda felt a chill. She was dreading their reaction, once she told them the truth. The edited version.

The cup rattled on the saucer in Magda's shaking hand. She took a sip. The coffee was laced with brandy and stung her lip. She forced a weak smile.

'This is good. Thank you.'

'It looks as if you need it, Magda,' Aniela said encouragingly.

Magda put down the coffee in slow motion, delaying the moment she would have to tell them. She took a deep breath.

'Aunt Emilia died four days ago.'

They both sat very still for a very long while, their wide-eyed look an eloquent expression of the turmoil going on in their minds. Aniela spoke first.

'B-but… I don't understand… When is the funeral? Why are you here?'

Magda cleared her throat.

'The funeral hadn't been arranged yet when I left.' She could see their expressions change from sympathy to puzzlement. She rushed on defensively. 'Please, believe me, I'd do anything to be there, to say farewell properly. I loved her. I loved her like my own mother. But it just became impossible…' her voice threatened to break. She took a quick sip of coffee. 'It really became impossible for me to stay any longer.'

Bronek shifted in his chair and rubbed is forehead. Magda felt acutely his bewilderment. Aniela leaned forward, her face and a lock of

16

hair catching a patch of light. Her eyes squinted with a sharp, unnerving look.

'What happened, Magda, that was so dreadful that you couldn't stay?'

Magda shuddered. 'I wish I didn't have to talk about it. It's about Uncle Zden.'

'What?' they both asked.

She could not put it off any longer. She said, 'He began to scare me. It got so bad that I had to get away.'

'What are you saying, Magda?' Aniela's eyes were round with alarm.

'He couldn't cope with Aunt Emilia's illness. When she was admitted to hospital and began to waste away, he became a different person. He would come home drunk most nights. Sometimes he would shout at me and say it was all my fault. I can't tell you how awful that was. I loved her. I loved him too before…' she shrugged helplessly, 'before he changed.'

Bronek shook his head in disbelief. Magda took another quick sip and continued, 'He said that Aunt Emilia should never have been burdened with looking after me. He said it had been additional stress for her and no doubt had added to her getting ill…'

'That's nonsense!' Bronek exclaimed. 'It had been entirely Emilia's decision. She must have been very happy to have you, Magda. I can only imagine the joy you must have brought into her life.' Bronek's words were like a warm embrace.

Aniela's expression softened.

'Oh, Magda, you poor child! Nothing that's happened has ever been your fault. You were only a small child then.' She moved closer to Magda and hugged her. 'Zden didn't hurt you, did he? In any way?'

For a split-second time stood still. Magda lowered her eyes when she replied, 'He frightened me lots of times. I began to avoid him. Not easy in a flat. I began to lock myself in my room, before he'd get home.'

She felt like a traitor having to say those things about him. She cringed at her deception of these two good people by telling them only half the truth. It was all his doing! But would they believe her? Was she in any way to blame? She felt hot and sticky and longed for a shower. A momentary shadow fell across the room of a lorry passing by in the street.

Bronek sighed and remarked, 'It is always so unpredictable how people will react to a death in the family. I'm just so sorry for you, Magda, that you've had to put up with Zden's awful behaviour, when it should have been him giving you support!'

There was a silence while they pondered their own thoughts, then Aniela said, 'Tell us about Emilia. It must have been really bad at the end.'

It was all so vivid, so intense in Magda's mind, so raw and painful. The worst day of her whole life. She nodded.

'It was horrible. You're on tenterhooks all the while. Waiting. Just waiting. You can't do anything else. It really wears you down.' She paused, overcome with the memory. 'Aunt Emilia was just skin and bones in the end. You'd hardly recognise her. They gave her morphine. Most of the time she was in and out of consciousness. But I believe she knew we were there.' He, restless and brooding, looking angry, and frightening Magda with his ominous silence. She did not tell them that. She continued, 'Auntie's hand went limp in mine when... I just knew the precise moment... Uncle Zden touched her face. There was no response, nothing. He did not say anything, just went to fetch the nurse. She did all the checks, said we could stay as long as we needed to. Said to wait for the doctor's official examination and for the death certificate.'

Magda's voice faltered and tears spilled down her cheeks. Bronek leaned forward to comfort her but she assured him, 'I'll be all right in a moment, Grandpa. This comes and goes...' She wiped away her tears. 'Uncle Zden broke down. It was dreadful to watch.' The image of him bent down was frighteningly clear in her mind, his face hidden in his hands, a chilling sound escaping his chest. 'When he composed himself, he said he had to go. He could not stand it any longer.'

'And he left you? Just like that? Where did he go?' Aniela did not hide her dismay.

'He said he'd go to his brother's. I stayed on at the hospital, saw the doctor, got the death certificate and then I went into town to meet my two best friends.' Magda spread her hands palms up. 'What do you do after such a blow? I was dizzy with the shock of it all. I had no idea what to do next. Seeing my friends helped, but I had to be home before Uncle Zden came back. I waited all evening. It got very late and there was still no sign of him.'

Magda told them briefly of her phone call to his brother's house, omitting the details that had made her cry. Aunt Lalka had picked up the receiver and in her usual manner could not refrain from snide remarks, even on this occasion. This was nothing new. The resentment had always been there in her perception of Zden's preferential treatment of Magda, the 'cuckoo baby', when he should have given all his attention and financial support to his own brother's children. Yes, Zden was with them, Lalka had told her, his true family where he belonged. She had

18

rung off, leaving Magda even more uncertain and anxious about his return home.

'It was scary waiting for him,' she continued. 'When he was that late, it usually meant only one thing. He'd come home drunk and very angry. I bolted myself in my room. I had started doing that recently. I know... it's awful. I heard him come in about ten. I heard him staggering about and his swearing getting louder. Then I heard him smashing plates and glass against the walls. Someone shouted through our front door. They'd be calling the police if he did not settle down. Amazingly, all went quiet after that. I waited for ages and listened through the keyhole. When I heard him snoring, I took that chance to run away. I gathered whatever I could, as fast as I could, and I left.'

Aniela and Bronek looked stunned. What would they say had she told them the whole truth? With a shaking hand she picked up the cup and drank the brandied coffee. The scab on her lip pulled painfully.

Aniela recovered first.

'My dear Magda, I'm horrified! It's utterly disgraceful how Zden has behaved. Bereavements happen all the time, but that's no licence for people to go berserk. You did the right thing coming to us.'

Bronek's hands were clenched and his eyes dark with anger.

'He needs some sense knocking into him!'

Strangely, his words heartened her. Aniela hugged her again.

'You poor child. Where did you go after that?'

Magda returned the hug. It felt so good and safe.

'I stayed with the Sisters of Mercy two nights. I did think about my Dad.' She paused, shaking her head. 'But I'd rather he didn't know. Not just yet, not till I've sorted myself out. The only safe place I could think of was here with you. I was so happy here last summer.'

Bronek's eyes shone. 'That was an excellent decision,' he said, and cleared his throat.

Magda could not think of words adequate enough to express her gratitude. She said reassuringly, 'It will only be for a few nights, until I find a job and accommodation.'

'What?' they both exclaimed. Aniela's head jerked back as if she had been slapped. 'What are you talking about?' she scolded Magda. 'Accommodation? Elsewhere? In some overcrowded hostel? When we've got a perfectly good room upstairs? You're family, Magda! I'd be ashamed to let you rough it, as if you weren't ours!'

Aniela's exaggeration amused Magda, despite her low spirit. She managed a smile.

'Thank you, Babcha. I'll never be able to thank you enough. But believe me, I'll manage as soon as I get a job. Any job. I'll be happy to do anything, so I can get on with my life.'

'That may well be.' Aniela sounded mollified. 'But for now you'll stay with us, until I'm satisfied that you're ready to start on your own. I've decided. No more arguments. Now, there's just one more thing. I know it's hard for you, but we must let Zden know that you're here, safe with us. He must be out of his mind with worry.'

Aniela's reasonable suggestion plunged Magda into terror. She did not want to speak to him or hear his voice ever. She shook her head with pleading eyes.

'Magda, you must,' Aniela spoke softly. 'What will his family think? You disappearing like that? As if you didn't care? For all you know, the police may already be looking for you.'

That thought had crossed Magda's mind, but she had been certain that he'd not involve the police in searching for her. Even more so after receiving her letter. Now, when she felt safe at long last, she did not want even his voice to break through into her place of refuge.

'Please, don't make me,' she begged.

'Aniela!' Bronek stepped in, 'Can't it wait till after lunch? You can see how upsetting this is for Magda.' He turned to her. 'And you must be starving!'

She was not starving; she felt no hunger at all, just her stomach clenching with unbearable anxiety. But Aniela tried to reason. 'Magda, I don't like leaving things… Listen, how about if I ring him? You don't have to say anything. I'll do the talking.'

Magda was helpless. There was nothing she could do to stop Aniela. She wrung her hands as she watched Aniela get up, pick up the receiver off the little table in the corner and look expectantly at her for his number. Her choked throat made it hard to speak. Watching Aniela press each number in turn was like waiting for a bomb to explode. Bronek leaned forward and patted her hand.

'Magda, don't worry. You've got us.'

She nodded vaguely, all her attention focussed on the receiver in Aniela's hand. The volume was on loud so they could all listen together. Magda glanced at the clock on the mantelpiece. It was about two-ish in Poland, an hour ahead of the British time. She prayed he'd be out. A man's voice came through. Not his. Magda slumped with relief.

'Slucham. Dopski speaking. Zden's brother.'

'Dziendobry. Aniela Sokolska. Emilia's aunt from Leicester.' Aniela launched straight into her speech. 'We've just heard the sad news. We are shocked. And very upset. Such a terrible illness. Poor Emilia! So much suffering and dying so young!' Aniela paused briefly to catch her breath. 'We just want you to know that Magda is with us. Safe and sound. We didn't want her uncle to worry. He's got enough to worry about. Such a dreadful time for him!'

A long silence followed. Magda wondered if he was still there or, God forbid, fetching Zden to the phone. Then his voice came through.

'Yes, he is taking it very badly. Very worrying. But good news about Magda. I'll tell him straight away. He's been out of his mind with worry. How is she?'

Aniela glanced at her, but Magda shook her head. She had no wish to speak to anyone close to Uncle Zden. Aniela continued, 'Magda is badly shaken by everything that's happened. On top of having to deal with Emilia's illness, she's had to put up with Zden's truly bad behaviour. No doubt, you know what I'm referring to.' Dear God, Magda's toes curled. If only they knew! Aniela continued, 'What Magda needs now is a good rest. She needs support. She's a young girl. It's like losing both her parents all over again. For the time being she'll be staying with us. And later... once she's recovered enough, she'll decide herself about her future.'

Magda was half-expecting Dopski to ring off, but his voice came through, surprisingly meek.

'I've seen a lot of my brother these past few days. I had no idea how bad his addiction had become. Frankly I'm not surprised that Magda ran away. It must have been hell for her.'

No one would ever know the extent of that hell, Magda reflected. At the same time a weight fell off her chest, at this welcome misunderstanding of the reason for her escape. Now the true reason need never be revealed.

Aniela said, 'She could not keep something like that from us. Especially that her visit came as a total surprise. Of course, we wanted to know everything that had happened.'

Dopski's voice came back, 'Tell Magda not to worry. I've already been to the doctor's with Zden. He gave him some mild sedatives. He's also booked him onto a rehabilitation course after the funeral. Zden has been very worried about Magda. He's been imagining all kinds of terrible things. The worst that she'd harmed herself. And the police knocking on the door... with bad news...'

Of course, he'd be worrying. About himself. About the consequences of his evil act. Magda could well imagine his incessant torture in the last few days, in addition to grieving for Emilia, in addition to organising her funeral. She felt no pity for him, but neither any satisfaction at his well-deserved inner hell. She felt totally exhausted. She caught Dopski's last few words, 'Emilia's funeral will be on Monday. Such a pity Magda won't be here...' He knew how to twist a knife inside her.

Magda hid her face in her hands and cried. She heard Aniela replacing the receiver and sensed her sitting down beside her. Her plump and comfortable arm rested on Magda's shoulders.

'My dear child, we'll pray for Emilia here on Monday. We'll ask our priest to say Mass for her. We'll be with her in spirit.' Such simple words yet such a lift to Magda's weary heart. She returned Aniela's hug. 'That makes me feel better already.'

Bronek got up and gently brushed Magda's cheek with the back of his hand. It was warm and comforting.

'It'll get better. Believe me, Marta. Give it time. But now, you must have something to eat.' He waited for them to get up, then followed them through to the kitchen.

'Bronek, it's Magda. Not Marta. Try to remember that,' Aniela reminded him.

Magda felt no hunger, yet the sight of the food on the kitchen table, the sliced ham and the cheese board, the fresh green salad with sliced tomatoes and cucumber, the grated carrot in mayonnaise, the diced sweet beetroot, but above all the heavenly smelling fresh bread, made her change her mind.

'This is a feast! Thank you, Babcha!' she said simply.

They sat down at the pine table with pine units surrounding them and the whole kitchen ambient with warmth and welcome. Bronek offered wine. Magda smiled and shook her head.

'Water is best. I must keep my mind clear.' She made an attempt at a lighter tone.

They enjoyed their food in silence for a while, Magda relishing the good, fresh taste after days on the run with irregular snacks, when Aniela stated decisively, 'I've been thinking. And please hear me out, Magda. You've been through a rough time lately. What you need is a good rest. You won't be good to anyone, Magda, least of all to yourself, if you don't allow yourself to recover. I don't mean recover from grief. That never leaves you completely. But you must get strong physically. A strong body helps mental strength. Don't you agree?' Aniela's blue eyes looked so fiercely into hers, Magda had to agree.

'I'm of the same mind,' Bronek added without hesitation, buttering his bread.

'So...' Aniela paused to chew and swallow, 'I suggest that you don't rush with getting a job straight away...'

'But, Babcha!' The anxiety was back in a flash. How could she explain that she'd go mad if she had nothing to do? That her unspeakable nightmares would take over her life, if she was left with nothing to fight them. She put down her knife and fork. 'Babcha, I need to be independent. That is really very important to me. Please. I can't be a burden to you.'

'We know that, Magda,' Aniela said gently, 'and we'll go along with your wishes. But what's the hurry? A week or two won't make any difference, except that you'll have a rest first. Treat it as a holiday... all right?'

'We'll go out some days.' Bronek got animated. 'There are so many nice places to see...'

Magda's eyes filled up. Yet again. Would the tears never stop?

'Babcha, Grandpa.' She steadied her voice. 'Thank you for your kind words. But I've just escaped a situation where I was perceived as the cuckoo baby in someone else's nest...'

'What do you mean?' Bronek's brow puckered.

It hurt her talking about it.

'Zden's family never liked me. Especially Aunt Lalka. She blamed me for taking his attention and his financial support away from their children. If it hadn't been for me, Zden and Emilia would have remained childless, and his brother and the family would have had the benefit of that.'

'But that's preposterous!' Aniela protested. 'Emilia was your very own blood family. It was on her insistence that you were made to stay with them. You were only a small child then. You had no say in any of it. And Zden never objected, as I recall.'

Magda nodded. It had been her Aunt Emilia's choice and decision. She had never stopped telling Magda how much she loved her and what it had meant to her to have a child of her own, even if only by proxy.

'She couldn't have been kinder to me. As I imagined my own mother would have been,' she said, swallowing hard. 'However, this is different. I'm grown up. I can look after myself. I'd never wish to cause anyone any trouble with my presence here.'

'Whatever do you mean? What bother?' Bronek stopped eating and looked perplexed.

'Grandpa.' Magda took a sip of water. Goodness, tears were threatening again. 'You have a family of your own. What would they say?'

They both looked at her with surprise and then they both smiled. Fascinating how their minds appeared to communicate and how they reacted simultaneously.

'My dear Magda,' Aniela said, 'I assure you, our Beata and Janusz lead such busy lives they have no time for pettiness. Their only concern is that we're well and happy. And so far, thank God, we're able to look after ourselves quite independently. We're still capable of making our own decisions. You'll see for yourself when they come to visit.'

Janusz and Beata lived abroad. They had both studied medicine, qualified and moved around frequently for advancement. Janusz was now a pulmonary consultant, living in Dublin with his lovely wife, Angela, a museum curator, and their two grown-up daughters. Beata was married to Captain Sebastian Jones, an orthopaedic surgeon in the army, and she herself practised as an army GP where they were stationed in Germany. They had two sons, primed from their earliest years for army life by their ambitious father.

Magda knew that neither Janusz's nor Beata's future was depending on the legacy left by their parents. Nevertheless, she did not want to be perceived by them as someone taking advantage of two elderly people.

'Babcha,' she said, 'I need to work. For my own peace of mind. That's really important to me. To feel independent. To stand on my own two feet.'

Aniela nodded in understanding.

'All right, Magda. We shall not argue over this. I think it's good that you think this way. But can I persuade you to do one thing? Take a rest from everything for a week or two. Be our guest. It will give you time to think about your future. To look around for a job. You mention accommodation. That's really not necessary.' And, before Magda could interrupt, Aniela carried on, 'Hear me out. What about your studies? You cannot abandon something so important. It all needs careful consideration, don't you agree?'

Of course, it all made sense and Magda agreed and was overwhelmed with gratitude and grief at the same time, for not being able to be totally honest with these two very kind people.

'I cannot thank you enough,' she said. One day, she promised herself, she'd do everything to repay their kindness somehow.

'Magda, my dear,' Aniela spoke gently, 'may I suggest that you finish your meal, take a rest, sleep, do whatever you need to do, and afterwards, when you've recovered a little, we can talk again.'

# CHAPTER 5

Magda woke up drenched in sweat, her heart hammering, as the nightmare of being chased by a faceless assailant faded into the darkness of her room. It was still night time, though it felt as if she had slept for hours. Her fingers searched for the bedside lamp and switch. When the light came on the clock showed one-twenty.

She should have listened to Aniela and taken the sleeping pills. They were still there on the locker, where Aniela had left them encouragingly, together with a glass of water. Magda hated taking pills. They nearly always stuck in her throat.

She pulled herself up, shaking and clammy, placed the pills on her tongue and thirstily emptied the glass. The cool trajectory of the water down to her stomach was strangely comforting. She slid back into her sleeping position and switched off the light. Would this be her life now, nightmares by night and tormenting anxieties by day? But this was only the fourth night since... too soon to hope for the miracle of a normal existence.

She screwed her eyes tight and willed the sleeping pills to work.

When Magda woke up, daylight was gilding the edges of the closed curtains and throwing a soft glow on the surrounding wall. Magda looked at the clock and was horrified to see it was noon. One o'clock in Poland! She had never slept that long! She sat up abruptly but a dizzy sensation made her slide back against the pillow. There was no need to panic. Aniela had wanted her to sleep. She would have woken her up by now, had it been necessary.

She took deliberate slow and deep breaths, but the heaviness on her chest would not shift. And suddenly, like a tornado, the nightmare tore into her mind: him looming over her, pushing her down, suffocating her with his weight, hurting her, again and again, her begging him and begging him to stop... Magda squeezed her eyes tight until there was nothing, only black space. After a while pin-points of light appeared and morphed into the faces of her most loved ones: Aunt Emilia, Dominik, Natalia. Tears filled her eyes.

Dominik would have received her letter by now. She felt his pain, his bewilderment, his deep sense of rejection. And she could do nothing to make him feel better. She'd never have the chance to explain.

It was easier with Natalia. She'd write to her soon, she promised herself.

Her dear Aunt Emilia. Such closeness, so many years spent together. Yet she could not be there for the final farewell. Another stream of tears.

She dried her eyes, uncurled herself and let her gaze wander around the ceiling. She must stop tormenting herself; she must look into the future. Think of this as a new beginning. Perhaps even change her name? Become another person. Would that change her luck? Would that make her let go of Dominik? Would it cure her of this unbearable yearning for him?

She drew the covers around her, this small action giving her a momentary sense of security. This had been her room the previous summer. It was spacious, with a high ceiling and a mullioned bay window looking out onto the street. She had been surprised by its old-fashioned look the first time she had slept here. All her family's friends in Poland, those who could afford to improve their houses or flats, had prided themselves in acquiring all the latest designs in furniture, kitchens and bathrooms. It was exhilarating to walk into shops and be spoilt for choice after nearly fifty years of general shortages, unrelentingly chronic under Soviet communism.

Here, in England, Bronek and Aniela had the choice and the means to change whatever they wished, yet they showed no desire for ostentatious living. This room was fresh-looking in white and palest greys, with a matching soft carpet, but all the furniture was dark wood, bought one item at a time, from a second-hand shop, when money was in short supply.

'When you've lost everything, my dear,' Bronek had explained, 'you appreciate all the more everything that you've got. This was our first furnished bedroom. It was my very own hard-earned money that made it possible. I'm rather attached to this furniture. Every piece is like an old friend.' Magda felt that too. She liked the old-fashioned quaintness of the bed with its solid wood head and foot rests, the double-door wardrobe, the dressing table with its age-spotted mirror, the lockers with their cleverly hidden drawers, and on them the smoked glass bedside lights, shaped like flames.

Aniela's soft singing floated upstairs together with muffled noises of kitchen work. Magda sat up and slid off the bed, forcing her mind to switch to the necessary practicalities of the next few days. She showered, washed and dried her hair and coaxed it into a tidy topknot. She dressed in the only remaining fresh clothes in her possession. New clothes were a priority. She thought of her father with a rush of emotion. Without his financial support over the years none of this would have been possible.

The next most important mission of the day was to go to the employment agency and register. She had every intention to start work straight away.

*

'What's the hurry?' Aniela asked, when Magda shared her thoughts with her downstairs in the kitchen. Aniela stopped icing the cake she'd just baked and gave Magda an appraising long look. 'You look very pale, and so thin! You need time to recover. And a month of hot dinners and heaped plates. That will put colour in your cheeks and flesh on your bones! And besides, it's Saturday. You won't find any offices open today. Next week will be early enough to start making enquiries.' Her tone softened. 'Stop worrying, Magda. Everything will get sorted, I promise. As for Zden, don't think about him. He's got his family and you've got us.'

Just hearing his name sent a current of fear through her.

Aniela got on with icing the cake, and Magda wished she could follow her instructions. If only she could shake off the horror of what had been done to her. If only she could wipe out that terrible night from her life and carry on as the person she had been the day before. Her loss was irreparable, but she could attempt to lessen her grief and pain by plunging all her energies into a job, the more demanding the better. She'd talk to Aniela again, later.

Aniela's vigour amazed her. She was sixty-eight, constantly mobile, attractively feminine with her smooth complexion, clear blue eyes, a pleasant roundness to her shape and still in possession of all her teeth. She put that down to the chronic lack of sugar in the meagre diet of her childhood years. Hard to imagine, she would remark with bitter humour, that anything good could have come out of her Siberian experience.

These days, despite her youthful appearance, she suffered the usual aches and pains linked to the inevitable approach of old age. Worst of all were the sporadic attacks of sciatica. Hence the sleeping pills, to ensure a few hours' respite from the pain. At the moment, she appeared to be enjoying a good spell of health.

Presently, Magda made herself useful with setting the table for lunch, while Aniela tidied up all her baking things. Magda felt at home in this warm, pine-furnished kitchen amidst the aromas of baking, which evoked memories of her once-carefree childhood. Two more cakes were cooling on the worktop, an apple and a cheese cake.

'Our friends are coming tonight,' Aniela said. 'You know them, the Barskis and the Demskis.' Magda remembered their coffee evenings from her previous visit. Aniela continued, 'Will you join us? They'll be pleased to see you. You don't have to say much, if you don't feel up to it. They all love to talk,' Aniela chuckled, 'as you well know. And they can be so funny. It may do you good and even take your mind off other things.' Aniela was so intuitive. Magda loved her.

'Of course, I'll join you, Babcha, and talk to them and help you make coffee.' Then she hesitated. 'They may ask about my visit. What should I say?'

Aniela looked up from the open fridge, from which she was taking out ham and cheese. She brought them to the table.

'They are our best friends, Magda. Like family. I'll tell them the truth.'

Magda's stomach contracted, but Aniela's words assured her, 'You don't have to say anything. I'll tell them simply about Zden's problem. They'll understand.'

Magda nodded. She trusted Aniela. The Barskis and the Demskis were her grandparents' closest friends. Magda knew this from the tales of their shared war-time experiences: their deportation to Russia, their long treks across Kazakhstan and Uzbekistan, their longed-for freedom in Persia, their waiting years for the war to end, while the men fought in Italy.

'Thank you, Babcha. I just don't want to be an embarrassment to you.'

Aniela gave her a hug.

'You could never be that!'

She took out more things from the fridge, while Magda finished setting the table with cutlery, serviettes and mugs.

'Is Grandpa coming home soon? Is he at the allotment?'

'That was his plan before Mrs Lenart rang. Some problem with a blocked drain. She's nearly ninety, bless her. Someone's got to help her.'

As she was saying this, the sound of Bronek's Volvo stopping at the front door could be heard. Magda's spirit lifted. The table was ready: the sliced ham and cheese, the mixed green salad, the sliced beetroot, the fresh bread and butter, all looking appetising.

Over lunch, Bronek gave a full account of his visit to the old lady, pleased that he was able to solve all the problems in one go. Indeed, there had been a blocked drain, but also a bulb that needed changing, a stronger screw to hold up the mirror, a loose tile in the kitchen and a leaking tap.

'I'm sure you've earned your place in Heaven,' Aniela teased.

'Sure, sure,' he replied drily, giving Magda a wink at the same time. 'They're waiting for me with open arms.'

'Just don't be in a hurry,' Aniela patted his arm affectionately.

He grinned. 'I don't think you need to worry. It'll take me years to atone for all my sins.'

Magda could have teased him too, but she knew too much to make a joke of the hint in his words. Once, during her previous visit, in a moment of openness, when retelling their hardships in Siberia, Aniela had told her something of Bronek's past. Like herself now, he had been carrying a secret, a terrible burden he'd rather forget. Magda would never betray Aniela's trust, nor resurrect Bronek's pain. She knew only too well that feeling of terror, at the very thought of having one's most guarded secret exposed. Perhaps, one day, Bronek would tell her himself.

She caught him looking at her with an air of expectancy, his knife and fork resting on his plate for a moment. His white hair and his grey eyes were aglow in the brightness reflecting from the polished table. He asked, 'Will you come with me Magda? I've got lots to show you on my allotment.'

She remembered with pleasure the afternoons she had spent with him last summer, assisting in his ever more imaginative schemes.

'Tomorrow?' she suggested to please him. She made a self-deprecating gesture. 'Look at me, Grandpa. I can't wear these old togs to church on Sunday. I've got to go into town this afternoon and buy something decent.'

'Just don't buy any rubbish,' Aniela admonished. 'If you're short of money I'll lend you some.'

Magda could not help but smile. This was such bliss, this ordinary conversation. For a moment she felt like her old self.

'Thank you, Babcha, but there's really no need. My Dad's been generous and I've got enough saved. I know where to look for bargains.'

Bronek gave her an approving nod.

Over tea and cake that followed lunch, Magda told them of her plans. In between the nightmares and the grief, she had forced herself to think of her immediate future. It felt surreal, as if she were mapping out someone else's life. But to survive and move on she had to become a new person. She was determined never to allow *him* to overshadow her future.

29

'As soon as I've registered at the employment agency,' she told them, 'I shall start looking for work.' Bronek glanced at her, as if intending to interrupt, but she rushed on. 'Please hear me out. I want to work through the summer, so I can start an A-level course in September. And then, if I could combine part-time work with studying, that would be perfect. I've been thinking a lot. With so many Poles in this country, there's bound to be a need for interpreters. I'd take further exams, whatever it takes to qualify. I've also been thinking about courses on teaching English to foreign students.'

She could tell with growing satisfaction that Aniela and Bronek were interested and impressed. His drawn out 'mmmm...' implied approval, and Aniela assured her, 'That's very good thinking, Magda. We'll help all we can. On one condition. Have a break first. For at least a week.'

She could not argue with that.

In the afternoon, Aniela accompanied her into town. Magda found the crowds overwhelming and the enclosed spaces of the shopping precincts, though huge, strangely claustrophobic. Yet the self-imposed activity of putting together a basic wardrobe of matching blouses, skirts and trousers soon became a pleasurable absorption, giving her respite from those other tormenting thoughts. Aniela insisted on treating her to a crisp linen jacket in pale blue, that would complement her other purchases.

'How can I ever repay you, Babcha?' Magda asked in earnest.

Aniela's smile was one of pleasure.

'Just be a good person. That is the best reward.'

On Sunday, dressed up in her new clothes, Magda accompanied Aniela and Bronek to the Polish church. The priest's friendly welcome and the fact that he had remembered her from the previous summer pleasantly surprised her. She was glad he was not a mind reader. He would have found a different person from the one he remembered. She wondered, a little incongruously, how double agents managed. All that deceit and the constant fear of being found out. She could never be a secret agent, and yet she was giving a convincing imitation of one.

Later in the day, going for a walk with Aniela and Bronek lifted her spirits. The charm of Aylestone Meadows, with the green open spaces, the copses of willows, the blossom-covered hedges, the streams, the horses grazing lazily – all those visual sensations filtered through her brain and like a balm quietened her anxieties. Magda was convinced that the colour green of the surrounding nature had magical powers. It was so good to feel normal again, even if only for the duration of their walk.

Despite her impatience to get on with finding a job, Magda had to admit that the leisurely pace of the first week imposed upon her was doing her good. The nightmares tormented her by night, but Aniela's sleeping pills fought them off. In the daytime, she made herself deliberately busy.

She took great pleasure in helping out with the house chores, food shopping, cooking, baking and the ever-necessary cleaning and tidying up, much to Aniela's protests at first, then to her acceptance and finally, her appreciation.

'My dear child, there's no need to wear yourself out!' She'd try to slow down Magda at first.

'Please, Babcha, I must!' Magda could not explain how this febrile and constant activity was sheer therapy for her.

She loved gardening with Bronek. He was seventy-three but still youthfully agile and seemingly immune to the aches associated with the gruelling exercise called gardening. His allotment was on a spacious strip of land, separated from the Aylestone Meadows by a paved pedestrian walk that had once been the Central Line. Most allotments had wood or metal-mesh fences around them, as well as naturally grown shrubs, hawthorn, laurel, yew and others forming additional divides. Fully grown trees sprang sporadically along the pathways, giving charm to the rural appearance of the allotments, some with very old and dilapidated sheds.

Bronek's allotment was a picture. Screened from the public walk by a hedge, it also had a breeze-block wall covered over with ivy. A giant and ancient oak tree dominated his garden but with no ill effects, as it stood back on the east side, exposing the vegetable and the flower beds to the sun all day. The ultra-accurate rectangular beds were resplendent with the colours of May flowers on one side of the central divide, and, on the other, equally precise rectangles of growing vegetables were showing off neat rows of sprouting potatoes, onions, carrots and radishes.

Magda loved getting down on her knees together with Bronek to get rid of the weeds and to plant new seedlings. She sensed he enjoyed her company too. She found his gardener's enthusiasm entertaining, but also surprisingly educating, for only a little while ago she could never have imagined being a gardener's apprentice.

He sat back on his heels and his eyes shone in anticipation when he spoke. 'And this year, Magda, I hope you'll stay long enough with us to see the dahlias in the autumn. The shapes and colours will take your breath away!'

'I have no doubt about that!' she assured him, enjoying his joy. 'They must be the best on this allotment.'

'Pah! This allotment? No, in the whole of Leicestershire!' His mock seriousness broke in a cheeky grin. His white hair looked like a stray cloud against the blue sky.

Some days Magda accompanied Bronek in his role as a handyman to friends older than himself. There was never a shortage of jobs. Payment was a cup of tea and cake and a long chat, extended eagerly when Magda showed interest. Their wartime stories were infinitely fascinating: the loss of their homes, families separated and lost, some in death, some miraculously reunited after the war, a new life in a foreign country, deprivations, difficult beginnings.

How did they manage to get through all that? Magda often wondered, forgetting her own grief for a while, her imagination following the wartime journeys of these old ladies, who had been young then, and whose minds, like hers, had been filled with great hopes and dreams for the future. They survived. They made new lives for themselves. There was a lesson there.

She plucked up courage one day to ask Mrs Morska exactly that, when Bronek was busy outside fixing the garden tap to a post, and she sat with the old lady in the kitchen. They drank coffee from the best china with gilded rims on the cups and saucers. Mrs Morska was a small shrunken lady of eighty-five, her lined face animated with the pleasure of having company. Her dark eyes, like black little marbles, fixed Magda with unabashed curiosity. She had been twenty when her family were rounded up in the middle of the night by Russian soldiers and packed off to Siberia. Her parents and her three younger siblings died from diseases and starvation. She and her one younger brother miraculously survived. Such multiple tragedy! Her own, Magda thought, seemed so minor in comparison.

'There were thousands of families like ours,' Mrs Morska said, rocking slightly. 'And there were deaths in every single family. No one escaped that. People say you get over it. You never get over the death of someone you've loved. To this day, every day, I think about my Mama and Tato. About my little sisters and brothers. They were only little children...' her voice trailed off, her eyes became moist, she sighed and rocked.

But then she looked at Magda; the far-away look gone, her expression attentive. 'I'm sorry about your auntie. It must be hard for you and it takes a long time to start feeling normal again. But it will get better, I promise. In my situation, I had to tell myself off and make myself get on with looking after my brother. Otherwise, I would have let my parents down. All their suffering would have been for nothing.' She stopped, nodded thoughtfully. Then she looked at Magda and her eyes smiled. 'I was very lucky. I met a good man. Like me, he lost members of his family. But he survived. I never stopped thanking God for him. And for my life here. And for my own children.'

Magda was overawed by this frail woman's strength of mind. Perhaps there was hope for her too? Except that the good man in her life had already been lost to her. And she could not contemplate sharing her life with anyone else.

*

One evening, when there was nothing on television that Bronek was keen to watch, he brought out his sketch book and watercolours. Magda sat with him at the table in the backroom, which overlooked a long strip of lawn, surrounded by a border of early summer flowers. Even with the French window wide open, this was a cosy room, his library, the walls lined with shelves of tightly packed books – history and art, architecture and gardening, and a stack of Bronek's old sketch books.

'Have a go with me,' he encouraged, setting out his pencils, pens, brushes, paints and jars of water.

'I just want to watch, Grandpa. I've not done anything like this since my school days. And you can imagine the level of that!'

'There's always room for improvement,' he said, sitting down and studying with narrowed eyes the view of his garden. 'That corner, with Aniela's summer house, the lilac tree and the peonies, looks very attractive.' He began to sketch in the shapes to form a composition to his liking, and, as he did, he talked. 'I started from zero, Magda. I went to a night school. It was technical drawing. Very disciplined. But I liked it. It stood me in good stead when I began to look for a better job later.'

Like most young Poles after the war, in a foreign country, Bronek had been keen to do any job to keep his young family going. At times he held two part-time jobs, working additional long hours to top up his earnings. In his late twenties, the placement he had acquired in a hosiery factory enabled him financially to enrol at an evening school for a technical drawing course. The completion of the course with excellent results and a diploma gave him the confidence to apply for a position at the city architect's office. He remained there for the rest of his working life until his retirement.

Magda picked up a sketch book from the top of the pile and turned the pages. Some were filled with minutely precise architectural drawings of buildings, bridges, landmarks and streets. Some, in surprising contrast, with free-flowing lines of landscapes, trees, flowers and birds.

'This is so clever!' she commented with honest admiration.

'Practice. It's all to do with practice. You could do it too,' Bronek said, not taking his eyes off the page, where the image of Aniela's summer house and the surrounding shrubs were taking shape with sure, strong pencil lines.

Magda watched fascinated. Bronek applied water colour in generous wet patches that created delicate shades as the colours mixed and dried.

'It's like magic,' she said.

'It is in a way,' he chuckled. 'Watercolours have a mind of their own.'

*

Another night Magda sat down with Aniela on the settee and watched her doing needlepoint work on a flower pattern in rich colours. When finished, this would be the top part of yet another cushion. The settee and the armchairs were padded with them, two-deep. The crocheted throws, the embroidered runners and tablecloths all bore testimony to Aniela's talents in a variety of hand-crafts.

'We made everything ourselves in our youth,' she told Magda while working the stitches into an intricate pattern of curly leaves and criss-cross lines of stalks and twigs. 'All the clothes I wore, all the cardigans, mine and our children's, everything was made and knitted by me. Materials were cheap in those days, especially when you bought fabric and wool at the market. I could dress us all for the fraction of the price of the ready-made clothes.'

When their children, Janusz and Beata, had started school, Aniela returned to work. The experience she had gained in the typing pool beforehand now proved crucially useful. She applied and obtained a position as the receptionist in a surgery, which over the years expanded to a medical centre and elevated her position to a manager, since she had been the longest-working member of the ever-changing team.

'Do you miss going to work?' Magda asked her.

Aniela laughed, and, threading the needle with another vibrant colour, replied, 'When would I find the time? Too many things to do.'

One of them was cleaning the church with two other ladies on Wednesday afternoons. Magda went with her and enjoyed the physical activity of sweeping up and mopping the floor, dusting the chairs and the windowsills, changing flowers, scrubbing the vases clean. She found it relaxing, listening to the friendly banter, with a generous dose of humour, and the two ladies' eagerness to tell her about their past and their recent visits to Poland. She was thankful they did not bother her with questions.

In the middle of the afternoon, the priest turned up to retrieve some papers from the sacristy and stopped by to chat. She liked his easy, engaging manner, yet it made it all the more difficult to sound sincere while she was holding back so much.

He had obliged willingly to say Mass for Aunt Emilia at the start of the week. Strangely, inexplicably Magda had felt great relief, a closeness to her aunt, and a reassurance that her aunt would understand the reason for Magda's absence at the funeral in Poland.

Presently, he gave her a crinkle-round-the-eyes smile. 'So, will you be stopping longer with your grandparents this time?'

'I hope so, if they'll put up with me.' She returned his smile.

'Good. Just don't abandon your studies, whatever you do. And there's always a vacancy for a teacher at our Saturday school, if you find any spare time. We've got the scouts and the guides, and a song and dance team. New people are always welcome.' Another encouraging smile.

'Thank you, Father. I'll bear that in mind.'

As Magda continued to sweep the floor after his departure, strange feelings of hope began to germinate in her soul. Perhaps she'd start feeling better in time. Perhaps each layer of new experiences would bandage and muffle the raw pain, until in time there would only remain a scar, where once a deep wound had been gouged.

\*

One Friday afternoon, Mrs Demska invited her and Aniela for tea. The Demskis' rose-covered cottage was in Grandview Road, once a country lane in the suburbs, now a desirable area with mature trees and an abundance of greenery dotted with flowering shrubs. The houses were impressive, each individually designed and set back from the lane with a sweeping drive. In Poland, Magda reflected, a road such as this would be known as the millionaires' row, for only those with an opportunity to spend most of their working lives abroad would have been able to own such properties.

The Demskis' house was one of the smaller properties, the white-washed walls offsetting the black beams and the climbing roses. The front garden was a master class in precision planting: the blue aubrietias, the white alyssum and the crimson geraniums standing to attention like the Queen's soldiers.

The interior's perfection was, therefore, no surprise to Magda. The palest neutral colours of the decor formed an elegant backdrop to crystal and porcelain vases, original paintings of landscapes and still nature, wood-carved figurines, colourful ceramic bowls and silver-framed family photographs. Mrs Demska, in a silk blouse, floaty skirt, high heels, pearls and her hair swept up in a neat chignon, looked dressed for a special occasion, rather than an afternoon tea.

She invited them out onto the veranda, where a wrought iron table was covered in white cloth and set with finest bone china and a plate of dainty cupcakes. The garden beyond, was a feast for their eyes with vivid colours, shades of green, all shapes and sizes of shrubs, garden features, a pond, a fountain and a bird table, the ones visible from the house – all the result of Mr Demski's gardening passion.

'I've never seen anything so beautiful,' Magda said with honest admiration, when they were seated and Mrs Demska began to pour tea.

'Is Michael not at home?' Aniela asked, looking automatically towards the end of the garden, hidden from view by acacia and willow trees.

Mrs Demska paused pouring as she replied, 'You know his obsession with the car. The slightest noise and he has to have it checked out immediately.' She glanced at her watch. 'He's been gone a while. But it doesn't matter. We can catch up and I'll just make a fresh pot when he comes back.'

She and Aniela found lots to talk about. It was hard to imagine that they had been friends for over sixty years: little girls all muffled up against the Siberian winter and forever hungry, forever waiting for the next meagre meal. Who would have guessed that, looking at them now? Two elegant ladies enjoying afternoon tea in an exquisite English garden. The peaceful beauty of this warm afternoon was rubbing off on Magda's mood and diluting the darkness in her soul. If only she could make the lightness stay, if only for a few hours.

She finished her tea, ate the last crumb on her plate and asked, 'May I take a walk down your garden path?'

'Of course, my dear.' Mrs Demska looked pleased. 'The garden is Michael's pride and joy. He rather likes showing off.'

'I bet he and Grandpa like to compete,' Magda hazarded a lighter tone.

'All the time,' Aniela laughed. 'Like little boys.'

'But that's great!' Magda rushed to Bronek's defence. 'And look at the results!'

'There's a summer house at the end of the garden,' Mrs Demska said. 'You can't see it from here, but I think you'll like it.' She gave her another encouraging smile.

Magda was in no doubt that she would. She skipped down the stone steps and followed the neat paved path around the various features, its meandering course ensuring the visitor would not miss any of the specially planned effects. She compared it with Bronek's garden, closed in on all sides by a red-brick wall that was covered in ivy, honeysuckle and clematis. She liked it all the more for making her feel safe inside its protected compound.

The timber summer house at the far and hidden end was indeed delightful, with its cushioned seats and open glass doors and windows. Magda sat down and breathed in with pleasure the scents of the drying wood and those of the acacia and the lilac blossom. Total peace, with only the sporadic buzz of bees and grass insects and the odd bird sound. She wished she could wrap herself in it and take it away with her like a protective blanket.

A mobile ring made her jump. It was piercing, like the noise of a house telephone. She heard a male voice answer it, in the neighbouring garden. Through the gaps in the recently cut hedge she could make out a gazebo, round and open with six sturdy poles holding up the domed roof. Inside its sheltered interior a young man was pacing up and down as he spoke to his mobile.

She had no wish to eavesdrop, but to move now would alert him to her presence. Magda cringed with discomfort. She had no choice but to stay very still and hope he'd take his conversation elsewhere.

'Thanks for getting back so quickly,' she heard him say. A pause as he listened, then, 'Just happened. Last night. I had to get away. Come home. Sort myself out. Any chance of seeing you tonight?'

Another pause, then, 'Well... what can I say? I'm gutted. Crushed. Who would have imagined it? What a difference a day makes.' Another long pause as he listened with the mobile against his ear.

He looked young, early twenties, pleasantly attractive with symmetrical features and dark hair curling behind his ears. His thin, long legs were encased in snugly hugging jeans and his pale blue shirt hung loosely from his shoulders. Magda could not see his eyes in the three-quarter profile, but when he turned her way she experienced a startling jolt at the piercing blueness in his gaze.

'Big thanks,' he said into his mobile. 'I appreciate that. See you at The Globe. Seven?' Another pause then, 'Of course, Julie must come too. I miss you both when I'm away.'

The moment he rang off his shoulders slumped, he sat down, rested his elbows on his knees and hid his face in his hands. Such an unwitting show of despair shocked Magda rigid. For a moment, she held back her breath. What could it be? An accident? A death? Some incident at work? So immersed she had been in her own trauma, she had become unaware of other crises, accidents, deaths, losses. They never stopped. Perhaps because of her own fragile state, she felt his pain. Tears stung her eyes.

Just then a young boy's voice pulled her out of her thoughts.

'James! Where are you?'

It came from where she imagined the house to be.

The young man sat upright but did not stand up straight away. He ran the back of his hand over his eyes and set his jaw firm.

'James!' The voice was close now and a young boy came into Magda's view, kicking the ball ahead of him. 'Where have you been? Why are you hiding from me?' He was about ten, with a much lighter, curly hair, and brown eyes.

'What's with the inquisition?' the man called James replied. 'Am I not allowed to have five minutes to myself?'

'Five minutes? You've been gone for hours! I've been looking everywhere for you!'

'How could it be hours, when I brought you from school only half an hour ago?'

'But every minute counts!' The boy spread out his hands in exasperation. 'You'll be gone again soon. And I want you to play ball with me. Please!' His pleading voice would have melted a frozen heart.

The young man came down towards him, ruffled his hair and challenged, 'OK. I'll race you to the patio and we can start from there.'

It was a relief when they ran off, kicking and chasing the ball, and Magda could leave the summer house unseen. She was intrigued by what she had heard and seen and guessed that the two were siblings. But were they? The age gap between them posed questions, but it was not unusual. She could ask Mrs Demska about her neighbours, yet she knew she would not. Somehow, having witnessed this stranger's distress had made her protective of him. He did not deserve to be gossiped about and she would not demean herself by blabbing. He was entitled to keep his secret as much as she so desperately wanted to guard hers.

For the rest of that day she could not get the young man out of her mind.

# CHAPTER 6

Premium job, the recruitment officer had described it as. The basic pay was regular, but one could increase that with additional double-pay hours on Sunday. This last consideration did not apply. Magda had a reverence for Sundays, born from family tradition and pride in the national history. For centuries, the Church had been the refuge for the oppressed and the only voice of opposition to the successive repressing regimes. The Church deserved support one day a week. Unless Magda's job involved saving people's lives on a Sunday, she could not justify making money on a holy day.

Her shift started at six in the morning. No big deal. The dawn broke at four and half an hour later, the sun was blazing at full power in this season. The best time of the year for getting up with the birds.

Bronek had offered to give her a lift to work, but she flatly refused. His old bicycle would make perfect transport for her. She had cleaned and oiled it with feverish zeal, this all-absorbing activity helping to stifle tormenting thoughts and the ever-present anxiety.

The Alfa Pie and Sausage factory was a sprawling rectangular building, its dowdy walls illuminated temporarily by the morning sunshine, on this otherwise soulless industrial estate. Between the car park and the side wall, there was a shelter for bicycles and motorbikes.

Magda chained hers to a stand and followed the other arriving workers to the main door. The entrance was a small vestibule with glass walls. This had been designed, as Magda soon discovered, to keep the indoor temperature close to freezing temperature at all times. The work room, a long hall with a low ceiling, was in effect a giant refrigerator. Two conveyor belts running the full length of the hall were flanked with people in white caps and overalls. They passed the meat, through all the stages of production, to the completion point and the packaging at the far end. A nauseous smell of raw meat permeated every cubic centimetre of the atmosphere.

In a flash of realisation, Magda knew that coming here had been a mistake. But she would not be beaten, not on her first day!

With a sinking feeling, she forced a smile at the manageress who approached her, a tall skinny woman, with flattened hair underneath the tightly tied net.

'Come with me,' she said. 'I'll show you to the changing room. Have you brought all your extra clothing as instructed?'

Magda nodded clutching her plastic bag, glad of Aniela's woolly cardigan and thick socks inside it, a requisite that should have made her think. Too late now.

The women's cloakroom, like the men's on the opposite side, was partitioned off in the adjoining part of the building. Further, in other rooms, there were sounds of operating machinery, probably large volumes of meat mixtures being churned, Magda guessed. The cloying odour hung everywhere, and there was no respite from the biting cold.

In the cloakroom, the manageress opened a metal locker from a row of them and passed Magda a white overall and a thick hairnet.

'Dress warm, me duck, and put these on last,' she instructed.

Magda dressed fast, piling on all the additional layers of clothing she had been asked to bring and tied the hairnet tight, ensuring no escaped hair hung around her face. The mirror did not reflect a flattering image, but what did that matter against the survival of such arctic conditions all day?

She was placed at the end of one of the long tables and her task was to cling-wrap the sausages, a dozen per pack, stick information labels on them and arrange them neatly in carton boxes ready for transportation.

The swarthy young man, possibly a Romanian, facing her from the opposite side of the conveyor belt, was evidently a master in this task. He worked with a fast and robotic precision, allowing himself at the same time to banter with his companion, a plump girl who gave Magda a suspicious look. Magda nodded, hoping to appear friendly and set about her work. Within minutes her face was stiff, her toes non-existent and her fingers, in their rubber gloves, like unbending sticks. The only thing warming her was her inner tension of keeping up with the mounting pile of sausages beside her.

The manageress came over and watched for a long while, making Magda nervous. When finally she moved away, Magda thought with trepidation of the long hours of painful endurance stretching out before her. How would she cope? At home, if everything had remained as before, she'd be sitting with Natalia at a lecture taking copious notes. Or writing an essay on metaphysical poets. Or attending a tutorial to discuss John Donne. Or just sat outside with her best friend on the sun-drenched green. *He* had robbed her of all that. How she hated *him*!

The workers were allowed short coffee breaks and half an hour for lunch, none, however, long enough to thaw out Magda's frozen limbs before returning to her task again. The twelve hours of the first day were unremitting misery.

When she cycled home in the full brightness of the evening summer sun, her skin and body revelled in the balmy air, and she could not believe it had stayed warm outside all day while she toiled in near-arctic conditions. The heat emanating from the buildings, the ground and the passing traffic was like the hot breath of a desert wind, as if compensating for the day's ordeal. She would persevere, she decided. She would tell Aniela and Bronek that her job was just fine.

*

On Thursday night, Bronek was waiting by the back gate as he swept the garden path. He stopped to take the bicycle from her and put it away in the garden shed.

'Don't touch me, Grandpa,' she warned him jokingly, 'or you'll smell like me.'

'We must have a talk,' he said, but she rushed past him to the back of the house, where the original brick coal-shed had been converted to an additional downstairs bathroom/utility room. She stripped off, dropping her clothes in a pile to be washed immediately.

She shivered with pleasure underneath the shower's warm stream, as she soaped away all traces of the foul smell from her skin and hair. Scrubbed clean and changed (she had prepared fresh clothes in advance to change into), she dried her hair, pushed the dirty clothes in the washing machine, switched it on, and only then did she go to greet Aniela and Bronek.

They were in the kitchen with the door wide open, letting in the fresh air, Aniela at the cooker and Bronek at the table with his *Telegraph*. She gave them both a hug before sitting down. Bronek folded the paper and cleared his throat.

'Magda, we must talk,' he said. Her heart missed a beat. Bad news from Poland? Zden?

'What about?'

Aniela turned around from the cooker.

'Magda, my dear, we can't watch you doing this and say nothing. You come home every night frozen like a fishfinger. Your clothes stink like the dishcloth at the butchers. You don't have to do this. You can do other jobs.'

Anxiety was back in a flash. 'But what shall I tell them? I've only just started this week.' Having to face the recruitment officer, give lame excuses, beg for another chance – it was a terrifying thought.

'Just tell them the truth,' Bronek said simply. 'Shutting yourself in a freezer all day can't be good for your health. Trust me, I know something about labouring in sub-zero temperatures. I'd never wish that for you.'

'But…' she cringed with the shame of looking like a failure.

'Tell them about your poor blood circulation.' Bronek was matter-of-fact. He picked up her hand. 'Look. That wouldn't be a lie. See how the tips of your fingers are still white, even after the shower? They will find you another job. That's their task. That's what they're there for. Don't look so worried.'

Magda's anxiety was not appeased but she did not argue. Quietly she was relieved that the decision had been made for her. No more frozen toes and painfully numb fingers. Whatever other job she was offered she was determined to tackle it with the same zeal, engage her mind totally, leaving no room for thoughts about *him*.

Next morning, with her heart beating fast, she sought out her manageress and told her truthfully that she had to finish early that afternoon, so she could visit the recruitment centre. To her enormous relief, the manageress showed no visible surprise or annoyance. She nodded, saying, 'Never mind, me duck. You're not the first one. I take it we won't be seeing you again. At least you're honest. You are a good worker.'

Magda was embarrassed. 'It's the cold,' she explained, showing her fingers, dead-white around the nails.

She finished the afternoon earlier, to give herself time to cycle to the recruitment agency, and arrived there much aware of the stink of raw meat trapped in her clothes. The man who saw her listened attentively, his eyes enlarged by the thick lenses of his spectacles. Magda was surprised by his calm manner and wondered how many times he'd heard this story before.

'OK, we'll find you something else,' he said. Was everyone so polite in public offices? Back home officialdom had still retained the heavy-handedness of the old communist arrogance, when Citizen Joe was just a worm to be stamped on.

The man's eyes scanned the computer screen, as Magda rubbed her fingers to bring them back to life.

'We've got a vacancy here,' he said. 'Small business. Sandwich making. The hours are eight to five.' He raised his questioning eyebrows over his thick glasses.

This sounded like paradise.

'I can start straight away,' Magda said eagerly.

'Eight sharp. Monday morning.' He gave Magda a printed sheet with all the particulars. The address was in the town centre. He added, 'Your boss's name is Scott Green. But he likes to be called Gordon.'

'Mr Gordon?' A strange request.

'No. Just Gordon. Like Ramsay.'

Magda had no idea what that was supposed to mean and wondered at the humorous twitch of the man's lips.

*

At ten to eight on Monday morning, Magda stood at the closed door of the 'First Stop'. Within a minute another girl joined her. At first Magda thought she was the first eager customer. She was small and thin, the most prominent part of her being a high ponytail of thick straight hair. Her oriental, almond-shaped eyes met Magda's in a friendly gaze.

'Do you work here?' she asked.

'My first day,' Magda said.

'Mine too. I'm Lin.'

'I'm Magda. We'll be working together,' she smiled, feeling pleased at the thought of a working companion. 'Fingers crossed that all goes well.'

Just then the door was unlocked and opened to reveal their boss. He was a big man, big shoulders, big hands, big rubbery lips, a white apron covering his prominent front and a tall chef's hat flopping to one side. For no reason, Zden flashed across Magda's mind, though this man looked nothing like him.

'From the agency?' He did not wait for an answer but led them hurriedly inside talking over his shoulder. 'I'm Gordon. Your boss. You follow my instructions to the last detail. Understand? I have strict rules. If you break them, you're out! Understand?' He stopped suddenly and the girls only just avoided bumping into him.

The narrow space inside was only big enough to accommodate five chairs in a row against the wall facing a long glass counter, underneath which were lined about fifteen open containers with a variety of sandwich fillings. On the worktop, behind the counter, fresh cucumbers, tomatoes and lettuce were waiting to be cut. Further along, there was a basket filled with cobs and sliced, wrapped loaves.

'On the wall, here,' he pointed his bulbous finger, 'there is a price list. Different prices for different fillings. Memorise them well. I don't tolerate

43

mistakes. Every mistake is money lost. Understand? The customers will start coming any minute now. There will be a lull mid-morning then a massive scramble between twelve and one. Get ready. Wash your hands. Put your aprons on. Get moving. Chop! Chop!'

Magda's head was reeling from all this instruction given at breakneck pace. She and Lin exchanged raised eyebrows, as they scrubbed their hands under running water in the backroom. There was a cooker with two simmering pots and a worktop crowded with Gordon's cooking paraphernalia.

No sooner had they put on their aprons when the first two customers arrived.

Lin saw to the lady. Magda's customer was a man dressed in a long coat, unshaved and smelling of tobacco. A flash of Zden's image again. She fixed her gaze on the man's dishevelled hair.

'The usual,' he said.

'Which is?' she prompted politely.

'Egg and bacon and tomato, naturally. And tea to take away.'

'White bread? Brown bread? Special?' she asked.

'Chop! Chop!' Gordon barked beside her. The customer gave a hollow laugh. She squirmed and felt tears welling up. She hated them both in that instant. Steady. Stay calm. She got on with making the requested sandwich. She packed it in a polystyrene box and made tea in a polystyrene cup. She checked the price list on the wall.

'Three-fifty, please.'

'Generous!' the long coat laughed.

'You stupid or what?' Gordon hissed, making her flinch. 'Three seventy-five, the usual price,' he corrected, taking the money from the customer.

Magda clenched her teeth. She saw how Lin's hands were shaking, as she hurried with making her sandwich. She must stay strong, for herself and for Lin. She must not allow this odious man to intimidate her. She pressed her lips together and shut her ears to Gordon's continuous mutterings and expletives. When the first hellish hour passed and there was a blessed lull, she forced herself to be civil to him. This made her feel in control.

'It would be perfect if the customers came one at a time,' she commented for something to say.

'That wouldn't pay your wages!' he barked. 'No standing around twiddling your thumbs! Here!' He gave them a cloth each. 'Wipe the surfaces at all times between the customers. You!' He jabbed the air in Lin's direction. 'You help me with the next lot of fillings. And you... you stay at the counter.'

44

'My name is Magda,' she reminded him, forcing herself to stand up to him while suppressing her fear. 'I'd like to make a suggestion. Since you know all the prices, Mr Gordon, wouldn't it make sense if you were in charge of the takings, and we got on with making the sandwiches? It would be quicker too.'

He flashed her a disdainful glance.

'I'm the chef here, not the till boy!'

Lin followed him into the backroom, sending Magda a desperate look.

'Don't worry,' Magda mouthed. 'You've got me!' She took a deep breath. Why was she being so nervous? This was silly, to allow this disgusting man to intimidate them. She and Lin could walk out at any time. There was no shortage of jobs at the agency. And Gordon would be left in the proverbial... This thought alone made her smile. She felt a sudden lift.

Around eleven, she and Lin were allowed a speedy cup of coffee, before the pressure started to mount again. Making sandwiches and cobs to order, their hands moved non-stop, as if electrically charged. Magda's shoulders ached. She felt dizzy with checking and rechecking the prices, all the while aware of Gordon's grumbling going on behind them.

By two o'clock in the afternoon, she was exhausted by the sheer tension around her. She'd had nothing to eat since before seven when leaving home, but she felt no hunger. Only a sinking disappointment. How was she to continue working with Gordon? What would she tell her grandparents? The recruitment officer? Anxiety was making her feel ill.

She finished serving a customer when another walked in, an office worker with a clean appearance, a white shirt and a tie. Lin leaned forward to take his order and Magda immediately got on with the job of wiping the surfaces. There was a crash. Magda's head jerked to see a bowl with sliced tomatoes smashed to smithereens at Lin's feet. Lin's face was frozen in terror.

'You idiot! Moron! Stupid cow!' Gordon burst from the back room, his huge features ugly in his temper. Lin's mouth trembled as she sidled up to Magda. Somehow, this small gesture of Lin's and the fact that there was a customer present gave Magda the courage to speak.

'Mr Gordon...' her voice sounded alien. She cleared her throat. 'No harm done. We'll clean up everything beautifully. In no time at all.' She gave the customer her most charming smile and Gordon appeared momentarily lost for words.

'Just a little hiccup,' the customer remarked amiably. 'Your sandwiches are still by far the very best in town.'

Gordon stepped forward, apparently mollified.

'Workforce, eh?' he muttered in disgust. 'What will you have, sir?'

Lin stayed close to Magda, as they both crouched behind the counter and began to clear the mess. By the time Gordon had served the customer, the debris had been removed, and the floor washed and wiped clean with not a trace of the recent disaster.

'That will cost you! You stupid bitch!' Gordon turned on Lin the moment the customer left the shop. She looked petrified, like a rabbit caught in the headlights.

In a split-second Magda was engulfed in blazing anger. There was no future, no past, just the present moment. The bastard! She could barely control the urge to punch him. Trembling with fury she stepped in between him and Lin. She saw puzzlement in his eyes, then his thick lips grimaced in a mocking grin. He folded his bulky arms on his protruding chest, almost pushing Magda back. She stood her ground, though the top of her head reached only the level of his nose. She guessed he was waiting for her to make the first move, and by God, how she'd enjoy sinking her teeth into his forearm. But no, she must surprise him.

'Mr Gordon,' she spoke softly, 'I've got something to tell you.'

A fleeting puzzlement crossed his features, but then he leered down on her in apparent contempt.

'Watch my lips,' he said. 'I'm not interested in anything you have to say.'

She swallowed hard to gain a moment, to make him wait.

'I think you will be.'

A split second's hesitation. 'What?' he barked.

Slow. Don't rush. One, two, three...

'In Poland, where I come from, the breeding and the good manners of an English gentleman are legendary. Pity you are not one. You are a bully. I cannot work in a place of constant harassment.' She stepped back, took off her apron and hung it on the door behind her. 'I'm leaving.'

It was satisfying, but also frightening to see his thick features turn purple.

'You can't! I won't allow it!' he shouted. 'The day's not over yet. You'll be sorry for this!'

She withstood his stare, her legs shaking, yet anger made her defiant.

'Mr Gordon.' She employed her most reasonable tone. 'This is a trial period, isn't it? Not just for us, but for you too.' She raised her eyebrows expressively. 'Please explain, how does your treatment of us promote good relations between the boss and his workers?'

His bulk inflated even more.

'You cheeky bitch! Bloody foreigner! You come over here and dictate your terms to me? You should be grateful I employ you. I was born and bred here!' He jabbed the air between them with his finger as he threw the words at her. She flinched but did not move back. She felt Lin step behind her.

'I'm leaving too,' Lin said, peeling off her apron.

He barred their exit.

'You won't get a penny for this morning's work!' he threatened. 'The agency will hear about this!'

'They certainly will!' Magda raised her voice. 'We are going there now!'

'Are you?' His sarcasm was like a threat. He stood so close to her now that she smelled all the odours on him: raw onions, salami and pickles, fried bacon.

'Please let us pass,' she asked politely, and as calmly as her shattered nerves would allow. He eyed them with hatred but made no move.

Two elderly ladies walked in and chattering to each other began to look through the glass counter at the array of fillings. Gordon hesitated, but their presence gave him no choice. As he went through to assist them, Magda and Lin picked up their belongings, and walked out of the shop.

The pavement was white in the sunshine. Spontaneously they clasped each other's hands and hurried on almost skipping.

'I need to recover first,' Magda said. 'Shall we sit in the Town Hall Square?'

They sat on a bench that faced the fountain and the grand entrance to the Town Hall. The square had a restful atmosphere on this warm day, with people sitting in small groups on the surrounding grass, some eating their snacks on benches, some stopping to chat by the fountain. Magda felt limp and drained of all emotion.

'Thank you,' Lin said. 'Thank you for sticking up for me. He was a horrible man. And you were so brave!'

The very notion of her being brave made Magda want to laugh, but instead, mortifyingly, her face crumpled, grief welled up and her eyes filled with tears. She rummaged in her hand bag for tissues.

'Magda,' Lin stroked her arm, 'don't let him upset you! He's not worth it. He's not worth a hundred of you, the disgusting man! So fat! And so ugly!' She gave an exaggerated shiver. 'I bet he's not even got one friend. Or a wife! Who'd ever want him?' Magda was touched by Lin's childlike loyalty. She nodded, dried her eyes, blew her nose, composed herself.

'I know all that, Lin. But I'm so angry! I feel right now as if I hate all men!' Even as she blurted out the words, she knew this was not true. She only really hated one man. And even Gordon was no match for him. She loved Dominik. She loved her Dad. Bronek was an angel. And she often thought about that young man, James, and wondered what his problem had been, and whether he had resolved it. He did not look like someone one would hate. But then, her uncle did not either.

Lin shook her head, her thick pony tail swinging.

'You don't mean that, Magda. You're just very upset. And rightly so.' She had a soft, girlish voice in character with her small stature. 'Listen, why don't we get some yummy sandwiches and drinks and sit out here, in the sun? There will be time to go back to the employment agency afterwards.' She angled her face to peer at Magda with her lively eyes the shape of dark almonds.

Magda managed a smile. It already felt as if she had known Lin for a very long time.

'You're very good to me, Lin. Thank you. We'll do just what you suggest.'

'And…' Lin added enthusiastically, 'we'll ask for a job with Colin Firth as our boss. And if we don't get it, we'll kidnap the employment man and hold him to ransom!'

At the recruitment agency, Magda requested to see the same person she saw the previous Friday. After a few minutes he appeared at his desk, his face bearing a trained look of concern, his eyes huge behind the thick lenses. They sat down facing him.

'Hello, it's me again.' Magda smiled apologetically. 'And my colleague. The two lambs you've sent to the wolf's den are back.'

'Sorry?' He looked perplexed.

'Haven't you had complaints about Mr Gordon before?' His expression remained blank but Magda continued. 'He is a bully. The rudest man I have ever met. It's not possible to work for him. Only if you're a masochist and enjoy being trodden on all day. Surely, we can't be the first to complain?'

The recruitment officer remained expressionless. He cleared his throat.

'Let's see what else we can find for you.' The word 'else' came out like a sigh. He tapped the keyboard and stared at the screen of his computer.

'All we want is to do a good day's work,' Magda assured him.

He did not reply but continued to study the screen. When he looked at them, it was with an air of being about to announce something of singular importance.

'They need help immediately at the hospital kitchen. The Royal. In the washing-up section. Would you...' – a prompting tone – 'consider that?'

Magda and Lin looked at each other and smiled.

'Nothing could be worse than working for Mr Gordon,' Lin said. 'When can we start?'

'Now?' the man's tone was persuasive. They nodded and he picked up the phone. 'I'll tell them you're on your way.'

Magda and Lin walked down Lower Brown Street towards the Infirmary. It was quiet here in the side street, away from the main traffic. Bright streaks of light fell out of the narrow gaps between the buildings and lay in narrow strips across the pavement. Magda got out her mobile and rang Aniela.

'Babcha, just to let you know, I don't know what time I'll be back tonight. Everything's changed. I'll explain later. I'm just on my way to help out in the hospital kitchen with my colleague Lin. I'll ring again if we're needed to stay longer.' She rang off before Aniela began to fret. She asked Lin, 'Do you need to ring anyone?'

Lin shook her head, her ponytail swinging.

'No. My room-mate Mei doesn't get back till very late. She wouldn't miss me. She works in a take-away. They're open till midnight.'

Magda asked, 'Wouldn't you like to work together in the same place?'

'I would, but there was only one vacancy there.'

Magda felt sorry for Lin.

'Where did you work before?'

'At my uncle's. He ran a small food shop with Chinese products. I came over two years ago. My home is in a small village near Chengdu. The pay for work over there is very small compared to here. I wanted to help my parents.'

Magda warmed to this slight-built Chinese girl even more. Her story was so similar to that of many Poles who were leaving their families at home to get better-paid work in England. Even despite the recent cataclysmic upheaval in her life, Magda felt luckier than Lin. She had only herself to worry about, and her kind grandparents to support her.

'So, why aren't you working for your uncle anymore, Lin?' An unnerving thought crossed her mind. Not another Uncle Zden!

49

'He died,' Lin said. 'It was sudden. A heart attack. His wife said I must go. She had her own family to worry about.'

'How awful for you!' Magda was shocked. Thought of her own wicked Aunt Lalka. 'So what did you do?'

'My friend, Mei, has a room in a big house. There's six other people there. I moved in with her. We share one room, but it's OK. I can save and send the money to my parents.'

Magda was moved and impressed. She wished to think of something supportive to say.

'Lin, we'll stick together. Let's hope this job will be OK. But if we have to leave, we'll go together, OK?'

Their place of work at the Infirmary was a long room with a low ceiling close to the kitchen in the basement. It was equipped with a conveyor belt that went through a dishwashing machine, not unlike a smaller version of an industrial car-wash. The hissing and rattling noise that it produced would drown out normal conversation. At each end of the room, there was an open double door with plastic flaps, one for the trolley with dirty plates and crockery to be wheeled in, and the other for trolleys with cleaned things to be taken away.

Two women in dark overalls were frantically spreading themselves over a number of tasks, receiving trolleys with dirty plates, scraping and disposing of the waste into plastic containers, separating the lids from the plates, sorting cutlery and mugs, sending all dirty items through the washing process in plastic baskets, and at the other end placing them clean on trays. Objects were mounting at both ends.

The manageress, a chubby woman with a ready smile, who had accompanied Magda and Lin from the reception to the basement, leaned close to them and shouted above the noise.

'As you can see, we need more hands. Can you two start at this end, and Britney and Sam can do the other end?' The shortened versions of the feminine English names baffled Magda. Sam sounded like a masculine name, but she guessed it was shortened for Samantha. There was never any confusion over Polish Christian names, as all the feminine names ended with an 'a'. The woman called Britney wiped her sweaty forehead with the back of her forearm, gave the manageress a lemony smirk and rushed to her companion at the other end. The clean end.

'Right.' The manageress turned to Magda and Lin. 'Put on your overalls.' She pointed at where they were hanging on the wall. 'Get started right away. Make sure the plates are scraped clean. We don't want bits clogging up the system. Some items may need washing twice.

Britney will bring them back to you.' She looked at the clock on the wall, large black numerals and a long minute hand moving jerkily. 'I must rush now, but I'll be back later.'

Magda and Lin set about their tasks immediately, aware of Britney and Sam working like ants at the other end. There was a feeling of urgency created by the continuous movement of the conveyor belt, its mechanism giving out thudding noises and squeaks, and the dish-washing section in the middle constantly hissing with strong jets of hot water. Swirling vapours rose to the ceiling before settling in droplets on Magda's hair and face. Within minutes her clothes, her hair, her face became damp and sticky. Her scalp prickled and her armpits itched. She brushed the itchiness off her face with the back of her hand and it was like spreading lard. Lin was doing the same spontaneously and they both laughed. This was still infinitely better than Gordon's company.

It was hard to imagine that, above them, there were several floors of hectic human activity. Here, Magda thought, it was like her hiding hole. Here, she felt safe. Here, *he'd* never find her. Her arms and her back ached, but every time she stretched and punched the air, she was punching *him*.

The length of the room and the continuous noise prevented Magda and Lin from engaging in conversation with the other two women, but now and again Britney would send them a thumbs-up sign or walk over with a plate or two that needed a second wash. It felt good to be free of an irate boss breathing down your neck and making you feel useless, because nerves would affect all your skills.

The manageress returned after an hour.

'How are you getting on?' She raised her voice to be heard.

'Fine!' Magda shouted back, licking the salty sweat off her lips 'What do we do for a toilet break?'

'Nothing. Just let it run. For a longer break you can de-activate.' She showed them the switch. 'Which shift would you prefer? The morning shift is from six to two o'clock in the afternoon. The afternoon shift is from two till ten o'clock at night.'

'The morning shift,' Magda replied without hesitation, thinking immediately of doing an additional job in the afternoons.

'Me too!' Lin shouted above the noise, and gave Magda a chummy smile.

Magda liked the idea of them working together. She liked Lin. They had only known each other for a few hours, but already Magda felt they could become friends. She was already thinking about asking Aniela if she could invite Lin for tea on Sunday.

# CHAPTER 7

For the next three weeks Magda came home from her shift smelling like steamed fish.

De-stacking and re-stacking trolleys with dishes, scraping waste into plastic bins, lifting loaded plastic baskets and sending them through the washing process made her discover muscles she did not know she had. Her arms ached, her back ached, her legs ached, but she liked working with Lin, and their supervisor was a friendly woman, worlds apart from Mr Gordon. Britney and Sam easily indulged in small talk but at breaks they preferred a smoke outside to sitting down to a coffee and sandwich. Magda and Lin did not mind; they made dreamy plans for their future jobs when they'd be stacking bank notes rather than plates.

Magda was sleeping a little better, her sleep less frequently broken with nightmares, which nevertheless haunted her at moments through the day. She pushed *him* out of her mind with deliberate thoughts of the people she loved. She created images in her mind of Dominik and Natalia in their favourite cafe in the Old Town Square in Krakow. She missed them with a deep ache and would have given anything for her life to return to how it was before. And all because of *him*. It was impossible to ever forgive *him*. It was impossible to ever stop hating *him*.

One afternoon, on returning home from her shift, and as usual reeking of dish-water, she found Aniela entertaining her friend, Mrs Demska, for afternoon tea.

All at once she remembered the young man called James. She had often wondered about him and about the problem that had obviously made him so upset, and whether he had been able to resolve it. She was certain of one thing, that nothing that he had suffered could be compared to what had been inflicted on her.

Mrs Demska, as ever, in her silks and fine jewellery, nibbled daintily at Aniela's best strawberry and cream cake, and drank from Aniela's best china, the cups with the golden rims. Her very presence made Magda squirm with self-consciousness of her own state.

She greeted her politely, just as Mrs Demska pinched her nose and fanned herself with a lace handkerchief before saying, 'My dear Magda! You cannot possibly continue to work in that place!'

'But I like it there,' Magda replied, amused, catching Aniela's discreet smile. 'Please excuse me. I'll join you as soon as I've made myself presentable.'

She showered, washed her hair, sprayed herself all over with a floral scent, changed into a white T-shirt and blue jeans and rejoined Aniela and Mrs Demska downstairs.

Mrs Demska patted the spot next to her on the settee.

'Come, sit down, Magda, I've got some good news for you.'

Good news? A sharp twinge of anxiety. She sat down next to Mrs Demska, catching her expensive scent, and clasped her hands on her lap, ready to listen. Aniela poured her a cup of tea, which she received with a grateful smile.

'Magda.' Mrs Demska took a long moment to savour her tea. 'A new hotel is just about to open off London Road.' She nodded knowingly. 'They'll be needing an army of staff. They are interviewing people this week for a variety of positions. I know Paul, the manager. I could put in a good word for you, if you're interested.'

Magda was struck dumb as thoughts raced around her brain.

'Interested? I'm... gobsmacked!' she managed to say at last. 'Mrs Demska... how can I thank you? It's so kind of you to think of me!'

Mrs Demska smiled happily, relishing her role of the messenger of good news. 'I was hoping you'd be pleased,' she said. 'I told Paul you'd see him tomorrow afternoon.'

'Tomorrow? So soon?' A rush of nervousness. 'But of course...' She was thinking fast. 'I must give notice first. My supervisor has been good to me. I can't let her down till she's found a replacement. And there's Lin. I don't want to leave her behind...'

Mrs Demska sat back enjoying the cake, enjoying Magda's consternation.

'It's only the interview tomorrow, Magda. I'm sure there will be time to put everything in order. And there will be room for Lin too.'

*

This was a month ago.

Magda liked her new job: a cleaner by day, a bar-attendant in the evenings. She liked her colleagues too, a team of girls of different nationalities. There was a Slovakian girl, a Ukrainian, two girls from the Philippines, Lin and herself. They were all conscientious hard workers, but lunchtimes were always fun. They all tried to outdo each other in telling amusing stories and would fall about laughing like schoolgirls. Magda surprised herself laughing with them, more and more. If only the nightmares would stop. If only she could erase those dreadful memories.

When Aniela and Bronek's daughter, Beata, came over from Germany one weekend, she voiced her reservations about Magda's long hours of work.

'Magda, darling, your hard work is commendable, but you need some healthy balance in your life. You need to get out and meet other young people.'

'But I've got them, Auntie, at work. We get on really well,' Magda assured her.

They had walked to the bottom of the garden and sat on the bench facing the back of the house. Beata wrinkled her pretty nose. She was in her mid-forties, a very attractive woman, with thick, short, golden hair and boyish, square hands, the hands of a doctor.

'Don't you get a little bored, doing this job?' she asked, unconvinced.

Magda shook her head.

'I promise you, the job's not boring. I have great company. Every day there's some excuse for chocolates or cakes. It's a wonder I don't look like a sumo wrestler yet.'

This elicited a begrudging laugh from Beata.

'Magda, you look like a waif. And that's exactly my point. You're doing too much.'

'Auntie, please, you mustn't worry about me. I've got to do it my way. Stand on my own two feet, for how could I ever repay your parents for their support? At least this way, it makes me feel as if I'm not a total burden to them.'

Beata patted her hand.

'You must never think that. I think fate has brought you along just at the right time. Mum and Dad are not getting younger, and Janusz and I live too far to be here straight away, if anything were to happen. Believe me, Magda, it gives me peace of mind, and I think Janusz too, to know that Mum and Dad have got someone here with their wits about them.'

Beata's thinking totally surprised Magda.

'I've never thought of it this way. I love doing things for them. My biggest worry is how to repay them properly, and when that day will come?'

Beata patted Magda's hand again.

'You're doing that already, Magda. Just knowing you're here is a load off my mind.'

*

Magda had no influence, it seemed, over her recurring nightmares. Before going to sleep every night, she made herself concentrate on the people she loved. With Natalia she visited all their childhood haunts; with Dominik she allowed her imagination to wander to what could have been, had they not been torn apart. His presence in her mind was at times so intense it followed her into her dreams, in which he held her tight and kissed her until she was weak with happiness. And yet, all the while, a dark shadow lurked close by and suddenly loomed into a giant menacing shape that dwarfed them and made her heart race and tear her chest with pain.

She would wake up shaking and sweaty and thankful, after a moment of clarity, that it had only been a bad dream.

This particular morning, the last Sunday in July, she woke up expecting a nightmare to be chasing her into wakefulness, but instead she was surprised by her own calm and the comforting brightness filtering into the room from around the edges of the curtains. She lay still for a long moment, before stretching her limbs.

Her mind automatically sought thoughts of Dominik. She sensed his presence everywhere: a face in the crowd, a scent, a voice, a tune drifting from an open shop, so many things made her think of him. She had endless conversations with him when at work hoovering the rooms, changing the beds, cleaning the bathrooms. Her mind would go over every minute of that fateful day. After the hospital. After all those hours spent at Aunt Emilia's bedside. After Uncle Zden had walked out and left her to deal with formalities. She had texted Dominik and Natalia and later they met for coffee in the Old Square. She could never have imagined then that she was seeing them for the last time. She could never have imagined what was about to follow. A cataclysm that turned her life upside down and gouged a bottomless pit between her and the man she loved.

Tears filled her eyes. This happened frequently. Would she ever find peace and respite from the constant longing?

She thought of Natalia. She had not written to her friend yet, but she would one day, she promised herself, when life became steady and normal, when she resumed her studies, when there was something praiseworthy to write about. She missed Aunt Emilia with an ache. If only once, just once, she could come back and tell Magda she was happy.

Magda checked the bedside clock. It was close to eight. She could hear muffled sounds of voices from downstairs. Aniela and Bronek believed life was too short to waste precious time on sleep beyond the light of dawn. Their very presence about the house filled her with a feeling of security.

She liked Sundays. She liked the leisurely pace of breakfast with Aniela and Bronek before getting ready for church at eleven. Bronek commented regularly on the political news from Poland he'd read in the *Polish Weekly*, or on the articles in *The Sunday Times* that questioned the wisdom of the government's latest strategy. Magda made an effort to give a semblance of informed conversation, at times playing the Devil's advocate, which made Bronek all the more eager to persuade her to his way of thinking. He wasn't fooled, but all the same she could see his pleasure when the argument was resolved with his opponent siding with him.

Aniela often commented on how the young ones these days had no sense of occasion and came to church dressed shabbily. It was true that some preferred jeans and casual tops to smart jackets, skirts or trousers, but Magda pointed out the girls made an effort with imaginative hair-styles and impossibly high-heeled shoes that made even the imperfect legs look good. To please Aniela, she always made an effort with her own appearance, wearing clean, crisp, co-ordinated clothes and tying her long hair into a neat topknot.

Magda sat up and at that precise moment it hit her: an overwhelming nausea and a cramp in her stomach. With one hand over her mouth and the other over her belly, she rushed to the bathroom and retched over the toilet bowl. It was ghastly: the spasms, the thick saliva, the copious watering of her eyes.

She rinsed her mouth and washed her face with litres of cold water, delaying the moment when she'd have to think. She buried her face in the towel and squeezed her eyes shut, pushing away that possibility which had haunted her in the past few weeks on top of everything else. The fear of *that* was her worst fear, worse than the grief of everything she had lost, worse than the hatred of the man who had robbed her of all things most precious, worse than her recurring nightmares, *that* fear was now becoming a reality which she could no longer ignore.

And even now, in the face of this most real possibility, there was an inner voice telling her that this was nothing more than an upset stomach. Something she'd eaten that had disagreed with her. Most probably something in the left-overs from last night's party at the hotel.

\*

'Shrimps! I never trust shrimps!' Bronek looked up from his paper, his brow knitting, when Magda declined a cooked breakfast. 'Did you eat shrimps last night?'

'There were no shrimps last night, Grandpa. I like shrimps. It could have been anything. Some spicy ingredient that disagreed with me.'

Magda's stomach was delicate, every movement making it unsteady. She sat down beside Aniela, who was spreading her toast with honey.

'Can I tempt you with anything here?' Aniela encouraged. There was the usual spread of ham and cheese and home-made jams. The sight of them and the smell of coffee made Magda feel queasier.

'Thank you, but I really have no appetite this morning. I'm sure by lunchtime, Babcha, I'll be ready for your roast,' she willed herself to hope.

'It'll be crispy roast pork,' Aniela said, 'your favourite, Magda. Lots of crackling.'

The very thought of that brought on another wave of nausea.

'I've got just the cure for all stomach bugs.' Bronek folded the paper and got up to fetch down a bottle from the dresser. The ruby liquid made of plum juice may have been refreshing to taste, but not when mixed with a high percentage of vodka. Bronek's well-intentioned eagerness made Magda smile, despite everything, but Aniela scolded him.

'Bronek! Really! On an empty stomach? On a Sunday morning? Before church?'

He sat down with mock sheepishness and sent Magda a mischievous grin, as he placed the bottle in the middle of the table.

'All right, then,' he conceded. 'Later. Just a little swig. It'll do you no harm, but may be a cure for your bug, Marta.'

'Magda,' Aniela corrected him. 'What will do Magda good right now is a little toast and mint tea.'

Strangely, the thought of this combination, especially the thought of burnt toast, did not make Magda's stomach flip.

'I think I'll be able to manage that,' she said brightly to please them.

The nausea passed by lunchtime. Magda felt enormous relief but no peace in her mind. She was hounded by a thousand 'what ifs'. The church service, the meeting in the hall afterwards with her grandparent's friends, and later the Sunday roast at home, the afternoon walk in the meadows, the long evening of Bronek's favourite programmes on the Polish channel, all the activities of the day were happening in another dimension, with her, like a spectator standing on the outside.

In bed that night, she struggled with the temptation to take one of Aniela's sleeping pills. Yet she dared not. In case there was another life to consider. Just in case. Exhaustion in the end brought a few hours' sleep, before the alarm woke her up at six. Even before she made the first move to get out of bed, nausea rose to her throat.

# CHAPTER 8

That week Magda was sick every morning.

Disbelief and revulsion gripped her in equal measures. How was that possible? How? When every cell in her body had screamed at him, rejected him, loathed him, wanted him dead that dreadful night? Now this, just when she was beginning to look forward to a more settled future.

If her condition was a fact (and she still hoped desperately that it was something else) then she was carrying his child. *His!* She wanted nothing of his! She would get rid of it. But the obvious and the quickest escape from this situation filled her with dread. Apart from her imagined messiness of the procedure, her strong Catholic upbringing conjured up images of little lost souls wandering in limbo for all eternity. Her only choice was to carry the child to the bitter end, then give it up for adoption.

Magda worked in a trance, performing all required tasks automatically, aware only of her inner turmoil that left her wrung out at the end of each day. At lunchtime, when she would sit with the rest of the girls in their basement common room, it was as if she were looking at them through a veil. She envied them their carefree chatter, feeling all the more weighed down with her terrifying burden.

Friday. She would finish her work earlier. She would go to Boots and find out for certain.

She was suddenly aware that Lin was talking to her, her lips delivering an excited barrage of words to the lively swing of her ponytail.

'Sorry, Lin?' Magda's fingers tightened around her cup of un-drunk mint tea. 'I was miles away.'

'I know.' Lin's cheeks dimpled. 'I was only saying would you like to come over on Sunday night to our house? Nothing posh. Not like your grandma's tea.' Her impish smile came with a self-deprecating shrug. She had been round to Magda's house a few times. 'Just a small get-together. Me and my friends.'

A get-together. Having to talk. Smile. Pretend. Magda could not do any of that. Besides, she could not imagine where she'd be on Sunday, once Aniela and Bronek knew the awful truth. She licked her lips, which were suddenly dry.

'Are you all right?' Lin's smile faded.

'Yes… thank you. Thank you, Lin, for the invite. I'd really love to come and meet your friends. But this Sunday I may have to go out with my Grandma. I think she's already got something planned.' This was not a lie. They were often out on Sundays.

'Going somewhere nice?' Lin asked.

Magda could barely concentrate.

'Their friends, most probably.' Soon they would know too. And the family. Beata, Janusz. Their children. What would they think of her? Magda felt sick.

'If your plans change,' Lin persisted, 'come over anyway.'

'Thank you, Lin. I'll let you know.'

*

At the end of her shift in the afternoon, Magda took a bus into town and before going home she stopped at Boots first. On shaky legs, she made her way to the pharmacy section. She had no idea where to look for the pregnancy testing kit, or what it looked like. Her eyes scanned nervously rows of small packets, bottles and jars, their colourful labels all looking similar, hundreds of them. She could be here for hours unless she asked for assistance. The very thought made her want to run.

And then she saw them; long, slim packages in the well-woman section, their brand names unambiguous, their small print, when she picked one, reassuring of the effectiveness. Which ones to trust? Were they all equally reliable? She picked the most expensive one. There was no room for mistakes.

Waiting in the queue to pay, she felt shaky, and when her turn came she was gripped with anxiety. She leaned over the counter and placing the package in front of the dispensing assistant she asked in whisper, 'Is this absolutely reliable?' Her question sounded stupid, but the woman's eyebrows lifted only a fraction.

She replied softly, 'Totally reliable.'

Two words, and a load fell off Magda's chest. The woman dropped the packet into a plastic bag, as if handling only aspirins. Magda paid hurriedly and with her eyes cast down hurried outside onto the street.

On the bus, she prayed for Bronek to be out. She could just about handle talking to Aniela first. To her relief he was not at home. Aniela was busy dusting and cleaning the front room. The window was wide open, the net curtain blowing in the warm breeze. Magda gave Aniela a hug, her stomach churning.

'Grandpa still at the allotment?' she asked with forced lightness.

Aniela leaned out of the window and shook the duster. The room smelled pleasantly of polish and lavender. She turned to Magda.

'Expect a giant salad this evening. Fancy a tea now?'

'I'll make it,' Magda offered. 'But first, I must get washed and changed.' She went into the kitchen, filled the kettle and switched it on. All the surfaces and the floor were gleaming in testimony to Aniela's meticulous attention. Another five minutes and the peace would be shattered. But perhaps not. She needed a miracle.

She ran upstairs and locked herself in the bathroom. With clumsy fingers, she unpacked the pregnancy testing kit and followed the instructions. Five minutes to wait. It was torture.

She showered and dried, feeling her neck ache with the tension. There was a tremor through her arms as she wrapped the towel around her and sat down on the toilet seat. With her eyes closed, she counted the last seconds before turning over the indicator. She opened her eyes and looked. Two blue lines.

It was still a shock to have her almost-absolute certainty confirmed. A strange limpness overwhelmed her, like defeat, but with it came unexpectedly a sense of relief. No more tormenting doubts.

She rose and, in a daze, went to her bedroom, where she dressed and combed her long hair, leaving it to dry naturally. She stared at herself in the mirror. She looked exactly the same as she did moments before. But she was no longer that person.

She placed her hand on her belly. There was still time to stop it. Destroy it. The temptation came frighteningly strong. The moment passed. She knew she could not do it. The price would have been too high. The haunting. The remorse. For the rest of her life.

She took a deep breath and went downstairs.

Aniela had already placed a plate of sliced lemon sponge on the kitchen table and was ready to make tea. Her face and her arms were the colour of dark honey from hours spent tending the back garden.

'Your favourite tea?' she asked.

Mint tea had become Magda's favourite drink since the previous Sunday, when she put on a pose of nursing an upset stomach. She did not disclose any further instances of vomiting, but to Aniela's delight developed a liking for the healthy herbal tea.

'Yes please. It's so refreshing in this hot weather,' she said.

Aniela brought over their two steaming mugs to the table and suggested sitting outside. Magda cleared her throat.

'Babcha, there's something I need to discuss with you. Better here, indoors. I don't want anyone else to hear it.'

Aniela leaned towards her, her blue eyes round in anticipation, her blond tinted curls framing her face.

'Good news, I hope Magda. For your sake. It wouldn't hurt fate to throw a smile your way.'

Magda squirmed. She waited for Aniela to be seated beside her at the table. She took a nervous sip of tea, aware of her beating heart, aware of the tension building up in Aniela's expectation.

'Babcha,' her voice did not sound like her own, 'it's not good news... I... I've no idea how to tell you.'

'Tell me what?' Aniela leaned closer. 'Just tell me simply. The only worst news is death. And it's not that, is it?'

Magda shook her head and kept her eyes down. Her clasped hands tested each other's strength, the knuckles shining white underneath the stretched skin.

'No, Babcha, it's not death. It's the opposite,' she said. She was jumping off a cliff. There was no return. 'I'm pregnant,' she said.

# CHAPTER 9

Once stated the words could not be unsaid. Magda was overcome with grief. She sat very still, head down, while tears trickled down her cheeks. She felt Aniela's arms, firm and soothing, hold her close, as she struggled to recover her composure. No outburst of shock from Aniela. No drama. Magda was weak with relief.

'That's life, Magda,' Aniela said simply. How could she be so calm? 'Don't despair so. Everything can be sorted. You must let your boyfriend know. You've never mentioned him. I can only guess that it's over between you and him, but it's his responsibility too. Who is he?'

'Babcha…' Magda shuddered. 'It's so complicated. I don't know where to begin…'

'At the beginning. Just tell me simply.' Aniela stroked Magda's hand.

The very thought of *him* made her feel unwell. She took a gulp of tea. She could barely utter his name.

'It was Uncle Zden. He did this to me.'

Aniela's head jerked back. Her eyes widened in horror and for a long while she just stared at Magda. Then slowly, her face came to life with an array of changing expressions.

'Zden?' Then louder. 'Zden?' With incredulity. 'Zden did this to you? But how's that possible? He was your guardian, for goodness' sake! You were like a daughter to him! Dear God! How did it ever come to this?'

'Babcha,' Magda cried out defensively, 'I've never ever done anything to make this happen. He raped me!'

She shocked herself with her own words. She shocked herself with the rawness of her pain, with the vivid memory of the things he did to her, of his brutal force, of his enslaving weight, of her helplessness and shame. She hugged herself and rocked in her wretchedness.

Then Aniela's arms were around her shoulders, and Magda sensed her agitation and her struggle to contain her shock.

'Magda, my dear Magda, my poor child…'

They said nothing for a while, just clung to each other. Aniela appeared to recover first. She sat upright and attempted her usual no-nonsense practical manner, but her voice shook with anger.

'I could murder him! The bastard! This is absolutely appalling!' She fell silent and her mouth trembled. She wrung her hands and closed her eyes, her expression pained as if she was fighting some internal battle. 'Magda,' she said at last, opening her eyes and looking at Magda with a fixed gaze. 'You're not on your own. You've got us! But tell me everything first.'

A weight fell off Magda's chest. At long last she'd be able to share all her worries with someone she could trust. She blew her nose and moved her chair closer to Aniela's. A bee was buzzing outside in the flowering basket. Such a normal soothing sound.

It was hard talking at first. Words came out in clusters, in stops and starts. But as Aniela listened, thoughtful, un-interrupting, absorbing every word, Magda's halting phrases settled into a coherent account of events: Emilia's diagnosis of terminal cancer, Zden's overreaction lapsing into habitual drinking, Magda's growing fear of his intimidating behaviour, and that horrific night after Emilia's death.

Magda could barely breathe when she finished speaking. They both remained quiet for a long time, Aniela's gaze fixed on some distant point beyond the window, and Magda rubbing her forehead as if that action could erase the ghastly images resurrected in her mind. She was still racked with utter disbelief.

'How could he do this to me? To anyone, Babcha? He'd been so good to me. All through my childhood. Made Aunt Lalka jealous. Stuck up for me when she called me the 'cuckoo child'. She was forever getting at him for caring more about me than his own nephews and nieces. Perhaps she'd been right all along. Perhaps that was all I was to him. A cuckoo child. An object...' Magda's eyes filled up and her voice faltered.

Aniela leaned towards her and spoke in an energetic yet comforting manner,

'My dear child, you must think only of yourself now, and of what is good for you. Have you thought what you're going to do now?'

Magda was prepared.

'Only a hundred times. I've thought of nothing else. I'll find accommodation elsewhere. I don't want to burden you with my problem. You've already done so much for me.'

Aniela's eyes widened in astonishment.

'What are you talking about? You'll do no such thing. Magda, how could you even think we'd turf you out now, when you'll be needing support? No, what I meant was, what are you going to do about Zden? What he did was a crime. A horrible crime. You should report it, really.'

Magda's heart began to hammer.

'No, Babcha, no! Please, no one must ever know. I feel so ashamed. Degraded. I don't want anyone to know. Please!' she took deep gasping breaths. Aniela placed her warm hand over hers and spoke soothingly,

'Magda... shh... I'm not going to say or do anything without your consent. Trust me.'

Magda felt suddenly limp, emptied of all strength. God, how desperate she was for this nightmare to be over, for her life to be simply normal.

'Babcha.' She spoke in a calmer manner. 'I don't want him to find out. Ever. I don't want him to have any claim on me. I've thought a lot about it. I'll carry this child and then give it up for adoption. I've no other choice. I don't want to be reminded of him for the rest of my life.'

She was expecting Aniela to nod in agreement but her Babcha took a moment to reply.

'Magda, you don't have to make any decisions in a hurry. You may find that in time you'll feel and think differently.'

'Never! I don't want his child! I don't want anything of his!'

Aniela's expression remained understanding, her tone gently persuasive. 'A child is not an object, Magda. He... she... will be a person not a possession. You may surprise yourself yet, how your feelings could change once the child is born.'

Magda sighed wearily.

'I know you mean to be kind, Babcha, but I've made up my mind. At this moment, my greatest worry is how am I going to tell Grandpa?'

Aniela gave her a hug, her scent of rose perfume, of recent baking and of lavender polish, soothing and reassuring.

'You must trust him,' she said. 'You could never imagine the things he saw and experienced in his youth. He was only a child in Siberia. He was forced to grow up fast and mature beyond his years. Many children were affected badly. Some could not cope with life afterwards. But Bronek somehow managed, and supported others around him. He was like a leader, like a guardian of our little group. I think' – Aniela's voice softened – 'he'll be even more protective when you tell him... He'll be mad with Zden, of course, and will want to kill him, but then when he settles down, he'll just want to sort things out in his own practical way.'

Magda looked up at the clock and dreaded Bronek's homecoming.

Bronek returned from his allotment around six, bearing gifts of all fresh produce: a giant lettuce, apple-sized tomatoes, a curved cucumber, radishes and spring onions. Magda made a fuss over the basket to please him. Her stomach was tight with tension and, as before, she had the feeling of standing on the edge of a precipice.

'I'll make the salad,' she offered brightly.

'Yours is the best!' He was, as ever, charming and approving of anything she did. Her spirit lifted a fraction as he went off to wash and change.

Over their supper of steamed salmon, new potatoes with dill and a bowl of mixed salad, Bronek told them of his colleagues from the allotment.

'You know, Aniela, that bloke with a scar over his eye...'

'Len.'

'That's right, Len. You'll never guess... He's got a friend on the allotment committee. And that friend informed him, secretly of course, that the chairman is thinking of taking Ted's allotment from him...'

'Ted's? But why?'

'Ted's not been very well lately. His plot is a bit overgrown. But not that bad as to snatch it from him! Anyway, that's not going to happen! Len, Raj and that lovely Jamaican lady... now, what's her name?' Bronek tapped his forehead. 'Anyway, tomorrow the four of us will weed Ted's garden before the chairman inspects it again. That'll teach him!' Bronek said with satisfaction as he buttered his bread.

'Good!' Aniela approved.

Magda only half-listened. This was excruciating, this small talk while she struggled with life-changing issues. And imagined Bronek's wrath when she told him.

She had never seen him angry, her kindly Grandpa. It scared her just thinking about it. And once he knew, she was certain he'd never look at her in the same way as before. Would he believe her absolute innocence? Or would he suspect she had led on a bereaved, broken man? She could not bear the thought of even a grain of doubt in her kind Grandpa's mind as to her honesty.

She helped to clear the table after the main course, and, when Aniela was ready to pour tea, Magda placed a plate of sliced lemon sponge before Bronek, knowing his weakness for Aniela's cakes.

'Magda, you help yourself first.' He held the plate for her, his mood ebullient. She took a slice but could not eat it. She sipped her mint tea and looked pleadingly at her Babcha. Aniela nodded and cleared her throat.

'Bronek, there's something Magda needs to tell you, but it's not easy for her.'

Bronek stopped eating, dabbed at his mouth with a napkin and turned all his attention at Magda. His manner towards her had always been warm and fatherly. She could not bear the thought of losing this bond between them.

'Grandpa…' her voice trembled. 'I'm too scared to tell you. I'm scared that you won't like me much when you know…'

'Know what?' He tilted his head, his voice gentle and encouraging.

'Bronek.' Aniela placed her hand on his arm. 'You know better than anyone how hard it is to talk about certain things.'

He appeared to stiffen and the look he gave Aniela was both alarmed and accusing.

'You haven't… have you?' he challenged her.

'It is your story to tell, not mine,' she said evasively.

All his previous cheerfulness was gone. His mouth set in a hard line and there was anger in his eyes.

'Those were terrible times! Nothing could compare to that!' he said.

Magda winced imagining his torment, but Aniela continued to stroke his arm as she spoke softly,

'Bronek, we are all family here. If we can't trust each other and share our troubles and offer each other support, who else can we turn to? Magda needs all our support now. Tell her about yourself. It'll make it easier for her to discuss her big problem with us.'

He kept his eyes down, his lined face, his white hair and something in the slump of his shoulders making him look vulnerable. Magda wished Aniela would not press him to reveal an episode from his past so as to make him more sympathetic to her present predicament. She almost blurted out, 'Stop! Don't torture yourself! I know everything! I just want you on my side!' But fear froze those words before they passed her lips. She waited for him to compose himself and wished none of this was happening.

'Bronek,' Aniela patted his hand, 'please say something.'

He looked up then and shrugged,

'What do you want me to say?'

'Just make it easier for Magda. You were a victim then, just as Magda is now.'

His expression became alert, his gaze sharp.

'Who has hurt you, Magda?'

Still, she could not speak. Tears filled her eyes and rolled down her cheeks. Nervously she wiped them with a tissue and felt a shift in his manner. He leaned closer over the table and when he spoke his tone conveyed a mixture of concern and anger.

'Who, Magda? Who has hurt you? Tell me what's happened.'

Magda's throat tightened even more. She took a gulp of tea, then another one. She breathed hard, bracing herself. But Aniela spoke before her, quietly, soothingly. 'Bronek, tell her about yourself first. She's very upset. Your story may give her a different perspective on her problems. We all three need to be involved.' She poured more tea into his cup.

He sat silent for a while, his hands clasped on the table, his gaze on the patterns of the wood-grain. It seemed for a moment as if he'd forgotten them. His voice made her start.

'Have you killed a man?' he asked.

# CHAPTER 10

Magda did not recoil. She knew his secret. She shook her head.

'Believe me, nothing could be worse than that,' he said. 'Nothing you tell me could shock me after what I've done.'

Magda coughed and took another big gulp of tea.

'Do you really want to hear my story?' he asked. She gave a nod. 'Then I hope it will give you confidence to tell me about your problem.'

Aniela topped up everyone's cup then sat back with folded arms ready to listen. There was a faint drone of a lawnmower a few doors away.

Bronek ran his fingers through his hair, leaving it ruffled, which gave him a boyish look. He had been once a defenceless little boy, Magda thought, this white-haired man with all his life's pitfalls etched in his craggy face and all the wisdom of his experiences locked in his intense gaze.

'We were small children when the Russians came to our village,' he began. 'They evicted whole families from their homes, packed us on cattle trains and sent us to Siberia. I was eight at the time. It was frightening. But what frightened me the most' – he looked up at Magda, his expression pained at the memory – 'was seeing the grown-ups cry. To a small child, as you know, a grown-up is almighty. But, when that grown-up looks frightened and confused, the child's world is shattered.'

He paused thoughtfully. 'But I remember some good things too. Once, someone gave me an apple. Another time, someone gave me a baked potato. I still remember that taste today.' His eyes glistened. 'The second summer we were there, and close to liberation, though we did not know it then, I was ten and working with other children on the embankment by the river. Can you imagine that now?' He raised his eyebrows at the very thought. 'Ten and twelve-year-olds wielding axes and saws? Health and safety...' he mused, 'I wonder if even today anyone bothers over there...'

He paused. 'The women's work was to push the logs off the embankment into the river. Stacks and stacks of logs. Trees had been cut down in the winter months. It was back-breaking work pushing the logs. Dangerous too, if you were caught between them. It would have been hard labour for strong and sturdy men, never mind weak and underfed women. Then one day...' He paused, his brow puckering. 'I saw a Russian guard molesting my mother. She was just getting on with her job, ankle-deep in mud on the edge of the bank. Her face was flushed and I could see she was close to tears with the effort of pushing the logs. He stood behind her and as she was bending over, he started prodding her bottom with his rifle. She cried and begged him to stop it. "Just let me get on with my job," she pleaded. "I've got mouths to feed. I've got to meet the target." But he just laughed at her, lifted her skirt with his rifle and started making lewd gestures.'

Bronek stopped and screwed his eyes tight. His shoulders and arms became rock-rigid. After a moment he opened his eyes and looked directly at Magda. 'I was possessed with such mad fury, I wanted to kill the man. I did not think; I just did what came automatically. I ran down the embankment and with all my force pushed the man out of the way. And then I watched in horror, as he lost his footing and fell into the river. The logs closed over him and he was gone. It all happened in a few seconds. Even if people had tried to save him, they wouldn't have had a chance.'

Magda held her breath. The lawnmower droned on a few doors away. Bronek's gaze was intense and his hands clasped hard on the table.

'Everyone around me stood frozen in terror. As if by a miracle, there were no other guards around. A woman nearby recovered first and urged me, "Quick, Bronek, quick! Get back to your work!" As I scrambled up the embankment the women got on with their jobs, as if nothing had happened and the children surrounded me, as if trying to hide me. Not one child said anything. Another woman came over and said to us, "Not a word to anyone. Remember, we could all be shot for this. When you're tempted to say anything, say to yourself, I'll be dead tomorrow. That will remind you." This incident was never mentioned. It just showed how scared people were. Even young children understood the danger.'

Bronek fell silent, and, though his story was terrifying, Magda could not help a smidgen of satisfaction, that retribution had been immediate in that incident. The bastard had got what he deserved. How often did that happen in life? Zden. She stiffened with loathing. If only she had half the chance...

Bronek looked wrung out, diminished, his shoulders sagging.

She asked, 'Grandpa, wasn't the guard missed? Weren't there questions asked?'

'We never found out,' Aniela answered for Bronek. 'For the next day "amnesty" was announced. And straight away people started to leave the camp. I like to think, for Bronek's sake, that the river current took the man along and threw him out to safety, somewhere else.'

'If that happened, wouldn't he have come back looking for Grandpa?' Magda reasoned.

'Perhaps he did.' Aniela said. 'Perhaps by that time we had left our camp. No one hung around for a moment longer than they had to. People left in droves, not just from our camp but from all the labour camps in the area. Even if the man came back searching for Bronek, he'd never find him in the crowds of children, all looking the same, skin and bones wrapped in rags.'

Bronek cleared his throat. 'I've had to live with this all my life. I've confessed this crime a hundred times. I've been given absolution every time. Every priest I've spoken to reassured me that I only did that to protect my mother, that I was a child, that the man was a threat, that there is nothing in our religion that stops us from defending ourselves. They made me sound almost like a hero. But, in my mind, this has stayed like a nightmare. Forever. That awful moment. Of him disappearing in the water. I see it as clearly as I saw it then. And that's sixty-three years ago! And yet...' He paused. 'I'd do the same thing again if anyone threatened the person I loved.'

Magda shivered. 'It scares me, Grandpa, when you talk like that. What I have to tell you will make you very angry.'

He sat up, but not rigidly, and his face softened as he spoke. 'Magda, you must never be afraid of me. I'm always on your side, and whatever problem you've got, we, that is, Aniela, you and me, we'll sort it out together. You'll see.'

Magda needed to hear those words to give her the push to start.

'Grandpa...' she began hesitantly, 'that day when Aunt Emilia died, something else happened. It was so horrible, so dreadful that I never wanted to think or talk about it, I just wanted to forget it all. In time, I hoped, because it's not possible to forget something like that...' This was torture. But Bronek did not interrupt; he watched her with a kind expression that encouraged her to talk.

'When Uncle Zden came home that night he was very drunk, very angry, out of control. He took it out on me.' Her throat was dry. She took a gulp of tea. Bronek leaned forward.

'What did he do?'

Her heart thumped in her chest, in her throat, in her head. 'The worst, Grandpa' – her voice dropped to a whisper – 'the worst a man can do to a woman.'

It was frightening to watch Bronek. First puzzlement, then a wide-eyed look, then naked fury as he got up abruptly, his chair scraping the floor. His hands clenched into hard fists. He barely controlled his voice.

'I'll kill him! I'll kill the bastard! I swear to God!'

Magda's heart pounded like a hammer.

Aniela waited a moment before speaking. Her voice was firm. 'Bronek, calm yourself down. Please, sit down. There's much to be discussed, but not like this.'

He did not appear to have heard her at all. He began to pace up and down the small kitchen floor, bristling with fury, his fists punching the space around him.

'Please, Grandpa.' Magda raised a small voice. He stopped abruptly and made her recoil, as he bent down to her.

His expression turned instantly soft and his voice contritely tender as he spoke to her. 'Magda, my dear Magda, don't be afraid of me.' He placed his hands on her shoulders tenderly. 'Don't ever be afraid of me. I'm here to protect you, not to hurt you. It's that bastard making me so angry. Just tell me what to do, and it'll give me great pleasure to beat the living daylights out of him!' He sat down beside her, his face twitching with suppressed emotions as he waited for her to speak.

Magda shook her head.

'Grandpa, that's not the end of it. I thought I could leave this nightmare behind, but I can't. I've just discovered... that... I'm expecting his baby.'

He did not respond with wild fury this time. He stared at her. He stared at Aniela, his accelerated thoughts reflecting in his changing expressions. His arms dropped down to his sides; he looked defeated. But only for a moment. He got up again, as if ready for action.

'God! I'd like to strangle him! But this changes everything. Magda, what would you like me to do?'

'I'd like you to sit down,' Aniela said, 'and hear Magda out.'

This gave Magda a moment to pull herself together. The worst was out in the open. The relief strengthened her conviction as regards her decision. So, when Bronek asked, 'Do you want him to know?' Magda answered readily, 'No, Grandpa, never! I don't want to have any links with him. I don't want to see him ever again! I don't want anyone to know. I want this to remain just between the three of us. Just our secret. Once the child is born and adopted, I want to get on with my own life. Free of him for ever.'

There was a silence between them as they sat for a while, immersed in their own thoughts. Then Bronek surprised her, as he unknowingly echoed Aniela's words. 'We shall respect your wishes, Magda. But you don't have to make any decision right now. These are important matters. Life-long decisions. You need to consider them thoroughly. You don't want to have regrets later.'

The change in his mood, so incredible, gave her the courage to insist, 'That's my decision, Grandpa. Believe me, I have thought long and hard about it. But we have a much more immediate matter to sort out first. Before long people will notice. Especially at the church. There will be talk. Gossip. I want to spare you all that.' She turned to Aniela. 'I know what you said before, Babcha, but I still think it will be best if I move out.'

'Out of the question!' Bronek's reaction was so vehement it made her flinch. Aniela covered Magda's hand with hers in a warm and comforting gesture.

'Nothing has to change, Magda,' she said. 'We'll just carry on as before.'

Their kindness was overwhelming and threatened another attack of tears. She waited for the moment to pass then controlled her voice to sound practical.

'What shall we tell the nosy parkers? There will be questions asked. We need to be prepared.'

Aniela patted her hand.

'You don't have to explain anything. You could have been engaged. And it didn't work out. Such things are common.'

Magda's heart fluttered, 'D'you know, Babcha, that wouldn't be a lie. I did lose someone very special because of this. Dominik. A medical student. I knew him only for a short while, but we were already like soul-mates. He came from a good family. They'd be horrified at this...' her voice trailed off.

'He doesn't know?' Aniela's voice conveyed surprise, but then she gave a nod of understanding.

Magda lowered her eyes.

'Nobody knows. Not even my best friend, Natalia. I thought it best if I simply disappeared. This way Dominik has a chance to find somebody else.'

'Oh, Magda...' Aniela was full of sympathy, 'if he loves you truly, he would be all the more understanding and loving.'

Magda shook her head.

'No, Babcha, I would complicate his life. His family's life too. I could not bear him knowing the truth about how this happened. This way I've left him wondering but not despising me. No doubt he'll find a girl more suitable for his family's approval.'

For a while nobody spoke, their faces illuminated by the glare from the polished pine, caught in the rays of the lowering sun. The back garden, seen through the open door, was a pattern of elongated shadows that cut across the lawn and across the borders of luminous summer flowers. Magda could only guess what her grandparents were thinking about her and Dominik, about Zden and what he had done, and about her decisions. Right now, she could not imagine what else she could have done to protect Dominik from a burden that would have been herself, or how to protect her own future from a living reminder of Zden's unspeakable crime. Only time would tell if her decisions were right.

Aniela got up to refill the teapot. Bronek turned to Magda.

'Believe me,' he said, 'everything passes. Even the worst things. And often, what you consider a total disaster can quite unexpectedly turn to your advantage.'

She nodded in acknowledgement of his well-meant words, but all she wished for was for this to be over, and for every trace of her predicament to be eliminated from her life. She remained quiet while they waited for the kettle to boil.

Aniela returned to the table with a fresh pot of tea and invited them to another slice of cake. Magda declined. Bronek took a piece but then absent-mindedly reduced it to crumbs on his plate, his concentration totally absorbed by his own thoughts.

Magda took a sip, licked her lips and asked timidly.

'What now? Don't I need to register with a doctor?'

Aniela immediately reassured her.

'Don't worry about that. I'll make an appointment at our surgery, with my own doctor, a lady, and I'll come with you, of course.'

Magda was struck with a fresh anxiety.

'What will she think of me?'

Aniela gave her hand a motherly squeeze.

'Don't worry about that, Magda. You've no idea how many hundreds of cases she has to deal with every year, some very difficult, some very upsetting. I know, I've worked in that surgery all my working life. Believe me, a pregnancy is one of the pleasant tasks to deal with, for any doctor.'

'Not in my case.'

Aniela gave her hand another motherly pat.

'My doctor is very sympathetic and efficient. You'll have to tell her everything.'

Magda's heart missed a beat.

'Do I have to?'

'Yes. Your medical history is very important. It is also confidential. No information will be passed onto anyone without your written and signed permission. But what's most important here is that, once she knows the whole truth, it will make her sympathetic to your decision about adoption. Trust me, she'll do everything to help you.'

Magda did not doubt Aniela's words. If only there was a way of sorting out this problem anonymously! But there was not. Magda felt sick at the thought of her shame being exposed, even if it were just one more person.

She took another sip of tea and consciously changed the subject.

'There's just one more thing I want to mention.' They looked up at her alarmed, but she hurried to explain, 'No, no… it's nothing serious. It's just that I've been thinking a lot about it recently. I'd like to change my name to an English name.'

'What for?' they exclaimed together.

Magda managed a smile.

'You'll laugh at me. It's sheer superstition. But I can't help thinking about it. Perhaps, with a new name, my luck will change too.'

'You don't believe that!' Aniela uttered with theatrical scorn and Bronek protested too, 'But I love your name! Magda.' His preoccupied expression melted in his wide smile.

Seeing him like this made Magda relax and hazard teasing him. 'So that is why you keep calling me Marta?' And, before he could protest, she patted his hand affectionately on the table and added in haste, 'But that's all right, Grandpa! Can't you see? By calling me another name, you're working the magic already. You and Babcha are my magic, my new good luck. A new name will be like a talisman.'

They looked bemused.

She added in earnest, 'Seriously, I thought it would be more practical. You know what it's like. Questions and explanations wherever you go. All that form-filling everywhere. An English name won't stick out. I'll be able to blend in with everyone else, wherever I go, just as it used to be at home. You can't imagine what it's like, till you're the odd one out.'

At the back of her mind, there was a voice of reassurance: a new identity in a new country would distance her from Zden. Of course, he could find her, if he set his mind on it, but she doubted he would. Nevertheless, a new name was like an additional barrier between her and *him*.

To her relief Bronek nodded in understanding.

'Magda's got a point,' he said. 'I remember only too well how it was with my name at the beginning. Bronislaw Sokolski. No one even attempted to say it. Explanations everywhere I went. It's only in recent years that things have changed. No one bats an eyelid now whether you're a Bronek, an Ahmet or a Nibelung.'

'And that is precisely my point,' Aniela said with emphasis. 'You don't have to change your name, Magda. Be proud of your name! Be proud to be Polish!'

'I am!' Magda replied hotly. 'Believe me, Babcha. In my head and in my heart, I could never be anyone else but a Polish girl. But the new name... it's something I need to do. It's like starting a new phase in my life. I hope it brings me luck. Please be happy for me, Babcha. I need you to approve.'

Aniela challenged her with a stubborn gaze, but then her expression softened and she spread her hands in good-natured resignation.

'What can I say? It's your life, Magda. You've got to do what's best for you. What will you call yourself?'

Magda had thought much about this too.

'Madeleine,' she said simply. 'It's the same name as Magda, from Magdalene. And I thought that Zielinska has a good connotation with Greenwood. *Zielen* and greenery. Madeleine Greenwood.'

'Hmmm...' Aniela took a moment to think. 'Yes, I suppose it sounds all right. Madeleine Greenwood. I shall have to get used to it. But,' she nodded, smiling, 'I believe it suits you.'

A few words and Magda's spirits lifted. Bronek looked distracted, his hair ruffled and sprinkled with crumbs where his fingers had attempted to smooth it down.

'Magda, my dear,' he said, 'Madeleine is a beautiful name, but for me you'll always be Marta... er... Magda,' he corrected himself.

Madeleine chuckled and Aniela's smile said it all.

*

In bed that night, Magda felt wrung out with weariness. She lay limp against the pillow, her arms inert beside her. She wished she could switch off her brain, empty her mind of all worries, eliminate forever the vivid memories she wished to forget, that almost nightly haunted her dreams.

'Time,' Aniela had comforted her, whenever unexpectedly Magda was overcome with grief. It could be in town, on a walk, while weeding the garden, while watching television. 'You need time, Magda. It's all still very recent and raw. A deep gash does not heal overnight. This is the same. You've been through a lot in a very short time. It will get better, believe me.'

'But why did this have to happen to me? Why? What have I done to deserve it?' Magda once sobbed in a moment of utter defeat.

Aniela had hugged her saying, 'Things like that and worse happen all the time. Not just to you. Life is like that. No one escapes unscathed one way or another. But I'll tell you something. You must never give up. You must always think like a child, always expect magic. We did, when we were small children at the mercy of our Russian captors. We did not understand why we were so far away from home, why we were always so cold and so hungry. But we still made up stories of what we wanted to be one day. You must give your spirit a chance to perk up. Make plans for the future. There's no harm in having lots of dreams. If one doesn't work out, there's plenty more that may come true for you.'

Her dreams for the future had been so clear only several weeks ago back home. She had it all sorted in her mind, the life with Dominik, happily married one day, settled in their flat in Krakow, immersed in work they loved, two children, a boy and a girl, family life with much travelling abroad, every Pole's dream. There was so much to dream about, so much to look forward to.

What now? The dreaded pregnancy. At least it had a deadline, a marking point in her life that would free her to make a fresh start. That very thought gave her a momentary buoyant lift to start imagining what that would be like. She was determined to finish her studies and find a satisfying job with a reasonable salary. She could not imagine returning home to Poland, certainly not to her town, where people knew her. What would it be like to stay long-term in a foreign country? Would the English people accept her? Would she be able to make friends?

Again, she found a comfort of sorts in Aniela's words. 'D'you know? Wherever I've been in the world I discovered that all people have certain things in common: they all want to live in peace, they all want a better future for their children and they all cherish genuine friends.'

But where would she find them, the English friends? The only English people she had met were the recruitment officer, the kind woman supervisor at the sausage factory, the terrifying Mr Gordon, Britney and Sam, the chain smokers at the hospital washing-up unit, and her present boss, Paul. He was a busy man and her contact with him was purely work-related. All her colleagues, with whom she got on very well, were foreign workers.

Magda closed her eyes and allowed random images to float across her mind. They were scenes from the English films that she had seen as part of her English studies. She had liked the characters of Darcy and Bridget as portrayed in the *Bridget Jones* films; she had liked Judi

Dench and Maggie Smith as the two eccentric 'Lavender Ladies'. She had enjoyed enormously the films that had been based on Jane Austen's novels. But this last category especially was a charming fantasy, bearing no resemblance to the present life in England. Why would anyone seek to befriend her when the Poles, arriving in droves, were generally perceived as a threat to the indigenous workforce?

She thought suddenly of the young man she had spied upon by chance from Mrs Demska's garden. He had looked so distressed at the time. There had been something about him that she liked instantly. It may have been simply the fact that her own delicate emotional state found instinctive empathy with his. She wondered if he had solved his problem by now. Whatever it had been, it could not have compared to hers. And, from what she had inadvertently eavesdropped, he appeared to have been speaking to a supportive friend on his mobile. Good luck to him, she thought.

She had been lucky too, she reflected with a sense of deep gratitude to someone above, for giving her two such kind people. Where would she be without them now? Having discussed her next step with them, she could now see some order being restored to her life. Next year at this time, with her big problem resolved, she could begin to look forward to her future.

# CHAPTER 11

## 2012 – Seven Years Later

Madeleine Greenwood stood behind the net curtain and looked down from her bedroom onto the street. It was a familiar sight: tall and substantial terraced houses with bay windows, recessed doorways, prettily tiled half way up, and wide pavements that were lined with equally spaced-out plane trees.

She checked both sides of the street. What had started as a compulsion was now a ritual, the pre-requisite to the start of a good day. She satisfied herself that there was no one lurking in the shadows. The few pedestrians rushing to work each morning had become, over a period of time, a reassuringly familiar sight. Already the bright sunshine held a promise of a warm day, as it shimmered through the fresh green of the tree crowns and bounced off the red-brick walls. Most of the windows had retained the bunting and their displays of flags, put up some weeks ago at the start of the Queen's Diamond Jubilee. It was now the end of April.

Madeleine picked up her fresh change of underwear and made her way to the bathroom. She could hear Aniela and Bronek already up and busy downstairs. There was something pleasantly reassuring in the soft sound of their muffled voices, in the aroma of coffee and toast permeating the staircase.

Ten minutes later, after an invigorating shower, she was back in her room checking her appearance in the long mirror hung on the wardrobe door. The navy dress, teamed with patent high-heeled shoes, gave her a business-like appearance. It mattered to her to be taken seriously. Around her neck she fastened a silver chain with a filigree butterfly, a precious memento – her mother's. She sat down at the dressing table, the old brown wood with the age-spotted mirror, and applied make-up to her eyes and lips. She had offered to replace the glass, but Bronek liked things to remain just as they were. He was sentimentally attached to his old possessions, acquired a long time ago with much scrimping and saving.

As she brushed her short hair into a neat bob, she saw a movement reflected in the mirror. Emily waking up.

Since her daughter's birth six years before, Madeleine could not stop berating herself for her hostile feelings towards her child throughout her pregnancy. Now, she could not imagine her life without Emily. The moment she had held her new-born daughter to her breast, and her baby's eyes opened and gazed at her with that puckered expression of total helplessness, Madeleine knew that she and her child could not be separated. The amazing thing was that Emily did not resemble or remind Madeleine of anyone. She was just herself. Emily. Unique. She needed protection and the best person to do that could only be herself. Madeleine was instantly convinced of that. As her baby's tiny body clung to her flesh, Madeleine was overcome with intense love and joy. For the first time in her life, here was a being that was entirely her own. No one could ever split them up.

Aniela had cried with happiness at Madeleine's decision and Bronek fell in love with Emily at a first glance and forever.

Presently, Madeleine watched her daughter's reflection in the mirror. A sleepy face above the bedclothes, ruffled hair, thin arms stretching out, a big yawn.

'Mama.' Emily sat up, hugging her knitted rabbit with long dangly ears. 'Is it time to get up?'

Madeleine came over and gave her child a cuddle, breathing in the warm smell of last night's bubble bath and talcum powder.

'Emily, look how sunny it is today. You can wear your summer uniform, your favourite blue dress with the pockets. And it will be much fun at school today. With all the playtimes outside!'

'And I'll play with Karishma!' Emily's eyes lit up, her face lively with anticipation, as she scrambled out of her bedclothes.

*

All was ready for Emily on the breakfast table: two spoonfuls of coco-pops, a small triangle of toast with peanut butter and an orange drink. Aniela knew Emily's food preferences thoroughly and happily indulged her. Madeleine guessed this was a way of recapturing Aniela's own grandchildren's childhood, when they came regularly to spend holidays with her and Bronek.

'How about having some of my delicious scrambled egg?' Bronek teased gently, his eyes sparkly underneath the bushy eyebrows. He was buttering a thick slice of sourdough bread.

Emily shook her head and gave him a smile of her stubby baby teeth.

'No, thank you, Grandpa. There's no room in my tummy.' She was a small and thin child and found a full plate daunting.

Madeleine made herself a toast and coffee and joined them at the table.

'You call this breakfast?' Aniela's scornful tone made it obvious what she thought. She was making herself a ham and cheese sandwich. 'If only you'd let me make you a proper breakfast, Magda! I've no idea what you exist on!'

Madeleine leaned over and kissed Aniela's pink and rounded cheek. 'At the weekend, Babcha, when we have time to enjoy it.'

'You need energy every day, even more in the weekdays when you're dashing from place to place,' Aniela stated sternly. She did that every morning. Dear Babcha Aniela. She loved feeding people. There was no doubt that this was her way of making up for the years of imposed hunger in her childhood. The Siberian years. Madeleine had offered countless times to help out in the kitchen, but her offer was rejected as an affront to Aniela's cooking talents. It was best not to argue.

'My dear girl,' Aniela would rebuff her. 'You've got your work and I've got mine. I love cooking. Don't deprive me of my little pleasure.'

Madeleine channelled her gratitude into helping out with the shopping, taking Aniela to appointments at the surgery or the dentist, sharing the heavier housework chores at the weekend. At seventy-five, Aniela was spritely and active, but, when her arthritic hip was giving her a hard time, she did not argue with Madeleine about carrying the shopping or vacuum-cleaning the staircase. The unwritten arrangement worked well.

This morning, as every morning, small talk accompanied the pleasant ambience of breakfast: talk of the latest news, the weather, the Queen's Jubilee, the forthcoming Olympics.

'In my school,' Emily announced, chewing her toast ten times, as instructed in her lesson on healthy eating, 'we have a white line on the grass. We practise long jumps all the time. I can jump that much!' She stretched out her thin arms and held them out for everyone to admire the length of her long jump.

'Emily, don't speak with your mouth full,' Madeleine reminded her, 'and keep your hands on the table.'

'Look! I swallowed!' Emily demonstrated by opening her mouth wide.

'Emily!' Madeleine gave her a stern look that had immediate effect. Emily took another bite of her toast and began to chew with her mouth firmly closed.

'She is a good girl.' Aniela stroked Emily's silky hair, caught neatly in a plait at the back of her neck. 'Keep on practising. We'll all come to watch you at the Olympics one day, Emily, when you grow up.'

'When will that be?' Emily's lively voice reflected the excitement in her eyes.

'Not the next ones, but the ones after that,' Aniela explained. 'The year 2020.'

Emily counted on her fingers. 'That's another eight years. I'll be... fourteen!' She laughed at the very thought of it. Then her expression changed. 'Mama, will you be back on time this afternoon?'

Madeleine looked at Aniela as she replied, 'I hope so, but...'

Aniela stepped in, 'Don't worry, Emily, I'll fetch you, if Mummy can't get back in time.'

'I'll give you a ring,' Madeleine said.

Bronek got up and moved to the oak dresser that stood against the wall and displayed a delicate china dinner service. He pressed his ear against the wall and listened. They watched him in silence, Emily with fascination, her brown eyes unblinking. They were used to this daily compulsion of his, and to Aniela's words that followed regularly, 'Bronek, my dear, do sit down and finish your breakfast. You know there's no one there.'

'Just checking.' He offered no explanations.

This bizarre behaviour had started about a year before.

'Spies. They're everywhere,' he would mutter mysteriously when challenged by Aniela, who was alarmed at the beginning when he started checking behind the shed, behind the summer house, behind the screening wall at the allotment, listening at the back gate, listening against the party wall.

On one of her weekend visits, their daughter Beata examined him.

'Don't worry, Mum,' she had comforted Aniela afterwards, 'Dad's managing really well for eighty. He's still doing everything he did twenty years ago. His mind may be starting to play tricks on him, but forgetfulness and distraction are common in old age. And this fixation of his about Russian spies is most probably linked to his childhood experiences. He's not likely to talk about it, and if your friends notice any changes in him, so what? They've been friends long enough to understand and to accept him as he is. If it eases your mind, I can go with him to your own GP, but she'll tell you the same things I've just told you now. Mum, the important thing is, he is still ever cheerful, ever optimistic, always kind and eager to help. He makes it so easy to love him.'

Madeleine agreed with Beata. Bronek's quirkiness did not diminish his naturally good nature. Like his daughter, Madeleine loved him all the more.

After breakfast, the usual hugs and goodbyes followed. Bronek, as always, bartered with Emily for more hugs. Madeleine slipped on her jacket, that matched her navy dress, and helped Emily into her summer school blazer. Just then, the sound of the letter box alerted them to the delivered post. Madeleine picked up the usual pile of advertisement leaflets and flyers, two letters from the bank for her grandparents, and a brown envelope with a large print of CRISIS for her. There was also a white long envelope with Polish stamps and her name and address on it. Her heartbeat quickened at the sight of the familiar handwriting. Even after all the years. Natalia's.

Madeleine's impulse was to tear open the envelope straight away. But there was no time. She dropped it into her handbag and led Emily outside to her car, a miniature, second-hand, red Ford Ka. Madeleine loved it, if objects could be loved. Without her Ka she wouldn't have been able to do the job she did. With Emily strapped safely in the back seat, Madeleine steered the car onto the main road.

Thoughts of Natalia flooded her mind. Her image was still so vivid despite the time of seven years separating them. So totally unexpected, this letter from her. What could she be writing about after all that time? A shiver of anticipation as well as foreboding ran down Madeleine's spine. She forced her mind to concentrate on the road, heavily congested with the morning traffic.

Emily's school could be accessed round the back streets and along a track that once had been the Great Central Line, but in the mornings Madeleine dropped Emily off on her way to work. She parked her Ka a little distance from the school gate and joined the procession of chatty mothers and their lively children, as they made their way up the path to the school playground. Emily clutched her hand and Madeleine was seized with acute tenderness at the sight of her daughter's neat hair parting and the plait resting on the back of her slender neck. It was always a wrench leaving her child, even if only for a few hours each day.

Emily lifted her earnest brown eyes and asked, 'Will you be back on time, Mama?'

Madeleine was never sure what surprises lay in store for her, but she did not want to leave Emily fretting all day.

'Of course, I'll be here,' she said firmly, 'but if by chance I get stuck in the traffic, Babcha will come to fetch you. You'll be good, won't you?'

Emily looked thoughtful, then her face lit up.

'Can Karishma come to play?'

'Of course.' Madeleine laughed, relieved it was so easy to satisfy her child.

The playground was a busy place, with children running around the groups of mothers, engaged in lively conversations. Madeleine knew a few and acknowledged them with a nod and a smile. A large proportion were non-English women, among them some Polish girls. She had exchanged pleasantries with them occasionally but had kept her distance. She had a dread of being asked personal questions, even though it was hard not having a close friend. Lin had filled that gap for a while, but after marrying she moved to London. Magda had missed Lin, only frequent texting kept them in touch. She never stopped missing Natalia. She had bitter regrets about not contacting her best friend and had thought of Natalia most days, but the cut-off from her past had had to be radical to protect herself and Emily. And now, this letter!

The sound of the bell stopped the children in their tracks, then, at the second signal, like a breaking swarm of bees, they assembled in lines in front of their waiting class teachers. Madeleine gave Emily a hug and watched her skip towards her friend Karishma.

Madeleine's first appointment was at a secondary school, an enormous U-shaped, two-storey building, with a spacious quadrangle for visitors' cars. Madeleine was obsessively punctual and liked arriving for her meetings with time to spare and wait in her car, rather than be stuck in the traffic. She always carried translation work with her and made good use of any waiting time, but now the only thing on her mind was Natalia's letter.

She could barely control the tremor in her hands, as her eyes scanned the neatly written page. Sweet relief swept over her. She read the letter the second time, slowly, carefully, enjoying every word. Natalia wrote:

*Dear Magda,*

*I've been wanting to get in touch with you a thousand times. I saw your Uncle Zden once, soon after you left. He said you'd had a nervous breakdown and it was best to leave it to you to make the first contact. He didn't look that good himself.*

*I waited. Life has moved on. I finished my studies, got my degree, and for the past three years I've been teaching English at St Casimir Grammar School.*

*The other day I was tidying out some old papers and found a letter from you written when you were visiting your grandparents in England that first time. Their address was on it and I took it as a sign to get in touch with you.*

*I want to share some good news with you. I'm getting married to Szymon, remember him? We've been together since our student days, since not long after you went away. He came into my life just at the right time and now I couldn't imagine my life without him. I'd be so very, very happy Magda, if you could come to our wedding. It's on 11<sup>th</sup> August.*

*Please write. I was distraught and missed you terribly after you left. I believed there must have been a very good reason for your long silence. Tell me everything. I'll be waiting.*

*With much love, as always, Natalia.*

Magda read the letter for the third time, her heart skipping madly, her anxieties receding to the back of her mind. She was seized with acute longing to see her friend, to tell her everything. But that was impossible. Her first duty was to her daughter, to keeping secret the identity of her father.

Natalia was getting married. Madeleine had never allowed herself that hope. She could not imagine trusting any man enough to share her troubled past with him. She would never give any man the chance to treat her with doubt, contempt, then the inevitable rejection. Keeping up the facade of an unmarried mother by choice gave her the image, she believed, of being in control of her life.

Yet, for the moment, Madeleine could not stop the bubbling elation at the mere fantasy of going to Natalia's wedding. She wanted to so much! Could it be made possible? She had much careful thinking to do.

She got out her translation papers but found it hard to concentrate. Among them was a variety of official forms that needed filling or checking for her clients, who were depending on her language skills. Her eyes skimmed them quickly: a woman's CV. She was applying for a carer's job. She had been a qualified nurse in Poland. Another was a letter of application by a middle-aged man for a manager's job in a warehouse. He had held a similar position at home, but the pay here was infinitely better. While taking on the first job available, checking and packaging shoes in a factory, he had also enrolled on an evening course to improve his English. He needed Madeleine to check the finer points. Most requests were similar.

At ten to ten, Madeleine walked into the reception area of the Mountblossom Academy and presented herself at the desk. The receptionist, a middle-aged woman with uncovered plump arms and gold-rimmed glasses, led Madeleine down a long corridor, her floral scent overcome at some point by drifting whiffs of cooking from another part of the building. An overpowering hush filled the lofty space around them with just a hint of distant muffled sounds.

'It's like inside a church,' Madeleine stage-whispered, and smiled.

'You should hear the kids when they change rooms.' The receptionist's eyebrows lifted expressively. But then she added with deadpan expression, 'Though of course we are proud of our code of excellent practice and exemplary behaviour.' Madeleine allowed herself a secret little smirk. Jargon. Wherever her services as an interpreter were required, she came across jargon upon jargon. Didn't the people hear themselves parroting each other?

They stopped at a door and the receptionist knocked before entering. The interview room was a small room furnished with a couple of easy chairs, a bookcase with colourfully illustrated hardbacks, and, in the middle, a table with six upright chairs. Two women were already seated with files opened before them. Short introductions followed, after which the receptionist withdrew.

Dr Jones was a white blonde with transparent-blue eyes, dressed in a black linen suit that sucked out all colour from her pale complexion. Mrs Wright, the social worker, wore a fixed smile and a bright pink jacket that intensified the colour of her ginger curls.

Dr Jones spoke first, with a business-like edge to her tone.

'No doubt, you're familiar with the procedure.'

'Yes, I am,' Madeleine replied pleasantly. 'My services have been used on numerous occasions at various schools. I'll do my best.'

Mrs Wright nodded as she made notes in her file. Then she addressed Dr Jones.

'Pity the father can't be here this morning. Doesn't like taking time off work.'

That did not surprise Madeleine. Every Pole she knew worked hard to secure a good job permanently.

From the snippets of exchanged remarks between the two women, Dr Jones's especially guarded, Madeleine pieced together a picture of a boy of twelve, with separated parents, a difficult family situation, and reports of bullying and self-harm. Even before she saw the boy for the first time, she was already feeling sorry for him. Her own Emily, though fatherless, had three people constantly involved in her upbringing.

The door opened and a young, friendly-looking woman, with bouncy hair and a bouncy step, walked in, steering a boy in front of her. Madeleine guessed she was the teacher's assistant. The boy looked small for his age. He gave Mrs Wright a fleeting thumbs-up sign of recognition, then his dark eyes darted suspiciously from Dr Jones to Madeleine. What was immediately noticeable was a bald patch, the size of a fifty pence piece, on the right side of his head, which he was fingering nervously. His nails were bitten to the quick. His arms were exposed in his summer shirt and visibly criss-crossed with scabbing cuts.

'Hello, Arek.' Dr Jones greeted him in a soft and welcoming voice. 'I'm here to have a chat with you. Would you like to sit in that chair facing me?'

Arek moved closer to his companion and shook his head. Madeleine translated into Polish.

'Arek, this nice lady here would like to have a talk with you. Would you like to sit on this chair beside me?'

Arek shot Madeleine a startled look and exclaimed in Polish 'Rozumiem pania! I can understand you!'

Madeleine translated his words. Mrs. Wright scribbled some more notes in her file. Dr Jones requested him again to sit at the table. When he did that without opposition, the teacher's assistant retreated to a chair at the side of the room. A smell of stale unwashed clothes breathed out of Arek's every movement and the stains down the front of his shirt looked ingrained with age. He eyed Madeleine with suspicion.

'Skad pani jest? Where are you from? Are you a new teacher?'

After translating this to Dr Jones, Madeleine was instructed to say, 'No, Arek. I'm an interpreter. I'm here to help you understand what this lady, Dr Jones, is going to say to you, and also your answers to her. It is important that you listen carefully and give her true answers, so she can help you.'

Mrs Wright's pen squeaked against the paper. Arek shot her a glance, remained silent for a long while, then asked, 'Why?'

With every question and answer on both sides and every word translated, the pitiful picture of his life emerged. His English was barely even basic because he'd not been in this country long enough to learn. His father brought him over from Poland after his mother had gone off with someone else. His father's girlfriend did not want him, as she'd already had a little girl of her own.

'She hates me, and I hate her!' Arek screwed his eyes menacingly.

'Why is that?' Dr Jones asked.

He shrugged, releasing another waft of staleness trapped in his clothes.

'I just do. She does not let me play with Marysia. She says I might hurt her. But I'd never do such a thing! Never! I only fight with my enemies!'

'And who are your enemies?'

Another shrug. Eyes cast down, a long stare at the floor. 'Some kids in this school.'

'What do they do?'

Arek made a fist and pressed it to his mouth then bit into the side of his thumb with the already half-eaten nail. 'They call me names and talk behind my back.'

Dr Jones made notes in her papers. Mrs Wright and the teacher's assistant remained very still.

'And at home, Arek, when you don't play with Marysia, what do you do then?' Dr Jones resumed her questions.

A big exaggerated sigh. 'They send me to my room.'

'What do you do in your room? How do you spend the time on your own?'

Arek's sullen expression relaxed. 'But I'm not on my own. I play games with Harry Potter. He's my best friend.'

Dr Jones looked gravely serious. 'Do you mean, you play games based on Harry Potter books?'

A vigorous shake of his head. 'That as well. But it wouldn't be much fun if he wasn't there. Look!' Arek stretched out his arms before her. 'All these crosses here are our secret signs. When I cross my arms like this…' – he demonstrated by shielding his face and clenching his fists – 'my enemies shit themselves with fright.' The room was deathly quiet.

Madeleine could well imagine Arek's ferocious expression frightening a small child, but his peers would have made fun of him.

'So…' Dr Jones resumed gently, 'when does Harry Potter come to visit you, Arek?'

Another shrug. 'All the time. He's here now. But no one can see him, only me! He's sitting right next to you.' Arek pointed at the empty chair between Dr Jones and Mrs Wright.

An hour later, after stopping briefly at the reception desk to fill in the necessary forms, Madeleine returned to her car and sat still for a long moment, unable to shake off the oppressive sadness. One of the cardinal rules that she and her colleagues were constantly reminded of was not to get involved emotionally with any cases. She'd have to have a heart of stone to remain untouched by Arek's plight. She thought of her own Emily and of how much love surrounded her child. Arek, Madeleine had been relieved to hear, had a grandmother in Poland. Perhaps there was some hope for him still?

She checked the messages on her mobile. There was one from Mr Bunting, the head co-ordinator at the Language Services, the agency she worked for.

'Ring me asap.'

She did. Mr Bunting, despite his jolly name, was as always curt and impatient.

'When's your next appointment?'

'Two this afternoon. The Royal. Discharge plan for an old lady.'

'Good. You're needed now. Your local police station. Some domestic incident this morning. They've got the duty solicitor. They need an interpreter. Now!'

His abruptness made it hard to warm to him, but apart from the weekly briefings she had very little to do with him. As always, she responded eagerly, 'I'm on my way.'

Madeleine introduced herself to the police officer at the reception desk, producing her identification card of an approved interpreter. He pressed the buzzer and presently a younger version of him came up the corridor, all eagerness and purpose in his long stride, his alert eyes appraising her with interest. His smile widened after introductions. She recognised that special look and was flattered. Yet years of nervous guardedness had taught her to respond with a coolly polite smile.

'Please take a seat.' He indicated a row of chairs in the waiting area. 'Mr Simms, the duty solicitor, is engaged with someone else at the moment, but I don't think he'll be much longer now.'

As Madeleine waited, amidst the sounds of frequent telephone calls and halted talk from the back room, her mind was haunted by Arek's urchin face, his ferociously screwed eyes, the bald patch on the side of his head. What hope was there for him? Everyone needed a Bronek or an Aniela in their lives. She had been so lucky, despite everything that had happened to her. So lucky! How would she ever be able to repay them?

The young officer reappeared. 'Mr Simms is ready for you.'

He led Madeleine down a narrow corridor at the end of which stood a man in a pin-striped suit, his right arm pulled down with the weight of a bulging briefcase. For a split second, he looked like Uncle Zden: tall, athletic, clean-cut features, greying hair professionally styled. A current of terror transfixed her. The moment passed, leaving her shaken.

He gave her a nod with a friendly expression and when he said, 'Pleased to meet you,' a weight fell off her chest. She replied with a polite smile. The young officer let them inside the interview room and closed the door staying outside.

The room was a small, square, empty space with only a table and four chairs in the middle. A plain-clothes officer was sitting opposite a big man, whose shaved head was dark with the stubble of regrowth and his black shirt was stretched taut over his bulging arms and chest muscles. There was a smell about him of yesterday's sweat mixed with cologne.

A uniformed officer was standing against a wall, arms crossed, his head outlined in the light from the small window.

After brief introductions, the plain-clothes officer handed Mr Simms some papers, saying, 'PC Bates will be outside if you need any assistance.'

He and the uniformed officer left the room, leaving Madeleine alone with the two men. Strangely, it was Mr Simms, Zden's look-alike, who was now the reassuring presence in the company of the other man. They sat down, the men facing each other across the table, and Madeleine on the side. The silence was unnerving while Mr Simms read through the papers and the other man fidgeted with his hands.

Finally, Mr Simms looked up. 'Mr Koval, I'm your representative solicitor,' he spoke to his client, 'and Miss Greenwood is here to interpret for us both.' Madeleine translated this into Polish, bracing herself to be sympathetic towards her fellow countryman. His appearance alone filled her with unease.

'Mr Simms will take your statement,' she said. 'It is my duty to inform you that everything you say, every single word, I'm under sworn obligation to translate to Mr Simms, and later, your sworn statement to the police.'

'O Kurva!' he exclaimed.

'Please!' Madeleine warned him. 'No swear words! You will make this hard for me and not in the least favourable to yourself.' She was glad to have Mr Simms close to her.

Koval shrugged and bit his thumb nail.

Mr Simms began. 'I shall read to you now the police report of the incident that has necessitated your arrest. And then I shall ask you some questions.' When Madeleine translated this, Koval nodded.

The police report stated that Koval had been arrested on suspicion of grievous bodily harm. At around seven in the morning before his wife left for work from their flat, neighbours had been alerted by her screams and those of their two small children. They called the police. On arrival, the police officers found Mrs Koval badly beaten about her face and her arm broken. She blamed her husband for her injuries, caused in a fit of rage. He had mistakenly accused her of an affair with her supervisor at a meat-processing factory where she worked. (Madeleine had a fleeting but very vivid memory of her experience of that kind of work and could not imagine hot passion flourishing in such arctic conditions.) Koval denied his wife's allegation, saying she had lunged at him, slipped, banged her head and broken her arm. The police called an ambulance for her, phoned her friend to collect the children and then arrested Koval on suspicion despite his protests of innocence.

Madeleine was disgusted by these allegations. She could barely look at him as she translated every sentence read out by Mr Simms.

'Ask him, Miss Greenwood, what would he like me to say in mitigation?'

Mitigation? A barbarian like him? Madeleine was speechless for a brief moment. As if guessing her inner reaction, Mr Simms added, 'Everyone's entitled to a fair hearing. And, since none of us were there to see what had actually happened, we must not jump to conclusions before all legal procedures have been carried out thoroughly.'

Madeleine boiled with anger. Reluctantly, she translated all Mr Simms's words. The accused looked up, his expression taking on a self-pleased look.

'I've got nothing to say in mitigation. She brought it all upon herself.' He spoke with a swagger. 'She thought she was being clever trying to get away from me. She slipped, she banged her face, she broke her arm. I'll tell you one thing though, if I lay my hands on that bastard, I'll break his bones!'

Madeleine squirmed with revulsion. Scum like him gave Poles a bad name. She translated every word and watched Mr Simms's features harden. His tone was icy when he spoke.

'It is alleged that you have caused your wife's injuries. Grievous bodily harm is a serious crime. This will not go down very well for you at the hearing. Is there anything you'd like me to say in your defence?'

Defence? This was sickening. Yet Madeleine had no choice but to do her job to her best ability.

Koval shrugged. 'There's nothing more to be said. She's brought it all upon herself. It's not likely to happen again. It's the end of the matter, as far as I'm concerned.'

Mr Simms looked amazingly calm.

'Except that it is not,' he said. 'The hearing will decide if you're eligible for bail.'

Koval looked suddenly confused, when Madeleine repeated this in Polish.

'What does it mean? What bail? But I must get back to work. I've already lost a day. I'll lose this job altogether if I don't show up. Mr

Solicitor!' He turned to Mr Simms. 'You must get me out of here. I drive big lorries. I was supposed to drive to Dover today!'

Mr Simms remained expressionless throughout the translation of Koval's plea, then gave him his advice. 'You can only get bail if the police decide that you are of no further danger to your wife, or anyone else for that matter. Only you know, Mr Koval, what actually happened. You'll get a fair hearing tomorrow. If you plead guilty as charged, you'll get a custodial sentence. If you plead not guilty and your case goes to trial and the jury decide on evidence that you are, then you'll get a much longer custodial sentence. I'll leave you with this thought to ruminate over till I'm called again to assist you.'

Madeleine translated sentence after sentence, her stomach clenching with fear at the heightening of Koval's palpable anger. But, before he could say anything else, Mr Simms stood up energetically and called out, 'Constable Bates!'

The door opened immediately and two officers walked in. Madeleine did not waste time in following Mr Simms.

'Miss Greenwood!' Koval shouted after her. 'Zrob Pani cos! Do something!' But the moment she and Mr Simms were out in the corridor, the door was shut behind them with Koval out of sight.

Mr Simms stopped and faced her with a thin smile, intending to defuse the tension, no doubt.

'That went well!'

She couldn't tell if he was sarcastic, but it mattered to her to say something that lay heavy on her chest.

'Mr Simms, I'm Polish too, but believe me, most of us here are law-abiding, hardworking people. I'm thoroughly ashamed of him!'

This time his smile was genuine.

'I know that. Everyone knows that. It's not the nationality that makes a person. It's their character.'

'What will happen to him? What if they let him out? He may do the same to his wife again. I fear for his children. They must be terrified!'

Mr Simms pulled up his heavy briefcase saying, 'I'll walk with you to the reception. Please be assured that he will not be allowed anywhere near his wife for a very long time.'

They walked in silence after that, Madeleine still agitated by Koval's attitude. As she signed out at the reception desk, Mr Simms waited.

'We will most probably need your services again,' he said. 'Thank you for doing a good job.'

She found herself turning pink at his praise. He did not look like her uncle at all. Whatever made her think of Zden in the first place?

'I try to do my best,' she said modestly. 'I assure you, people like him are an exception in the Polish community, not the norm.'

'I know,' his tone was friendly. 'A Polish man has renovated my friends' kitchen for them recently. Worked like a Trojan.' Madeleine smiled inwardly at the comparison while Mr Simms continued. 'They could not praise him enough. He was exceptionally intelligent, practical and inventive, and no hitch along the way was too much trouble or impossible for him to solve.'

That did not surprise Madeleine. Decades of oppression and chronic shortages in her post-war country had produced a nation of inventors, struggling daily to outwit the system in order to survive.

'I'm pleased to hear that,' she said.

'I'm pleased to have met you,' Mr Simms replied, then politely bade her farewell.

# CHAPTER 12

Madeleine's last appointment took her mind off Arek and Koval. The old Polish lady, discharged from a short hospital stay after a suspected heart problem, cried with gratitude as she thanked the staff, while her much-relieved daughter made careful notes of Madeleine's translated instructions regarding the medication sent home with them.

As she waited in the school playground, Madeleine's thoughts turned to Natalia's letter. She was already anticipating Aniela's reaction; she'd be pressing her to go to her friend's wedding. Her mind began to fantasise about a joyful reunion and precious time spent with her best friend. Yet overshadowing her excitement was the ever-present unease whenever she thought of home and the connection with *him*.

The school bell was followed by the spilling out of children from their classrooms. Emily and Karishma skipped to her, holding hands and bubbling with excitement. Karishma's mother appeared from around a group of chatting mothers, like a ray of sunshine from behind the clouds with her bright orange silk scarf draped over her shoulders. She was small and slender, making it hard to imagine she had produced four children. Two boys, one older and one younger than Karishma, were following close behind, and there was a baby girl in the pushchair.

'Thank you, Madeleine.' She smiled, revealing her very white teeth. 'Karishma, she cannot wait to go to your house. What time do I fetch her?'

'Don't worry about that. We'll bring Karishma home at seven. Ready for bed.'

She nodded and hugged her daughter. 'You be a good girl, OK?'

'She is always a good girl,' Madeleine assured Karishma's mother, watching her glow with pride.

At home, Aniela was already busy in the kitchen preparing the evening meal.

'I've got some exciting news,' Madeleine could not stop herself as soon as she was alone with her, 'but I'll see to the girls first and then we can talk.'

93

She took a tray outside with juice and biscuits and placed it on the patio table. Emily and Karishma were already playing hopscotch on the grid marked out in white paint, their plaits bouncing as they skipped. Madeleine returned to Aniela and stood beside her at the cooker.

'Can I help with anything?' This daily question was rhetorical, but she asked it any way in case one day Aniela relented.

'Tell me your news.' Aniela turned from the cooker rubbing her back, her face pink from the warmth.

Madeleine perched on the stool her heart quickening.

'Babcha, I received a letter from Natalia. She's getting married in August. She's asked me to come to her wedding.'

Aniela's eyes widened and a broad smile lifted her cheeks.

'But that's wonderful news! You must go!'

'Just like that?'

Aniela sat down at the table with her, from where they could see Emily and Karishma through the open door.

'My dear Magda, you can't live in hiding forever. You've done nothing wrong. You don't owe anyone any explanations. Those who love you will accept you on your terms. But you may find that when you see Natalia you'll be ready to tell her more than you think.'

'I really wish I could! But just even thinking about it fills me with dread. And shame. And... I just wish I never had to think about it again!'

Aniela leaned towards her and lowered her voice.

'Magda, Emily can stay with us when you go. What the eyes can't see... you know the saying. You won't have to stress yourself for nothing. Just be ready with plausible answers in case the questions get too snoopy. You can edit your story any way you find suitable for the occasion. That's not deceit, that's being discreet.'

Madeleine nodded to please Aniela, but she was not at all convinced. She had never left Emily except when going to work.

'It's like denying Emily's existence, though. How could I do that? I've got so much to be thankful for.'

Aniela got up slowly and rubbed her back. She returned to the simmering pot on the cooker.

'Magda, you've got plenty of time to think it over. Write to Natalia tonight. Tell her you'll come.' She sounded so sure, Madeleine wished she could feel that brave.

'But what if... what if I run into him?'

They never discussed Zden but Aniela knew she meant him. She turned around, stirring spoon in her hand.

'Krakow is a big place,' she stated, matter-of-factly. 'What is the chance of that? Look how many people we know in Leicester. And how many times do we bump into anyone we know? But, in the unlikely event of this happening, you just ignore him and walk on. By the time he's realised, it will be too late. I rather think, Magda, that he'd be the one to avoid you at all cost, even if he saw you first.'

Aniela's sensible words brought her no relief.

'What about Dominik?' she fretted. The passage of time had not diminished her guilt of how she had left him so abruptly, with no explanation except for that feeble letter.

'I would imagine that by now Dominik has moved on and lives a happy life,' Aniela said sensibly.

Magda wished that for him too, despite the prickle of regret every time she imagined him with somebody else.

'So much to think about.' Madeleine got up with a sigh.

She tried hard to concentrate on her translations while uncertainties distracted her. She was sitting at her desk by the French window that opened onto the back garden and frequently looked up from her work to watch Emily and Karishma playing outside. The garden was a long strip of green, walled in from all sides, with climbing ivy and clematis covering the red brick, and the borders filled with seasonal perennials all round. The fading daffodils were now lost in a blue stream of the bluebells and forget-me-nots, dotted with red and pink tulips. A central paved path ran the full length to the end, where facing each other across the path, stood Bronek's shed and Aniela's summer house. This was everyone's favourite place for an afternoon tea in good weather.

Bronek had installed a swing for Emily and a small sandpit close to his shed. An inflatable paddling pool was also at hand on hot summer days. But this afternoon the girls were busy competing with each other in hopscotch and ever-more imaginative skills with their skipping ropes. From time to time, Madeleine waved to them as she attempted to continue with her work.

She had mastered the formal language of official documents so that translating CVs had become routine work. But booklets and information flyers from various companies took longer, for they were as diverse as transport and cosmetics or pharmaceuticals and sports equipment. Madeleine had armed herself with a thesaurus and Polish–English dictionaries and tackled everything sent to her with stubborn determination. Whenever frustration threatened with self-pity, she only had to look up to Aniela and Bronek and remind herself of the obstacles they had to conquer before achieving basic normality in their lives.

An outburst of the girls' laughter made her look up. Bronek had just come through the back gate. He was immediately besieged by Emily and Karishma, vying with each other to tell their own news first. He carried a large bunch of red and yellow tulips, the earliest yield of the year from his toils on the allotment. Madeleine watched his white head stoop down to the girls' level and his hand produce two packets of sweets from his pocket. She guessed he was telling them to save the treats for after dinner, for they began skipping ahead of him and waving their packets like flags.

Madeleine stood up to meet them on the doorstep.

'Mama, Mama, look!' Emily was jumping up and down, with Karishma copying her every move.

Madeleine placed her hands on their heads to calm them down.

'Let's go set the table,' she suggested brightly. They raced off amidst squeals of eagerness and Madeleine made a fuss of Bronek's flowers.

'Grandpa, they surely deserve first prize!'

'Sorry?' These days most things said to Bronek had to be said twice. It took him longer to absorb the merest comment.

'Your flowers, Grandpa. They are the best!'

His look of concentration dissolved in a grin.

'I think so too, and I'm not ashamed to boast. I hope the committee will notice too.' His face crinkled at this pleasant thought. 'Will you come with me on Saturday?'

'Of course! You know how Emily loves playing "dens" in your shed, especially when Karishma comes along too.'

'Sorry?' His brow puckered again.

'We'll both come, Grandpa. And Karishma. They'll be company for each other.'

He nodded then looked beyond her towards the kitchen, from where excited chatter and busy noises of table setting could be heard.

'I better wash and change,' he said with a twinkle in his eyes, 'or I'll be banned from the kitchen.'

Madeleine watched him for a moment before returning to her desk. He appeared more distracted these days. His hearing appeared less sharp. It seemed that old age was catching up with him. She tidied up, collected all loose sheets and filed them accordingly, then placed the files in cardboard boxes that were marked alphabetically and stacked beside her desk.

Her mind was still a jumble of the day's events. Yet dominating them were thoughts of Natalia and her imminent wedding and all the complicated issues to be addressed and somehow resolved, if Madeleine were to attend.

Tonight, she would write to Natalia. For the first time in seven years.

*

After reading Emily two bed-time stories, *The Ugly Duckling* in Polish and *Paddington Bear* in English, Madeleine settled her for the night and went downstairs to her desk. Aniela and Bronek were watching television in the front room. Madeleine had already formed some idea of what to write to Natalia.

*My dearest Natalia,*

*Your letter was a most wonderful surprise. I cannot thank you enough for thinking about me. I'm so happy about your forthcoming wedding and it will be a great joy to me to share that special day with you. Of course I remember Szymon, please tell me everything about him in your next letter.*

*It is true to say that I was in a very 'bad place' when I left home after my Aunt Emilia's death. It took me a long time to recover – and all thanks to my very kind Grandparents. But afterwards, I found it hard to re-establish contact, even with my dearest friends like you. I'm still tormented with guilt. Please forgive me, Natalia. I hope to make it up to you in whatever way I can.*

*I managed to complete my studies here. I've got a certificate that entitles me to teach English to foreign students, but at the moment I work as an interpreter and as a translator of a variety of scripts. It's very interesting work and much of it I can do at home.*

*Do you see anything of Dominik these days? It was horrible what I did, disappearing from his life so suddenly, and I can't forgive myself for that, but the events at that time were truly beyond my control. I hope to explain everything when we meet.*

*I'll write again soon.*

*With much love, Magda*

Madeleine re-read her letter several times and wished she could have said more. But not yet. Not on paper. She needed to talk to Natalia, face to face. For that reason, and for the time being, she did not suggest a telephone conversation. Instead of her number, she added her e-mail address at the bottom of the page.

She joined Aniela and Bronek in the front room, where they were so absorbed in watching Bronek's favourite programme that they were sitting in the dark with the curtains still drawn back and their faces lit up with the flickering light off the screen. Madeleine had never got rid of the feeling of being somewhat exposed and therefore vulnerable if watched from the outside. She drew the curtains and switched on the Tiffany lamp in the corner of the room, which immediately cast a soft and calming glow around the room.

'Come, sit down with us, Magda. This is really good.' Bronek was as excited as a little boy.

'Shh… Bronek. You're missing the next bit,' Aniela admonished.

It was a thriller on Polish television, set in the old and picturesque city of Sandomierz, with the priest-detective driving the plot in every episode of the popular serial.

'They make it far too easy,' Bronek commented. 'I already know who killed the old man!'

'Shh… Bronek! I don't want to know!' Aniela reprimanded him.

'But it's obvious, isn't it? It's written all over their faces, those two sisters!'

'Bronek, please, no more telling!' Aniela covered her ears.

Bronek was silent for thirty seconds.

'And why have they cast such an ugly actor for the good policeman?'

'Because… 'Aniela huffed with utter impatience, 'not everyone is so lucky to be as gorgeous as you!'

Bronek gave Madeleine a mischievous wink, and at that moment the telephone rang. Aniela sighed with desperation.

'It's all right, Babcha. I'll take it,' Madeleine got up to her feet. She picked up the receiver in the hall. It was Aniela's friend, Mrs Demska. They spoke to each other naturally in Polish. Madeleine said that Aniela would ring her later, but Mrs Demska stopped her, 'Nie, nie trzeba. No need, Magda, it's actually you that I want to speak to.'

'Me?'

'Yes, my dear. Please forgive me if I've acted out of turn, but I thought, no harm asking.'

'About what?'

Mrs Demska took a deep breath, 'It's my neighbour, Jean Hammond. But actually, it's about her son Josh. It's like this: he's recovering from glandular fever, which has left him very weak. His doctor says it may take him weeks to recover fully. He's in the lower-sixth. His course work is piling up. He needs practical help with finishing his work on time. When Jean mentioned about advertising for a tutor, I thought about you straight away… Sorry… I meant well. I know you're busy with your own work, but I thought, if you could help Josh even in a small way, Jean won't be worrying so much, and it will be extra money for you.'

It took a moment to absorb Mrs Demska's words and all the implications of fitting another commitment into Madeleine's already very full week. But what had sharpened her interest was the word 'neighbour'.

'Jean Hammond? Is that next door to you, Mrs Demska? The big house?'

'Yes, that's the one.'

A vivid memory rushed back. Madeleine had never forgotten the young man who had looked so distressed when she had seen him by pure chance from Mrs. Demska's garden, all those years ago. He was called James. So, Josh must be the little boy who had run up to him with a ball. Of course, he'd be a teenager now.

Madeleine was gripped with uncertainty.

'It's so good of you to think about me, Mrs Demska, but I'm not sure if I'd be the right person. I'd hate to not live up to their expectations and disappoint you too.'

'But you wouldn't, Magda, I assure you. I have great confidence in you,' Mrs Demska's voice vibrated with enthusiasm. 'Why don't you see Jean and Josh first, discuss it with them and then decide? I think she would be sympathetic to whatever arrangement suits you best. She too had to juggle time between work and looking after her boys.'

'Do you know her well?' Madeleine asked.

'Jean? I've been her neighbour for over twenty years. You must have heard me mention her before. She's still working so there's not much time to socialise but we always have a chat when we meet in the drive. She's a radiologist, at the Infirmary.'

'A doctor?' This piece of information increased Madeleine's uncertainty. As a youngster, she'd always been in awe of officials and highly ranked professional people. Nepotism had been rife in communist Poland, but even now, in her new democratic country, some of the old habits remained – much was still arranged through connections, while the arrogance of officialdom towards the ordinary citizen was not uncommon.

'Is that a problem, that Jean's a doctor?' Mrs Demska asked.

'No.' Madeleine did not say how a humiliating dismissal would make her feel. 'Is it just her and her son?'

'Jean is a widow,' Mrs Demska said. 'Her younger son, Josh, the one you'll be helping, I hope, is a charming boy. You'll have no problems with him. Jean's older son, James, lives in London. It's only the two of them in that big house.'

Strangely, just those few words made Madeleine hesitate in favour of helping out a mother and her son. She'd always had Aniela and Bronek for support. Not everyone was so lucky.

At the back of her mind there was a seed of curiosity about the older son, James. And sympathy. She could not erase that picture from her mind of him sitting bent down in utter dejection, his face hidden in his cupped hands. She had known grief. She had known despair. She had a need to know if his life had been sorted. She would never lower herself to prying; she would only observe.

'All right, Mrs Demska. I'll give it a go. Thank you again for thinking about me.'

'You won't regret it, I promise.' Mrs Demska sounded glad. 'Shall I tell Jean, tomorrow at eight?'

# CHAPTER 13

In Grandview Road, Madeleine passed Mrs Demska's Rose Cottage and parked her Ka by the gated entrance to Jean Hammond's property. Walking up the drive, she could not help but admire the expansive and solid structure, the tall mullioned windows and a turret on one corner of the building. She wondered what it was like living in a house with so much space. Her experience was that of having grown up in the confines of a second-floor flat, two small bedrooms, a lounge and a kitchen in one bigger room.

She felt her confidence waning.

The porch with its wide-arched entrance was flanked with tubs spilling over with white gardenias. Madeleine pressed the doorbell and waited, her heart beating faster. Was it a mistake coming here? Would she make a good impression? Would they trust her to do a good job? Already she cringed at the imagined rejection.

She had a sudden urge to run away. But too late. The heavy, metal-studded door was pulled back. In a split second, she composed herself to act with chirpy eagerness, but the rehearsed words stuck in her mouth.

Before her stood not her imagined middle-aged Jean Hammond, but he, the man called James. He was tall and slim, as she remembered him, clean-cut in a white shirt and smart jeans, thick black hair curling behind his ears, regular features and now, at close up, intense blue eyes.

'Oh…' Madeleine hesitated. 'I'm here to see Mrs. Hammond.'

'That's right, we've been expecting you.' His voice was vigorous, his tone polite. Quintessentially English. 'Madeleine Greenwood, isn't it? Please come in.'

She was aware of his eyes scrutinising her as she stepped in past him, her nostrils catching a whiff of an aftershave. She waited for him to lead her. He introduced himself.

'I'm James, the older brother.'

She nearly said, 'I know,' and wished she could be straight with him.

'I'm pleased to meet you,' she said, annoyingly self-conscious but glad at the same time, knowing that the pastel pink trouser suit offset her dark looks attractively and would have made a good impression. It had been drummed into her, even as a child, that she must always take the trouble with her appearance for the sake of those who had to look at her. For Mrs Demska's sake (and indirectly for Aniela's), she had made a special effort to impress Jean Hammond.

'It's this way.' James indicated towards a half-open door. There were three other doors leading off from the square vestibule, which had a shiny tiled floor, a display of trailing plants in tall vases and original watercolours on white walls.

They entered the lounge, a long L-shaped room. Through the French window there was a clear view of the back garden, its expanse of lawn surrounded by a variety of trees and shrubs. Part of the lounge served as the dining room, its mahogany table polished to a mirror. Looking down from the walls were still-lifes and portraits in oils.

A boy of about seventeen was reclining in an armchair. His navy trousers and a pale blue shirt were visibly baggy over his limp and thin limbs. Unlike his older brother's thick black hair, his was much lighter, softer and curling around his boyish face. He greeted Madeleine with a friendly grin, his hazel eyes reflecting the light from outside.

'Hi! I'm Josh.' He lifted his hand with an effort, letting it drop back gently. 'I'm sorry I can't get up.' His voice was hoarse.

'Please, don't trouble yourself,' Madeleine walked over and touched his hand. 'I'm Madeleine Greenwood.'

'Yes, I know.' Then he chuckled, his hand instinctively protecting his throat. He shook his head. 'I'm sorry. I'm just laughing at myself. I'm sure my mother told me everything. I should have paid more attention. It's just that I'd been expecting someone much older. We even took bets on it. James and I...'

'Josh, really...' James cut him short and Madeleine thought there was the tiniest hint of embarrassment in his voice. She found that amusing and felt her nervousness drop a notch.

'Who won?' she asked.

'I did.' James inclined his head almost apologetically and she could not tell if he was serious. 'With Josh, anyone over thirty is old.'

'That's not true!' Josh protested, his voice breaking in a coughing attack. He swallowed hard and wiped his eyes. 'It's just that none of my teachers at school look so young!'

Madeleine smiled at his artlessness. She felt her tension relax.

'I've got a little time before I reach thirty,' she said. 'And maybe for that reason I'm not the person your mother's looking for.'

'You are!' Josh cried emphatically and coughed, his eyes watering again. 'Sorry about this. Please sit down, Miss Greenwood. Please, let's talk.'

His spontaneous politeness was disarming.

'Call me Madeleine,' she said. 'No one is formal these days.' Madeleine had found that puzzling at first, virtual strangers calling each other by their first names straight after introduction. That would have been considered impolite and rather presumptuous in her own country. Even with her own grandparents' friends after all the years, she still addressed them as Mr and Mrs out of reverence for their age.

'OK, Madeleine. That's a lovely name.'

This made her truly laugh, his transparent eagerness, and she berated herself for all her initial doubts.

There were two easy chairs angled towards Josh. Madeleine and James sat down. She assumed their mother would be joining them shortly, having heard, no doubt, from wherever she was in this vast house, Madeleine's arrival.

'So how did your illness come about?' she asked

Josh swallowed hard and held his hand against his throat. James answered for him.

'A school trip to Paris at the end of last term. They stayed at a youth hostel. It only takes one unclean utensil, apparently. That's Josh's explanation.' He raised an eyebrow. 'They don't call it a kissing disease for nothing.' His tone was deadpan.

'Ha! Ha! Very funny!' Josh managed hoarsely and smiled at Madeleine. Why had she been so nervous before? They appeared like two normal brothers sparring with each other, yet so polite towards her.

She had once trusted Uncle Zden too. She got that wrong.

But this was different, she convinced herself. Josh, in his present state was no threat to anyone. And James... She sensed a deep reserve in him. She couldn't imagine... but could one imagine that with anyone you thought you knew so well? She gave him a surreptitious sideways glance and noted the shape of his hands, square yet attractive with their very clean and neatly cut nails.

She became aware of a silent pause. She spoke to appear friendly, 'We always used to have an outbreak of glandular fever among the first years at the university. I was lucky. I never had that pleasure. Have you been very ill with it, Josh?'

'Just a bit,' he nodded. James shifted in his easy chair and spoke for his brother.

'Had our mother worried sick. Not an amusing thing to do.' It was hard to tell if his seriousness was genuine.

'Well, I didn't go looking for it, did I?' Josh's muted voice conveyed his indignation. 'Yeah! It was hilarious! Swollen throat, swollen tonsils, swollen spleen! Top of the world feeling. And the crutches! What a thrill!'

'OK, you've made your point.' James raised his hand in surrender, then looked at Madeleine, the crinkling around his eyes hinting at a dash of humour. 'That's why we need help.' The blue of his eyes was so intense, she lowered her gaze. She sat up straight, business-like and looked pointedly towards the door.

'Am I too early for your mother? Is she not home yet?' she asked.

'Well, actually,' Josh said, 'she's been and gone.'

'Gone?' All her body tensed. The old fear was back. She was alone in a big house with two males. Ridiculous fear, but one did not reason with instinct.

'It's nothing new,' James explained, matter-of-factly. He sounded genuine, but was it just pretence? 'In her line of work, she's often called out in an emergency. Outside her set working hours. Tonight, for example. There's been an accident. Lots of X-rays required. The person on duty was taken ill. Mother stepped in. Sod's Law!' He shrugged.

Madeleine got up ready to go.

'I'll come back another time when she's here.'

'No need to waste your time. Please sit down, Madeleine.' The way he spoke her name and the merest touch of pleading in his voice did strange things to her. Her legs felt weak and she sat down, unable to turn her eyes away from his gaze without appearing rude. She noted his very blue irises and the black eyelashes. An Irish trait, she thought, perhaps a throwback to some distant relative. All this flashed through her mind as she listened to his words. 'Josh will tell you everything you need to know, and then you can decide if you want to take this on.' She nodded, relieved to turn her attention to Josh.

Josh shifted in his armchair, sliding back limply into his previous reclining position. He smiled self-deprecatingly and spread his hands. They were smooth-skinned with long tapering fingers, almost like a girl's. He took a deep breath before speaking haltingly.

'Nothing's easy for me at the moment. I feel tired most of the time. I can't read for too long or write or concentrate even on the computer. But' – another deep breath – 'my doctor has promised it's only temporary. I hope to be back at school before the end of the term, with all my assignments completed on time. I can't do that on my own in my present state.'

How could one refuse this plea? Madeleine found her reservations melting away.

'So, what would you like me to do?'

Josh thought for a moment. 'I think I can cope with Latin. It's mainly translations.'

'Latin?' Madeleine was pleasantly surprised.

'Yes, my school is one of the very few that still teach Latin.'

'I liked Latin,' she said. 'It's so logical. Like mathematics. Once you learn the rules, it's easy to work out the meaning in a script.'

'And there's IT. But that's OK. It's the English lit. and history that take up so much time with all that reading and essays to write...' Josh spread his hands helplessly.

'Some practical assistance would be great,' James said, two vertical lines forming on his brow. 'If you have the patience to take down his notes, go over his essays with him or even just read to him, that would be enormously helpful. I'd do it myself, if I lived at home. And mother works long hours, some evenings too. Josh is on his own a lot of the time, normally,' he added as an aside, 'every teen's dream. But not such a good idea at the moment.'

'I want to do well, Madeleine,' Josh's hoarseness did not diminish his enthusiasm. 'My personal tutor has urged me to apply for Oxford. He'd like me to have a go at the Greats.'

'The Greats?'

Josh smiled. 'Yes, the Greats. Peculiar to Oxford. Greek and Roman history, literature and philosophy.'

'O... K...' she nodded cautiously.

'And later, politics and economics. I want to go into journalism.'

'No pressure then.' She liked him. He had it all worked out. He was already aiming high. At seventeen. 'That's great, Josh. I'm impressed.' She noticed his self-conscious smile. 'But, in the circumstances, I'm not sure I'd be the right person to help you. You need someone with experience and good knowledge of the subjects you've just mentioned.'

Josh's smile changed to a look of puzzlement, but before he uttered a word James came in, all the authority of the older brother strong in every word.

'That's all in the future. What Josh needs now is immediate support. I only saw mother briefly tonight. But she said Mrs Demska spoke very highly of you. We have no reason to doubt her. And,' – he looked intensely into her eyes – 'we'll make it worthwhile to you.'

It wasn't the payment that bothered her. It was the constant uncertainty with anything new or different in her life. But here, she sensed, their need was genuine. It would appear cruel to be playing hard to get.

Madeleine licked her lips. His gaze had a disturbing effect on her. Not unpleasant at all. She had to remain business-like.

'My interpreter's salary is nothing to brag about. If you can match that, that'll be fine. I do this work because it fits with my family commitments.'

'Ah, yes...' James gave her another lingering look. 'Mother mentioned something about your little girl.'

Madeleine wondered what else Mrs Demska had told Jean Hammond, but without annoyance. It was inevitable that people talked. She nodded.

'Yes, Emily. She's six. I've been very lucky. My grandparents couldn't have been kinder. I owe them a lot.' She met James's gaze. He looked thoughtful.

Josh readjusted himself to a more comfortable position, gave his laboured breathing time to slow down then smiled to her.

'Madeleine, I guess it's a yes. So glad we don't have to advertise and interview strangers.'

'But I am a stranger!' She laughed and felt the tension go.

'Not anymore!' James leaned towards her looking earnest. 'I'll find out what home tutors charge in London and I'll match that, if it's all right with you.'

She felt herself colouring.

'Thank you for your trust in me. But shall we have a trial period first? So neither side feels bad if things don't work out?'

'I already know,' Josh said, 'that it won't be necessary.'

'When can you start?' James came straight to the point, and Madeleine felt strangely pleased being needed by them.

'I've already got a kind of an established routine,' she said, thinking ahead that Mr Bunting could call someone else in her place when necessary, 'How often would you like me to come?'

'Every day,' both brothers said at once, looked at each other and laughed. James for the first time. His face was transformed. Madeleine could well imagine that women found him attractive.

She said, 'I work most mornings as an interpreter. Some afternoons as well, when my boss runs out of people. But generally speaking, I'm at home in the afternoons and evenings working on translations. This gives me flexibility to fetch Emily from school. So, would early afternoons suit you, Josh?'

Josh looked pleased and James remarked, 'No time for hobbies, then?'

She shrugged and smiled. Josh asked, 'When can you start?'

They agreed on the following Monday, then he invited Madeleine to stay for coffee.

'James makes a wicked cup of coffee!'

'Wicked?'

'Perfect! You don't know what you're missing until you've tried.'

She returned his grin and got up.

'I'm sure everything James does is perfect!' That came out wrong. What possessed her to say it? She cringed at her own words, and could well imagine what he thought of her, and was annoyed with herself for even caring about his opinion of her. James got up too, making it obvious, she thought, that he was not going to stop her.

She looked at Josh. 'Thank you for offering coffee, but I really must go. I'll see you on Monday.'

'Just one more thing,' Josh said, lifting his hand as if to stop her. 'Mrs Demska said that you're Polish.'

'Can't you tell from my accent?' she grinned.

'Your English is impeccable.' This came from James and she was at once flattered and self-conscious.

'But your name?' Josh persisted. 'That's not Polish.'

'No,' she smiled.

'What is it then? In Polish? And why did you change it?'

'Josh! What's this? The third degree?' James stopped his brother with a reprimanding stare.

'It's all right.' Madeleine laughed. 'It's no big secret. I changed it to make life easier for myself, as I perceived it at the time. But now I can see, it was not necessary. My name is Magda Zielinska.'

They were quiet for a brief moment before Josh spoke first.

'I like it. It sounds exotic. May I call you Magda?' He made her laugh again.

'Of course! Everyone calls me that at home.'

She said her goodbyes and felt Josh watching her, as James accompanied her out of the room into the hall, his tall frame towering over her. The silence between them was awkward and she racked her brain to say something sociable but nothing clever came to mind. At the entrance, she turned to him to say goodbye but he indicated with a gesture that he would go with her to the car. As their feet crunched across the gravel in the silence between them, the last rays of the evening sun threw long shadows across the drive. She cleared her throat.

'I like your brother already. He sounds like a really nice lad. So unlike a typical rebellious teenager.'

'He has his moments. As you've just witnessed,' James said, and she detected a smidgen of indulgence in his tone. Then he was serious again. 'Mother and I both worry about him. I can go back now on Sunday, knowing that something's been sorted out for him. You can see how he is at the moment. Shouldn't be left on his own so much. Having regular visits from you will be a big favour not just for him, but for mother and me.'

She was taken aback by his words but his sincerity sent a warm glow through her body.

'Josh sounds like a sensible boy. I can't imagine he'd do anything silly. Perhaps you worry too much?'

They stopped at her Ka at the open gate and James inclined his head as if to give her a good look.

'It's a habit,' he said. 'There's no one else to worry about them.'

'And who worries about you?' She squirmed at her own question. This sounded as if she were prying. In her embarrassment, she plunged her hand inside her handbag and rummaged for her car key.

'I manage well on my own,' he said, and she did not look up to read his expression. 'My big worry is Josh at the moment. He's got to be very careful not to knock his spleen. It's still swollen and the worst scenario would be if it burst.'

'That sounds horrific!' She looked up at James and felt a strong need to believe that he was a truly good man. But so had been Zden; to his wife, to his brother's family, to herself, until that horrific, inexplicable incident. Could anyone be capable of such extremes? Could James? With held-in breath she banished that thought from her mind.

'Is there anything wrong?' He was speaking to her, and catching his clear, mesmerising gaze, she had to look away.

'No, nothing's wrong. I was just thinking about what you've said and about Josh's problems.' She forced a smile. 'I can't stop you worrying, but I hope my daily visits will be of some help.'

The unexpected softening of his features jumbled up her thoughts.

'Thank you,' he said. 'I'm only here some weekends, but I'll leave instructions with mother regarding your payment and...'

'No, please don't worry about that! There will be time for that later...' and feeling a little flustered she said the first thing that came to her mind. 'Do you live somewhere nice? In London, I mean.'

He gave her another of his thoughtful looks.

'It's OK. I suppose. A flat in Putney.'

Bright and lively images filled her mind. London by night, London by day. Theatres, museums, galleries, busy streets, open spaces of Hyde Park.

'I don't think I'd find time to work if I lived in London,' she said.

He grinned. 'I dream of being a millionaire every day when I'm stuck behind my desk.'

'Is it that bad?' she returned his smile.

He shook his head. 'No. I actually love my job.' And then they both spoke at once.

'It was lovely…' she began.

'Do you ever…?' he asked, then laughed. 'You first.'

Madeleine smiled. 'All I wanted to say before I go, it was nice meeting you.' Just being polite.

'Really?' It was clear he knew she was just being polite. 'But if that is so, perhaps when you're in London next time and need a guide…' he made a mock bow.

Madeleine shook her head. Why was he saying that? 'Thank you. It's a kind offer. But I've simply got too much on at the moment.' And for the next ten years, she thought.

'That's all right. No worries then,' he said lightly.

All at once, she felt regret at the loss of an opportunity.

'I must be going,' she said. 'Have a good week.'

'And you too.' He stepped aside for her to get inside her Ka.

As she drove off, she saw him in the wing mirror watching her until she reached the end of the lane. She turned into the main road and lost him from view.

She drove automatically, her senses guiding her through the traffic, the lights, the crossroads, the changing lanes, while all the time her mind was trying to make sense of this brief closeness between them. Nothing had actually happened. Polite words, unspoken thoughts. Then why this agitation, why the bubbly feeling? She had not felt like that since Dominik.

Seven years had passed, and there had not been a day without thoughts about him. Natalia's letter awakened a myriad of memories. It comforted Madeleine to repeat Aniela's words to herself, that he had moved on, made a new life for himself, found happiness with somebody else, but it also hurt to think how it could have been. No time for self-pity, she told herself firmly. A single life for her was a safe life, with no expected explanations, no fear of condemnation and the inevitable rejection.

There had been boys who had shown interest in her while she was studying her A-level subjects. Later, when she juggled time between childcare and hard work to achieve her degree in English, men made passes at her, some subtle, some off-putting, but she could let them off gently with a genuine excuse. She was already attached and she had a small child.

The 'attachment' part was not a lie; her emotional tie to Dominik had never weakened. Its strength had given her the much-craved stability to pursue her studies, and later, to focus on her work and give Emily all her attention without distractions. But, above all, staying single and discreet gave her full control of her own life.

This thought alone was already distancing her from James.

*

The following evening Madeleine rang Mrs Demska.

'Just to thank you again for thinking about me.'

'Have you agreed?' Mrs Demska was all eagerness.

'Yes. I'll give it a go. But Jean Hammond wasn't there. Just her sons.'

'James? James was there too? How did you find him?'

'All right.' There was a pause while Mrs Demska was waiting to hear more. Madeleine added, 'Very polite. Cool. English. But Josh is very likeable. Very open and direct.'

'You'll like them both, Magda. I assure you. James had to grow up fast when their father died. Such cruel irony. He was such a good man, a well-respected doctor, saved others but could not save himself. He died of leukaemia.'

A pang of sympathy brought back her own memories. 'When was that?' Madeleine asked.

'When Josh was only four.'

So, James's distress she had secretly witnessed had not been for that reason. Like herself, he must have had other bad times in his life. It would be easy to ask Mrs Demska, but shamelessly insensitive to display such curiosity.

Madeleine said, 'It's evident that James is very protective of Josh.'

'Yes. He was young himself when it all happened, but he took his role as the older brother very seriously. It must have been quite an effort for him to share all the house chores and look after Josh when he was in the sixth form. But he did well, went onto the London School of Economics and is now one of the top men in an accountants' firm.' Mrs Demska spoke with pride, as if describing her own son, and Madeleine tried to imagine James as a teenager, having to cope with much more than teenagers normally do. Not unlike herself in a way, yet with no shameful secret attached.

'His mother must be proud of him,' Madeleine said.

'Yes, in her own down-to-earth way. She doesn't lavish praise. She believes that helping each other should be the norm. Not only within the family. She's a dedicated doctor. Just as his father was.'

Madeleine wondered, not that it mattered at all, what she'd make of her past.

'They don't look like brothers,' she commented, 'but maybe I'll see similarities when I get to know them better.'

'It happens in some families,' Mrs Demska said. 'Strong genes on both sides. James is more like his mother in looks. Josh was a surprise baby, later on in their marriage. Took after his father. It's good to think his father had that joy before his untimely death.'

There was a lesson there, Madeleine thought. Make the most of your life. You don't know what's ahead of you, in a day, a week, a month. But when you've rebuilt your ruined life, and secured it on a safe plateau, was it sensible to start seeking new adventures?

On an impulse she asked, 'Is James with anyone?'

'Jean hasn't said. But then he lives away. Comes home only sometimes. So who knows? I'm very fond of James. Keep my fingers crossed for him.' For some inexplicable reason, Madeleine was touched by these words.

'Mrs Demska, I mustn't take any more of your time. I'm very grateful to you and only hope I can live up to your expectations. And theirs!' Madeleine gave a big sigh.

'I have no doubt you will!'

# CHAPTER 14

'I knew it! They're spying on me even here!' Bronek was agitated. He squinted against the sunlight, inspecting the damage.

It was clear to Madeleine what had happened. The breeze-block wall, which had already been in place when Bronek took over the allotment years ago, was beginning to crumble with age. Overshadowed by the branches of the tower-like oak tree, overgrown with ivy and flanked on the outer side by a hedgerow, it formed an additional screen from the public footpath. Madeleine guessed Bronek felt safe and happy on his allotment, in his belief that the wall hid him from spying eyes. Luckily, he did not mind at all fellow allotment keepers and would happily stop to chat with them.

'Grandpa.' She spoke gently. 'I honestly don't think that anyone's been here to spoil things for you. Look, there's a gaping hole there! Where the brick was. Not surprising. It's a very old wall.' The grey brick with its rough, uneven corners lay on the surface of the wrought-iron table that stood pushed against the wall. And trailing down from the wall were ribbons of torn ivy that had come away with the weight of the brick. 'But don't worry, Grandpa, we shall soon fix it. A tub of ready-mixed cement should do it.'

'And I'll help!' Emily offered, her eyes huge with eagerness.

'Me too!' Karishma did a hop in anticipation. She was dressed in a long red satin dress and strappy sandals. Madeleine always kept a change of practical clothes for her when she came to the allotment with them.

Except for the brick on the table, nothing else looked disturbed. Madeleine picked up the brick, climbed up on a chair and held the brick against the gap in the wall.

'See, Grandpa? It fits. Some animal, perhaps a fox, must have climbed on top and disturbed the loose brick.'

He surveyed the scene carefully, his squinting gaze wandering up and down the wall and back and checking the ground around the table.

'I suppose it could have been a fox,' he conceded. 'I've seen one sunning itself right on the roof of my shed.'

'I think it was a fox,' Emily agreed with him, and Karishma added, 'Or maybe a tiger!' and made everyone laugh.

'I suggest,' Madeleine said, 'that for safety's sake we move the table and the chairs away from that wall and close to the shed.'

The shed stood on the opposite side of the allotment between the vegetable and the flower plots. There was room on the sunning deck to accommodate additional garden furniture. Bronek and Madeleine picked up the table, and Emily and Karishma one chair between them. When everything had been put in place, Madeleine said to Bronek, 'There! It's even more convenient, close to the shed.' Apart from Bronek's gardening equipment, some of Emily's special things were stored there too: a small child's wooden chair, which Bronek had painted lilac, and all her colourful sandpit toys.

Emily was already dressed in her gardening pink dungarees and pink wellingtons. Madeleine folded Karishma's satin dress in a bag and dressed her in a T-shirt and Emily's dungarees that she had grown out of. Karishma was smaller than Emily and last year's wellingtons fitted her tiny feet comfortably.

'There!' Madeleine gave her a hug, feeling her bird-like bones and smelling the baby powder on her skin. 'You're now all ready for work!' Karishma shivered eagerly, her black eyes shining like marbles.

While the girls set out marking their sand garden with pebbles, Bronek still looked distracted and thoughtful. He brought out the spade and the trowel and stood still surveying the wall.

'What's bothering you, Grandpa?' Madeleine asked, ready to get on with anything under his direction. He did not respond straight away, but when Emily tickled his hand, that appeared to awaken his attention. He picked her up, gave her a hug, and putting her down teased, 'I bet you and Karishma can't make a prettier flower garden than mine!'

'We can!' she giggled and skipped off to the side of the shed where Karishma was crouching in the sandpit, marking out a pattern with a stick.

He picked up his spade and hoe and led Madeleine to a plot that he had prepared for planting the day before. He lowered his voice. 'I've just had a terrifying thought. What if that brick had fallen on one of us?'

Madeleine had thought that too. Emily. Karishma. But she was not going to be hysterical.

'Grandpa, it didn't. Nothing's happened.'

'But what if it did? Another time?'

She knew he was not going to like what she was about to say. 'Grandpa, if you want to stop worrying, then there is only one solution. Get rid of the wall.'

He shook his head with a look of alarm. 'Magda, you know I can't!'

It was hard to understand his illness. Most of the time he spoke and behaved and reasoned and reacted as most people would have done. But this fixation of his about Russian spies, about being watched, made a cruel mockery of all his common sense.

'Grandpa,' she said, 'let's get all the things you need for repairing the wall and I'll come with you one evening. We'll strip the wall of all ivy and repair every single crack.'

His face brightened and his eyes shone.

'Would you really do that with me?'

'Just say when.'

Now that Bronek's fears had been allayed for the time being, he set about his work with Madeleine in tow, a willing supporter. In truth, Bronek preferred to do all the work himself, simply enjoying her company. She made herself useful by passing him various things and tidying up the weeds into the sack.

His potatoes were already growing in raised rows. This time, he was planting the beans and the peas, and marking the spots with cane rods, against which the seedlings would grow later. The radishes and the beetroot were showing their baby green leaves just above the ground, the onions their spiky presence and the cabbages were already at the two-leaf stage.

'Your allotment is a picture,' Madeleine praised him. The flower strip was especially eye-catching with its blanket of forget-me-nots, above which rose white tulips looking more like peonies with their multiple waxy petals edged with pink. The air was fragrant with the scents of dry soil and bursting growth around them, heightened by the midday warmth.

Bronek stretched from his crouched position and rubbed his back.

'When I'm here, Magda,' he said, his shining eyes scanning the surrounding allotments with a dreamy gaze, 'it reminds me of our land at home. It's like my own piece of land. I love it here. My skin crawls at the thought of some unwanted individuals invading my little corner.' He threw a surreptitious look at the screening wall.

'We are safe here,' Madeleine told him firmly. 'Trust me. There's nothing to worry about.'

They continued to work together, Emily and Karishma searching for wild flowers on grassy strips close to them, to make their sand garden pretty. At lunchtime, Madeleine brought out a thermos flask with tea, juice for the girls and packed sandwiches and cakes. They sat around the table in pleasant tranquillity, enjoying their refreshments, even Emily and Karishma forgetting to chatter for a while.

It was the first weekend in May and, quite suddenly, benign warm weather dispelled the cold nights and days. Voices of other gardeners on their allotments drifted on air, and, with the sun high in the sky, it already felt like the summer.

'If only we could harness this weather for good,' Bronek said, closing his eyes against the brightness.

Emily and Karishma got their scrapbooks out, and with renewed energy chatted excitedly as they drew around the various leaves they had collected. Emily tapped Bronek's arm.

'Grandpa, my picture wants a bird here, on this spot. Can you draw me a robin?'

Bronek's face lifted amiably and with a few sure lines he made a robin appear, sitting on one of Emily's leaves, a round body, a fluffy breast, an open beak as if the bird was singing.

'That is the best robin I have ever seen!' Emily stated with the seriousness of a judge. He chuckled.

Karishma touched Bronek's arm shyly.

'Can you draw me a rabbit?'

He patted her head, saying, 'Anything for my two most favourite girls!'

Within seconds, Bronek's skilled squiggles produced a furry rabbit with whiskers that appeared to move.

'I want to draw like this,' Karishma said.

'All right.' Bronek placed his hand over hers and together they drew another rabbit. 'Now all you have to do is practise many times,' he said.

'How many?' Her huge dark eyes were serious.

'As many times as the numbers you can count.'

Karishma thought for a moment.

'I can count to a hundred. I sometimes get muddled after that.'

He patted her head and smiled.

'All you need to do is draw just one rabbit a day.' They all looked up spontaneously to the chirping high up in the oak tree. 'I think someone else is waiting for a portrait of themselves,' Bronek joked. The fragrance of the burgeoning hedgerow blossom was all around them.

'Mama!' Emily lifted her head from her drawing. 'Will you be teaching Josh to draw?'

Madeleine smiled with a wave of tenderness for her child.

'Josh is a big boy, Emily. The work he does is very grown up. He can do it all by himself, but he needs help at the moment, because he's been ill and doesn't feel very strong.'

'When will he be strong?' Emily's lips pursed in concentration.

115

'It may take a little while. Perhaps till half term. Perhaps till the summer.'

Emily stopped drawing and looked at Madeleine.

'And after that, will you not see him again?'

'Why do you ask?' Madeleine was curious, but Emily's shrug and a deep sigh indicated that it was obvious.

'Because, if I was Josh, I'd be very sad if I couldn't see you again.'

Before Madeleine thought of an answer, Bronek stroked Emily's head, his big hand as light as a feather.

'This would never happen,' he said soothingly. 'Whatever made you think of that?'

Emily continued to colour. 'I just did.'

They carried on making small talk but Madeleine's inner peace was disturbed. She had always been careful not to allow her insecurities to overshadow Emily's childhood. When her daughter had started pre-school and saw fathers fetching their children at the end of the morning, she had asked, 'Have I got a daddy?'

Madeleine had been dreading that question but she was prepared.

'Yes, you have got a daddy, Emily. Everyone has. But he lives far away.'

'Where?'

'Poland.'

'Why? Why isn't he here with us?'

'Because…' She made it sound casual. 'Sometimes people stop being friends and can't live together. But you've got me, Emily, and Babcha, and Grandpa. We are so lucky to be living together, all four of us, aren't we?'

'When can I see him?'

Madeleine answered in her calm story-telling tone.

'When you're grown-up, Emily. When you won't need me to travel with you anymore. Then you can go on your own and visit Daddy.' Madeleine could not imagine how this was going to happen, how she'd ever be able to tell her daughter the truth.

Emily's probing gaze turned serious and thoughtful.

'That's a long time to wait. Why can't he visit us now?'

'Because…' – a moment of frantic thinking, then a little truth – 'because, Emily, he's not been very well.'

'Was it the chicken pox?'

'No, it wasn't the chicken pox.' The truth. A little at a time. 'Sometimes, Emily, things can go wrong inside a person's head. No one can see what's wrong, but it takes a long time to get better. We'll just have to wait, won't we?'

For the time being, Emily's curiosity had been satisfied. Madeleine had heard her talking to Karishma.

'My daddy lives in Poland. He's poorly. That's why he can't visit me yet.'

'What's wrong with him?'

'It's a secret illness. Inside his head. No one can see what it is.'

'Oh!'

And the subject was never raised again. Madeleine felt a touch of guilt at her daughter's innocent interpretation; she'd never lie deliberately to her child. She was convinced that was not a lie, for how else would one explain his appalling behaviour unless he was deranged?

Presently she watched Emily and Karishma making laborious drawings in their scrapbooks. Emily's was an attempt to depict Bronek's allotment: gigantic flowers dwarfing minute vegetables. She wondered if Emily was anxious sometimes about losing her.

'Emily,' she said, 'you must never worry about me going away. Anywhere. Except when I go to work. And you're used to that. Besides, where would I go? I would never leave you.'

Emily carried on drawing, not looking up and only after a while she said, 'I know that, Mama.'

Karishma tapped her shoulder.

'My mummy never goes anywhere.' Her eyes were huge and earnest. 'You could live with me when your Mummy is away.' Emily nodded, not looking up, and Madeleine was touched.

'You are a good friend, Karishma. You too can stay with us. Even when your mummy is not away.' Or when, she thought to herself, she's in hospital having another baby.

Her words produced happy giggles, while her own thoughts turned to Natalia's wedding. She knew now, with a nervous flutter in her stomach, that if she were to make that trip to Poland, she would have to take Emily with her.

*

'Emily!' Madeleine called out. 'Your Grandpa Adam is on Skype!'

Every night Madeleine had been checking her e-mails for a reply from Natalia. Tonight, when she switched on the laptop, there was a signal from her father on Skype. It was always with a little nervousness that she approached her father even on the screen. His kindness, his fatherly sense of duty, his unfailing financial support could not be faulted – she would be eternally grateful for all those things. But there was a terseness about him, a too-direct openness when he challenged the level of her achievements. Like most Polish fathers, he was expecting her to have ever new goals. So, she had a degree, she was an interpreter, she could be a teacher of English to foreign students, all very good, but what about pursuing her own career further? Why not go on and do a master's, secure a post of university lecturer, become a professor at one of the prestigious universities? She did not argue. She listened politely.

He had the same high expectations of his other two children: Jarek, at twenty-one, was half way through law school, and Dana, at eighteen, was preparing for exams that would secure her a place in marine biology studies. Madeleine had visited them with Emily, when Emily was three, and they all, including Adela, her father's caring wife, had made a big fuss of them. It had been a wrench to leave them and that was when her father had suggested Skype.

It was a mixed blessing. Madeleine loved the frequent contact with his family, but dreaded his persistent questioning about her future plans.

He was smiling to her now from the screen, a handsome man in his mid-fifties, thick dark hair, dark brown eyes (like her own), a pale lemon shirt against the background of shelves packed with books. By now, Emily had climbed on Madeleine's lap and was waving to her Grandpa Adam.

'What have you been up to, Emily?' he asked, leaning closer, distorting his face.

'Gardening with Grandpa Bronek.' Emily wriggled.

'It's been a glorious day.' Madeleine added.

'Now's the time to make the most of the good weather,' her father admonished. 'Are you keeping up with all your sports activities, Emily? Lots of cycling, lots of swimming, running, long walks. All good for your health and for strengthening your bones.'

Emily nodded and Madeleine remembered, now with affection, but then with enduring stoicism, the exhausting daily routines during their annual meetings: the visits to museums and zoos, the trips to historical beauty spots, the adventure of boats, the excitement of trains, every minute of their time spent together filled with activity. She would return home to her Aunt Emilia longing for a rest before the start of a new school term.

'Tato,' she assured him now, 'Emily is active all the time. She is healthy and has grown another inch since we spoke last time.'

'Good, good, that's what I like to hear.' He loved Emily. From their first encounter Madeleine could feel his emotional tie with his granddaughter: the gentle way he picked up the three-year-old child, showed her around the garden, holding her lovingly to his chest, yet giving her space to touch the flowers, watch a humming bird or stoop down to the pond and plunge her hand in the clear water with the swimming goldfish. It had been a great relief to her, and also a puzzle, that, after the initial shock at the news of her pregnancy, he had accepted her explanation and never badgered her again to reveal the identity of Emily's father. She had told him at the time that it had been a big mistake and that she would never seek contact with that man again.

'Believe me, Tato, Emily is infinitely better off without him.'

'All right, we'll leave it as it is, if that is your wish. As long as there's no come-back from him.'

'I assure you, there never will be.'

She had imagined all too graphically her father's wrath had he been told the truth. Terrible thoughts of retribution, murder, trial and her father's sentence behind bars. Too frightful to even think about. They never touched the subject again.

Presently his grainy image asked her, 'So, what's new?'

She told him about her new additional job as a home tutor.

'That's all very well, Magda, but the more you take on, the further back you're pushing your studies. If it's the cost that's stopping you, then just tell me when you need the money.'

She knew that. She had a feeling that his eagerness to help her out financially was his way of dealing with the regret of his absence during her formative years.

'Thank you, Tato. I assure you, when I feel the right time for that has come, I'll talk to you about it. At the moment I've got too much on, and Emily still needs me.' As if on cue Emily threw her arm possessively around Madeleine's neck.

Madeleine told him about Natalia's wedding.

'Are you excited about going back?' he asked.

'Yes, and apprehensive.'

'Don't be. It's all in the past now. Are you likely to see... Zden?'

'No.' She held Emily closer.

'Who's Zden?' Emily asked.

'No one important.'

'Magda.' Her father's tone became gentler. 'Carrying all that anger for so long is not good for you. Have you never thought of getting in touch with him? He's most probably been cured of his addiction and must be bitterly regretting his behaviour towards you. I imagine he'd be greatly relieved if you were the one to get in touch first.'

She was not sure Zden would be so ecstatic to be reminded of his crime. In any event, that problem was his; she wanted nothing to do with him.

'He was a big presence in your childhood,' her father continued. 'Doesn't that count for anything? It was like a double bereavement for him, losing Emilia, then you disappearing from his life.' He went on to quote, 'To err is human, to forgive divine.'

'I'm not divine, Tato.' Magda said. And never would be. Some things could never be forgiven.

# CHAPTER 15

Madeleine was a touch apprehensive when she pressed the doorbell. She had been looking forward to her first session with Josh, but now her confidence failed her, not so much on account of being alone with Josh (in his present state he was no threat to anyone) but because she feared her assistance might not meet his mother's expectations, or, worse still, his older brother's, James. It mattered to her that they should be pleased. A trial period, she reminded herself: she could be the first to walk away, before giving them the chance to reject her.

Josh was on crutches when he opened the door.

'See what I'm reduced to?' He greeted her with a self-conscious grin and a rasp in his voice. His hair was tousled and his face, though unblemished by teenage spots, was pasty. Yet his white shirt, open at the neck, gave him a clean and fresh appearance. Even on crutches and slightly stooping, he was a head taller than Madeleine. She could not help a passing thought that in normal circumstances he'd have been stronger than her, but these were not normal circumstances, she assured herself, and she had nothing to fear.

'Bear with me,' he added, shuffling his way shakily across the hall. His breathing was laboured and beads of sweat appeared on his forehead. Poor lad, she thought, and all at once all her previous misgivings dissolved in her sympathy.

'Is there anything I can do to help?' she asked.

'Just be patient with me.'

He led her to a room, obviously a study with its shelves of books, a desk, a swivel chair, two laptops and a telephone. Just above the desk there was a window giving a wide-lens view of the back garden, which Madeleine had glimpsed on the previous occasion – a long expanse of green with a colourful border of flowering shrubs. A small portable radio was on, its music as soft as an echo.

Josh flopped into a padded chair with additional cushions for support, and for a few moments just breathed deeply, recovering from his effort.

'Please sit down.' He indicated the swivel chair close to his. He wiped his forehead with the cuff of his sleeve and rested his hand against his throat. 'Mother's left some sandwiches for you, Magda...' he smiled as he said her name in Polish, 'in case you've not had time to eat.'

She was surprised.

'That's very kind of her. But please tell her not to go to such trouble again. I always grab a snack before I come here. When do you think I'll see her?'

'You tell me,' he chuckled huskily. 'I should be used to her irregular hours. And normally I don't mind. But now...' He spread his hands expressively. 'Days can seem very long on my own.'

He sounded vulnerable, almost like Emily, and Madeleine felt a rush of feeling for him. She had been silly to have worried so much before.

She said cheerfully, 'You'll have me to put up with from now on. I think that alone will speed up your recovery.'

His husky laughter sounded sincere.

'Let's not make it too speedy,' he said. 'How was your morning?'

He sounded genuinely interested, so she told him, feeling her previous awkwardness dispel completely. She had spent the morning with a young Polish couple, whose premature baby needed special treatment. She had come away feeling glad for them, having seen relief and hope in their faces, after she had translated the consultant's proposed treatment and a positive prognosis. Her second appointment was equally satisfying: a Polish boy with threatening peritonitis caught just in time. When Madeleine was leaving, the boy was in a comfortable post-operative state and the distraught mother could dry her tears on being reassured of his complete recovery.

Josh lay back against the cushions listening absorbed, his dark thoughtful eyes expressing concern. It was easy to like him. She had a good feeling that they'd get on well together. She asked, 'Josh, can I get you anything before we start. A drink?'

His face livened up.

'A cool drink please. Anything as long as it's wet. After my lunch and a ton of pills, I could drink a tank of... anything!' As Madeleine rose, Josh instructed her where to find things in the kitchen. 'There's a marked tin with ginger nuts. My favourites. Fruit drinks in the fridge. And please make yourself a coffee or a tea.'

The kitchen was a sizeable room with an island in the middle that served as a breakfast table. All the kitchen furniture and fittings were in brilliant white, looking ultra-clean. The sunlight streaming through a bouquet of golden roses on the windowsill was like a splash of paint on white canvas. Madeleine liked it all but felt like an intruder. This was Jean's kitchen and she had yet to meet her.

She poured a fruit drink for Josh, made herself instant coffee, placed a few ginger nuts on a plate and rejoined Josh in the study. She found him in exactly the same place and position, as she had left him.

'Right! Where shall we begin?' she asked, intent on making herself sound business-like. He munched his biscuit and smiled.

'Just having company is a treat. Days on your own…' He made a sad-clown face. 'Especially with mother's crazy hours. James comes home only some weekends and all my friends are at school.' He placed his hand on a wad of sheets. 'An essay on Dickens. Needs checking over.'

'Very good,' she praised him. 'I'll take it home with me. Pity to waste practical time. What would you like me to do now?' She took a sip of coffee.

Josh stretched out his arm towards a thick book on the edge of his desk and pulled it towards him. He opened it on the marked chapter.

'Could you read this chapter to me so I can make notes?' Mistaking her raised eyebrows for a challenging look he added quickly, 'I know what you must think. Why can't he do it himself? I can, of course, but I'd be tired and asleep within minutes.' Poor lad, she thought, and smiled.

'No, Josh, I wasn't thinking that at all. I was thinking how easy my first task is. Are you sure this is what your mother had in mind?'

Josh shook his head.

'It was James's idea. He felt I should have support and that I shouldn't be on my own so much. My friend, Matt, brings me notes and instructions for assignments at the end of each week. Then the rest is up to me, how and when I do it.'

This was a normal family with people caring about each other. Her previous apprehension seemed silly now.

'All right, Josh, I'll do whatever is needed, as long as all three of you are pleased with my help.' She picked up the heavy book and placed it on her lap. It was entitled simply 'Napoleon'.

'Napoleon!' she exclaimed and, catching Josh's bemused look, she said, 'Josh, I can tell you stories about him that you won't find in many history books!'

'Really? What stories? Some racy ones?' He made an attempt to sit up only to slide back into his previous languid position. 'Was history your special subject too?'

'I liked it very much at school. You see… we Poles viewed Napoleon differently from the English. Poland was going through a very rough time in Napoleon's era – constant partitions by her greedy neighbours, over a hundred years of enemy dominance in all. When Napoleon's armies crossed Poland on their way to Moscow, the Polish aristocracy saw this as a chance to make the most of his friendly disposition towards the Polish nation. I'll tell you more about that later. This chapter, I see,' – she thumbed through the marked pages – 'is about his rise to power after his victory in Italy.'

She stopped and waited for Josh to organise himself with the tablet. 'I shall be reading slowly. Stop me any time you need me to clarify anything.' She began,

*'At the age of twenty-six, Napoleon was appointed General of the French Army for the second time. His enforced retirement from the army was short-lived. His enemies in the frequently changing French Government were replaced with people mindful of his previous victories over the Spanish and the English in Toulon. Eager to make use of Napoleon's military talents, they recalled him to service when their Italian campaign became too drawn out for comfort.'*

For nearly an hour Madeleine read, stopping for Josh to catch up when details needed repeating. He changed his position many times but found it hard to sit still for too long. Madeleine could see he was tiring.

'Perhaps two hours is too long for you, Josh?' She placed a marker inside the book and closed it. 'Would you rather I left now, so you could lie down for a rest?'

He rubbed his forehead.

'Don't go, Magda. You don't have to do anything. Just stay with me.' His directness was disarming.

'All right. But there must be something useful I could do.'

He thought for a moment.

'I should get up every hour or so and move around for a bit. To build up strength – so my doctor advised. Would you like to see my workout room? James has bought me an exercise bike and a rowing machine. I hate to disappoint him but it's a bit too late for the Olympics!'

She laughed. The start of the Olympics was only weeks away.

'I wish I had an older brother like your James,' she said to please him. Those electric blue eyes, she thought.

'Yeah! All my mates want him too.' Slowly, shakily, Josh raised himself and leaning on his crutches led Madeleine out and across the square hall to a small room, which could have been a walk-in wardrobe before but was now empty except for a thick rubber mat on the floor, an exercise bike and a rowing machine.

'Bear with me,' Josh said, leaning his crutches against the wall. With an effort he climbed onto the bike. There was nothing Madeleine could do but watch as he struggled and admire his determination. Settled safely Josh began to pedal, very slowly at first, then, as the speed increased, he grinned mischievously.

'Easy-peasy, when you set it on the highest gear!'

Madeleine wished James was here to see this. She asked, 'Is James pleased with your progress?'

'He'd better be! I practise slavishly every hour. But the rowing machine is too tough. I tried it once and nearly died!'

'Oh Josh! Should you be doing this when no one else is about?' She was instantly concerned.

He stopped and smiled.

'Then I'd be waiting forever. Trust me, Magda, I really am very careful. Even if I wanted to, I'm not able to rush with anything.' He climbed down carefully and leaned on his crutches.

When they were settled back in the study, Josh in his cushioned armchair, limp with exhaustion, Madeleine said, 'Shall I read you a bit more? You can just listen, and I shall make notes for you by tomorrow.'

'Thanks, but I'd rather listen to one of your stories. About Napoleon's private life.' His voice was husky. 'It'll make a change from all those tedious dates and bloody battles.' He grinned. 'I mean "bloody" as an adjective.'

'I know,' she laughed. 'I think all children at school find dates hard to remember. Things that happened centuries ago, when you're only ten. I managed to remember mine only because I liked to draw them. I kept a book with all their portraits, names and dates and imagined they were my other family. Strangely, it was easier to remember all those adopted great uncles and aunts.'

Josh looked amused. 'Was Napoleon one of your favourite uncles?'

'No. He was not my favourite. But I was fascinated by his relationship with Marie Walewska. We covered that period in Polish history when I was fourteen. I suppose it stuck especially in my young and innocent mind, because I couldn't work out why the Church had approved of that affair, at the time. Of course, as we well know, morality is often diluted for political expediency.'

'Ermm... can you explain?' Josh grinned good-naturedly. Madeleine laughed at herself for getting too serious. She could not help it. Marie Walewska's story had that effect on her.

'Even before Marie met Napoleon,' Madeleine said, 'her teen years were shrouded in mystery. Her family were comfortably well-off landowners. They owned villages. They had an army of people working for them. They had home tutors for their children. Marie's piano teacher, by the way, was Mr Chopin, the famous Frederic's father. Unfortunately, Marie's father died prematurely, leaving his wife to run the estate. Not an easy task, since Marie's two older brothers were in the army. So, when the wealthy Count Walewski asked for Marie's hand in marriage, her mother and her brothers were naturally very pleased, seeing this as a great opportunity to secure their own wealth as well as having an experienced man to help the widow run the estate.'

'Was Marie pleased with this arrangement?' Josh asked. 'I'd hate to be a girl in those days.' He grinned at himself lopsidedly. 'Not that there's any chance of that happening, anyway. But for those girls… for Marie… it must have been revolting! You couldn't imagine that happening now.'

'It still does happen, Josh,' Madeleine said. 'Arranged marriages are still practised in some ethnic societies. And it happens among the wealthy too. Precisely for the purpose of capitalising on the combined wealth. But at least the wealthy girls are smart enough these days to exert bargains to their own advantage. But poor Marie had no such choice. Especially since she was only sixteen and Count Walewski sixty-eight!'

'Gross!' Josh made a face. 'How could they do that to her? Her own family? So, what did she do?'

'Strangely, Walewski did not press for an immediate wedding and Marie was relieved to delay things for the time being. I would imagine that he had no shortage of amusements in Warsaw, where he spent a lot of time, and that Marie most probably and desperately hoped that something would happen to stop this arranged marriage altogether. And indeed, a strange chain of events has left the historians puzzled. Close to Christmas 1804, when Marie was eighteen, Christmas festivities were suddenly cancelled in their country home on account of Marie's mysterious illness. A few weeks later, at the beginning of February, she was escorted by her eldest brother Joseph to church, where the marriage to Count Walewski took place. It is reported that she was overcome with such grief, she could barely say her wedding vows. Immediately after the ceremony, Walewski whisked her off to Italy for a honeymoon.'

'Gross!' Josh repeated making a 'sick' sign with his hand against his mouth. 'An old man of seventy?… And a girl of eighteen?'

'Precisely.' Madeleine knew something about that. She blacked out the memory. 'However, they came back to the Walewski castle in June, in time for Marie to give birth to a baby boy. Now, work this out for yourself. No prize for your conclusion.'

Josh's hazel eyes questioned hers for a moment, but Madeleine only smiled. He said, 'It's obvious, isn't it? She was already pregnant when she married Walewski. But why would he marry her, knowing it wasn't his child?'

Madeleine shrugged. She had often wished that Emily was Dominik's.

'Who knows?' she said. 'He may have needed an heir. He had only two spinster sisters living with him in his castle. It is reported that they treated Marie like their own daughter and her little boy like their own grandchild. And Walewski was proud to be perceived by his contemporaries as a youthful and virile man, still capable of producing a child. Not to mention the fact that his beautiful wife was the envy of all his friends.'

'But what about the man she loved? I guess he'd have been her own age? Why didn't he come forward and fight for her?' Josh was indignant.

'Again.' Madeleine shrugged. 'The historians can only guess that he may have been a Russian aristocrat, serving in the army, and stationed in Warsaw at the time. Marie's grandson actually mentions this in his book, that Marie had enjoyed a friendship with a young Russian called Rudolph. Strangely, all her three sons were given "Rudolph" as their second name.'

'Then why didn't he marry her, and save her from this nightmare?' Josh asked.

'Because… in those days of the occupation by Poland's three neighbours, the Russians, the Prussians and the Austrians, it would have been perceived as the utmost treachery for an aristocratic lady to marry the enemy.'

Josh pondered her words, his gaze turning distant before he said, 'Aren't we lucky, living in our times? I wouldn't stand for it – I mean someone else dictating to me what I should do with my life!'

'And that's how it should be,' Madeleine replied. 'But sometimes unexpected circumstances force you to do things that you wouldn't do otherwise.'

'Like you and Emily? I mean, on your own?' Josh said, then, realising in an instant what he should not have said, rushed to apologise, 'Sorry, Magda… I didn't mean it… to come out like this… Sorry…'

He looked so contrite she smiled, despite the jolt his words gave her. It's nothing, she told herself, just a young boy, being curious. 'You've not said anything wrong, Josh. It's natural that people wonder. I wonder all the time what makes other people tick. Unexpected things happen all the time, and when they happen to you you think it's the end of your world. But life goes on, you learn to adjust to new situations, and the important thing is, to turn any adversity to your advantage. So you are the one in control of your life.'

'Is that what you had to do?' Again, a touch of anxiety, but his question, seemingly probing, was just honestly direct.

'Not just me, Josh. Everyone has to do it. Many times in their lifetime.'

'Was it hard for you? I mean deciding to go it alone?'

'No,' she said without hesitation, sticking in her mind to the agreed version with Aniela of her imagined relationship that did not work out. 'I'm very happy for things to stay just as they are.'

'But... isn't it a bit lonely?' His concern was touching. She smiled.

'Don't worry about me Josh. I'm never on my own.' She looked at her watch. 'It's actually time for me to go.'

'What about Napoleon? You haven't finished telling me Marie's story.'

'It's a long story. I'll tell you more another time.'

'So, you'll come back tomorrow? You're not cross with me for asking too many questions? James often tells me off for my lack of finesse. My big mouth!' He made a mock gesture of zipping up his lips, then added hurriedly, 'So, we're still OK to carry on working together?'

It did not require a genius to work out Josh's needs: he was unwell, he was stuck in the house on his own all day, he was desperate for company. His childlike directness was proof, she thought, of how at ease he felt with her from the start, and this thought pleased her and dispelled all her previous uncertainties.

'We're still OK,' she assured him with a chuckle. 'Now, don't do anything silly when I'm gone. I don't want to come back to a bandaged-up mummy.'

'You know me,' he replied in a suave tone, 'or perhaps you don't know me yet. Genius and wisdom personified.'

*

'Look, Mama! It's Grandpa over there!' Emily let go of Madeleine's hand and ran towards Bronek, who was standing very still, looking lost at the end of the long aisle between the tinned soups and the pasta/rice sections.

Madeleine had just collected Emily from school and had stopped at the local supermarket on the way home. She followed Emily in between other shoppers' trolleys and watched Bronek's face light up when he turned and saw them. He bent down and gave Emily a hug, and she in turn threw her arms possessively around his waist. His basket was full of packages with pasta and rice.

'Has Babcha run out?' she asked amiably, secretly surprised, as this was unlikely. Aniela's pantry shelves were always well stocked up. She had never been able to eliminate her secret fear of food shortages or the memories of her near-starvation in Siberia.

Bronek looked puzzled, his white hair ruffled where he had combed it with his fingers.

'I did remember it then,' he rubbed his forehead, 'when I was going out. Aniela asked me to get it on the way home. But I've been at the church all afternoon, you know, helping to clean and dust. Then I did the lawn. It was like a meadow around the car park. By the time I'd finished with all the jobs, I clean forgot what it was I was supposed to get. I think it was the rice. But maybe pasta. But look at all these different brands. Hundreds of them! How am I supposed to know which one is the one that Aniela wants?'

Madeleine got her mobile out and, as she pressed the home number and held the mobile to her ear, she rested her hand on his shoulder.

'Don't worry, Grandpa, we'll soon get this sorted.'

She heard Aniela at the other end and explained Bronek's dilemma. Aniela was puzzled.

'Rice? Pasta?' There was a pause. 'Poor Bronek. Some confusion again. I was cooking rice this morning. To make golombki. Perhaps I'd said something. Perhaps there was some connection there. No problem. Bronek can get a packet of each anyway. It'll make him feel good.'

'Any particular brand?'

'Not necessarily. But to make it easier for him, tell him an Italian egg pasta and basmati rice.'

Madeleine switched off the mobile and gave Bronek a wide smile.

'You were right, Grandpa. Babcha needs both.' She helped to put back all the unwanted packages, then followed by the relieved-looking Bronek and skipping Emily by his side, she went to look for the things that she had come for.

*

At home, Madeleine checked her e-mails. Among them was one from Natalia. All the cells in her body tingled as she waited for Natalia's message to appear on the screen.

*My dearest Magda,*

*What a joy to receive news from you after all the years! I cannot believe that I'll be seeing you in August. Now I'm counting the days for two reasons: my wedding and your visit.*

*I admire you for having settled in so well in a foreign country, for having completed your studies and now doing a job that you enjoy. You say nothing of your private life, and I cannot imagine you being short of admirers.*

*As for Dominik, don't worry about him. He's doing his second year of internship and will most probably specialise in lung diseases. He married last year, and already they've got a six-month-old little boy.*

*My Szymon's choice was Accident and Emergency. As you can imagine, very demanding of time and energy, but he thrives on being needed and on putting things right. Of course, I'm the one picking up emotional pieces when things go wrong, but I've no excuse to complain as I'm the one with the best job. My students love learning English and dream of visiting England at the first possible opportunity.*

*My dearest Magda, please tell me everything, so I can picture you in your new life.*

*With much love, Natalia.*

Madeleine wished she could tell Natalia everything, and she would, but not just yet. She had nearly three months to think it over. What touched her the most in Natalia's e-mail was the news about Dominik. She was very glad for him (and not without a huge dose of relief) that he had got on with his life without her, finished his medical studies, had found someone to love and to love him, and was now a proud father of a baby boy. She was truly happy for him, yet something heavy landed on her chest and she could not stop a sudden gush of tears.

Luckily, Emily was playing outside, Aniela was busy at the cooker and Bronek was catching up with *The Telegraph* at the kitchen table. By suppertime, Madeleine was composed and presenting her cheerful face.

They had golombki for supper, a delicious fried meat and rice mixture wrapped in cabbage leaves and cooked in tomato sauce.

'Babcha, yours are the best!' Madeleine declared with feeling. Even Emily managed to eat a whole one. 'It must have taken you all day to make them. How did you manage to stand for so long?'

'I didn't!' Aniela said smugly, 'Once I'd prepared the filling and softened the leaves, I sat on the stool to make them and I listened to the radio!'

'You're amazing!' Madeleine said, omitting to say 'for your age'.

'I couldn't imagine spending hours preparing food that was eaten in minutes. You're our very own Nigella!'

'I just wish I had her youth and energy,' Aniela sighed with a heaven-sent gaze.

'Babcha,' Emily clapped her hands with excitement, 'you could teach people to cook on television!'

'She'd have a job teaching me,' Bronek said with a mock-wry expression, 'I'd rather you continue cooking just for us, Aniela. And I'll see to all the other stuff, unfit for your fair hands.'

'And what might that be?' Aniela challenged him. But he only smiled, lifting his eyebrows and squinting his keen grey eyes at Madeleine.

'Will you have the time, some time, to come with me to the allotment?'

'Bronek…' Aniela tried to stop him from saying more, but Emily clapped her hands and cried excitedly,

'And me too!'

Bronek gave Aniela a triumphant look.

'I've already told Manu, my Indian friend about it. He's keen to help me repair the wall. I've got a tub of ready-mixed mortar. I just need a boss to oversee it all.'

'But you're the best boss, Grandpa!' Madeleine protested cheerfully. Aniela was less cheerful.

'Bronek,' she said, as if she meant business, 'you know what I think about that wall. It's too old. It's crumbling. Get rid of it before it falls on anyone!'

Bronek shrugged and carried on eating the remains of his meal. Keeping his eyes down he said, 'You know, Aniela, that I can't do it. You know the wall has got to be there. Trust me, I shall make it as strong and as solid as a rock.'

Aniela shot a helpless glance towards Madeleine, who felt compelled immediately to say something calming.

'Babcha, please don't worry. I'm sure Grandpa will make an excellent job of it. And Grandpa, I will come with you, and if you wish, check every single brick, so we're both sure that the wall is a hundred per cent safe!'

'A hundred and fifty!' Emily added for good measure.

# CHAPTER 16

Things were not going to plan. Madeleine rang up Josh earlier in the day to warn him she'd be late.

'I'm interpreting in court. The case is taking longer than expected. I'll come over after I've fetched Emily from school.'

She could not ask Aniela to help out, as she and Bronek were visiting friends in Melton Mowbray. It was one of those days when everything conspired against her. She tried to quash her frustration by reminding herself that things hadn't been that bad lately: at home, at work, with Josh. Bronek's wall on his allotment had been fixed, much to his joy and Aniela's relief; Mr Bunting appeared less snappy towards her, especially when he relied on her support at inconvenient times to others; and the trial period with Josh had proved unnecessary. There had been a good rapport between them from the very first session and she could not find one trace of teenage rebelliousness in him. Perhaps he saved that for impressing his peers. With her he was always polite and very easy to like.

'Are we there yet?' Emily asked from the back seat.

'Just five more minutes,' Madeleine promised resigned to the snail's pace in the traffic jam on both sides of the outer circle, built for the purpose of avoiding traffic jams. The car in front jerked into action only for a pushy Audi to jump the queue and squeeze into the tight space before her. She was not used to swearing, but 'Sugar!' came spontaneously.

'Mama, why are you saying sugar?' came from the back seat.

'Maybe... because I fancy something sweet.' Resigned, she waited for the next movement in the traffic.

Her thoughts returned to the man in court. She felt sorry for him. She had a feeling he had been set up by his flatmates. His own countrymen. They had all come here to better their lot. He had trusted them, like his substitute family. And they broke that trust in a most perfidious way. A stash of cocaine had been discovered in a sock in his drawer. He swore on oath he knew nothing about it. The trial was to continue the next day.

In the lunchtime break, there had been the usual mid-week meeting of Mr Bunting's team: interpreters in Urdu, Gujarati, Romanian, Latvian, Serbo-Croat, Polish and others, if free to attend. Madeleine went dutifully, as her appointment happened to be close to the agency premises. There was little chance of getting to know her colleagues personally during those brief weekly meetings; Mr Bunting discouraged that, insisting that any unresolved problems arising in the course of their work had to be directed exclusively to him. The team was regularly reminded of the utmost professionalism expected of them, of their absolute impartiality and total confidentiality. When they dispersed after the meeting, Madeleine would not see them for another week. It was hard not having a close work colleague. She saw hundreds of people in the course of her work but never long enough for the acquaintance to grow into a friendship.

'Mama, is Josh waiting for you?' Emily's voice pulled her out of her thoughts.

'Yes, Emily, he knows we are coming, and he knows we'll be a little late, and he knows what a good girl you are and how you'll be busy colouring when I work with him.'

'I can help you, Mama. I can teach him how to draw birds. Grandpa showed me.'

'Good girl, Emily. We'll see if there's time for that at the end of his lesson,' Madeleine replied, coming off the main road, at last, into Grandview Road. With a sigh of relief, she parked by the main entrance of the Hammond's house. She took out Emily's bag of colouring books and crayons and together they approached the front door, Emily skipping impatiently by her side.

Madeleine warned her, pressing the bell, 'It sometimes takes Josh a long time to come to the door. He is on crutches.'

She was surprised to hear a rapid clicking of heels before the door opened, and guessed his mother was at home. A wave of nervousness swept over her. And indeed, when the door opened, it was to reveal a good-looking middle-aged woman. She was wearing a navy trouser suit, as if she had only just arrived from work, and there was an air of briskness and authority about her, even as she surveyed Madeleine and Emily.

'I'm Madeleine,' Madeleine introduced herself.

'I know.' The woman's blue eyes (almost as piercing as James's) appraised her unhurriedly. 'And I'm Jean.' Her features were attractively regular and there were two artful white streaks in her raven, short-cut and shaped bob.

'I'm… not… usually this late,' Madeleine stuttered.

'I know.' A slow smile softened her mouth. 'Please come in. I'm so glad I'm at home this time at least to meet you at long last.'

Madeleine felt a great need to explain her lateness.

'It was a complicated day. I had no control over it. Except to walk away. But I couldn't do that, once I'd committed myself.' Emily tugged at her hand. Madeleine looked down at her daughter's upturned face. 'And this is my Emily. I don't usually bring her with me. She'll be no trouble, while I work with Josh.'

'Please come inside,' Jean repeated showing them inside the hall. 'Don't worry about anything. We'll find some interesting things for Emily to do.'

No need, Madeleine wanted to say, but refrained from explaining.

By Josh's half-open door, Jean stopped and said, 'I think some drinks would be good to start with. A juice drink, perhaps?' She looked down at Emily then at Madeleine. 'Tea? Coffee?'

'Coffee would be most welcome, thank you,' Madeleine admitted, and Emily did a hop at her side.

'Thank you, Mrs Hammond,' she said, as she had been instructed.

There was a flicker in Jean's eyes and a twitch in her mouth. Seriously she said, 'Go in. See Josh. He's been waiting all afternoon.' (Ouch!) 'I'll be along shortly.'

As usual, Josh was half-reclining against the cushions in his easy chair. He looked pale and the curls around his forehead were damp.

'Ah! Emily! What a lovely surprise!' He raised his hand in greeting.

Emily looked up uncertainly at Madeleine.

'Where's the little boy Josh that you help to read, Mama?' Madeleine and Josh exchanged smiles.

'This is Josh, Emily. He's a big boy, remember? I told you we read grown-up books together, about history and about famous writers. He's got to be very clever and remember lots of things, so he can get top marks in his exams.'

'Like me in my spelling test at school?'

'Something like that.'

Emily looked at Josh with more interest. He smiled and picked up his tablet.

'Would you like to play a game with me?' he asked. She nodded and stepped up right beside him. Once he explained the rules of 'The Runaway Train' and she got engrossed in pressing all the correct keys, he and Madeleine exchanged small talk until Jean came back.

She had changed into a pale pink shirt and navy slacks and carried a tray of drinks and biscuits. Once they had settled with their refreshments,

Emily holding her glass of orange carefully with both hands, Jean said, 'Madeleine, I'm sorry I missed you that first time. I'm glad my boys have persuaded you to take on this task. It can't be easy for you pulling everything else all in, and this too.'

Madeleine detected empathy in Jean's brisk manner and felt herself warming to her.

'It's no more than you do, Mrs Hammond.'

'Call me Jean.'

Madeleine nodded. 'My grandparents help me a lot. I gather you were on your own when Josh was Emily's age.'

'We had James,' Josh boasted amiably.

Jean gave Emily an appraising glance before turning to Madeleine.

'James was only a young lad at the time,' she said, 'and one could say that wasn't fair on him. But life isn't always fair. It's what you make of it that counts.'

'I agree,' Madeleine said. Jean was quiet for a moment and Madeleine wondered what her impressions were of herself and Emily. Back home, she knew she'd not have been able to escape prurient speculation as to Emily's father. Here, in this country, she had found a far more tolerant attitude towards unmarried mothers. It mattered to her, she could not explain why, that Jean should think well of her and Emily.

Jean stood up energetically and announced, 'Right, time for me to leave you two to get on with your work, and we'll get on with ours, Emily, shall we?' She turned to Emily. 'I've got some gardening to do. Will you help me with that?'

Emily slid off her chair, her eyes sparkling, and returned her empty glass to the tray.

'I help Grandpa all the time!'

'Good!' Jean said. She assured Madeleine, 'Emily won't get dirty. It's only bagging the grass on the lawn that has been cut this afternoon.'

'Emily will enjoy that,' Madeleine said to please Jean, who was not to know that Emily was capable of entertaining herself for hours. Nevertheless, she was touched by Jean's interest in her child.

She cleared the cups and mugs before sitting down with Josh.

'So, what will it be today?' she asked.

He gave a long, slow breath.

'It's been a long day. My brain feels dead. I'm not sure that the Industrial Revolution can resurrect it.' He paused. 'I've been reading George Eliot's *Middlemarch*. I wish it could have been Ian Rankin or Robert Harris.' He smiled a tired smile.

'Shall I read you a bit? We can stop any time.'

'OK. I suppose I'd better look diligent for mother's sake.'

They worked together for an hour, but Josh found it hard to concentrate or to formulate pertinent comments and questions.

'Enough for today,' Madeleine decided. 'I'll make up the time to you on other days.' She checked her watch. Quarter to five. Not the best time of the day for sharp concentration.

Josh did not argue, just lay back against the cushions. He had dark shadows under his eyes.

'Sorry I feel so lousy today, Magda. Just don't go without me saying goodbye to Emily.'

Madeleine found the back door as instructed and stepped out onto a patio shaded by a canopy of hanging wisteria. It looked pretty and peaceful. At the far end of the lawn, she could see Emily holding up a green sack and Jean filling it with cut grass. Emily's excited chatter floated towards her on air.

She walked over to them. Emily's face was hot and damp tendrils stuck to her forehead and neck. Jean's face was flushed too when she straightened and waited for Madeleine.

'I don't want to go yet, Mama,' Emily announced, leaving a green streak from her finger on her cheek. 'There's all that grass to tidy up first.'

'You've already done such a lot, Emily,' Jean said. 'I'm sure there will be another big job waiting when you come next time.' She turned to Madeleine. 'Was it hard going? Have you finished for today?' Her tone was matter of fact, summing up the situation.

But Madeleine was anxious to explain.

'Josh is too tired. Another hour would be a waste of time, but I'll make up the time on other days.'

'Don't worry, Madeleine. I think we've all had a long day. You too, Emily.' She picked a blade of grass off Emily's hair. 'Come back another day and we'll do more jobs together.'

People made well-meant promises to Emily, which they forgot. But Emily remembered and pestered Madeleine with daily reminders. Was Jean just being pleasant? Emily tugged Madeleine's hand, 'Can I come again, Mama? Please. I promise to be good.'

'I know you're a good girl,' Jean said seriously. 'I'll let your mum know when I'm at home in the afternoon next time, so you can come too. How's that?'

At least this was straightforward, Madeleine thought.

'When will that be?' Emily asked.

'I don't know this very minute, but when I do, I'll let your mum know.' This satisfied Emily.

They strolled back indoors to say goodbye to Josh and found him fast asleep in his armchair. Emily blew him a kiss before they tiptoed out and said their polite farewells in the porch. When Madeleine drove back home, it was with a feeling that she had not shown herself at her best to Jean. Jean could justifiably reconsider employing her against the demands of her other commitments and find someone else with more spare time to help Josh. That very thought dampened her already low spirits, in addition to her imagined rejection. She had grown to like Josh. She would miss him.

At home, she prepared a simple meal of pizza and green salad, Emily's favourite. Afterwards, while Emily watched CBBC, Madeleine made an attempt to get on with her translations but found it hard to concentrate. Besides, the house felt empty and dead with Aniela and Bronek out. She had realised from the very beginning that this family life she had been enjoying with them would not last forever; there was a difference of two generations in age between them; the implication of that did not require a genius to work out. What would she do when they were no longer here? The practicalities of everyday life did not bother her; she was an expert at coping with those. But once Emily was grown up and gone too? She could not visualise her future as anything other than a solitary existence. She'd have to join some evening classes! Dancing? No. Involved pairing up. Drawing and painting was a possibility. As long as no one pried into her life. Learning a new language would be a challenge. The harder the better. Chinese? Greek? Which of the two would ensure a large class? Less of a chance of getting too intimate with anyone.

She watched children's television with Emily until it was bedtime. She bathed her, read her a story and returned to her translations with no more enthusiasm than before. When her mobile rang, her immediate thought was Mr Bunting. She could not oblige him tonight, not until Aniela and Bronek were back. She did not recognise the number. She pressed and a male voice came on. Her heart stopped for a second and then ran like mad.

'Hello, Madeleine. It's James.'

'James?' She could hardly speak. 'Josh's James?'

'Josh's James.' His voice rang with amusement. 'My mother asked me to ring you.'

Panic. She was giving her the sack.

'Your mother? Is there anything wrong?'

'Nothing's wrong, Madeleine. She was concerned about you.'

Jean? Worried about her? This was astonishing. A load fell off her chest.

'Why? I mean… that's very kind of her. I'm not used to people worrying about me… I mean… I'm glad everything is all right. I thought

137

for a moment that something's happened with Josh. He wasn't too well today, and my day was all higgledy-piggledy, and nothing went right and I was late for Josh, but I'll make it up to him over the next few days…'

She paused to take breath and James's voice came through firm, 'Stop, Madeleine, stop! That is precisely why I've been told to ring you. Mother thought that you looked a bit… unhappy with the way things turned out today despite your best efforts. She did not want you to worry. There's always the next day and the next. Josh will also be better disposed as time goes on…'

They were such understanding people. She was overcome with thankfulness and would have hugged Jean, not that Jean looked like the hugging type. She did not know what to say, but was suddenly aware of that pressing, sombre and bleak mood dissolving in a wonderful buoyancy that spread out from her chest.

'Thank you, James,' she said simply. 'Thank you for taking the trouble.'

'No trouble at all. It's a pleasure. I'm glad mother rang me.'

'She's very perceptive. Or, I'm too transparent.'

'Both are virtues,' he said. A pause, then, 'Are you happy to continue with Josh?'

'I love working with him. Truly. Such pleasure after all my other tasks. What about you? Busy life?'

'A bit. I've been travelling a lot lately. Just now I'm in Hamburg.'

Madeleine was astonished.

'You sound as if you're in the next room. Exciting trip?'

'Run of the mill. Meetings by day and a hotel room by night.'

She pictured him all alone, but perhaps he was not. None of her business, what did it matter? She heard him say, 'We must catch up, next time I'm in Leicester.'

Really? Was he just being polite?

'That would be nice.' She was polite too. 'Fingers crossed that Josh's recovery won't take too long.'

'Fingers crossed,' he said.

When Aniela and Bronek walked through the front door she had the urge to skip like Emily.

'Did you miss me?' Bronek teased, his bear hug wrapping her in his warmth and Old Spice. Madeleine gave Aniela a big hug too and kissed her on her apple-rosy cheek.

'I missed you both,' she said. 'The house feels empty when you're not around.'

# CHAPTER 17

Bronek was enjoying a good phase, and with him Aniela, the woman with angelic patience. He was no less forgetful and every morning searched for things he had hidden in a safe place the day before, but, since the wall in his allotment had been fortified, he appeared less preoccupied with the KGB agents spying on him.

Madeleine was therefore startled when one afternoon after fetching Emily from school he surprised her by coming out suddenly from behind the tree close to the front of their house.

'Grandpa, who are you hiding from?' She walked up towards him with Emily skipping ahead of her.

He stooped down towards her and lowered his voice.

'There's a stranger in our street. I don't like that. I've no idea who he is, but I've seen him walking up and down several times this week.' Bronek looked genuinely concerned.

'Grandpa,' Madeleine said soothingly, 'do you remember last Saturday? Do you remember the removal van and the new people moving into number ninety-six? That's probably our new neighbour getting to know our street.'

Bronek's furrowed brow would not relax and his pursed mouth would not respond to her smile.

'Are you sure about that, Magda?'

'I'm guessing, Grandpa, but I think I'm guessing right. Please, don't worry yourself for nothing.'

'It's not nothing, if he is one of them! You've no idea, Magda! You've got to be vigilant at all times!'

Magda looked up and down the street. A soft breeze was rustling the leaves above them, a car went slowly by, mothers were walking home with their schoolchildren, some pushing prams. It looked a normal May afternoon, soft and warm, nothing sinister about it. Madeleine had an idea.

'Grandpa, if you like, we could go to them later on tonight, knock on their door, take them a box of chocolates and say welcome to our street.'

'Yes! Let's do that, Grandpa!' Emily skipped beside him, holding onto his hand. But he still looked unconvinced.

'That's one way of checking who they are,' Madeleine continued, 'and you'll see for yourself if it's the same man you keep seeing in the street.'

'Yes,' Bronek reasoned, 'at least I'll see him close up, but that still won't solve anything if he is one of them. They are masters of disguise.'

However, Bronek had been persuaded eventually to go along with Madeleine's suggestion and she was still thinking about it now as she was driving to Josh's house. The evening had finished far more successfully than she could have imagined. Their new neighbours were pleasantly surprised with their gifts of Aniela's cake and a box of chocolates, and it turned out that the man had been injured badly in Afghanistan, had recovered, but could no longer work in the building trade and had been working from home instead, doing prescribed exercises to keep his body agile as well as taking regular walks. Hence the reason for his frequent presence in the street.

In Bronek's eyes the new neighbour became an instant hero. Anyone fighting the evil of oppression deserved a medal and life-long recognition.

Unlike the man she had been required to interpret for at the police station earlier in the day. Bronek would have been thoroughly ashamed of his countryman. The young Pole, after a night of drunken brawling, had stolen a car, enjoyed a police chase and only sobered up with the shock of crashing into some law-abiding citizen's newly built wall.

When Madeleine met him in the interview room at the police station, it was indeed hard to remain unbiased, as instructed by Mr Bunting. A beery and sweaty aura emanated from him that made Madeleine feel nauseous. She marvelled at the calm of the two police officers. The man was wearing a stained singlet with printed words 'Funk me' across his chest. His exposed arms were tattooed with an army of scorpions and spiders. The very sight of them gave Madeleine the shudders. His head was shaved, with the exception of a narrow swathe of thick hair running from his forehead, over and down the back of his head, which looked like an animal pelt. But it was his insolent manner that made Madeleine itch to give him a sobering smack. She hissed at him when the formalities were over.

'You're giving the Poles a bad name. You should be ashamed of yourself!'

He was taken aback then lowered his gaze, saying nothing.

'What did you say to him?' one of the officers asked.

'That he should be ashamed of himself.' The officer gave a thin smile.

'We'd be out of a job if all people had a conscience.'

'Believe me,' she said with feeling, 'most Poles are decent people.'

'I believe you,' he said. 'It's always the few that spoil it for the majority.'

*

Madeleine's spirits lifted as she turned into Josh's tree-lined avenue. Since that time when she had been late and he had been too tired for a meaningful tutorial, they'd had a few good sessions, and Madeleine had a feeling that his mother was pleased. James too, apparently. Every time he rang Josh, he sent his best regards to her.

Used to his slow progress on crutches, she waited in the porch and looked around. The flowering shrubs and trees were bathed in sunshine and the warm air was heavy with the fragrance of lilac and acacias. They could sit out on the patio, Madeleine thought, already planning to pad out a deck chair with cushions for Josh.

She rang the doorbell again. He was taking much longer than usual. Sudden anxiety gripped her. She lowered herself to the flap of the letterbox, pushed it back and looked inside. She called out his name. Just then he came into view shuffling laboriously inch by inch, bent double, with one arm cradling his abdomen, and with the other hanging onto his crutch.

'Josh!' she cried out panicked. 'I'm here! I'll help you! If you could just open the door!'

It was excruciating watching him move towards her, agony etched on his pallid face, his lips clamped to stifle his cry. She willed him with all her might to reach the door and to turn the key. The moment this happened, she was inside the hall talking fast, 'Don't move, Josh. I'm getting you a chair!' She was back in an instant with a padded chair from his study, helped him to lower himself down on it and crouched down beside him.

'Could it be your spleen?' she guessed.

'I think so... I feel so sick... the pain is unbearable...' His face was contorted in agony.

'I'm calling an ambulance!'

He did not protest, just leaned his head on his arm that was holding on to the crutch and listened to Madeleine's emergency phone call.

'The ambulance is on its way, Josh. Can I get you anything? Water? Tea?'

He shook his head. 'The very thought makes me want to vomit.'

She got up and fetched a dry and a wet paper towel. She moistened his parched lips with the wet tissue and with the dry towel she wiped the sweat off his face. He moaned with pain.

'Just a few minutes, Josh. I'll let your mum know.' She dialled Jean's number and left a voicemail message.

They didn't talk while waiting. Madeleine wished she could soothe Josh's pain, as she did Emily's on countless occasions, just holding her close and stroking her head. Very gently she stroked his shoulder. He did not shake off her hand.

The ambulance arrived with astonishing speed and backed up right in front of the porch. The young paramedics, a man and a woman, wasted no time. A few questions, a gentle examination and Josh was on a stretcher being transported inside the ambulance.

'I want my friend to come with me,' Josh pleaded. 'There's no one else at home.'

'I can call a family member,' the paramedic woman offered.

'I've already done that,' Madeleine replied for Josh. 'His mother. Dr Hammond in radiology. I expect she'll be waiting.'

'Oh right!' the woman said amicably. 'Hop in with me.' She waited for Madeleine to bang the front door shut while the man climbed up to the driver's seat and started the engine.

At the hospital, Madeleine walked alongside with Josh, as he was being wheeled to the examination room. He had stayed very still throughout the journey, lying bent double on his side with suppressed moans escaping his chest every time the pain peaked. The examination chamber was crammed with curtained cubicles and relatives waiting outside them. They were met by a young doctor and a mature nurse, who took over from the paramedic and wheeled Josh inside an empty cubicle. Drawing the curtains around them she asked Madeleine, 'Are you family?'

'No, but I expect Josh's mother will come soon. She knows he's here.'

'Do you mind waiting outside?' She meant outside the curtain.

Madeleine obliged and felt suddenly very much alone in this crowded room. She felt helpless; there was nothing more she could do except pray. Please, God, let him recover. Soon. For his mother. For his brother. Please, please! She imagined, with a mother's pain, if this had been Emily behind that curtain. Her eyes stung and as she turned away she saw Jean, in her dark suit and standing out from the moving crowd, coming towards her.

Madeleine indicated the curtain and Jean slipped behind it. The general hubbub in the room made it impossible to follow any conversation in the cubicle except for the odd word. Madeleine had no wish to eavesdrop, but she felt she should wait until Jean reappeared with the assurance that all would be well. She watched other patients being wheeled in, mute and stoic in pain, their companions' faces drawn with concern, the nurses calm and reassuring. It was hard to imagine that this unending flow of human suffering went on every single day, of every week, of every month alongside the busy life of the city on the other side of the hospital wall. A sobering thought for any time of self-pity, she thought.

The curtain twitched and Jean came out. She looked tired, but her expression softened when she turned to Madeleine.

'It's the spleen. But it's not ruptured. And no operation is necessary,' she sighed with relief. 'They'll be doing a blood test and a CT scan, and keep him overnight. The painkiller they've given him is already doing wonders.' She sighed again. A weight lifted off Madeleine's chest.

'Could I see him before I go?' she asked.

Jean pulled back the curtain and Madeleine slipped inside the cubicle. There were tubes and monitors and bleeping sounds and a breathing mask over Josh's mouth and nose. He looked vulnerable, unlike the jaunty and amusing teenager that she got to know. The doctor and the nurse had their heads down over Josh's notes but acknowledged her with a nod. Josh's drowsy eyes opened at the rustle of her entrance.

'Please don't go,' he whispered.

'I'll come back later. You must rest now, Josh,' she said.

'Promise?'

'Of course!'

Outside the cubicle Jean said, 'Madeleine, how can I ever…' Her voice faltered. Spontaneously Madeleine clasped her hand.

'I'm just glad I was there. Anyone else would have done the same.'

Jean held her hand in a warm tight clasp, as she recovered from her moment of weakness. When she spoke again it was with the composure of a practical woman.

'Madeleine, we'll meet soon and talk. Now, how will you get home? I expect you've left your car at our house?'

Jean's concern sounded suddenly funny in the scheme of things. Or was it the relief that made Madeleine want to laugh? She gave Jean a sympathetic smile.

'That's absolutely no problem at all for me. I'll just get the bus to your house. Fetch the car. And I'll be back tonight.'

*

'Mama, does this look like Josh?' Emily was sitting with Madeleine at her work desk close to the French window, putting finishing touches on her 'Get well' card for Josh. Madeleine looked up from her translation.

'It's a lovely picture,' she said diplomatically. The stick person with a pancake face, oversized shorts, and a curly scribble on top of his head appeared to be kicking a ball the size of an inflated balloon. 'Make him smiley,' Madeleine suggested. 'That will cheer up Josh no end.'

A wide U-shaped smile was squiggled on in a flash, and indeed the stick figure became a character.

'When can I see him?' Emily asked.

'As soon as he is better. I'll take you to his house. Now, what will you write inside the card?'

Emily thought for a moment chewing on her pencil. 'Do... you... want... to... play... with... me... and... Karishma?' She enunciated each word in readiness for writing.

'I'm sure he'd be delighted with this, but he's not well enough to play with anyone. Shall we just wish him well and write something like... "I'm sorry that you're in hospital. Get well soon",' Madeleine suggested.

'Or,' Emily corrected, 'get well as fast as the speed of light!'

'That's very clever, Emily, but cards don't usually have messages like that.'

'Why not? Don't people want poorly people to get better fast? The faster the better. And nothing is faster than light. Miss Jones at school said so.'

'All right, Emily,' Madeleine gave her a hug. 'I'll help you write your message just as you want it.' She wrote it out clearly on a piece of paper and Emily copied it carefully, letter by wobbly letter inside the card for Josh.

They tidied up their desk, washed their hands and joined Aniela and Bronek in the kitchen. It was six o'clock, close to the evening meal. Madeleine knew better than to meddle with Aniela's cooking, so she sat down next to Bronek, while Emily got down to setting the table, her favourite job – knives and forks, serviettes and drinking glasses.

Bronek folded away his paper saying, 'You've had quite a day today!'

'Yes, but it's all sorted. Josh is in good hands, the best place for him.'

Bronek leaned towards her conspiratorially, his eyes swivelling under his brow towards the wall behind the dresser, the spot he listened to daily for the sound of hidden spies.

'Is Josh well-guarded in his ward?' he asked in a whisper.

Madeleine patted his sun-bronzed arm. He was still so good looking for his age, she thought, the cloud of white hair falling over his forehead, the neat features unspoilt by the lines, the still good teeth, all his own, his frame un-stooping, that of a much younger man. But his mental state – that was so unfair!

Aniela looked over her shoulder, catching Madeleine's gaze, and Madeleine saw helplessness in her eyes.

'Grandpa,' she said, 'believe me, Josh is being looked after well and guarded at all times.'

'So was Litvinenko.'

'But Josh is of no interest to the KGB. He's just a young English boy. Getting on with his life, getting on with his school work.'

'Ah! That is just when they catch them. Young and impressionable. For all you know they may already be keeping an eye on him, ready to entice him, the moment he leaves home.'

'Grandpa, that may be the case. But I know Josh. I'd know if there was something strange going on.'

'Can you be certain of that, Magda? Can you be certain of anything?'

There was no answer to that. She caught Emily's fascinated gaze and suggested, 'Emily, could you fetch something for me? You know the boxes of pens I have in my drawer? There are little notebooks too. Could you fetch me one of each? A pen and a notebook?' Emily nodded and went off and Madeleine turned to Bronek. His grey eyes looked intensely into hers.

'My dear Magda, I worry about you. I worry about Emily. They know when to strike and they strike hard. It's always the ones that you love.'

'Bronek!' Aniela snapped, sending him a reprimanding look from stirring the pot. 'Don't say such things!'

And Madeleine, despite her familiarity with Bronek's state of mind, felt a chill down her back. Emily returned with a notebook and a pen, gave them to Madeleine and threw her arms around her mama's waist.

'Grandpa, why are you worried about Mama and me?'

'Worried?' Bronek sat up as if waking from a trance. 'No, my sweet Emily, I'm not worried at all. Nothing bad could happen today. Because its number is not divisible by three.' Emily thought for a while then counted on her fingers.

'You mean like eight or eleven?'

'You've got it! My clever girl!'

'But then, what about Josh? It's not been a lucky day for him!' Emily pointed out.

'Ah! That's where you're mistaken. It's been a very lucky day for him. Your mama came just at the right time and saved him from a very bad thing. Don't you agree?'

Emily nodded satisfied and Madeleine was sure she heard Aniela sigh with relief. The meal was ready to serve: noodles, chicken stew, and glazed carrots.

'Grandpa, all your favourite things,' Madeleine remarked, helping Aniela bring the food to the table.

After the meal Madeleine helped to wash up, dry and tidy up, allowing Emily, ever eager, to be useful too, while Bronek retired to the front room to watch his favourite priest-detective on Polish television. It was a blessing that he enjoyed this series so much and could follow the plots and remember the characters. Some of the modern serials were presented like pieces of a jigsaw that the viewer had to put together to make sense of the plot. Bronek could not follow these and invariably fell asleep.

When Emily went outside to play, Aniela said hopefully, 'I wish Josh was well enough to have some of my cake. What will you take him, Magda?'

'Nothing, Babcha. I don't think he's in an eating mood just yet.' Seeing Aniela's disappointment, Madeleine added, 'Don't worry Babcha, there will be lots of opportunities yet to feed him up.'

'Do you think so?' Aniela wasn't convinced. 'What will happen now? About your job, I mean?'

Madeleine shrugged. 'It was only going to be temporary, anyway. I expect I may be needed for a while longer when he recovers after this hospital stay.' She gave Aniela a hug. 'What is it that you're worrying about, Babcha?'

Aniela shook her head.

'I'm not worrying, and it's nothing, Magda. It's just seeing you so happy doing this job and spending time with someone closer to your age. I had this feeling, this hope, I suppose, that maybe there was a chance for you to meet other young people. I mean people your own age...'

Madeleine gave her another hug and chuckled.

'I know, Babcha, that you want to marry me off...'

'No, Magda, no! It's not that! It's just that time is passing by... and... I just want you to be happy.'

'I know that. And I couldn't be happier anywhere else.'

Madeleine showered and changed into a dress and matching high wedges. The evening had turned balmy, a chance to wear something light. The cotton dress was pale pastel pink and fitted smoothly around her thin waist. She brushed her hair into a fluffy bob, applied fresh lipstick and mascara, sprayed perfume onto her hairline and neck, and folded a thin cardigan into her handbag, in case it turned cool later.

She found Aniela sitting on the patio, watching Emily playing hopscotch. She gave her another hug, saying, 'I'm really grateful, Babcha.'

'It's only right that you should visit Josh,' Aniela replied. 'It will please his mother too. A doctor or not, she'll be worried sick, like any other mother. I can only imagine how I'd feel if this was one of mine.'

'Me too,' Madeleine replied, watching Emily hop to her heart's content. She added, 'With Emily, it's the usual…'

'Bath, story, sleep,' Aniela finished for her. 'I know it all, Magda. She'll be no problem. And if for any reason they need you to stay longer, just stay. Don't worry about anything.'

'Thank you, Babcha. You're an angel!'

*

Madeleine had texted Jean earlier for the number of Josh's ward. She parked her Ka in the street between two giant four-by-fours, which looked sinister with their black paintwork and their black glass windows. She thought her little red Ka was infinitely prettier and locked it up with affection and concern for its safety, as if it were her little pet.

At the hospital, the endless corridors, the crowds of people moving about, looking for lifts, looking for directions made her think of earlier on, when she had come with Josh. She realised afterwards, when travelling on the bus, that she had been in shock, doing things instinctively, perhaps even looking detached. The sway of the bus had suddenly made her feel shaky and slightly sick then. On arrival at home Aniela forced her to have a swig of cherry vodka, followed by camomile tea. And it had worked!

She followed the signs to Josh's ward, suddenly remembering her visits to Aunt Emilia. And that awful day! She blanked it out instantly. Even after all the years, the pain of that memory was still so raw.

There were six beds on Josh's ward, men patients of mixed ages with their visitors standing or sitting around them. Madeleine saw Josh from the entrance, propped up against pillows, looking comfortable and surprisingly well, after the drama earlier in the day. Her heart missed a beat. Sitting beside him was James.

He looked up at the same time she saw him, stood up and watched her approach. She had a strange feeling of floating towards him, as if for a split-second there was no one else in the room. Then his arm was light on her shoulder, a natural and deft hug followed and he stepped back. She could have imagined it, it happened so quickly, except for the pleasurable sensation throughout her body.

He was saying, 'Madeleine, so good of you to come. You're quite the heroine today. Look, Josh is already looking so much better!'

In her confusion, she did not notice at first that Josh was smiling, that his face was a normal colour, even a little flushed, that his sparkly eyes expressed his gladness at seeing her. She walked up to him and gave his free hand a gentle squeeze with both hers. The top part of his left hand had a canula inserted and plastered over the vein.

'Josh,' she said, feeling a bubble expanding her chest, 'you gave us such a fright! You've no idea what a relief it is to see you looking so good!'

'I know.' His voice was still husky. 'It's a miracle! At home you swallow thousands of painkillers and you still feel like death. Here, one injection and you're ready to sprint!'

'You've got enough long corridors here to practise,' she teased, at the same time as James offered her his seat and fetched another chair. He sat down beside her, she very much aware of his closeness. 'So, what next, Josh? When are you coming home?' she asked. The two visitors by the next bed burst out laughing and then just as suddenly quietened down. Good news, no doubt, or just relief. Josh rolled his eyes and grinned.

'Tomorrow, hopefully,' he said. 'I've had all the tests done. I've had injections and pills. They've just got to be sure, I suppose, that I'm ready to be sent home.'

'That must be such a relief for your mum!'

'Yes,' James said, and she was obliged to turn and look at him. His eyes focussed directly on hers, giving her a melting sensation. She kept her expression serious, desperate to look normal. James continued, 'It's a great relief for me too. It was lucky I was not abroad. I took the first train to Leicester after Mother rang. Madeleine... we owe you... lots!' He said it simply, matter-of-factly, but she found herself going hot in the face.

'Don't mention it. Anyone would have done the same.'

He smiled, still looking at her with that unhurried, considered look. She looked away but returned her gaze as he spoke.

'Some trial period you've had with Josh... You've not been put off?'

'Not in the least!' This sounded like a nervous reaction. Josh came to the rescue.

'Magda, you mustn't be! I mean put off! I forbid it!' His voice was hoarse but his tone impassioned. 'We've still got lots to do. And you haven't finished telling me that story yet!'

'What story?' James looked amused and intrigued at the same time.

'Ah...' Josh raised his finger mysteriously. 'It's a secret between Magda and me.'

Madeleine laughed at that, feeling the tension loosen within her. It was a good feeling to be needed by them.

'Give yourself time to recover, Josh. I'll be ready any time when you are. I'm not planning on going away anywhere in term time. My grandma would have something to say if I took Emily away from school.'

'Is she the boss in your house?' James asked with a deadpan expression, and she could not tell if he was serious.

'The kindest boss you could wish for,' Madeleine replied with feeling.

A nurse came to the man on the other side of Josh's bed, drew the curtain around him and asked the relatives to bear with her while she administered an injection. After this short distraction, James turned his attention to Madeleine.

'Have you got your summer break planned?' he asked. Just the look of interest in his eyes made her feel like a teenager being asked on her first date. She forced herself to focus.

'Just a few days away. In Poland. My best friend is getting married in August. What about you?'

James and Josh exchanged glances then they both talked at the same time and laughed, James giving way to his younger brother.

'We've got a summer house in Polperro, Cornwall,' Josh said. 'We've been going there ever since I remember. A lot with Dad, when I was a toddler. Mother loves it there. But we also go off together, that's James and me, cycling in Sweden or France.'

'I'm green with envy!' Madeleine pressed her hand to her chest and chuckled. 'My last great achievement in cycling was seven years ago, when I first came to Leicester and had to get myself to work from A to B. I've graduated to being Emily's companion on her cycling meanderings in Aylestone Meadows!'

'I've got a better idea,' Josh spoke with an enthusiasm that enlivened his fragile voice. 'Let's go together to Rutland Water. You don't even have to take your own bike with you. They've got everything for hire there! Well… almost everything!'

'Sounds like a great idea!' she said to please him. 'This reminds me.' She took Emily's card out of her bag. Josh studied it and looked amused.

'A most original message. Yours?' He looked up.

'All her own. Emily knows very much her own mind.'

'Like her mother?' James quizzed with a hint of fun.

She smiled back but her tone was serious when she answered him, 'I can only hope that she'll always be herself and not anyone's double.'

The moment her words were out, she thought she detected a questioning look in James's eyes. Perhaps she shouldn't have said so much.

But he only smiled back and spoke lightly. 'We're all individuals. And thank goodness for that!' He gave Josh a meaningful look and Josh sent him a funny face back. 'Even twins,' he continued, 'with all their similarities develop very separate traits.' He paused and looked at Madeleine unhurriedly. 'There is of course, the ever-ongoing debate between nature and nurture. But in the end it is often a random event that shapes one's future. However, I do believe that nurturing support stands a person in good stead. With Emily, knowing her own mind, as you put it, Madeleine, can only be a good thing.'

What was James trying to say? That the environment had a stronger influence on the character of a growing child than the child's inherited genes? Was he having a guess at her past? He'd never be able to guess the awfulness of the truth. Every single day she had prayed that no traits of Zden's would become apparent in Emily as she grew up.

'Like any mother, I try to do my best by Emily,' she said feebly, before changing the subject. 'Anyone for a drink? I can fetch some from the machine. I saw one on the way.'

'Don't go, Magda. Stay. The visit will be over too soon,' Josh said. 'I just need to quiz James about a thing or two before he disappears for another twelve months!'

'OK.' She smiled and remained in her seat, giving a performance of observing others on the ward, so as to appear discreet. Josh and James exchanged small talk about their shared familiar things and the people they knew. That buoyant feeling she had felt before was gone and in its place her old uncertainty was creeping in, and a feeling of exclusion from James and Josh's world. This was silly! Only a few weeks ago she'd had only the merest awareness of their existence, and that only because of a moment's random eavesdropping upon them seven years ago! And in a few weeks more she and they would go their separate ways, and life would return to its previous pattern. Already the very thought of that felt like a pang of loss.

'Magda?' She was suddenly aware of Josh speaking to her. 'You seemed miles away!'

'Was I?' She shook her head, gathering all her attention for the present moment. 'I'm listening.' She gave him a broad smile, aware of James's gaze on her.

'I was just saying,' Josh was informing her, 'that mother will be at home with me for the next couple of days. I'll give you a ring as soon as things feel a little more normal.'

'Don't rush with anything,' she said. 'I'll be ready when you are.'

At the end of the visiting time, Madeleine picked up her chair and took it to the stack outside the ward, and waited in the corridor for James, so he and Josh would have some brotherly time together. She watched people pass by, but, when James appeared striding towards her, all long legs and energy, she experienced the same exquisite mood lift as before when entering the ward and seeing him by Josh's bedside. She was about to comment about Josh's improved condition, but he spoke first as he stopped beside her.

'Madeleine, I've got a request. Please say yes. Let's go somewhere for a bite to eat. I've not eaten since lunchtime. Just a coffee on the train. Shall we go?' He indicated that they should walk on and, as she attempted to keep up with his long strides down the corridor, her mind worked overtime trying to make sense of what he'd just said. Had she heard him correctly?

'Go out? To eat? Now?' In her mind she was returning home to some more translations, perhaps a little television and some bed-time reading. His words had made a jumble of her thoughts.

'Is that a problem?' James stopped abruptly and looked into her eyes. That brilliant blue stare!

'No... no problem at all.' She could hardly tell him that she had never been out to eat. Not alone with anyone. And not for lack of invitations. Only for the fear of getting involved. Her occasional indulgence had been the theatre or the cinema, children's stuff with Emily or adult performances with Aniela. 'No, no problem,' she repeated with feigned confidence. 'It's just that I've already eaten and this... is a bit of a surprise.'

'Then you'll come.' This wasn't a question, just a sure statement.

'I'll just ring Aniela, my grandma. Emily's babysitter tonight.' Madeleine rummaged in her handbag for the mobile.

'Will she mind?' James asked, concern creeping into his voice. If only he knew. Aniela would squeal with excitement at the prospect of Madeleine being taken out!

'No,' she said honestly. 'Grandma won't mind at all. Emily will be asleep by now, anyway.'

They found a secluded spot at the end of one of the long corridors and Madeleine dialled her home number. When Aniela answered, she said, 'Babcha, I'll be home a little later.'

'Is everything all right?'

'Everything is fine. Josh is so much better. They are keeping him overnight for observation, but he'll probably be sent home tomorrow.'

'That's really good news. So, where are you now?'

She may as well plunge in.

'Babcha... James, Josh's brother has come from London. I'm just going with him for a bite to eat. Not me. Him. He's hardly eaten anything all day.'

151

There was silence at the other end.

'Babcha, can you hear me?'

'Yes. I heard you.' There was excitement in Aniela's voice. 'Enjoy your evening. And don't rush home!' Madeleine suppressed a fizzy feeling when she switched off her phone and turned to James.

'I've got my Ka nearby. Is that OK? You've seen it. You need to be a bit of a contortionist to get in.'

'I'll do my best.' His laughter did strange things to her legs.

# CHAPTER 18

They found an old pub in town with good traditional food on the menu. James ordered a gammon steak with roast potatoes and salad, and a glass of wine. Madeleine declined the wine but asked for a coffee and an apple tart.

'So…' James leaned back comfortably against his back rest and placed his hands on the table. Madeleine liked his hands, a touch sinewy, a touch square, yet with shapely fingers and nails cut straight. 'How's life for you in Leicester, Madeleine? How are you finding living here?'

She gave him a polite smile but felt herself relaxing. The amber light above them cast a soft glow on their table, making her think of scenes in romantic films. It felt like being in one of them, with an ambience of discreet lighting, soft background music and hushed voices of other customers drifting unobtrusive.

She had braced herself against his questions. It was inevitable that he should ask her things, if only to keep the conversation alive.

'The answer to your question is easy.' She smiled. 'I find English people very tolerant. I find them very polite, but I'm never quite certain what they really think. With a Pole you know exactly where you stand. We don't mince words. But then, there's always a price to pay for absolute honesty.'

He smiled back and gave her one of his unhurried looks, which made her self-conscious. She looked down and adjusted the napkin alongside the knife and fork.

'But don't you think,' he said, 'it's not always possible to be totally honest? There are so many considerations and so many different situations when diplomatic handling seems the wise thing to do. Edited truths are often the safer option.'

'I totally agree with you,' Madeleine said readily, relief lifting her inner self. It would never do for him to know the truth about her. 'That is why,' she continued, 'I love listening, whenever I have the chance, to *Question Time*. It's so civilised, and so orderly, even when the opposing sides would happily strangle each other. I can't help laughing at times.

Especially when I compare debates in our Polish Parliament. It's like an insult contest in the playground!'

'I can't believe that!' James laughed. He asked, 'So where in Poland did you come from?'

'Krakow. I was born there and lived there till I was eighteen. A difficult family situation left me on my own. I was extremely lucky to have had relatives in Leicester. My Grandma Aniela and my real grandma were sisters. I came here, to Aniela and her husband, Bronek. That was seven years ago.'

'That would have been... 2005?' James's expression turned thoughtful and he was quiet for the merest moment. In that moment, a memory flashed through Madeleine's mind: the young man in utter distress, hiding in the gazebo at the far end of his garden. Presently James spoke. 'I'm really sorry that you've had to come over because of necessity rather than choice. But I hope this has been a good decision for you in the long run.'

'Yes,' she replied simply. 'I'm glad to be here. What about you, James. Don't you miss Leicester?'

He leaned over intimately.

'I do. My flat in London is comfortable enough and I know a crowd of people through work, but my best friends are still the ones I grew up with, here in my home town.' He smiled. 'Tell me about your work.'

This was easy. She described her typical day. He listened holding her gaze, folding and unfolding the napkin, as if his fingers led a separate life. His wine arrived and her coffee. Talking felt less stilted over their drinks.

'Tell me about Emily,' he said after a pause in their conversation. She met his gaze with outward calm while her thoughts did wild somersaults. How much to say? How much to hold back? Here goes.

'She is six. Good-natured. I'm very lucky. Especially with my grandparents. Without their assistance I wouldn't have been able to get back on my feet as quickly as I did. I finished my studies, got my degree, found work and did all that before Emily started pre-school.'

James just kept looking at her saying nothing for a long time. So typically cool and polite and English.

'Goodness, Madeleine!' he said at last. 'That took some doing! What about Emily's father? Didn't he feel obliged to help?' His praise dissolved instantly in his question, causing an eruption of panic within her. She took a hasty and generous gulp of coffee but could not control the tremor in her hand as she replaced the cup on the saucer. He noticed, and she lowered her eyes, miserable and mortified. Then suddenly both his hands were covering hers, holding them down gently on the table.

'I'm sorry, Madeleine. You're visibly upset. I was just making conversation.'

'I know.' She raised her eyes to him, he withdrew his hands and she missed his touch. 'It's not your fault at all, James. I can't talk about it. Perhaps another time.' Never, she thought. 'Let's talk about cheerful things.'

He picked up his glass and took a sip of wine.

'Madeleine, if it's any consolation, we all have experiences we'd rather forget.' Nothing he could tell her about himself could match her past. Sure, losing his father so young and having to look after his brother had been a challenge. And whatever had upset him to that extent (his gazebo retreat she had witnessed by accident) must have been serious, but nothing as horrific as that inexplicable violence forced upon her.

'I'm sure you're right,' she said. 'No doubt you have a few grievances of your own.'

He shrugged and fleetingly looked away, before smiling at her.

'Let's talk about cheerful things,' he quoted her. 'Have you seen any good films lately?'

They both laughed and when their orders arrived they were exchanging small talk about their work, their colleagues, the Queen's Diamond Jubilee celebrations and the Olympics in London. Madeleine could not stop marvelling at how different James was to that first impression she'd had of him of being aloof and coolly polite. He spoke to her with the same candour and warmth as Josh did, which she had found so endearing. She could well imagine girls being attracted to him, swarms of them, yet there was no mention of anyone special. If James was indeed still single, then why was that his choice? Such a waste!

At the end of the evening she offered to share the cost of the meal, but he laughed it off.

'Next time, Madeleine, when we dine at the Ritz.'

'When I'm rich and famous? Next century, then!'

'I don't mind waiting.' He grinned but she sensed a seriousness in his words that made her busy herself with her handbag.

Outside it was still light, the start of the longest days in the year heralding the summer. Madeleine drove James home in her Ka and was amused by his gallant remarks about the amazing compactness of her deceptively miniature car.

'I bet you wouldn't swap yours for mine!' she challenged.

'Mine's good for my long legs.' He gave a clownish shrug. 'I had to leave it behind today. It was quicker by train. That means a really early start tomorrow.'

When she stopped by his front door, he said, 'I'll most probably be back for the bank holiday. Could I see you then?'

He surprised her. She answered with automatic politeness. 'That would be very nice, James. Can I let you know nearer the time? Aniela's daughter Beata may be over from Germany.' This last thought came suddenly to the rescue. 'We're not sure yet about our plans.'

'That's all right. No worries. I've got your mobile number. Will you mind if I ring?' He did not give up. She felt a frisson of pleasure as well as uncertainty. Should she be doing that? Giving him false hopes? Dear God! Why was fate doing this to her yet again? Tempting her with possibilities that were just outside her reach?

'Feel free to ring me any time, James,' she spoke across her warning instinct. 'I hope to have something to report as soon as Josh is back on his feet.'

He raised his eyes from his mobile that he was scrolling to check her number.

'I hope we'll find lots of other things to talk about, apart from Josh,' he smiled. His eyes wandered slowly across her face and she felt as if she were melting under his scrutiny. In a romantic film this would be the moment when the hero takes the heroine in his arms and their lips fuse. She almost sagged with relief when he spoke. 'Madeleine, after the initial fright earlier in the day, this has been the best evening I've enjoyed for a long time. Thank you for everything. For being there for Josh. For mother. I'm sure she'll thank you herself.'

'She already has. I can guess her feelings. I know how I'd feel if this was Emily.'

He gave her again that soft look that made something flutter in her chest.

'Get home safely and keep in touch.' He got out of her tiny car, impressively agile considering his long legs, and bent down to say good night. She watched him in the mirror as she drove off. The dusk had changed the sky to a lilac colour, which made her think she had never seen such a beautiful evening sky before.

*

This particular afternoon, Bronek was sitting on the front wall, shielding his eyes from the bright sun, when Madeleine arrived home, her head full of the day's events. Even through Emily's cheerful chatter on the back seat, Madeleine was unable to switch off her thoughts from the morning's case. A mother of two young children had committed suicide, overdosing on her sleeping pills and half a bottle of vodka. Her husband found her on the kitchen floor and their children playing unattended in their bedroom when he returned from his night shift.

All morning, Madeleine's interpreting skills had been required by the attending police, the medics, the social services, the shocked husband and the family friend, who drew up a coherent picture of the causes that had led to this tragedy. The dead woman suffered with depression. It would have been better for her to return home to Poland, but she could not leave her husband behind, believing that he was having an affair.

It was agreed that, for the time being, until the children's grandmother came over from Poland to take care of them, the family friend would take them under her wing, together with her own two. Their father's bereft expression haunted Madeleine for the rest of the day. Later, after her services were no longer required, she escaped to a nearby cafe for a fix of strong coffee. She felt totally wrung out.

What rotten luck! What a disaster for this family! She could well imagine how they had hoped for a better life, dreamed of a better future for their children, how hard it must have been for them to leave home. Like the majority of Poles arriving in England, they would have taken on any job, often two or three with part-time hours, working all hours to achieve their dreamed of success. But such sacrifice came at a cost. Homesickness was the worst. Many got depressed, unable to cope with the big change in their lives, the alien environment, the foreign language, everything so different and strange, and the distance from home and their supportive families they had left behind. Some looked for solace in drink, some with dubious company, both such remedies giving only a passing relief while throwing lives into a spiral of self-destruction.

Each tragic case that Madeleine had come across was a reminder of her own luck. She must guard what she had at all cost; she must not allow romantic dreams to weaken her resolve. And yet, that evening spent with James brought feelings of longing in unguarded moments, thoughts of how her life could be, so different from her set-out existence.

'Mama! Why is Grandpa sitting on the wall?' Emily's voice pulled her back to the present. Madeleine switched off the engine and got Emily out of the car and together they approached Bronek.

'Grandpa, are you sunbathing?'

Bronek smiled self-consciously, slid off the wall and gave them both a hug.

'The front door banged shut on me. All my keys are indoors.'

'Poor Grandpa!' Emily hugged him around the waist. 'But don't worry. We've come just in time for the rescue. You don't have to sleep outside all night!'

'No, indeed. I'm very lucky to have such a good guardian angel!' He stroked her head. She giggled.

'No, Grandpa, I'm your Sherlock Holmes, remember?'

'How could I forget?'

Madeleine opened the front door and they all went inside. The sound of running water made her rush to its source. It was in the kitchen. A bucket left in the sink was overflowing under a tap. She turned it off and gave Bronek a reassuring look.

'It's all right. Nothing's happened.'

'I wasn't expecting to be locked out,' he said defensively. 'I was just filling the bucket with water to give the car a rinse.'

A number of little incidents occurred daily because Bronek seemed unable to think ahead. He was forgetful and easily distracted. Lights were often left on all night, as he was the last one to go to bed. The television was still running in the morning, when Aniela got up first. There had been sink overflows in the bathroom when running taps had been forgotten. The toaster switch was often mistaken for the kettle switch and the seconds in the microwave for minutes. The boiling liquids would spatter the microwave walls like a miniature volcano. These things happened usually in Aniela's absence, which she thoughtfully arranged to be infrequent, but even when she was at home she could not shadow her husband every minute of the day.

'Where's Babcha?' Madeleine asked, drying her hands on the towel.

'Sorry?' A brief pause, as he appeared to struggle to remember, then, 'At Irena's. You know Irena.' Madeleine remembered a ninety-year-old from the church, always leaning on a stick. 'Some problem with her knee. She was expecting a nurse to visit. She wanted Aniela to be there. So I took her.' His driving skills were still reliable. Strange, Madeleine thought, how there was no rhyme or reason to nature's choice when it came to dishing out old-age surprises.

'What time do you have to fetch Babcha back?'

He looked at the kitchen clock and shrugged.

'I can't remember what she's said. I'll ring her.'

'It's all right, Grandpa. I'll do that. Emily, make Grandpa a drink.' She dialled Aniela's mobile number while Emily grasped his hand and led him to sit down at the kitchen table.

Emulating Madeleine's concern, she asked him, 'Would you like some orange juice?' and proceeded to get the glasses out and the carton from the fridge.

'Ah, Babcha.' Madeleine responded to Aniela's voice. 'Are you waiting to be fetched?'

'Has he forgotten about me?'

'No, Babcha, everything's all right. Grandpa will just finish his drink and he'll be on his way.'

They all took a long sip of their cooling drinks before Bronek confessed with a sheepish smile, 'I've just got to find my keys first.'

This had become a daily ritual, the quest for misplaced things. Emily had become quite a sleuth in finding her grandpa's lost things: the keys, his wallet, his mobile, his scarves in winter, his small boxes of seeds in the summer, and any other things that were not attached to him by flesh. She slid off the chair and scanned all the kitchen surfaces at her level, while Madeleine looked around the shelves, the windowsill, the cooker, the fridge and any possible surface that his hand may have accidentally brushed.

Bronek emptied his pockets – a garden string, a penknife, a handful of receipts, a few scrunched paper tissues and a bag of seeds. He looked baffled.

'When was the last time you had the keys?' Madeleine asked.

'Sorry?' He stopped still, looked down hard at his trousers, then a smile of relief transformed his face. He slapped his forehead.

'Of course! I totally forgot!' Saying this, he dashed off through the open kitchen door. Madeleine and Emily ran after him and stopped on the patio. There on the washing line, buoyed like sails by the breeze, were his navy trousers flying. Of course, Madeleine should have noticed straight away that the brown trousers he was wearing did not match his blue shirt. (Aniela always checked his colour co-ordination before he went out anywhere.)

He retrieved the car keys from the flapping trousers and retraced his steps hurriedly.

'No time to change now. I forgot the other trousers got wet and the keys were in the pocket. But all's well now. I'd better dash off or Babcha will bite my head off!' This made Emily laugh.

They watched him drive off, Madeleine with affection. At eighty, he could have been mistaken for a much younger man: straight posture, sprightly gait and a becoming mop of white hair. Such a pity about his mind. And yet his mind appeared selective in its retrieval system: incidents from his past he could recount in the smallest details and yet all the simple repetitive actions of his daily life proved a challenge to him.

'Mama.' Emily squeezed Madeleine's hand. 'Can we go swimming now?'

'Right away!'
'And take Karishma?'
'Of course!'

\*

Madeleine missed her afternoons with Josh. Her days were filled with appointments around the city, some run of the mill, some absorbing, demanding of her language skills as well as testing her emotions, but nothing compared to the satisfaction she had felt when helping Josh with his work. Despite his frail pre-hospital condition, he had worked with true grit, producing an essay on Napoleon's strategic victories in Europe and another one on Dickensian heroes and villains. It was child's play typing them for him.

He texted her most days. He was recovering well with the help of the energy-boosting vitamins and prescribed medication; his throat was no longer sore and his voice less husky, he informed her. As soon as he was able to move about without the fear of falling over, he'd call her.

James had not got in touch, despite asking if he could do so. She balanced her disappointment with self-persuasive common sense that it was for the best. Yet little flashes of fragments of the evening spent with him kept coming back. Perhaps, she told herself, this had a purpose to free her of her obsession with Dominik. She still thought of him with fondness, but she noticed a certain lack of sadness whenever she thought of him these days, as if she had been absolved from carrying a torch for him. He had moved on; it was time she did too.

When Josh rang her asking her if she could come towards the end of the week, she could not hide her joy.

'Josh, this is really good news. I'm fully booked these next two days, but Friday lunch will be fine! I shall be expecting a party!'

'You'll be surprised!' he laughed mysteriously.

\*

There was a dark green Jaguar parked by the garage next to the Hammonds' house. With a quickened heartbeat, Madeleine wondered if James was home for the weekend. Holding her breath, she pressed the doorbell.

It was a warm day with the sun drawing out the scents of the earth and of the flowering shrubs and Madeleine felt just right in her light cotton summer dress, the colour of pale primroses.

She was not surprised when James opened the door, yet seeing him did not diminish the strange effect he had on her. Especially when his eyes held her gaze for a long moment before a wide smile split his face.

'It's so good to see you, Madeleine. It seems like ages since the other evening.' He sounded sincere. Why hadn't he called? 'Please, come in. Josh has been waiting since the crack of dawn!' That made her smile.

'Impossible! Not when you're his age. But I missed him too.' She stepped inside, noting how the ends of his raven hair curled behind his ears, how the open collar of his crisp white shirt gave him that aura of freshness, which she wanted to breathe in and keep. She made a move to go on, but he stopped her with a touch on her elbow.

'I'm so glad we are back on track. I worried you may have been put off.'

'Why?' This did surprise her. James worried? 'I'm very fond of Josh. I'm happy to come for as long as he needs my help.'

'And you can still fit it all in, with all your commitments?'

'We all have to juggle time. No doubt you do too.' This came out terse. She did not mean it to. She cringed. He gave her a puzzled look but she continued briskly, to cover up her discomfort. 'Shall we go see Josh?' James stopped her.

'Just as I guessed,' he said gently. 'You must tell me if it's all too much for you. For that reason, Madeleine, I did not pester you with phone calls.'

She raised her eyes to him. She wished he had. Pester her with phone calls. She'd always find time for him. His expression of concern was so transparently genuine; she felt compelled to make amends if only with a few kinder words, but just then she heard Josh's voice and a woman's in conversation in his study.

'Is your mother at home?' she asked, her spirit rising.

But before he answered, the door of the study opened wide and a young woman, tall and willowy with blond hair cascading down her shoulders, came out, laughing at something she'd obviously just shared with Josh. She was still laughing loud as she approached Madeleine and James.

# CHAPTER 19

'You must be Madeleine,' the young woman said, extending her hand. 'Josh's tutor. How clever of you. To be bilingual. And teaching.' Madeleine detected a patronising undertone. 'I'm Fiona, I work with James.' Her eyes swept over him possessively.

'Pleased to meet you,' Madeleine said, shaking her hand, soft and exquisitely manicured. James stepped so close beside her she was aware of his scent, like pine in the summer breeze.

'Madeleine's been a godsend,' he said, then, looking directly at her, he added, 'in more ways than one.' A butterfly fluttered in her chest.

She could not think of anything to say except, 'I'd better go see Josh.'

James stepped aside for her to pass.

'I'll be outside, if you need me for anything,' he said. 'The lawn needs attention.'

His gaze lingered as if he was expecting her to say more, but Fiona butted in chirpily, 'I'll give you a hand, James.'

Pull the other one, Madeleine thought. Fiona, in her silk blouse, designer slacks and wedges as high as the Shard. She breathed a sigh of relief when they went and she was free to go to Josh. He was sitting upright against a stack of cushions, his brown eyes shining like conkers, eagerness touching his cheeks with a hint of colour.

'Josh! You're looking so good!' Madeleine exclaimed. 'By the looks of it you won't be needing me much longer!' She sat down in her usual seat facing him.

'Don't say that, Magda.' His voice was less croaky. 'Even when I do go back to school, I'd still like you to come and help me.' His cheeks dimpled. 'Shall we start with coffee?'

'OK,' she said. 'The usual?'

She came back with two steaming mugs and two biscuits each.

'So, how's it been going?' she asked settling herself down. 'I've got your two essays typed up.' She took the two files out of her briefcase as her eyes wandered magnetically towards the window. James was trimming the edge of the lawn and willowy Fiona was standing beside him, teetering on her wedges, her elegant hands eloquently expressive while she was making a point in their conversation. Madeleine was suddenly aware of Josh speaking to her.

'I've started my next essay on Victorian writers...' Josh stopped and followed her gaze.

'I'm sorry, Josh, I am listening. Just a momentary inattention. My head's still filled with this morning's meeting.'

'It's OK,' Josh assured her in his usual easy manner, then glancing towards the window he added, 'James came home this morning. To extend the weekend. He's planning a barbecue tomorrow. Three of my friends are coming. Also, my mother's friend. Will you come, Magda?'

'Me?' She was taken aback. 'Oh... thank you, Josh. That's really nice of you to think about me. But, weekends are busy. Besides, I won't know anyone here.'

'You know mother, James and me. We'll look after you. Promise.' That dimpled smile again.

She looked towards the window.

'James looks busy.'

Josh shook his head.

'Fiona's his work mate. There was a muddle with her weekend plans. I didn't quite get the gist of the full story. Anyway, James took pity on her, invited her over "to experience the delights of a provincial town", as he put it.' Josh looked amused and none of this should have mattered to Madeleine, but it felt as if a cloud had darkened the sky.

'Is she an accountant too?'

'PA to one of the bosses. So...' He changed the subject. 'Will you come tomorrow?'

Madeleine made a show of hesitating for Josh's sake, her mind already made up to stay away.

'Emily goes to the Polish School on Saturday mornings. Then we go with Grandpa to his allotment.'

'I'm sure he won't mind if you give it a miss just once.' (Madeleine was sure he'd be delighted for her to have found company her own age.) 'Bring Emily here straight after school. Mum's friend will be here with her granddaughter Daisy. She's seven. Perfect company for Emily.'

'And your mum knows about all these wonderful plans of yours?'

'It was her idea.' His gaze was expectant, his earnestness disarming, but Madeleine knew she could not do it. Fiona's presence was too unsettling. Why waste time on useless emotions?

She answered evasively, 'Thank you very much, Josh. I'd love to come. I'll ring you tonight to confirm. But now, let's get on with our work.'

163

They looked over his English essay and Josh pointed out the sections he wanted Madeleine to check especially. She gave him a few suggestions, after which she read three long extracts from Victorian novels, *Middlemarch, Tess of the d'Urbervilles* and *David Copperfield*, 'in the context of required comparisons of the narrative structures and character development'.

'Phew!' Josh plunged his fingers into his hair and pushed it back off his brow. 'That was intense! More coffee? Tea?'

Madeleine's throat was parched. She went to the kitchen, switched on the kettle and while waiting for the water to boil, she washed the mugs and watched James and Fiona through the window. They had moved to the furthest part of the garden, close to that memorable gazebo. James was crouching over the flower border, apparently weeding. He'd tire himself out in this position, Madeleine thought with a touch of superiority, hard on thighs and calves, hard to maintain for long. She could teach him a thing or two about practical gardening, she thought with a sudden lift of amusement. Fiona was standing over him gesticulating in her monologue and throwing back her head now and again to shake her long tresses into place.

Madeleine felt a brief but strong feeling of longing. She wished to change places with Fiona, if only for a few minutes, and be there with James inside the orbit of his attention. But then what?

She made two coffees and went back to Josh. He was just finishing texting his friends. He looked up at her, excitement livening up his face.

'I've just told them, you're coming too. To the barbecue, tomorrow.'

She felt like a traitor. 'Why would they be interested in me?'

He laughed a happy, amused laugh.

'They'd all like a personal tutor like you, Magda. They think I've won the lottery!'

She laughed at the absurdity of it all. Teenage crushes! She remembered her own. When her world was still so innocent. When she was fourteen. When the object of her desire was an altar boy, Jacek, safe to adore from a distance.

'Thank you for your faith in me, Josh. Now, shall we get back to work?'

He took a sip of coffee. 'In my research reading on Napoleon I got to 1806. His armies were marching towards the east.'

'That was the time his armies marched across Poland towards the Russian border,' Madeleine remarked.

'You never finished telling me Marie Walewska's story.'

'It's not in the curriculum.'

'But it gives a fuller picture of his life. You said yourself how little is mentioned about her in the history books. It'll give me an edge knowing things others don't.'

Madeleine smiled at that. 'Competitive, I like that, Josh. OK, I'll tell you a bit more.' She took a generous gulp of coffee.

'You may remember, Marie had been married off to Count Walewski, when she was only eighteen and he seventy. Now, this is two years later. With him constantly away in Warsaw, Marie threw herself into a women's patriotic movement, helping the injured soldiers and their families. Her very first meeting with Napoleon was like something out of a fairy tale. When news of his approach to Warsaw went around like wildfire, Marie and her friend Elizabeth joined the hundreds of others lining the streets in Bronie, a little town close to the Walewski estate. Napoleon's coach happened to stop right in front of them. His companion General Duroc spotted the two aristocratic ladies and was immediately smitten by Marie's beauty – so the story goes. He invited Marie inside the emperor's coach, who in turn was enchanted by her entreaty to be the saviour of her country, to free Poland from her Russian oppressor.

'A ball in Warsaw was arranged, the Walewskis were invited and Marie was favoured by Napoleon all night. The ball finished with a crushing blow for her. Her hero, whom she revered as the most noble of all men, asked her to spend the night with him. She was devastated and rushed out to be taken home to the Walewski estate.'

'What about her husband?' Josh asked. 'Didn't he do anything?'

Madeleine shrugged. 'Most historians conclude,' she said, 'that he must have been complicit in this affair, because three days later, after unanswered messages from Napoleon, Marie was visited by Prince Czartoryski and a high-ranking representative from the Church, to persuade her to become Napoleon's mistress.'

'Really? That's gross! How old was Napoleon?' Josh asked.

'Thirty-seven.'

'Yuk! From one old man to another!'

Madeleine laughed at that.

'Thirty-seven is young, Josh. You'll find out for yourself one day.'

'That's another twenty years before I'm that old! But perhaps by then medicine will discover a remedy for old age. But what happened next to poor Marie?'

'She had no choice but to bow under their pressure. For the good of the country, they said. She'd be like the biblical Esther; they made it sound so noble.' Madeleine paused. 'Awful, wasn't it? It was like being sold. Even an aristocratic woman became nothing more than currency in a political deal.'

'And did Napoleon keep his part of the bargain?'

'In a small way. He created the Duchy of Warsaw, which for the freedom-starved Poles was like a promise of greater things to come. But that was later. In the meantime, Marie became Napoleon's mistress, and was expected to accompany him in his quarters close to the battlefields. When she became pregnant with his child, he sent her back to the safety of the Walewski estate. She gave birth to a baby boy, just as he was getting married to the Austrian princess, Marie-Louise, again for political reasons. Any hopes Marie may have had of becoming his wife were totally dashed.'

Madeleine stopped to drink her coffee. How was it possible to love and remain devoted to a man who had so unashamedly used her? She would rather die than be connected in any way with Zden.

'In the next few years,' Madeleine picked up the story, 'Napoleon looked after Marie and her two sons in his own way, installing them in a comfortable house in Paris. In his final defeat, when everyone else had abandoned him, she was the only loyal and devoted friend. She even visited him in his exile in Elba, so he could see his son, and all that in secret from Marie-Louise. It was only when he was finally exiled to the remote island of St Helena that she was freed from this relationship. She was still only in her mid-twenties then.'

'What a sad tale! I hope something good happened to her after that. Did she find somebody else? Did she find someone her own age?'

Madeleine smiled and looked at her watch.

'I'll finish her story another time, Josh. I'd better be making tracks.' She looked towards the window and James at the far end of the garden. Everyone longed for happiness. Some were luckier than others.

'Will I see you tomorrow?' Josh asked eagerly. His childlike candour never failed to touch her.

'Don't worry, I'll be back. I'll just go say goodbye to James.' And Fiona, she should have added.

Outside on the patio, the wisteria was rampant with hanging long shoots and strong-scented flowers. Beyond, the sun had intensified all the tones of green, making the white, pink and purple rhododendrons stand out vividly against their leafy background.

Madeleine waved to James to catch his attention. Fiona saw her first but remained in place, apparently composing a bouquet of cut lilac. Her hair shone like wild silk in the sun and Madeleine felt an annoying jab of envy. Stupid, really, for she could have had any colour out of the bottle.

James put down the long-handled edge-trimmer and Madeleine watched him walk towards her with his long, energetic strides. It gave her pleasure just to be looking at him and she wished she could feel at ease with him as she did with Josh.

'I just wanted to say goodbye before I go,' she said when he joined her on the patio.

'But we'll be seeing you tomorrow, Madeleine? Josh told you, no doubt, about the barbecue?' His piercing blue eyes were as earnest as his brother's.

'He did, and thank you for the invite, but...'

He interrupted before she said any more, 'We'd love to see you. Mother especially. There's just one more thing, before you go. Just bear with me a second.' He went inside through the French windows and came back with an envelope, evidently prepared earlier. 'A cheque for you.'

All of a sudden Madeleine felt embarrassed.

'No need, James. It can wait till Josh starts school again. For his sake, I hope it will be soon.'

'It's yours, Madeleine. You've earned it. All three of us are grateful. Please take it and let me know if the amount is satisfactory.' The warmth in his voice made her feel that this was between friends.

'Thank you,' she said, and as he handed her the envelope their fingers touched. It was electric. She spoke automatically. 'It's been a pleasure and you're paying me for it!'

'Your time is precious, Madeleine. Don't undervalue that.' He spoke like an accountant. 'If it weren't you, we'd be paying someone else. We're all glad it's you! So there!'

She giggled and looked nervously at her watch.

'Thank you. I really must go.'

He walked with her to the car and watched her drive off as he did last time. And again, as before, she was overcome with regret that she could not allow their acquaintance to develop further. Her past would have been a turn-off for any man. And somehow it mattered to her that he should never find out the whole truth about her.

Despite the increased Friday afternoon traffic, she got to Emily's school with five minutes to spare. She opened James's envelope. His handwritten note on the back of his business card was simple:

*Madeleine, I checked what home tutors charge here, in London, and rounded up the figure. I trust this will be to your satisfaction. See you tomorrow. James.*

Madeleine stared at the cheque in disbelief. The figure was three times the amount she would have earned for the same number of hours

167

as an interpreter. Her heart beat fast. This was a mistake. Obviously. But how come, when James was an accountant? She needed to speak to him. She had no choice but to accept their invite to the barbecue tomorrow.

*

'Bronek, your fresh change of clothes is ready on the bed,' Aniela said, cutting her cheese cake into squares.

'I don't understand this!' Bronek's finger was jabbing at the article in *The Telegraph*, spread out on the kitchen table. 'They've let him out? A dangerous man like that? And what is the first thing he does? Kills an innocent passer-by!'

'And get the wine ready!' Aniela reminded him.

'Who's going to be responsible for that?' Bronek followed his own train of thought.

'The glasses are washed and clean. Just put them on a tray,' Aniela said, getting out the dessert plates and the teaspoons.

'What is the matter with those people and their idiotic decisions? Have they no common sense?'

'And don't forget to splash on some aftershave!'

Madeleine waited for an opportune moment to make her announcement. She was wiping clean the porcelain cups and saucers.

'Babcha! Grandpa! I've got an invite!'

'Bronek, please go get changed now! They'll be here soon!' Aniela stopped, turned around and looked at Madeleine.

'What did you say, Magda?'

Bronek looked up from the paper, lingering thoughts giving him a distracted appearance.

'I said,' Madeleine repeated, smiling, 'I've got an invite. To a barbecue. Tomorrow. At Josh's house.'

Aniela folded the tea towel and pulled down her sleeves. She was dressed up for her friends, the Barskis. The Demskis were away this weekend, so it would be just the four of them tonight. Her white silk blouse, her flowery skirt in tones of blue and the pearls made her look so attractive, Madeleine thought, despite her age. Her face was visibly getting animated as Madeleine's words sank in.

'I hope you said yes! You must go, of course! Do you know who else is going to be there?'

Madeleine glanced towards the open back door, through which she could see Emily and Karishma thinking up ever more difficult tricks with their skipping ropes.

'Josh's friends, I imagine. And James too. He's down for the weekend.'

Aniela's excitement lifted her brows up to her fringe.

'That's wonderful, Magda! It's high time you made friends with people your own age!'

'I'll take you there myself,' Bronek offered getting up. 'I suppose I better go to get changed.'

As he disappeared up the stairs, Madeleine helped Aniela to take things to the coffee table in the front room, the two plates of cut cake, the porcelain cups and saucers, the dessert plates and forks, the linen serviettes ironed flat like cardboard.

When they were back in the kitchen Madeleine said, 'I want to go, Babcha, but the very thought of being asked all those questions... It's such hard work being charming and evasive at the same time.'

'Just stick to our agreed version,' Aniela said practically, giving the worktop one last wipe. 'You'll find that, once you ask a question, people are quite happy to talk about themselves.'

Madeleine laughed. She had met compulsive talkers before and in a way she had been grateful. They had saved her from having to say too much about herself.

'It's just that... the Hammonds have been kind to me. I hate the thought of deceiving them in any way.'

Aniela came up to Madeleine and gave her a hug.

'You worry far too much. Take one step at a time. I'm sure they already like you for all you've done for Josh. Everyone's entitled to keep certain things private. That's not deception, that's just being discreet.'

Bronek came down in a pastel blue shirt that enlivened the colour of his eyes. His white hair brushed back from his tanned forehead gave him a noble appearance. He smelled of Old Spice, abundantly applied, no doubt, on Aniela's instructions.

'You look great!' Madeleine said sincerely, knowing the little praise would please him. And indeed, a smile rounded his cheeks and lit up his eyes.

'Stay with us, Magda, when they come. They like talking to you and they like Emily.'

Madeleine picked up a posy of roses and took it through to the front room to place in the middle of the coffee table. Bronek followed her, sat himself on the settee and switched on the television. It was his favourite Polish serial. 'They like this too,' he said excitedly. 'We can watch this together. See?' he pointed at the character who was a corrupt village administrator. 'So many years after communism and there are still bastards like him!'

Madeleine hovered at the door.

'I'll come back and sit with you and your friends for a while, after I've taken Karishma home. But later. I still have some things to finish.'

'Don't be long, we need a chairperson in our meetings!' he said with a twinkle in his eyes.

Their Friday get-togethers were indeed animated, usually fervently put forward theories on spies, infiltration, Putin's Russia and never trusting a communist. Reminiscing about their past was a regular theme too; Madeleine knew by heart all about their enforced wartime journeys, about their difficult beginnings on arrival in England in the late 1940s. She could not understand their need to relive the times of their most painful experiences. She wanted to forget hers. But perhaps this was precisely the remedy for expiating the pain and blunting the memory.

*

Later, she could not fall asleep. She heard the Barskis leave at about half past ten, followed by careful creeping of Aniela and Bronek's feet up the stairs, which did not stop the old wooden treads from groaning. After finishing some of the translation work, she sent her regular e-mail to her father, and another one to Natalia. She read with hungry absorption any messages Natalia sent her, wishing the time away to Natalia's wedding, at the same time dreading telling her friend about Emily. She had imagined the scene in a hundred different ways and composed in her mind a hundred different openings to her confession. But for the moment that could be pushed away.

The next day's barbecue at James's house was the more immediate issue to occupy her mind. If only, in some way, she could get rid of the burden of her past. For if, by any chance, James showed her interest, when was the right time to tell him the truth? At the very beginning? A sure put-off and a hasty end to any possible relationship. After a few weeks? Months? This could only be followed by accusations of dishonesty and enticement. Suspicions too that in some way she had contributed to Zden's abominable treatment of her.

But why was she even having such thoughts? Despite what Josh had told her about Fiona, no one really knew how close she and James were. This thought brought her no relief, just doubled her anguish.

The bright sunshine next day lifted her spirits. With Emily attending the Saturday School at the Polish Centre, Madeleine spent the morning translating a leaflet for a pharmaceutical company: the usual warnings about all the possible side effects of this particular drug. It was a wonder there were people brave enough to take any medication at all.

Aniela had gone into town, and Bronek, after dropping her off, had planned to visit an elderly widow, who was worried sick about banging noises in the bathroom pipes. Bronek, the ever-ready knight on his charger (the Volvo) had assured the poor woman that there were no ghosts in her house, only air in the pipes.

At noon, Madeleine tidied up her desk, made herself a coffee and changed. She checked her appearance in the long mirror, not quite the designer-clad sophistication of Fiona but it would have to do. Anyway, she thought the pastel pink suited her, the linen jacket and the slim-leg trousers. The freshly washed hair formed a fluffy bob around her face, a bit like a mop. So what? She could grow her hair too, if she so wanted, and dye it any colour!

In the car park at the Polish Centre she chatted to some of the other waiting parents, before the wide double door was opened and the children came out walking as they had been instructed to do. Only the first few steps, then they all dispersed and ran to their parents.

'Mama! Mama!' Emily skipped with excitement beside her. 'I'm going to be a Krakowianka girl in the Krakowiak dance at the end of the term. Will you make a costume for me? Here's a letter for you!' She thrust a piece of paper at Madeleine. It was a request to the parents with instructions for making such a costume. A tall order, Madeleine thought with a smile, but she had had one too when Emily's age. 'We'll ask Grandma Aniela to help out. She loves making things like that.'

'Can we go into town now, to get all the things?' Emily jumped in anticipation. Madeleine held her hand and led her to the car.

'We'll go into town Emily, but not right now. Have you forgotten where we're going?'

Emily shook her head vigorously and smiled a big smile displaying a double gap and the tops of adult teeth growing.

'And you will be a very good girl, as I have asked you, OK?'

'And always remember to say please and thank you,' Emily added seriously as Madeleine strapped her in the back seat.

# CHAPTER 20

Next to James's Jaguar, two more cars were parked in front of the garage. As Madeleine got out of her Ka, a pleasant aroma of barbecued food drifted towards her, together with a muffled chatter of voices from beyond the side gate, which had been left open for the visitors.

Madeleine picked up the bottle of Shiraz from the back seat and handed Emily the box of cherry liqueurs to present to Jean. She felt a jab of nervousness as they walked down the shaded side of the house towards the patio. Her heart missed a beat the moment they stepped onto the crazy paving and revealed their presence to everyone. Three garden tables had been set out underneath the canopy of wisteria, and around them sat groups of people, evidently enjoying their talk and drinks.

Her eyes caught James first, perhaps because he was not sitting down. He was standing by the open grill at the side of the patio, with a male companion. He looked up and waved with an inviting smile. Something fluttered inside her. Just then Josh called from his table.

'Over here, Madeleine!' He did not call her Magda in company, she noted. Sitting around him were three teenage boys, their animated chatter stopping as they eyed her with undisguised interest.

'Josh!' Emily made a move to run to him, but at the same time Jean got up from her table and approached them in her brisk manner, the white streak in her raven hair falling over her brow. She was dressed in a navy cotton dress, with large white buttons and large white beads to match. Simple, yet classy, Madeleine thought.

'Madeleine! I'm so glad you've made it!' She sounded truly sincere, and bending down to Emily she said, 'Hello Emily. No jobs today. Just lots of fun!'

Emily smiled shyly and lifted the box of chocolates to her.

'These are for you,' she said.

'Are they? That's very kind. Come with me, Emily. Let me introduce you to my friends.'

She took Emily's hand and Madeleine followed, her peripheral vision catching sight of Fiona at another table, talking animatedly to a dark-haired girl.

'This is my friend Sue.' Jean introduced her friend, a pleasantly plump woman, with an expertly made-up face and silver highlights in her blonde hair. Sitting next to her was a young girl of about Emily's age, obviously her granddaughter. Her sturdy body and her uncovered plump arms testified to her good appetite. Even the ringlets of her very light hair were thick and curled tight.

'And I'm Daisy,' she introduced herself, sliding off her chair, and clasping Emily's hand. 'Will you play with me? Over there?' She pointed her outstretched arm towards the end of the garden. Emily looked uncertain for a moment, but Madeleine answered for her.

'Of course Emily will play with you, Daisy, but we must say hello to everyone first. Will you come with us?' Daisy nodded eagerly. Madeleine deposited the wine on Jean's table and smiled. 'I'll be back.'

They stopped at Fiona's table. Her companion had crinkly dark hair that stood out in artistic disarray around her heart-shaped face. She lifted her lively, conker-brown eyes and looked up at Madeleine with interest. Fiona interrupted her own monologue and her voice sounded sincere enough when she spoke to Madeleine.

'Ah, we've already met! Madeleine, isn't it?' She turned to her companion. 'And this is Julie!'

The dark-haired girl shook Madeleine's hand. It was a welcoming handshake.

'I'm really pleased to meet you.'

'It's my pleasure to meet you too,' Madeleine replied, feeling a good vibe.

'And this must be?' Fiona continued, studying Emily and Daisy as if they were house pets. 'Now, which one is Emily and which is Daisy?'

Daisy laughed out loud, her white curls shaking. 'I'm Daisy! You saw me before! Did you forget?'

Emily smoothed down her pink dungaree with the frilly pockets.

'I'm Emily,' she spoke seriously.

'What a lovely name,' Fiona said, her blue-shadowed eyes scrutinising her like a painting. 'A definitely good name. I approve. Is that after Emily Brontë, or perhaps more recently after Emily Blunt? The actress. Have you heard of her?'

Emily's eyes widened. She shook her head and explained.

'Everyone calls me Emily. But my real name is Emilia. Like Emilia Plater's name. She lived in Poland a long time ago. She was very brave.

She went to fight like the men against the enemy. And she was killed. She was only a young girl.'

There was a moment's silence when Daisy patted Emily's hand and Fiona appeared to have forgotten her words.

Her dark-haired companion spoke first. 'Well done, Emily! I wish all my children at school remembered their history lessons as well as you do.' There was an innate warmth in her manner which made Madeleine like her. Julie smiled and angled her head towards James and his companion standing at the at the grill. 'And that is my husband, Mark, over there beside James. He likes to imagine he can become a cook by osmosis in one day.'

Madeleine laughed. 'Two chefs are absolutely essential at a barbecue.'

'We'll soon find out,' Fiona said. 'I volunteered to help.'

'They wouldn't have the satisfaction of proving themselves, Fiona, if you were in charge.' Julie turned to Madeleine. 'They've always had to compete. We've been friends since our infant days.'

'That must be wonderful!' Madeleine said, thinking of her own childhood friends.

'It is. We often meet up when James is home from London,' Julie said.

'And this weekend, they've even allowed me inside their club,' Fiona remarked peevishly.

'It's not a club,' Julie laughed. 'Just an old friendship. We come and go, but each time we meet up it's as if we've never been apart.'

It would have been like that for her and Natalia, Madeleine thought, and for their friends. She excused herself.

'I'll come back. I'll just talk to Josh.'

At his table, Josh introduced his friends. 'Seb, Matt and Tim.'

Seb brushed back the fringe from his eyes self-consciously. Matt gave her a wide grin, his slightly chubby cheeks dimpling. Tim, tall and lanky hunched towards her and held out his hand to shake hers. The other two followed suit immediately. Madeleine smiled. She remembered clearly her own teen angst over a myriad of uncertainties. She guessed she had been the subject of their man-conversation.

'Please, don't let me disturb you,' she said. 'I'm sure you've got a lot of catching-up to do. After Josh's long absence from school. I'm pleased to meet his friends.'

'And I'm glad you found time to come,' Josh said with his usual openness. 'Hi Emily! How was your Polish School today?'

Emily leaned forward, only her hand held back in Daisy's possessive clasp.

'It was nice,' she said. 'I did some reading and writing in Polish. Then we drew maps and we had to write the city names in the right places.'

'Goodness!' Josh exclaimed. 'It sounds like a lot of hard work!'

'No!' Emily giggled. 'It was all easy. In my real school I'm writing a book. One page every day.'

'Me too!' Daisy announced with a little skip, her curls bouncing.

'Really?' Matt sounded suitably impressed. 'You are two very clever girls! What are your books about?'

'My book is about birds!' Daisy stated importantly. 'We've got a bird table outside our classroom. I have to note down each one that comes to feed. Then we look them up on the internet and then we write about them. There will be a prize for the best book at the end of the term.'

'Wow!' Matt was overawed. 'No prizes for guessing who'll be the winner!' Daisy did another little skip, still holding onto Emily's hand. He turned to Emily. 'And what is your story about?'

With her free hand Emily stroked the ruffles on her pockets and looked seriously thoughtful.

'My book is about a little girl in India. She cannot go to school. She has to do all the house work because her mum is ill.'

Josh's friends expressed wonder and encouragement, which made Emily self-conscious yet pleased at the same time.

Madeleine said, 'Please excuse us, gentlemen,' (this made them giggle) 'we've yet to say hello to James and his friend.'

James was standing at the grill turning over chicken portions, pork ribs and sausages. Even in the heat surrounding the grill he looked fresh and unflustered in his white shirt, the sleeves rolled up, his arms masculine, attractive. He raised his eyes and smiled and her heart quickened.

'I'm so pleased you've come,' he said. For a split second, only he existed. She turned to his companion. Mark wore knee-length navy shorts and a matching Aertex shirt. He greeted Madeleine with a vigorous handshake and a wide smile that showed two rows of strong teeth. His lingering look made her feel that they'd been talking about her. She was getting paranoid!

Though not as tall as James, he had an athlete's body with not a spare ounce of flesh visible. He stooped down to the girls.

'I've heard you two are very good in sport.'

They nodded eagerly, Daisy saying first, 'I can do headstands!'

'And I practise long jumps,' Emily added quickly.

'That's very impressive! A ball game will be easy-peasy for someone like you two. It just so happens that I've got a ball with me. Shall we play?' He retrieved a ball from behind the overhanging cover of the serving table that was laden with salads, cold meats and a sumptuous cheese board. Madeleine watched him dribble the ball expertly on the patio then across the lawn to the far end with Emily and Daisy chasing after him, their excited shouts following behind them.

She was alone with James. 'I didn't expect a child-minding service as well,' she joked.

He put down the forked utensil and smiled. 'Pleased to be of service.' He made a mock bow. 'Let me get you a drink.'

She declined wine on account of driving. He brought her a soft drink and looked towards where Mark was entertaining Emily and Daisy.

'Little Daisy and Mark have been friends ever since she could run. He teaches science, but in his spare time he runs a sports club at his school. No problems with discipline there.'

'I bet all the kids love him,' Madeleine said.

'Love whom?' It was Fiona, materialising beside James. Madeleine squirmed.

'I'm just singing Mark's praises,' she said. Fiona looked in Mark's direction.

'I've told him he is being wasted here. Out in the sticks.'

Madeleine took a hurried sip as James laughed out loud.

'We can't all live in London, Fiona. What about our own Loughborough? A centre of excellence for the training athletes and future Olympians. The Olympics will soon prove that!'

'We'll see!' Fiona replied testily and changed the subject. 'Here, let me!' She took the platter from James's hands and held it for him as he began to arrange the barbecued meat pieces on it. 'Shall I announce the food is ready, or will you?' She moved off without waiting for his answer, and he continued to turn over the remaining pieces on the grill. There was no need for any announcements, for Jean and Sue got up first and were soon followed by Josh's friends. Unhurriedly, James continued to turn over the remaining pieces on the grill and Madeleine wondered at his relationship with Fiona. Just a work colleague? A friend? Or something more than that? This sobering thought pulled her back to reality.

He asked, 'Was it a problem for you juggling time this weekend? To come here?'

She replied a touch brusquely, 'I had to find time, James. That cheque you gave me. It's some mistake. It can't be right.'

'Why?' He looked genuinely surprised. She could not tell if he was serious when he asked, 'Wasn't it enough?'

'You know I can't accept it, unless it covers the next few weeks as well.'

He smiled then.

'Was that your only reason for coming here today?'

Was he teasing her?

'We must sort it out,' she insisted.

'What must you sort out?' Fiona was beside him again with two plates. She handed him one which he passed to Madeleine.

He said, 'We'll talk about it later. Now, let's have something to eat.'

Madeleine stepped aside for Fiona, and when James made a gesture for her to follow she said, 'I'll join you in a minute. I'll talk to Julie first.'

While Fiona was busy at the serving table, Madeleine sat down beside the dark-haired girl with the heart-shaped face.

'I think Josh is smitten with you,' Julie said amicably. 'You've made quite an impression on him.'

Madeleine glanced in his direction. He was enjoying his friends' company, all cracking jokes with youthful exuberance. They were filling their plates and piling food on his until it resembled a miniature Everest.

'He makes my work easy,' she said. 'I wish all my other work was as enjoyable.'

'People are fascinated by your background,' Julie said. 'How often do you go home to Poland?'

A twinge of anxiety. Madeleine suppressed it.

'My home is here now,' she said. 'I've not got any close relatives in Poland.'

'I'm sorry,' Julie said.

'Please don't be. I love living here.'

Julie glanced in Mark's direction at the far end of the garden where he was playing ball games with Emily and Daisy. Now and again Emily waved with shouts of, 'Look, Mama, look!'

'You've got a lovely daughter,' Julie said, and Madeleine shrank inwardly, guessing where this was going to lead.

'Thank you,' she said. 'My grandparents give me a lot of support.'

'Your grandparents? They live here? When did they leave Poland?'

Madeleine was used to giving a brief outline of her family's history: those who had been taken by the Russians to Siberia soon after the start of the war, those who had been deported to Germany, and the ones left behind in their own country only to suffer Soviet communism for the next fifty years. 'Grandma Aniela is my real grandmother's sister. After all her forced travels during the war, she and her husband settled in this country. Apart from my own father in the States, they are the closest family I've got.'

'Your father's in the States? Wouldn't you rather be out there with him?' Julie asked.

Madeleine smiled, shaking her head.

'We've been apart for too long. He is happy and settled there. With his new family. We keep in touch all the time. I've been to visit him several times. And Skype is a great invention. It's like seeing him every week in person.' She took a sip of her soft drink. 'What about yourself? Tell me about you and Mark.'

From the corner of her eye she could see Fiona monopolising James by the serving table. She concentrated her attention on Julie.

'Our lives are very ordinary,' Julie was saying, sipping her wine, giving a shrug of her thin shoulders. 'We had a carefree childhood. We went to the same schools. Mark and James and me. Mark went on to do science at Manchester. I got a degree in biology. But I always loved young children, so I now teach a class of ten-year-olds.'

'That's quite a challenge, these days,' Madeleine said with feeling.

'Depends on the area. I'm very lucky. It's a small village school. Everyone knows everybody else and the children are quite responsive to reasoning. Mark and I usually go cycling in our summer holidays. This August we're planning to go to Spain. But first we must make the most of the Olympics. We've got tickets for some of the events.'

'Have you? Really? I wish I had thought of it in time!' Madeleine said, knowing she'd never have gone on her own.

'Thought of what in time?' James stood at their table. Madeleine looked up and squinted at the brightness between the leaves in the canopy.

'Tickets for the Olympics,' she said.

'It's not too late,' Julie encouraged. 'Even if you don't get the best seats, nothing can beat the atmosphere of the real thing.'

'Which events would you like to see?' James asked.

'Me?' His question surprised her. 'I love gymnastics. The rhythmic gymnastics especially. I could watch that forever.'

'I'd make enquiries,' Julie said.

'It's all right,' Madeleine smiled. 'I'll make sure to see it all on the television.'

'Not quite the same...' James began. At that moment Mark joined them and two smiling faces appeared at the edge of the table.

'Mama! I kicked the ball fifteen times!' Emily boasted.

'I counted twelve,' Mark teased her.

But she ignored him and added, 'And I caught it ten times!'

'And I caught it twenty times!' Daisy's eyes challenged anyone to disagree.

'Well done!' Julie praised them both, then, getting up, suggested, 'Shall we all get something to eat?'

Emily looked up at Madeleine.

'Please can I sit with Daisy, Mama?'

'Of course.' Madeleine patted her daughter's head. 'But shall we get something on our plates first? Everything looks so yummy!'

After everyone got settled at their respective tables, with full plates, refilled glasses and continued talk, Madeleine found herself sitting next to James, with Fiona on his other side and Julie and Mark facing them. Their topic of conversation returned to the Olympics.

'I've got a spare ticket for the opening ceremony,' Fiona announced. 'Any eager takers?'

'Are you kidding?' Mark laughed. 'Let's draw lots, but not before I mark the longest straw!'

'And you'd go without me?' Julie chided him. She turned to Fiona. 'Keep it for your best friend.'

'All my friends got theirs,' Fiona said. She looked at James. 'Have you got yours yet?'

'No,' James replied. 'I honestly could not think that far ahead. My schedule's been pretty busy and the next few weeks look just as bad.'

She shrugged. 'Your loss.'

He took a swig of beer.

'So much is happening this summer,' he said. 'Are any of you going to London for the Queen's Jubilee celebrations? It's going to be spectacular, so all the media promise. With the open-air concert and the pageant down the Thames.'

'All I can think of,' Mark replied, biting into a chicken leg, 'is the crammed underground, crammed streets and all those exhaust fumes poisoning my lungs. No thanks!'

'Don't be silly, Mark,' Julie chuckled, 'of course we're thinking about it. About going to London, I mean. A lot will depend on the weather.'

'If you made that your condition every time,' James pointed out, 'you'd never venture out anywhere!'

Madeleine listened. All her recreational outings were related to Emily's needs. Fiona sat up and stretched her slender neck as if preparing to announce something important.

'We've got a room booked with balcony at a hotel that overlooks the Thames. We'll have a grand view of the pageant, especially the royal barge.' She could not help a self-satisfied smirk.

'Any room for little me?' Mark quipped.

She ignored him. She turned her attention on Madeleine, looking past James. 'And what about you? What exotic holidays have you got planned this summer?'

Despite her patronising tone, Madeleine was amused.

'I'm going for a week to Poland in August. My friend is getting married.'

'That's plenty exotic enough for me!' Julie stated brightly and Madeleine wanted to hug her for it. 'And' – she turned to Madeleine – 'I want to see all the wedding photos when you come back!'

The conversation turned to the subject of weddings and the extortionate cost of arranging one, each section of the preparations invoiced by separate people. The sums mentioned were ridiculously beyond Madeleine's scope of possibilities, not that this was ever going to affect her. Fiona appeared to enjoy enormously recounting horror stories of her friends' weddings that had not gone to plan: a collapsed marquee under the pressure of a freak deluge, an unexpected menu muddled up with another wedding menu, a wedding car that had been hit by a lorry when on the way to fetch the bride to the church. Madeleine turned to James and spoke discreetly so as not to interrupt Fiona's torrent of words.

'I'll leave you for a minute. I'll have a chat with your mum.'

'She'll like that,' he said, getting up to hold back the chair for her. Such old-fashioned gentility. She loved it.

Before sitting down with Jean, she walked over to Josh's group. They were high-spirited, evidently making the most of their time together. They went quiet at her approach and raised their grinning faces to her.

'Please carry on,' she said. 'I just want to see how Josh is today.'

'He's absolutely fine!' Matt assured her, but then clamping his hand around his neck, he added with a painful expression, 'but I'm not so sure about me. I feel a fever coming on. A long stay at home. Definitely a case for home tuition!'

'Ha! Ha! Can you see me rolling about on the floor?' Seb threw his head back and swiped the fringe off his eyes. 'Ignore him, Madeleine. If you're looking to tutor a suave and sophisticated student, then I'm your man!'

'Nonsense!' Tim got up, his long and lanky frame hunching protectively over Madeleine.

'Don't listen to either of them, immature kids! I make an excellent minder, if you ever need one. No one messes with me!' He pulled himself up to his full impressive height.

Madeleine laughed. She said to Josh, 'I can see you're enjoying yourself.'

He nodded, his cheeks dimpled, his eyes shining with amusement.

Madeleine joined Jean's table and was invited to sit down. Sue moved her chair to make room for her between them. Emily and Daisy were absorbed in excited chatter and their plates looked as if they had been licked clean. Even Emily's!

Emily looked up at her and pointing at her clean plate exclaimed proudly, 'Look, Mama, look!'

Jean smiled. 'The girls have done really well,' she said. 'I don't think their plates need washing.' This made them giggle.

'Can we go to play now?' Daisy asked. Sue nodded, her silver-touched hair catching patches of light. 'But don't go pestering Mark, Daisy. Wait for him to finish eating. He'll come over when he's ready.'

Madeleine watched Emily and Daisy skip off hand in hand and she was glad she had brought her daughter to this most enjoyable afternoon.

'Madeleine,' Jean said, leaning towards her, 'it's so good to meet like this. Not having to rush off. To have time for a normal chat, at long last.' She gave her a steady, considered look of her clear blue eyes, not as piercing as James's. 'I'm glad you could make it today. We owe you such a lot!'

Madeleine shook her head, smiling.

'If you mean going with Josh to the hospital, anyone would have done the same.'

Jean nodded, combing back with her fingers the white streak of hair.

'I hope so. But it's not just that. The first time you came to our house and I couldn't be here to meet you, I worried you may have been put off. You know, a young boy and just his older brother. I wasn't sure how that would impress you. Basia Demska spoke so highly of you, I kept my fingers crossed you'd at least give it a chance.'

Madeleine could not believe Jean's words. She'd actually been wanted, really wanted, here in this family. She smiled, feeling a warmth spread inside her chest.

'No, I wasn't put off.' (Just terribly nervous.) 'I found Josh unexpectedly charming. So unusual for a teenage boy. And James was straight and to the point. I know where I stand with people like him.'

'Really? I'm relieved to hear that.' There seemed a note of doubt in Jean's tone. 'It's just that James can sound officious, when he doesn't mean that. It's his work habit spilling over into his private life.'

'Oh, Jean! He's never that! Officious? What are you saying?' Sue jumped to James's defence and Madeleine loved her at that moment. 'All those Saturday kids! They're all crazy about him. An officious person wouldn't last a minute there!'

'Saturday kids?' Madeleine asked intrigued.

Sue flickered her mascaraed eyelashes and glanced at the far end of the garden, where Mark was playing ball games with Emily and Daisy. She also glanced towards James's table, where Fiona was holding court, much to the amusement and lively commentating from her audience. There was no chance James would have overheard any of his mother's and Sue's conversation, Madeleine noted with relief.

'It all started,' Sue was saying, 'when my Peter, James, Mark and Julie were in the Scouts and Guides. They did voluntary work on Saturdays for a charity that helps parents with disabled children. Most of the time it was just keeping the children minded and amused for a couple of hours to give the parents a break, but sometimes they helped with organised outings.'

'They did that? In their free time?' Madeleine was astonished. She imagined there were similar charity bodies in Poland, but she had never come across anyone who was involved in this kind of voluntary work. It was fashionable for students to tend to graves in their summer holidays, especially in old cemeteries, where heroes had been buried throughout the centuries of oppression, forgotten and their graves overgrown with naturally rampant nature.

All of a sudden, she thought how insular and self-centred her own life had been. It had been dictated such by necessity, but nevertheless it would have been a noble thing to do to think of others. But when would she find the time, in her already crammed work schedule? These people had made time.

'And do they still do it?' she asked, throwing a surreptitious look towards James's table.

'Most Saturdays,' Sue confirmed. 'They have a rota. They need some Saturdays for other things.'

'What about James?' Madeleine asked Jean. 'With living in London.'

'He still does it,' Jean said, 'whenever he comes home at the weekends. And in London, where he lives, he's been helping out a similar charity.'

It was a side to James she'd never have guessed.

'I'm full of admiration,' she said honestly. 'When do they find the time to do all this?'

'I can only speak for James,' Jean said, brushing back her falling fringe. 'He was taught by necessity to make time for things he didn't always like to do.'

'And you forget, Jean,' Sue pointed out, 'how young James was at the time. And how lucky you were to have a teenager with so much common sense.' Madeleine guessed Sue was referring to the time of Jean's husband's death.

Jean glanced towards James's table.

'You're right, Sue. I suppose I should give him his due,' she said musingly.

'Should? Oh, Jean! This should come naturally!' Sue gave a huge, expressive sigh of impatience.

'But they know what I think and feel about them. My two boys,' Jean said defensively.

'Only if you tell them. Often enough. No child is too old for a mother's praise!' Sue concluded with 'I rest my case!' tone.

Jean sighed, shrugged and turned to Madeleine.

'I only put up with this from Sue because we've known each other for so long. And we work together. It wouldn't do to fall out!' She gave Sue a pointedly wry smile, shifted in her chair, took a sip of wine and asked Madeleine, 'Can we talk about your work? Where are you based? How often are you required to do interpreting? How does the whole thing work?'

Madeleine gave them a brief account of the many places where her skills were required and they both listened with interest and asked questions. They also asked her about her grandparents, and Jean remarked how identical their story was to Basia Demska's past. They did not ask any searching questions about her own background. Madeleine guessed that Mrs Demska may have already told Jean certain things and that would have been the version edited by Aniela. She was relieved she did not have to rack her brain with evasive answers.

Half way through their conversation, Josh's friends came round with bowls of ice cream topped with diced fresh fruit. Madeleine looked in Emily's direction and saw her sitting in the gazebo with Mark and Daisy enjoying their desserts. James was serving his table, with Julie giving the odd polite nod to Fiona's excited monologue. She wasn't missing anything there, she comforted herself. Only James. She looked up at Matt and Seb.

'This is so lovely,' she said, 'thank you, boys.' They sauntered away smiling mysteriously.

Madeleine was surprised when she checked her watch how quickly time had flown. Josh's friends were getting up to go. She took her cue from them, not wishing to be the last one to leave. At James's table, she chatted with Mark and Julie for a while and wished Fiona a pleasant end to the weekend in Leicester (yearning in her heart to change places with her).

For a short while, she had James all to herself when he walked her and Emily to the car. After strapping Emily in the car seat, Madeleine straightened up to face him. The air around them was heavy with Maytime scents, bringing sharply back childhood memories of summers spent in the country. The shaded area by the garage gave an intimate feel to their shared presence.

'I never got the chance to sort things out with you about the cheque,' she said.

'There's nothing to sort out,' he replied, the expression in his eyes so soft it made her knees wobble. 'It's all correct, Madeleine, based on my research into the matter.' He smiled reassuringly. 'I'm not going away forever. I'll see you again soon, I hope. You worry too much.'

'That makes two of us, by all accounts.' She raised her eyebrows a touch challengingly.

He smiled again.

'We've got something in common then.'

For a split second she felt intense affinity with him. If only... Dear God, she had so much baggage with her. Too much!

'James...' she halted to control her voice, 'it's been a truly lovely afternoon. Thanks for everything.'

Josh's three friends came out of the side gate, laughing uncontrollably at something that Seb was telling them. Their laughter settled to polite jollity as they approached James and Madeleine.

'Great afternoon, James,' Matt said. 'Cheers!'

'Cheers!' Seb and Tim confirmed. 'And lovely to have met you, Madeleine,' Tim added.

'Likewise,' Madeleine replied, all her previous tension slipping away, as she watched the boys walking towards the gate, their feet making crunching sounds on the gravel.

James bent down to the open window at Emily's level.

'Did you have a nice time too?' he asked. Emily nodded.

'I'd like to play again with Daisy and Mark.'

'Then you shall have to visit us again,' he said. Madeleine was certain that James meant what he said, but what was the point of saying it, when there was little chance of them visiting the Hammonds again, socially. Her acquaintance with them was based on a temporary business arrangement that would cease as soon as Josh returned to school.

James straightened up and looked down straight into her eyes, his silhouette etched sharply against the luminous sky beyond the trees.

'Madeleine, would you fancy an outing to Rutland Water sometime? As soon as Josh is better, so he and Emily can come with us. Naturally.'

She was so taken aback she could not think of anything to say, except, 'Why?'

'Because…' he laughed, 'the country air by the water will do us all good.'

'B… but…' Questions flooded her mind. When would he find the time? With all his hundred commitments and hundreds of people in his life. Fiona? Why was he even asking her? 'James.' She affected a reasonable tone. 'You've already rewarded me generously for what I do for Josh. There really is no need to do anything else.'

A puzzled look crossed his features.

'Don't say that, Madeleine. I just thought that the four of us could spend a pleasant afternoon together. Cycling round the lake. I know Josh would love it. I'm sure Emily would like it too.'

She felt like a fool now. To save her face she asked, 'Haven't you more important things to do in your spare time?'

He shrugged.

'I see enough people during the week. Some weekends too, when deadlines have to be met. It's bliss to get away from it all, though; don't get me wrong, I do enjoy my work.' He sounded sincere. Where did Fiona fit into all this?

Madeleine said graciously, 'Thank you, James, for the offer. It's certainly tempting, it's just that…'

He didn't let her finish.

'It's settled then. May I contact you next time I come home? We could agree details, but, if Josh is not quite ready then, I'm sure we can think of other things to do.'

What could she say? She felt like putty under his spell.

'That will be very nice, James. I shall look forward to that.'

At this point, if she had known him longer, she would have given him a hug. She wanted to. And more than that. Much more.

She smiled graciously and got in her car.

# CHAPTER 21

Within days of reading Emily's letter from the Polish Saturday School, Aniela had bought all the materials, ribbons, sequins and colourful beads for making a little girl's costume from the Krakow region. By the end of the week, the floral skirt, gathered at the waist and its hemline trimmed with bands of silky ribbons, red, blue, green and white, was finished. Also, a white fine cotton blouse had been sewn and finished with a frilly lace collar and cuffs. The black velvet sleeveless bodice was waiting to be lined, and then the real fun would begin: sewing on those shiny beads and sequins in shapes of flowers and leaves, with curving stems between them.

'I'll be very happy to help,' Madeleine offered, while sitting with Emily and Aniela at the sewing table in the spare bedroom.

'Me too!' Emily was shivering with excitement, her fingers stirring the beads in the bowl.

'Thank you.' Aniela's gaze rose above the rim of her spectacles. 'The only problem is, that I can only do this work in daylight, and that is when you are both out.'

'Oh!' Emily's disappointment sounded like a cry.

'But don't worry, Emily,' Aniela said kindly, biting off the end of the thread with her teeth, still healthy and strong despite Aniela's deprivations throughout her childhood. She put it down to the total absence of anything indulgently sweet during the wartime years and the ration times that followed. 'I'll cut you a velvet ribbon for a scarf for Rabbit, and you can decorate it with beads and sequins any way you like.'

'Oh, can I?' Emily's mouth parted in wonder.

'And I can help you with that,' Madeleine promised, smiling at Aniela's deft diplomacy. She knew Aniela was keen to finish the whole project herself.

After supper, Emily tried on the new skirt and the frilly lace blouse and twirled around on the kitchen floor for everyone to admire her dance moves.

'Excellent!' Bronek clapped. 'You'll be the queen of the ball!'

Emily giggled.

'No, Grandpa, there's no queen in our dance. I'll be a Krakowianka from Krakow.' She could have been, Madeleine thought nostalgically, remembering her own childhood concerts and the brightly coloured costumes, the dances and the songs. If things had worked out differently.

'You'll be the prettiest Krakowianka ever!' Bronek said. He was having a good phase lately with no major adverse incidents. One night he forgot to lock the car. By amazing luck, the car was still in its place in the morning and the only thing missing from the glove compartment was the change he kept for incidental parking. After that, Aniela made a point of checking the car each night before bedtime. They had all got used to the daily search for his missing keys, also for his mobile, which he accused of camouflage trickery, by hiding in plain sight against a dark background.

Madeleine's e-mail inbox was punctuated (staidly) with well-meant epistles from her father and (excitedly) with accounts of wedding preparations from Natalia. Each time a new one arrived, despite the joy of their renewed closeness, Madeleine's stomach felt sick with anxiety. The only way to eliminate this problem was to tell Natalia the truth. And she had determined to do it when she saw her friend face to face. But before then she had to say something; she could not turn up to her friend's wedding with an unexplained child by her side.

Every night she told herself she'd do it, and every night her e-mail took on an entirely different form and mood. She set herself a deadline, and when that evening arrived she could barely eat anything of the meal, or concentrate on the small talk, as her mind rewrote hundreds of versions of her e-mail to Natalia.

Aniela's sixth sense picked up on Madeleine's anxiety and as soon as Bronek and Emily were out in the garden she asked her directly, 'What's worrying you, Magda? Has it been a bad day?'

Madeleine stopped in mid-track of wiping the plate dry and reined in her scattered thoughts.

'No, Babcha, it's been a good day. It's just that... I'm so looking forward to Natalia's wedding... but I've not told her yet... you know, about Emily.'

Aniela's wide-eyed look couldn't have been more expressive of surprise and disapproval. She took the tea-towel and the plate from Madeleine's hands and urged impatiently, 'Go! Do it now! Write to her. No sense in putting it off and tormenting yourself like that. And she needs to know beforehand. She'll have enough to think about without surprise revelations before the big day!'

Of course, Aniela was right.

'I want to, Babcha, it's just that I don't want any of the worst facts to be recorded on the computer.'

'Then just simply tell her that. Tell her she'll get the full story when you two meet.'

Such a simple solution; why had she been agonising over it for so long? She gave Aniela a heartfelt hug, went to the backroom, sat at her computer and began to type.

*My Dear Natalia,*

*I can't wait to see you. I'm counting the days and crossing off the windows in my calendar. There is just one thing I want you to know, and if that changes your mind about my presence at your wedding, I shall fully understand.*

*I've got a six-year-old daughter, Emily. I can't write about her father just now, but I'll tell you everything when we meet. I promise. You'll understand my strange behaviour seven years ago, when I left home so suddenly. And no, that had nothing to do with Dominik. He knows nothing of this, and I beg you, please keep it this way till I see you.*

*If you still wish me to visit you, then I'd like to bring Emily with me. With much love, as always,*

*Magda.*

She pressed SEND before allowing herself time to hesitate.

Natalia's response came back the very same evening.

*My Dear Magda,*

*What a shock! Surprise! Joy! Of course you must come over with your little daughter. I can't wait to see you both. Send me some photos, please.*

*Love and hugs to you both,*

*Natalia*

Madeleine felt as if she had surfaced from the bottom of a dark lake onto a warm, sunlit surface, with gentle waves lapping against a sandy, safe shore.

\*

It was the day of the Queen's Diamond Jubilee river pageant. Madeleine heard her mobile ping. It lay on the coffee table beside her, next to the glass of wine and a plate of nibbles.

'Mama! You've got a message,' Emily informed her, not taking her eyes off the television screen. She was sitting on the settee between Aniela and Mrs Barska, watching the river pageant floating along the Thames. Bronek and Mr Barski, comfortable in their armchairs and sipping wine, watched too, this not preventing them from a running commentary, which appeared to drive Mrs Barska to the limits of her endurance with frequent reminders of Cicho! Quiet, please!

Madeleine picked up the mobile, her spirits dropping in anticipation. Please, don't let it be Mr Bunting, not today! She had been called out in emergencies before, when no one else wished to be available on a Sunday night. Accidents did not choose convenient times.

Her eyes scanned the message and her heart skipped. She sent a lightning gaze around the room, checking no one had noticed its effect on her, but they were all totally absorbed in the action unfolding before them on the screen.

The message was short:

*May I ring you later? Will you be free to speak? James.*

She sent back a simple 'Yes', but the moment it was gone her mind could not rest. What could be so urgent that he needed to speak to her on a Sunday? Today of all days? Since the barbecue, he had not been in touch with her, despite suggesting a trip to Rutland Water. And she never asked Josh about him, abhorring the very notion of appearing nosy or needy. She had felt disappointed with James's silence, but persuaded herself that this was for the best. For what expectations could either of them build on a phantom relationship that had no chance of materialising?

She imagined James now with Fiona's crowd watching the royal pageant from a grandstand view of a hotel balcony overlooking the Thames. Why would he be thinking about her now?

As the cavalcade of colourful boats, representing a plethora of names, charities, companies and commercial networks, sailed down the Thames, its banks thronged with thousands of onlookers, all Madeleine could think of was that somewhere there was James. A feeling of regret assailed her. In normal circumstances, she would be out having fun with people her own age.

But when she looked at Emily, her child's cheeks rosy in all the excitement, the momentary feeling of self-pity passed. She had a lot to be thankful for. The noise of jubilation filled the space above the river, and with it Madeleine's spirits rose. The intermittent rain could not dampen the people's joy.

Mrs Barska remarked, 'What a dreadful day for such a special occasion!' She was wearing her Sunday best, a pale grey silky dress that complimented her white hair especially styled the day before. Her feet were exceptionally small and looked dainty and young in the high-heeled sandals.

Madeleine could not imagine being that age, but, if she were, she hoped she'd look like Mrs Barska. She said amiably, 'Nothing seems to dampen the spirit of the British. They always rise to the occasion.'

Mrs Barska gave a mock shudder.

'I'm glad I'm not out there soaking in the rain.'

Her husband, all smart and sleek in his light grey suit, raised his glass, smiling.

'Here's to the best hotel!'

Emily looked at him, puzzled.

'Uncle, what made you think this is a hotel?'

He chuckled.

'Emily, don't you agree it is like the best hotel ever, with all this lovely food and drinks?' Madeleine's thoughts escaped to that other hotel overlooking the Thames. Fiona and James. How she wished...

'Oh look!' Aniela cried, 'There's the Queen's boat!'

All talking stopped and they all leaned forward for a better look. The royal barge was festooned with swags of red and purple material; the Queen stood out distinctive all in white, and the Duke in his naval uniform still presented a handsome figure.

'Amazing at his age,' Bronek remarked. 'Ninety-one! Done enough escorting all his life. Always a step behind.'

'Wouldn't you do the same for me?' Aniela challenged impishly.

'I thought I already did. And that without you wearing a crown!' Bronek chuckled. She made a face at him and he raised his glass to her.

Next to the royal couple stood Prince Charles and Camilla, he smartly uniformed, she sporting a large hat that matched her off-white outfit.

'Does he ever, I wonder, think about Diana?' Aniela mused.

'It would be unnatural if he did not,' Madeleine said, her own past momentarily flashing across her mind. She blanked it out and focussed on the screen.

'She'd be so proud of her boys,' Mrs Barska said. Prince William and Prince Harry, both tall and slim, were exceedingly handsome young men, Madeleine thought. Katherine, thin and willowy, was magnificent in her all-red outfit. Mrs Barska continued to comment, 'And Kate is so beautiful.

Diana would have loved her. She looks frozen, poor thing. Fashion before comfort.' She gave another expressive shudder.

Talk continued on the subject of the royals, as the cameras followed the course of their barge down the river. The barge concluding the long procession carried young singers from the Royal College of Music. There was just a group of them but the volume of their voices rose high and strong and filled all the air above the river and the buildings. The rain poured on them, splashing their faces, soaking their clothes, but it could not dampen their youthful exuberance. 'Land of Hope and Glory' rang out loud and clear, and 'Rule Britannia' trailed after them, as their boat disappeared from view.

On the first note of the National Anthem, Aniela and Bronek stood up. Their friends and Madeleine did the same, Emily leaning against her, looking spellbound.

When the pictures faded and the credits began to roll Bronek raised his glass and waited for everyone to have their drinks ready. He then proposed solemnly, 'Na zdrowie Krolowej! The Queen's health!'

'The Queen's health,' they all repeated before sitting down.

'And to think…' Mrs Barska said disapprovingly, 'that there are people who want to do away with all this tradition!'

'A year under Putin would cure them of their whinges,' her husband added. 'No one else in the world has what we've got in this country. Why do all the tourists flock to Buckingham Palace or Windsor? Why do they wait hours to see the changing of the guard, or hope for a glimpse of any of the royals? I somehow cannot picture crowds rushing to see Berlusconi, or even Merkel, for that matter.'

Madeleine chuckled. She was fascinated by this older generation's reverence for the royal family. In Poland there was nothing comparable for the people to admire with such loyalty. Only national heroes in the face of communist repression for five long decades: Lech Walesa and Pope John Paul, the Polish Pope. Even now, as the nation strived to rebuild its economy, the Church remained its guardian and its driving force.

As if guessing her thoughts Bronek said, 'I can't imagine anyone disliking the Queen. Elizabeth was only a young girl when we arrived in England after the war. Her wedding gave everyone such a lift. It was beautiful and glamorous and brightened up no end those grey post-war days. It also brought some sense of hope, I suppose, a visible sign that things were getting better. We all needed that. Especially us, Poles, after all those years of wandering about so many other countries.'

'I've always admired her,' Aniela said. 'For me, she's always been a symbol of continuity. I like it when things stay the same. You know where you are and what to expect. We've never had that in Poland. Perhaps just those few years between the wars, but what of it? The Germans came, the Russians came, and the upheaval started all over again. Anyway, that's enough of that!' She stood up. She too was dressed up for the occasion, a silky lilac dress with ivory flower patterns and two strings of pearls around her neck. 'Just to remind everyone, there's plenty more food in the kitchen. Don't let it go cold!'

Emily giggled and pulled at her hand.

'But it's already cold, Babcha!'

'Oh, so it is!' Aniela laughed. 'Good on you to have spotted it!'

They all trooped out into the kitchen, except for Madeleine, who stayed behind to collect used plates and crumpled serviettes. Her mobile rang. It was James.

With a quickened heartbeat she said, 'Give me a second, James, to find a quiet spot. We've got visitors.'

She made her way past the chattering group in the kitchen and out into the back garden. It had stopped raining, but the air was damp. She stood underneath the wide eave of the back extension, from which hung a basket with scarlet geraniums and trailing ivy.

'I'm with you now, James. Is it still pouring hard in London?'

'London?' There was a pause. 'I've no idea. I'm here, in Leicester.'

'In Leicester?' Her heart did another flip. 'But I thought…' She could not tell him what she had thought, imagined, him and Fiona. 'I thought you were with your friends in London watching the Jubilee celebrations live.'

He was quiet for a moment. She pictured him thinking.

'No, I never had such plans.'

'I thought Fiona had invited you.'

Another pause. And then, as if remembering, he chortled. 'No, if you mean that invite at the barbecue, that was just Fiona's idea of spicing up the conversation. She's got her own circle of friends. I very rarely go out with them. That weekend she and her partner were having new floors put in their flat. He was away on a working weekend and had actually asked me if I could bring Fiona to our rural Leicester for those three days.'

So, that's all it had been. A weight lifted off Madeleine's chest, and for no reason at all she felt deliriously happy. And tongue-tied. She could not think of what else to say.

'So… is there anything… is it about Josh?' It occurred to her that perhaps Josh was ready to return to school. Though he did not suggest anything of the sort when she saw him the last time.

'Madeleine,' James's tone was full of purpose, 'I know it's short notice, but could you possibly be free tonight? Remember my friends Mark and

Julie? I'm meeting them later at the High Cross. Some restaurant they really like. Could you please come to join us? I'd really like that.'

Every cell in her body tingled. Was she dreaming? And just as quickly caution crept in. She must not give him false hopes.

'James, thank you for asking, and I honestly appreciate it but...'

He cut in.

'Please, Madeleine, don't say no. Go and ask your Grandma now. I'm sure Emily will like an evening with her grandparents too. And please ring me back. I'll be waiting.' He rang off before she could say another word.

It felt like being a teenager again, asked on a first date. She wanted to go, she so much wanted to go. But would that be fair on him? She'd have to insist, she'd have to make it quite clear, that they could be no more than just friends. With that resolution in mind, she returned to the kitchen and waited until everyone refilled their plates from the cold buffet spread and returned to the front room.

Left alone with Aniela and Emily picking crumbs off the cake plate, she said, 'To byl James. It was James. He's asked me to go out with him and his friends tonight.'

It took Aniela a moment to absorb this, and then her preoccupied 'hostess' expression melted in a smile of delight.

'Powiedzialas Tak! You said yes, of course!'

Madeleine shrugged exhaling a long sigh.

'Oh, Magda! Ring him this minute! Tell him you'll come!'

'Will Josh be there?' Emily asked. 'Can I come too?'

'Moje sloneczko. My dearest sunshine,' Aniela stroked her head, 'Josh is not well enough to go out yet. And you'd get tired and very bored staying out so late at night with adults. I think we'll find better things to do here. You can choose your favourite film and we'll watch it together.'

Emily nodded and then asked Madeleine, 'Will it be like when you have a meeting with Mr Bunting?'

'Not quite.' (And thank goodness for that, Madeleine thought.) 'It will be a meeting with James and his friends.'

'It's nice to have friends,' Aniela said. 'It's like you and Karishma. Grown-ups need friends too. Today, for example, it just wouldn't feel like a party if our friends weren't here.' She looked at Madeleine. 'Go, ring him now!'

# CHAPTER 22

Madeleine was ready at eight, as arranged: a pastel pink dress with a print of white outlines of flowers, white sandals and a white shawl against the dampness of the evening. James had insisted on picking her up. Aniela was excited about meeting him and Madeleine resigned herself to her Babcha's over-imagined speculations in the face of her own well-justified resolve. For the time being, and for the sake of harmony, she allowed herself to go with the flow.

And yet her heart quickened when she opened the door and his appraising eyes made no secret of his admiration. He wore a navy linen jacket and a sky-blue shirt, and everything about him was fresh and crisp, and made her acutely aware of how good-looking he was.

She led him to the front room, where Bronek and Aniela were watching television with Emily and Rabbit cuddling up between them. Bronek stood up to greet him, after which James stooped down to Aniela to shake her hand.

'Hello,' he said to Emily, and shook Rabbit's paw, which made Emily giggle. 'Please, don't let me disturb you,' he said, deftly standing back close to the door.

'Not at all,' Bronek assured him. 'We've done nothing else but watch television all day.' Madeleine sensed in his tone that he already liked James. He invited James to sit down.

'Thank you, perhaps another time.' James smiled. 'We'll have to be going soon.' He looked at Emily. 'Did you enjoy watching the Queen?'

Emily nodded with a self-conscious smile, hugging Rabbit closer. Then raising her head, as if about to recite something, she said, 'My Mama is going to take me to Buckingham Palace in the summer holidays!'

'Indeed?' James replied with an approving tone. 'Then you must let me know when, so I can be your guide. There are so many things to see. Would you fancy a visit to the Natural History Museum?'

'The one with the dinosaurs?'

'The same!'

Emily gave a squeaky, happy laugh. Madeleine had not been prepared for this. Why was James making such promises? She butted in before it got out of hand.

'Emily, summer holidays are a long way off yet. James may be very busy just at the time when we visit London. We'll take a map with us and find all the places we want to see.'

James chuckled and looked at her, making it plain he guessed her thoughts. Light-heartedly he said, 'I'd always make time for my friends from Leicester.'

Madeleine caught Aniela's look, that look, silently reprimanding her. OK! OK! Her raised eyebrows signalled back. James did not appear to notice as he continued to talk to Emily.

'Do you like reading, Emily?'

She nodded and began telling him about her favourite stories. From the flat pocket on the side of his jacket, he brought out a slim volume and placed it on Emily's lap.

'Can you read the title?'

Bronek, observing quietly from the side, leaned forward as Emily exclaimed, 'I know this story! It's *Winnie the Pooh*! I've got a big book of Winnie and his friends, with lots of pictures!'

'The Walt Disney version,' Madeleine explained, 'but your book, James, looks like a very special edition. Don't part with it so lightly!'

He laughed.

'I know where to find it if I get the urge to read it again!'

Why was he being so generous? This was making her nervous. Aniela looked up at him, and with her most charming smile, declared, 'This is the most beautiful and original gift. What do you say, Emily?'

'Thank you,' Emily said promptly. 'Thank you very much. I like this book already.' Her small fingers pinched the pages with care and turned them over, revealing the child-friendly script interspersed with the iconic pen drawings.

Moments like this one made Madeleine proud of her daughter. She said to James, 'It's very kind of you. I wouldn't part so easily with my childhood treasures.'

He looked at her and smiled.

'I know this book has found a good home.'

*

The Almanac in High Cross was packed out when they arrived, with groups of young people, drinks in their hands, standing around the entrance amidst tumultuous gaiety. James clasped Madeleine's hand and made way for her through the crowd indoors past the bar, where a spacious area was divided into smaller sections with tables, and even smaller alcoves with leather seats and coffee tables. He let go of her hand but the tingling sensation lingered as he steered her towards a corner, from where Julie and Mark were waving to them.

*Did James feel anything too?* Madeleine wondered.

Mark stood up to greet them and gave her a peck on the cheek as if they had been old friends. She liked that, feeling part of their group, and even more so when Julie gave her a warm hug.

'So glad you could make it,' Julie said, and it sounded sincere.

'Thank you,' Madeleine replied sitting down next to Julie on the leather two-seater. James and Mark sat down facing them. Madeleine added, 'So kind of you to have thought about me.'

Julie gave her a wide smile and glanced at James.

'A foursome seemed like the perfect number.'

Small talk followed amidst sorting out the drinks, then James and Mark got up to fetch them and Madeleine was left alone with Julie. Despite this being a busy evening with all tables occupied, their corner felt quieter and it was possible to talk.

'Was it a problem for you to go out at such short notice?' Julie asked, her big brown eyes appraising Madeleine's face unhurriedly.

'I'm very lucky,' Madeleine answered. 'It's as if Emily's got three parents. And she is equally happy staying with any of us.'

'I thought how well adjusted she was when I saw her at James's barbecue,' Julie said pleasantly.

'We watched the Queen all afternoon. Emily loved it. No doubt your class will have plenty to say and to write about after this weekend,' Madeleine said.

Julie nodded, her dark wiry curls shaking with the movement.

'An exciting summer for us this year. With so much going on. The Queen's Jubilee and soon it will be the Olympics. And then the holidays.' She paused. 'I don't usually mention our long summer break. It's often a bone of contention, especially for those who only get a fortnight's break in the summer.' Madeleine nodded as Julie continued, 'Believe me, Madeleine, mine's not a job where you have strict cut-off points. I'm there at school at quarter to eight, preparing stuff for the day. Mainly print-out sheets. Thirty-two for the class. This is followed by brief meetings most days. The school day is officially over at three, but again most days there are meetings on a variety of subjects in the curriculum. Then there's all the marking, thirty-two books of English and maths. There are other subjects too. I stay at school till five and take all the unfinished work home with me. There's still the preparation for the next day. It's relentless, but…' she smiled, 'I love my work, as long as the kids behave themselves.'

Madeleine gave another nod.

'I hope Emily has someone like you when she moves up to the junior school.'

They continued talking about their respective jobs until James and Mark came back with the drinks. Madeleine sensed James's gaze on her and when she looked up she had a fleeting sensation that his inner excitement matched hers. It was with such careful precision that he placed the drinks down on the coffee table in front of them and then he laughed out loud at something Mark said. They continued to parry good-naturedly when they sat down, with his gaze frequently darting towards her. Madeleine had not seen him like this before, as if something was fizzing inside him, so different to that other image of a serious, controlled, matter-of-fact man.

They studied the menu and when the waitress appeared Madeleine asked for a paté on toast from the starter menu. She felt no hunger at all, just a chest-expanding bubbling inside her.

'Won't you consider something more substantial?' James asked.

'I can recommend the lasagne,' Julie suggested.

'Perhaps another time,' Madeleine replied graciously, realising too late the implication in her words.

James caught her eye and smiled. He and Mark ordered lamb shanks, Julie her favourite lasagne.

'Here's to us.' Mark raised his glass, after the waitress was gone, and insisted on clinking it with everyone else's, much to their amusement. 'To lots more of the Queen's days and Bank Holidays and our get-togethers!' He tasted his beer with froth sticking to his upper lip. He licked it off with theatrical relish.

'Tongue like a lizard's.' Julie laughed wickedly.

'Has its uses!' Mark flicked back his overgrown fringe and took another sip. 'Such bliss being away from the mayhem at the end of the school year. At least the exams are over now, but there are still all those reports to write and all those parents' evenings to get through!' He caught Julie's expression and smiled cheekily. 'What?'

'You know you love all the drama!' she said. 'Not to mention the after-school football and the cycling clubs. And the Saturdays with the Scouts. I wish you could find just a teeny-weeny bit of time to finish all those DIY jobs.'

'DIY?' Madeleine asked.

'Do It Yourself,' James explained with a grin. 'To be fair, Julie, I think Mark has already done wonders to your house. The best in the street!'

'Well, you would say that, wouldn't you?' Julie replied unimpressed, giving him a mock-stern teacher look. She looked at Madeleine. 'No job in our house gets finished in one go. I'm forced to remind him, then I turn out to be the baddie, always nagging!'

Madeleine laughed. Mark leaned forward above the coffee table, jabbing a finger in the air.

'May I remind you, my dear wife, who it is actually who is out most nights? Rock choir. Painting classes. Not to mention the gossip brigade masquerading as the reading group!'

Julie shrugged her thin shoulders and beamed a wide smile.

'If you wanted a domestic, then you should have married one!' Their dialogue disintegrated into a playground word-slinging match, but Madeleine had a sudden serious reflection of what a boring, stay-at-home nonentity she had become.

She asked, 'How do you find time to do all those things?'

Julie's wide brown eyes looked into hers and her cheeks began to turn pink.

'I didn't mean...' she tried to explain, 'it's different for you, Madeleine. I haven't got your responsibility of bringing up a child. On your own...' Her voice trailed off, and she was obviously uncomfortable at having overlooked Madeleine's particular situation.

'It's all right, Julie,' Madeleine assured her, 'I'm far more fortunate than most mothers on their own. I get support. But I still cannot find time purely for relaxation.'

'What? Not at all? But you must!' Julie's well-meant indignation made Madeleine laugh.

'The fact is, Julie, I don't seem to be able to find any spare time. I work on my translations any time when I don't do anything else. It's like an addictive gap-filler.' How could she explain that at the beginning only the all-consuming work deadened all other sensations, that working all hours until her body and her mind were numb with exhaustion made her think less of the things she wanted to forget. 'It's become a habit,' she said. 'When I arrived in England, I came with nothing. My adopted grandparents were wonderful, but my first goal was to find work, to become independent. I got into the habit of working all hours. It stayed.' She smiled and took a sip of wine. 'Sorry to be so boring!'

'Not at all!' James leaned forward. 'I admire self-made people.'

'I'm hardly that!' she giggled, her seriousness fading. 'Let's not exaggerate. But I do,' she looked at Julie, 'go to the cinema or to the theatre with Aniela, sometimes. And Bronek loves it when Emily and I go to the allotment with him on Saturday afternoons.'

'An allotment?' Mark gave out a shivering sigh of pleasure. 'Ah, that's my dream. To grow my very own organic food!'

Julie gave him a wry 'dream-on' look and smiled at Madeleine. 'I've no idea when he'd fit that in. Would have to stop sleeping altogether!'

The waitress appeared and led them to their table. When they were seated in the soft orange glow from the overhead light, with hushed voices rising from the neighbouring tables, Julie said to Madeleine, 'Tell us about your planned visit to Poland. You mentioned a wedding last time we met.'

A perfectly innocent request, yet Madeleine's stomach tightened. She took a sip of wine and held onto the long stem of glass, ensuring her hand stayed still.

'My friend, Natalia, is getting married. We were at school together. Then at university.'

'Will you be her bridesmaid?' Julie's eyes were wide with glee.

'No, it wouldn't be practical.' Madeleine was anxious to give a plausible explanation. 'She needs someone over there to help, at such a busy time.'

'Do you go home often?' Mark asked, sweeping back his fringe off his inquisitive eyes.

Madeleine shook her head, catching James's gaze. No doubt, he wanted to know more about her past too. She chose her words carefully.

'My home is here now. My Aunt Emilia who brought me up died seven years ago. That was when I came to England. The apartment where we lived belongs to her husband now.' Calling him 'her husband' surprisingly distanced him and blanked out his face. She was able to carry on talking. 'I couldn't and had no wish to stay on. His family had always been resentful of the fact that I, no blood relation of his, had financial support from him that should have been entirely their own children's. That was untrue. I did not need anything from him. My father paid money into my account regularly, and Aunt Emilia looked after my affairs. Now they can have him and all his money to themselves!'

Enough said. Perhaps too much? Mark and Julie remained pensive and James spoke gently. 'I'm sorry, Madeleine, to hear all this. I'd never have guessed that...' His voice trailed off. And a lot of other things you'd never guess, Madeleine thought. She took a sip of wine.

'It's all right now,' she smiled reassuringly. 'That's all behind me now.' Not quite, but the other things would remain buried.

Their food arrived and for a while their attention focussed on their chosen dishes. Madeleine munched small morsels of the paté on toast. It was good, but she felt no hunger at all, and when James refilled her glass she was glad to take generous gulps of wine. A pleasant sensation relaxed her stomach and her legs became weightless.

Talk was high-spirited and she listened with envy to her three friends joking at each other's expense, such easy familiarity born of years of close friendship. She remembered vividly her childhood friends, and in their teens the same friends approaching adulthood with ever-new adventures and discoveries. They had felt so grown-up then and so keen to outdo each other in their perceived adult sophistication. Some began to smoke and some, Madeleine knew, indulged in recreational drugs. That was one thing that Madeleine had never touched.

'A penny for your thoughts,' she heard Julie say.

She pulled back her reflections and focussed on the present.

'To tell you the truth, I was just thinking how lucky you are. The three of you. I've had such close friends once. But, unless you make the effort of keeping in touch often, distance can really loosen that very close bond.'

'But you'll be seeing them all shortly, won't you?' Julie said hopefully.

'Yes, it will be lovely! I can hardly wait,' Madeleine replied, knowing that, apart from Natalia, there was little hope of rekindling all those other extinct friendships.

They finished their main courses and ordered some light desserts. Madeleine was persuaded to have a crème brûlée.

'Anyone can manage it, even on a full stomach,' Julie promised. Then, while James and Mark continued to spar on some technical point relating to the men's athletic team, Julie asked suddenly, 'Does Emily's father live in Poland? Does she see him sometimes?' A perfectly natural and polite question. Madeleine's stomach knotted. James stopped talking and in that momentary silence Julie must have realised her unintentional faux pas. 'Gosh, Madeleine! I'm sorry! I shouldn't have asked. It's personal. I know!'

Making a fuss would have made it worse. Madeleine affected an unruffled pose.

'It's all right, Julie. We don't talk about him. For a very good reason. But, as you've asked, no, Emily has no contact with him.'

'None at all?' James asked, and she thought she detected just a smidgen of disapproval.

'No.'

He gave her a long stare as if trying to read her mind.

'Is that fair?' he asked quietly.

No, it wasn't fair. But *he* did not deserve fairness. It wasn't fair to Emily. It wasn't fair what *he* had done to her, Madeleine. It was damn criminal! Her only protection from the nightmare of her past was to write *him* off entirely from her life.

Madeleine licked her lips aware that James was waiting for her to say more. Stick to the version inventively bent for Emily's sake.

'It's complicated,' she said, steadying her voice. 'He's not well. I don't mean physically.' She paused to let the meaning sink in. 'For the time being, Emily is too young to understand and travel on her own to see him.' She noticed James's expression soften as he considered her words.

'I'm so sorry to hear that,' he said as before. 'You've given her a stable life, Madeleine. Things have a way of working out. One day, when she is able to make up her own mind, she'll decide what to do.'

This was not going to happen, but Madeleine was overcome with a deep feeling for James, and gratitude for his words of support. For a second too long she could not take her eyes off him. If only things were different, she knew without hesitation that James would have been her man.

*

Later, after having had said their goodbyes to Mark and Julie with promises to meet up soon, James drove Madeleine home. The street was quiet and dark underneath the swathe of clouds, remnants of the previous downpours; some lights were still on in some houses, but Aniela and Bronek were morning people and would have been in bed by now.

James stopped his car in a space past Bronek's Volvo.

'Pity the evening is over, so soon!' He turned to look at her, and she was aware of an intensity in his voice. 'Madeleine, can we do it again? Next time I'm home? Just you and me. I'd love to spend more time with you.'

Now was the time to tell him. She clasped her hands hard.

'James, I really enjoyed it tonight. And I liked your friends. Very much. And thanks, for including me with them. But' – her mouth was drying up – 'please don't waste your time on me if you want more out of our friendship. I've been through a bad time. I'm not ready for a relationship. I don't want to give you false hopes. I don't want to hurt you.'

James's hands resting on the steering wheel gripped it hard as he looked ahead into the darkness, but when he turned his head to her they relaxed their grip and slid down.

'Madeleine.' There was tenderness and understanding in his tone. 'If it's just a matter of time, then I'm prepared to wait. Give us a chance. I may grow on you yet. What would you say to that?'

God, he was so good. She did not deserve him. Yet his words made her smile.

'James, you've already grown on me, as you put it.' If only he knew how much. 'But I'm not so sure you'd see me the same way if I told you everything about myself. I want to, I really do, but it's too painful to talk about.' And it was, but the pain she feared the most was his rejection once he knew the truth. That seed of doubt in his mind that somehow Madeleine had contributed to her own disaster.

She was aware of him looking at her and she lifted her gaze from the clasped hands on her lap to him. There was a faint scent about him, cologne and clean hair and a hint of the evening dank air trapped in his clothes and she inhaled it all, wanting him to pull her close to him and tell her everything would be all right. But it could never be. Because he could never be told the truth.

'Madeleine.' His tone was kind, but firm. 'I won't press you to tell me anything, but I hope you will one day. Because only that will free you from the past and allow you to move on. You deserve to be happy, and I believe, and please forgive me if I sound presumptuous, I believe I could make you happy, if only you'll allow me.' And before she could respond to that he carried on in a lighter tone. 'You know… when Mrs Demska first mentioned you and mother discussed things with me, about asking you to help Josh, I had this picture of you in my mind, and I'm sorry, it's so shallow, of this Plain Jane who got herself into trouble and couldn't marry the bloke for some reason. But even then, I thought how brave of the Plain Jane to have had the child and bring it up on her own. And then I saw you. That first time. I was astonished. I could not understand why you hadn't been snapped up years ago!'

His words lightened her mood. She laughed despite herself.

'Oh, James, how you exaggerate!' Then she added seriously. 'I've just got too much baggage. It wouldn't be fair to dump it on you.'

'We've all got baggage, Madeleine.'

'And you too, James?'

'What makes you think that anyone is exempt from life's painful knocks?'

She wondered if he was referring to that time all those years ago, when she had seen him so distressed, a total stranger to her then. She wanted to know everything about him, certain that nothing could diminish her fascination with him. But prodding him now would be unwise. Perhaps like her, he too had buried things in his past that he did not wish anyone to uncover.

Undeterred by her long moment of silence, he spoke softly, 'Remember the old adage? Life is for the living. It's a waste otherwise, if you don't make the effort to live your life to the full.'

'With mistakes along the way?'

'That's just being human. No shame in that. You learn from your mistakes.'

She knew all this, except that the most awful, shameful mistake had not been hers, and she had been burdened with it, for life.

'Madeleine.' James's voice rose with renewed energy. 'Please come out with me again, and with Julie and Mark. I know they like you very much. I'd like that very much too.' Even by street light, his eyes appeared to glow with renewed hope.

If only he knew that all evening she had been spellbound by his closeness, she was aware of his every movement, of his every expression, of his scent, of his hands, the way his elegant fingers curled around the wine glass, the sound of his voice, the choice of his words and her fancied hidden meaning in them. She recognised those feelings. This was how it had been falling in love before. She never imagined she could feel like that again. But she had to let it go.

'James… I don't know what else to say… Please have a think about it. You can text me, that's only if you feel inclined. You promised to text me before, and you never did.'

'Is that a reprimand?' The tenseness in his voice was gone, as if he'd won an invisible battle. 'Madeleine, I wanted to text you so many times, but I did not want to appear pushy. I did not want to frighten you off before tonight. But now… I feel as if we know each other that little bit more. I hope so.'

He inclined his head again to look straight into her eyes. 'I've got a brilliant idea. I've got a busy time ahead of me, a few trips abroad. But I'll be back in Leicester for the reception of the Olympic Torch. How about if we make an evening of that? You and Emily, Josh and me?'

His beguiling persuasiveness broke her resolve. How could she refuse? Only this one more time, she told herself. Anyway, it was still a little way off. Anything could happen. Not in her life, but in his, so densely populated with smart London girls.

She nodded, 'All right, James. Just a friendly outing. That will be something nice to look forward to.'

He smiled then, a broad, relaxed smile and even in the semi-darkness she was aware of his suppressed inner delight. She had a sudden strong need to hold him close, to kiss him. But he made no attempt to touch her, not even her hand. And she could have cried with wanting him to do that.

'Thank you for the lovely evening, James,' she said, and with that she got out of the car. He waited, watching her until she opened the door, until she was safe inside. She waved to him as he drove off.

A heaviness settled in her heart. Would there ever come a time when she'd feel confident to trust a man with her past? And not fear his rejection? Would James perceive her, if he ever found out the truth, as she perceived herself, defiled, used, imperfect? If Dominik had deserved the perfect best from her, did not James deserve that too?

# CHAPTER 23

James texted frequently, as promised, and every time her mobile pinged something leapt inside her then dropped with disappointment when the message was from someone else. He had been thrown into a flurry of appointments abroad, in Brussels and Frankfurt, where some of the firm's clients were based. His choice of words never failed to amuse her. He also made it clear how he missed her and looked forward to his next visit home. She thought of that too, with bursts of intense feelings for him, reined in by the constant, nagging anxiety.

She informed him of Josh's steady progress. His return to school looked certain before the end of the month. She was truly glad for Josh, yet already saddened in her mind at the loss of that link that Josh had become between her and James.

Her own days were a whirlwind of dashing around to numerous places across the city, where her interpreting skills were required. Some cases affected her, despite Mr Bunting's regular reminders to remain professionally detached. It was hard to remain unmoved where young children were involved: accidents, serious illnesses, tragic loss of a parent, sometimes both. All these people, her own countrymen, had come to England with dreams of bettering their lives. Her own dilemma diminished to an insignificant niggle in the face of such devastating blows. And yet her niggle was still a worry: if only she could find a magical way of being honest with James and not lose him.

The evenings, the long June evenings, stretching daylight until late, were a welcome slow-down time. She exchanged e-mails with Natalia, ever more ebullient at the prospect of their imminent reunion, while watching Emily and Karishma playing in the back garden from her writing desk. Some evenings, after supper, the three of them would sit around Aniela and watch mesmerised, as her handiwork was being completed before their very eyes.

One evening, after the last bead was sewn on and secured underneath with a treble knot, Aniela cut off the thread, spread the sleeveless black velour jacket across her lap and declared, 'Time to try it on, Emily.'

Dressed fully in her Krakowianka costume, Emily stood stiffly in the middle of the lounge, her face beaming nevertheless. The finishing touch was a crown of flowers with long ribbons cascading down her back over the lacey blouse with puffed out sleeves, the richly embroidered velvet jacket, the flowery skirt with a band of ribbons around the hem and a see-through organdie apron tied in a big bow at the back.

'Give us a twirl,' Bronek said, turning down the sound of his favourite serial, his recently frequent preoccupied expression dissolving in a big, relaxed smile.

Emily obliged self-consciously with a peel of laughter bursting from her. Karishma came right up to her and with one careful finger touched the sequins and the beads on the rich embroidery.

'I wish I could have a dress just like this. Exactly the same!' She turned her huge, black-marble eyes at Madeleine.

'But you have,' Madeleine reminded her. 'Your beautiful blue and green and gold sari. For special occasions.' Indeed, the colours of Karishma's dress could be compared to a kingfisher's feathers.

Karishma did not look convinced.

'Karishma,' Aniela said cheerfully, 'when it's Emily's concert day, we'll ask your mum to dress you in your special sari and we'll take you with us to Emily's concert. Your dress will be as beautiful as any other costumes there. Will you come with us?'

Karishma nodded and a shy smile crept to her lips.

'I wish I had Emily's dress,' she said.

*

They were sitting at the kitchen table with the morning sunshine bursting through the open door.

'Grandpa.' Emily stopped eating her toast and looked carefully at Bronek's wrist and arm. 'Why are you wearing two shirts on top of one another?'

Bronek's brow puckered, as he examined the double layer of cuffs and his fingers checked automatically the two collars around his neck.

'So I am!' he exclaimed in genuine surprise. 'How did that happen?' He proceeded to take off the top shirt, ruffling his hair in the process. He hung the shirt over the back of his chair, smoothed down his hair with his fingers and gave Emily a conspiratorial smile.

'It's a good job you noticed, Emily.' Emily wriggled her shoulders with pleasure at his praise.

Aniela placed his cooked breakfast before him, but remained standing, squinting at him pointedly.

'Bronek, didn't you feel just a little too hot to give you a clue that perhaps you were wearing too many layers?' She spoke gently as if teaching a child.

'No.' He shook his head, puzzled. 'I didn't notice a thing.'

'And,' she remained standing above him, 'have you found your car keys yet?'

He shrugged.

'I cannot think what could have happened to them. One minute I had them, the next minute they were gone.'

'I know!' Emily sounded eager to be helpful. 'Perhaps you're a magician, Grandpa, and you don't even know it. Perhaps you can make things disappear. We just need to know what the secret words are that will bring them back.'

Madeleine was amused but she kept a serious face. Bronek smiled.

'It's a total mystery, Emily.'

'It's no mystery, Bronek.' Aniela's tone conveyed her enduring patience. 'You just have to be systematic and always leave them in the same place!'

'And I keep telling you, Aniela, I would if I could remember!'

Madeleine sensed his frustration and assured him quickly, 'We'll all help you look for them, now eat your breakfast before it gets cold.'

'No need!' Aniela announced like a victor and brought a bunch of keys out of her apron pocket. She placed them on the table before Bronek and sat down. 'Guess where they were?' she asked.

'No idea,' he was bemused.

'In the fridge! Between the ham and the cheese! Just as well I keep them wrapped. I'd hate the thought of some unclean metal touching them directly!'

Bronek slapped his forehead and made Emily laugh.

'Of course! That must have been when I was getting things out on the table for breakfast!'

With this crisis over, talk turned to mundane matters.

Emily licked the jam off her fingers and asked, 'Mama, will you be sad when you don't see Josh anymore?'

'It won't be quite anymore, because we shall still be friends, and I expect he'll want to see you again. And I'll have more time now to fetch you from school every afternoon.'

This prospect lit up Emily's eyes, then she looked at Aniela.

'But I still like Babcha to come with you.'

'We can take turns,' Aniela said, 'but this afternoon I think your mama would like to fetch you.'

'I'll be there, Emily,' Madeleine assured her, finishing her toast and coffee. 'I've only got two appointments, both at the hospital. A man with unexplained injuries, and a lady waiting for an operation. Then my last session with Josh.' She glanced at the clock. 'Time to go, Emily.'

Emily made soft eyes at her.

'Can Karishma come to play?'

'Of course she can,' Aniela answered for Madeleine, 'and I'll make you your favourite dessert.'

'Apple fritters?'

'Hundreds!'

Madeleine hugged Bronek, who had that preoccupied, far-away look about him again.

'Have a good day and stop worrying.'

'I need to check that wall again,' he answered thoughtfully. 'Who knows what's hiding behind it?'

*

Josh opened the door. Without the crutches he was even taller, his long thin limbs moving gracefully, his cheeks dimpling at the sight of her.

'So good to see you looking so well, Josh,' Madeleine said warmly, walking with him towards the study.

'Whatever shall we talk about today?' he joked.

'Isn't there an essay on Jane Austen to check? And some notes on the British Empire?'

He groaned.

Jean's voice called out from the kitchen.

'Just coming!' And before Madeleine and Josh were seated, she breezed in with a tray of three coffees and biscuits. As always, she had that scrubbed, no-nonsense look about her, neat cropped hair, straight navy slacks, a sky-blue shirt. She placed the tray on the tidied end of Josh's desk and said, 'Just so happens I've got a day off today. So glad I could be here on your last day, Madeleine.' She handed them their coffees as they sat down. She sat opposite Madeleine and fixed her with a steady gaze. 'We're indebted to you. If there's anything at any time we could do for you, we'd be very happy to reciprocate.'

Madeleine was pleasantly taken aback by Jean's words.

'That's kind of you to say,' she replied, 'but I only did what I would have done in any other job. It's all thanks to Josh that our combined efforts produced good results.'

Josh raised his shoulders and spread his hands in mock impersonation of a genius who can't help his superior intelligence.

Madeleine smiled at him.

'You must be dying to get back to your friends at school.'

'Just a little,' he grinned. 'Texting is not quite the same.' No, Madeleine thought, yet every text from James made her excited like a teenager.

'What about you, Madeleine?' Jean asked, sitting up straight as she raised her coffee cup to her lips. 'No doubt you'll be getting back to your old routine?'

'I rather think so. My boss is always short of people. Especially at the weekends. Not many people are willing to step in on a Saturday or a Sunday. Emily is good and hardly ever complains, but I have to be careful not to overdo it. Very occasionally she cries and that makes me feel awful.'

Jean nodded and looked at Josh.

'I remember those days, even now. James had just started university and Josh was in the infants.' She paused, as if to think for a second before saying, 'That was the time when I could have really done with another pair of hands.'

'My grandparents help a lot,' Madeleine said. 'They are like parents to both Emily and me.' She wondered what Jean was thinking. Was she worried about James's possible involvement with her? Taking on the responsibility of someone else's child? Madeleine would have gladly reassured Jean that she had nothing to fear. She had no designs on James. Only deep-hidden yearnings that could never be fulfilled.

'I'll leave you to get on with your work,' Jean said, getting up. 'And I must make the most of my day at home. I'll see you, Madeleine, before you leave.'

'Of course.'

When Jean was gone, Madeleine tidied up the tray and placed it aside, away from Josh's desk. She sat next to him as he was opening his first file.

'Right, let's have a look at the amendments to your essay,' she said, studying his face discreetly, looking for a likeness to James. They were not in the least alike, except for the fact of both being very tall and slim, but just being so close to him made her feel closer to his brother.

They spent nearly an hour going through the twenty printed pages, editing or expanding on points where necessary. Madeleine could see that Josh was beginning to tire. Even with the window open wide, his forehead was damp, his hair sticking to it.

'Shall I make you a drink?' she offered.

'Thanks. I'm OK.' He unscrewed the top of the small water bottle, 'But you go and make yourself one.'

She fetched a glass of water and sat down beside him. Jean must have been doing her own things in another part of the house, for there were no audible signs of her presence.

'No rush. When you're ready,' Madeleine said to Josh.

'I get little reminders now and again, that I mustn't run before I can walk,' he explained, taking a few gulps from the bottle. 'Give me a minute or two, and I'll be fine!'

She sipped her water in silence, thinking how pleasant it was to work for people who appreciated her efforts.

'Magda,' Josh said after a while, 'you never told me the end of Marie Walewska's story. If you don't tell it me now, I shall be forever left wondering what happened to her.'

Madeleine smiled.

'All you need to do is google her name.'

He rolled his eyes, then grinned.

'It's never quite the same. Go on, indulge me, while I brace myself for the next hour's marathon.'

'Does it really feel that bad?'

'Sometimes.' That beguiling smile again. 'But never when I'm working with you.'

'Thank you.' It sounded formal but his compliment, whether genuine or just a nicety, gave her a good feeling. She wondered if he spoke of her in those terms to James. She nodded. 'All right, I'll tell you the rest of Marie's story, but it's not a happy ending.'

'I'm intrigued all the more,' Josh said.

Madeleine gathered her thoughts.

'Marie remained faithful to Napoleon, though God knows why. While always stuck in the background she endured the humiliation of his marriage to Marie Therese, then the birth of their son, then the rumours of other women arranged for him during his battle trails. He'd come back to Paris always expecting her to be there for him, just like the ever-faithful Penelope.' Madeleine's expression was clear what she thought of that. 'There must be some psychological explanation for this misplaced loyalty on her part, but it totally escapes me.'

'Perhaps,' Josh hazarded, 'in her mind she was the only one and true wife to him? And nothing else mattered?'

Josh surprised Madeleine with his mature insight.

'I suppose,' she conceded, 'in any adverse situation one should stay focussed on the positive aspects, even if only for self-preservation.'

Perhaps that was what she should have done: focussed in her thoughts on the life with Zden before that awful event, when he had been her kind and devoted uncle. It had been a good life and she had much to be thankful for. But he wiped it all out with just one unspeakable deed. She did not have Marie's forgiving nature.

'Anyway,' Madeleine continued, 'all through his disastrous defeats that eventually brought his downfall, she visited him in Paris when his own generals had abandoned him. She visited him in his exile on the island of Elba, bringing to him their little son, and that in great secrecy from his royal wife, Marie Therese. Marie continued to live in Paris and only after Napoleon had been exiled to the remote island of St Helena, and all contact with him had become impossible, and there was no chance of ever seeing him again, was she freed from his influence.'

There were no such inaccessible islands any more. Zden would always remain within easy reach if he chose to contact her. But he had not. Perhaps he never would. Perhaps, like Marie, she should turn her thoughts away from the past and look to the future.

'What did Marie do after that?' Josh asked.

'She continued to live in Paris. Men found her very attractive. Two men fought a duel over her. One was wounded and Marie felt obliged to look after him in his recovery. He was Count d'Ornano. He asked her to marry him, she accepted and it looked as if she had found her true love. She gave birth to their son a year later. Another little boy with Rudolph for his second name. All her three boys had been given that name, all three from different fathers. This has always been a puzzle for the historians.'

'Have you got a theory about that, Magda?' Josh raised his eyebrows quizzically.

'Not a theory. Just a thought,' Madeleine took a sip of water. 'I can only guess that Marie never got over her first love. Despite being forced to do all the things that were against her will, she had stayed true in her heart to the man she loved. Giving all her three sons his name was an expression of defiance against her oppressors. It must have given her great satisfaction that she had outwitted them all, and had had the last laugh, after all. And a scrap of independence, if only symbolic.'

'Good for her!' Josh stated with his usual exuberance. 'What happened to her in the end?'

'Something very sad. But not uncommon in those days. There were complications after her childbirth and she died. She was only twenty-eight.'

'That's younger than James!' Josh cried. 'And that would only give me another eleven years! And I don't feel as if I've started living yet!'

Madeleine gave him an amused smile.

'Don't worry, Josh, everything is still before you!'

'Like those notes on the British Empire,' Josh said with a clownish frown.

'Come on, Josh, the sooner we get down to it, the sooner it will get done.'

They worked together cross-checking Josh's research notes on the places, the dates and the pivotal figures who shaped the Empire's power and destiny. When they turned over the last page of Josh's densely written manuscript, Madeleine remarked, 'You've done a truly thorough job. Well done!'

Josh smiled wryly, 'Now it's just a small matter of writing the essay.'

'You'll do it, Josh. Perfectly!'

She looked at her watch and he said, 'I know you've got to go soon. But don't stop visiting us, Magda. It would feel really strange if you weren't around anymore. You won't mind if I text you sometimes?'

She wanted to hug him.

'Of course, you can text me any time you wish, Josh. I'll want to know how you get on at school.'

'And we've got that date together with James and Emily.' His cheeks dimpled.

'Has James twisted your arm?' Madeleine laughed. 'Please, Josh, don't feel obliged.'

'I wouldn't miss it for anything. I think it will be a very exciting evening.' His eyes shone with a hint of a double meaning. Or did she just imagine it?

In the hallway, he called out to his mother and the sound of Jean's busy steps preceded her appearance.

'Thank you, Madeleine, thank you for everything you have done.' Her manner of speech, as always, was clipped and precise, but there was warmth in her voice. 'James has left you an envelope.'

'I feel embarrassed taking it,' Madeleine spoke honestly. 'Working with Josh did not feel like work at all.'

'You deserve every penny.' Jean spoke emphatically. 'And don't forget us.'

'As if I could!' Madeleine smiled, thinking at the same time that she would have to let go of this acquaintance gently, for James's sake. She felt like a hypocrite, but this was for their good.

When she got to Emily's school, she opened James's envelope before getting out of the car. The cheque, as before, was far more generous than her expectations. He had slipped in a note with it.

*Madeleine, how can I thank you enough? Please let me do it my way. I'm looking forward to seeing you soon. James.*

# CHAPTER 24

The evening of the arrival of the Olympic torch in Leicester was only days away. Madeleine wished she had the power to stop time long enough to resolve her problem. She knew that the only way out of the tangle of her anxieties was to be totally honest with James, but then her imagined hurt in his face and his rejection of her filled her with such a sick feeling, she could not bear to even think about it. The constant indecision niggled like a toothache that would not go away.

One evening, after Emily had been tucked up in bed for the night, and Bronek was watching his favourite crime serial (amazingly, despite his distractedness, he always managed to guess who the culprit was from the beginning), Madeleine came into the kitchen, where Aniela was tidying up all her baking utensils, with the newly baked apple and honey cakes cooling on the wire racks.

'Babcha.' Madeleine slumped down on the chair. 'I'm exhausted from thinking so much.'

Aniela put away the last of the spoons and the spatulas, hung the towel over the radiator and sat down beside her.

'I know what you're going to say, Magda. Stop tormenting yourself. Just tell him. Tell James the truth.'

Since meeting James, Aniela made no secret of her opinion of him. She thought him eye-catchingly handsome, charming and polite, but most of all she admired his background: good family, good education and a good profession.

'Just think, Magda.' She would look up dreamily from the washing-up. 'How your life would change, if James married you.'

Magda laughed it off.

'Babcha, it's not going to happen.'

'And why not?' Aniela had a challenging way despite her small stature.

'Because it's simply not possible.'

And this evening she repeated her reservations, slowly, rationally, to which Aniela listened with the odd nod, her rigid back and folded arms implying a difference of opinion.

'Magda, all this is irrelevant,' she said. 'If he truly loves you, nothing will put him off.'

'I fear it will. And once things are said openly, they cannot be unsaid. From then on I'll be known as the girl who got raped.'

Aniela shook her head.

'I cannot imagine James being indiscreet. His very profession depends on him being trustworthy. Magda, believe me, in life, sometimes the things you fear the most never happen.'

Madeleine hugged herself and rocked.

'I wish there was an easy way of telling him. He's asked me to see him again. He suggested meeting in town, together with Emily and Josh, to welcome the Olympic Torch. I'd be a spoilsport if I refused to go.'

Aniela's eyes lit up.

'Sounds like a family outing. Oh, Magda, don't you see? He's prepared to put up with gooseberries as long as he can spend time with you.'

Madeleine smiled at Aniela's interpretation of James's arrangement.

'Maybe,' she conceded, 'but the longer I keep on seeing him, the more hope he'll have of our relationship developing further. I can't describe how bad that makes me feel.' No, not even Aniela, her lovely and dear Babcha, could imagine the nightmares that Madeleine was still reliving after all the years.

'Magda.' Aniela spoke with renewed energy. 'You must give James a chance. What's the worst that can happen? Him stopping seeing you? You'll recover. Two months ago you didn't even know of his existence.' (She did; that memory of a distressed young man had never faded away.) 'And if he were to reject you, then would you really want a man who judged you for someone else's crime?'

Aniela made it sound so simple. Magda gave a deep sigh. Aniela patted her hand.

'Trust fate, Magda. There will come the right moment when you tell him everything.'

*

The evening before the awaited event, James rang Madeleine. Just hearing his voice, manly and strong with purpose, released a myriad of sensations within her.

'Madeleine, about tomorrow night.' He came straight to the point. 'I'll pick you up and Emily. I think that will be better than looking for each other in town. I expect there will be crowds.'

'I hadn't thought about that.' She hadn't, too busy thinking about resolving her dilemma. 'A good idea, James. Thank you. Emily's very excited.'

'And you?' A teasing note.

'Who wouldn't be?' she replied politely. 'It's a unique occasion. I'm very much looking forward to it.' And aching with longing.

'It will be an evening to remember,' he promised. 'And otherwise, how are things? Did you have a good day?'

She told him briefly about visiting a school where she was the interpreter for the head, the social worker and a little Polish girl with suspected abuse bruises on her body. She heard James sigh.

'That's so grim,' he said. 'Here we are immersed in our own affairs with no idea about the lives of others. All those individual little worlds rolling alongside ours, so many never discovered.'

Like mine forever hidden for the shame of it, she reflected before asking him, 'And you, James? Busy day?'

'Run of the mill. Office work with my assistant. Reams of spreadsheets. Cross-checking expenditures and profits. Just a tad stressful when your clients are worth millions.'

'Dizzy-eyed then, with all that concentration?'

'Just a bit.'

They talked for a while about nothing much, Madeleine sensing his reluctance to ring off. And the moment he did, it felt like a momentary sense of loss.

*

James knocked on Madeleine's door punctually, as prearranged. She waved to Josh, who was sitting in the front seat, before showing James inside. Aniela and Bronek greeted him with smiles and handshakes, and he in turn asked if they would like to come into town too. Making two short journeys was no problem at all, he assured them. No wonder Aniela was smitten with him. She declined graciously blaming her back.

'It can rebel quite suddenly when I'm standing around for too long. Besides, at my height, the best view I'd get is of other people's backs.'

And Bronek explained his problem. 'Crowds give me claustrophobia. But thanks for the offer. I'll be watching all that on our news tonight. From the comfort of my armchair.' A happy grin creased his face.

James bent down to Emily. She was leaning shyly against Madeleine's thigh and clutching Rabbit to her chest.

'Shall we go?' he asked, offering his hand. Emily placed hers in his naturally and went with him. Madeleine's chest expanded with joy. She picked up the child-safety seat in the hall and followed them outside. Emily's shyness dissolved in a fit of giggles on discovering Josh waiting in the passenger seat. All the way into town he kept her amused with stories of his friend Matt's dog and his antics. James did not seem to mind at all, just smiled every time he caught Madeleine's gaze in the mirror.

He parked his Jaguar close to the centre and together they walked towards the Clock Tower. Crowds were already lining the streets, three people deep. A clear central passage had been created with metal barriers, so that the procession could pass through without obstacles. Already colourful bands, singers, dancers, street performers, acrobats and gymnasts were forming a non-ending chain of entertainment, inviting deafening cheers from the crowds. The carnival atmosphere made the waiting a pleasant pastime.

Madeleine and Emily, James and Josh managed to secure a spot close to the barrier, and every time the crowd's cheering shot up a hundred decibels James picked up Emily to point out the happy recipients of so much ovation. Madeleine was charmed with the natural ease with which James handled Emily and was much relieved with Emily's willing co-operation. The surrounding noise was making it impossible to hold any conversation for longer than a few moments. Madeleine gave in to the joyful spirit of this occasion and banished all nagging thoughts from her mind.

Suddenly there was an upsurge of cheering. The approaching flame was spotted in the distance. Madeleine leaned forward over the barrier craning her neck.

'They're coming! Emily, they're coming!' she shouted with uncontrolled delight.

'I can see it!' Emily shouted back from the height of James's shoulders, her legs dangling down his chest. He looked as excited as a small boy, and Josh next to him was cheering with all his might, waving his arm vigorously.

It was over in a flash. The girl running with the flame whizzed past them with a group of athletes close on her heels. If you blinked, you would have missed the torch. After all the cheering, there was an audible collective sigh of satisfaction. People began to disperse.

James lifted Emily off his shoulders and placed her down on the pavement. She leaned against his thigh, seeking to hold his hand. He took it and stooped down to her level.

'Now, how about something to eat?' He spoke as if addressing an adult. 'I'm sure all that cheering has made you hungry, Emily. I am ravenous! I could eat a horse!' This made her laugh and display her little white teeth with the new gap.

Madeleine was overcome with tenderness for him. A suspicious person would have interpreted his gentle handling of Emily as a devious way into Madeleine's heart, but in the short time she got to know him he had convinced her of his transparent honesty. He was what one saw: straight and to the point. And with a talent for dealing with young children.

As they started moving, keeping close together, she couldn't help remarking, half-jokingly, 'Where did you learn your childcaring skills?'

'I was the guinea pig,' Josh quipped.

'And you've survived,' James pointed out. Madeleine laughed.

'Rather well,' she said, and holding Emily by her other hand she added, 'Wouldn't it be nice to have a big brother looking after you, Emily?'

'But we already have, Mama. We have James and Josh,' Emily explained with her clear logic. James caught Madeleine's eye and grinned.

Making their way between the milling groups of people, they walked to an Italian restaurant in a street off the city centre. They were seated by the window, giving Emily a fascinating view of the great numbers of pedestrians passing by. James ordered the drinks while they decided about the toppings on their pizzas. Madeleine asked for just one to share with Emily.

'With mushrooms and ham?' Emily reminded her.

As they tucked into their chosen toppings on the flat crispy dough, small talk flowed easily. Josh was happy to be back at school with his friends, the end-of-the-year exams were over and the holiday break was only a fortnight away.

'And are you fully recovered, Josh?' Madeleine asked.

'I have moments,' he replied with his cheerful smile. 'But that's good and sobering. Reminds me to be sensible. And take it easy. Which I will soon, hanging out with my friends in the holidays.'

'Not going away, then?'

'We'll have to go to Cornwall at some point,' James joined in, 'to check everything's OK with the house. Though we've got our good neighbour, George, to keep an eye on things.'

'And can you really leave your work behind?' Madeleine asked with a tease of a smile. 'I mean, really forget about it while you're out there, James?'

'No,' Josh said curtly, nevertheless giving James a challenging grin.

James nailed his brother with a withering look.

'I do leave my work behind, Josh. Or is your mind going prematurely senile? What about all our cycling holidays? Have you forgotten?'

'I haven't forgotten your evening sessions with your laptop.'

'But that's only in the evening. As you well know, there's always something urgent waiting.'

'Like what?' Madeleine asked, attending to cutting Emily's pizza section into smaller pieces.

James chewed his thoughtfully before replying.

'Our company services a number of mega big corporations. The run-of-the-mill stuff is done in the office, but when big meetings are called, that is always extremely urgent.' He emphasised 'extremely' with a grave expression, then laughed. 'Not really. Not life-threatening extremely, but no one has the patience to wait these days. And time costs money. So, it's skates on and dash off to be there on time together with the lawyers when big contracts are signed.'

'Wow!' Madeleine said.

'You're mocking me.' James made a clownish face.

'Not at all!' Madeleine was serious. 'I'm impressed with what you do. I can't imagine handling numbers all day, every day. Don't you get dizzy with it all? And bored?'

James put down his knife and fork and laughed. As if she had said something truly amusing. Emily stopped eating and looked at him wide-eyed.

'Madeleine.' He spoke in a tone reserved for explaining simple facts. 'But mathematics is the most reliable science, don't you agree? I love numbers. I trust numbers. There's sheer poetry in their patterns. If you follow their formulas, numbers will never let you down.'

'Wow!' Madeleine said again and this time she smiled. But then she added in earnest, 'Seriously, I think, James, that you should be employed to teach maths at school. I wish my maths teacher was like you and not the dragon I had, who made me quake every time I got the answer wrong!'

'You're taking the p...' He stopped, correcting himself. 'You're making fun of me, Madeleine. That is so below the belt!'

She laughed and shook her head. If only he knew how aware she was of him, of his every movement, every facial expression, the sound of his voice, his scent, every detail about him was being picked up by her senses. To anyone observing them they would have looked like a family enjoying a night out. Josh was tirelessly attentive to Emily, entertaining her with photos of amusing cats and dogs on his Twitter feed. For that alone, she loved him.

How could she ever find the right moment to tell James about herself? Already she pictured this lovely scene before her, shattering into pieces that could never be put together again. Anxiety returned to the pit of her stomach. She took a generous gulp of her cool drink and pushed all bad thoughts away.

At the end of the meal Josh got up and bade them goodnight.

'I'm meeting up with Matt in the High Cross,' he said. 'Enjoy the rest of the evening. See you soon, Magda. And Emily.' He shook her small hand ceremoniously, which made her giggle.

When he was gone, she returned to cuddling Rabbit, a sleepy look descending down her face.

'We'll get you home to bed in no time at all, Emily,' James promised, and when they got up to go he picked her up and she rested limply against his shoulder.

'James, there's really no need to do this,' Madeleine said gently. 'You'll find Emily weighs more than she looks.'

He gave her a smug smile.

'Are you doubting my strength?'

In the car park, Madeleine settled and strapped Emily in her seat, before joining James at the front. As they drove out of the car park, she said, 'James, it's been a truly lovely evening. Thank you for everything.'

He shot her a sideways glance with a smile.

'We can have many more, Madeleine. Just say when.'

Her stomach tightened. He truly deserved someone better than her.

'I'd hate to impose on your time. So busy, by all accounts.'

He chuckled.

'You must know, Madeleine, that that's not an issue.'

She did not know what to say. She asked, 'Tell me about tomorrow. About the week ahead of you.'

'I'm staying at home tonight, but it's an early start tomorrow. I've got to catch a train to Brussels at midday.' He looked at her. 'You know, Madeleine, it's so easy these days to go to Paris on the Eurostar. If you ever…' He did not finish but looked boyishly happy, as if in anticipation, the light of the street lamps playing on his features, his car gliding smoothly down the one-way lane.

'It's a lovely idea, James.' Madeleine looked over her shoulder, checking on Emily, playing for time. Emily was fast asleep, her head drooping to one side. Madeleine felt utterly miserable having to say what she did. 'James, I'd love to. I'd really love to. But I can't. Please take it from me. It's for your own good.'

He gave her another sideway glance and a challenging smile.

'You may change your mind. And I'm a patient man. I don't give up easily.'

Close to the city hospital, James slowed down to allow an ambulance to overtake.

'Another emergency. Another poor soul,' he remarked. 'My mother's off duty tonight, but that department never sleeps.'

Dusk was falling when they arrived at Madeleine's front door. There was the glow of subdued lighting along the curtains' edges, indicating that Aniela and Bronek were watching television in the front room.

'Will you come in?' Madeleine asked.

'Only to help you carry Emily upstairs,' he replied practically. 'But, before we do that, I've got something to show you.'

'For me?' Intrigued, she watched him bring out an envelope from his breast pocket.

'Please open it,' he said.

All her anxiety melted away for the moment. She looked inside the envelope and pulled out two tickets. Her eyes scanned the print, but her mind could not absorb the meaning at first. Then her heart did a somersault.

'I can't believe this!' she suppressed a squeal in her voice. 'Women's gymnastics! In London! At the North Greenwich Arena! Live! James, how did you know? How did you know it's my favourite sport?'

James's face was transformed with pleasure at surprising her this way.

'Madeleine, you told me yourself. At the barbecue. Remember?'

'And you remembered!' She shook her head, incredulous. 'I don't know what to say! It's such a shock! The best surprise I've had for a long time!'

He did not hide his joy.

'Then you'll come?'

Her common sense told her to stop it all now, but how could she? After he had gone to all that trouble for her? Just one more time, she told herself, then she would tell him. He'd distance himself after that, anyway.

'James, I'm overwhelmed. Thank you, thank you so much! You've no idea... and please, keep the tickets safe.' She returned them to him and as she did so, he clasped her hand and pressed it to his lips. A shower of hot drops ran the length of her body. She could hardly breathe.

He let go of her hand, saying, 'You've made me so happy!'

'And you me,' she said, unable to push back a prod of anxiety.

James helped Madeleine unstrap Emily from her seat, then, resting the sleeping child against his shoulder, he followed Madeleine indoors. Aniela called out from the front room.

'It's all right, Babcha!' Madeleine assured her in a hushed voice. I'll be back in a sec. Just taking Emily to bed.'

She led James up the stairs to her room, where he placed Emily on the bed. She did not stir.

He turned to Madeleine. 'Right, I'd better go,' he whispered, lingering on uncertainly. She had the urge to throw her arms around him and feel the length of his body against hers. And then he surprised her. Yet again. His hands, his strong warm hands, were suddenly cupping her face and his lips touched hers. It was electrifying. Over in a flash. Leaving her breathless, as he was saying, 'I must go...'

She followed him on shaky legs down the stairs and waved him off, almost tripping on Aniela, who had suddenly materialised in the hall behind her.

'And?' Aniela's wide-eyed look could not have been more explicit.

'Oh, Babcha!' Madeleine sighed, grappling with all her emotions, 'I haven't said anything to him yet. Not about that! I couldn't. He's invited me to go with him to London. To the women's gymnastics! He's already bought the tickets! What could I say? How could I refuse?'

Aniela rubbed her hands with theatrical glee.

'Oh, Magda! What a wonderful chance! Don't fret. Just go!'

# CHAPTER 25

On the day of the start of the Olympics, Madeleine hoped to finish work early, so she and Emily and Aniela and Bronek could spend the evening watching the opening ceremony. The press had been whipping up the public's interest with promises of a spectacular show. With Danny Boyle as the mastermind behind the scenes, expectations were high and the waiting feverish.

But, more than the expected pleasure of watching the opening event, it was the thought of the following day that had kept Madeleine awake late each night with thoughts of her train journey to St Pancras, of James awaiting her, of them travelling on together to the Olympic Village. And then the gymnastics! Live! She could already see it and feel it all in her mind, the gymnasts' breathtaking routines in their determined spirit to win.

She could have been one of them, when still a young teenager, if her uncle had had his way. But Aunt Emilia had considered her physical well-being far more important than the uncertain possibility of her fame in sport. She had allowed Madeleine to continue but only for as long as the weekly gymnastics sessions remained a source of pleasure. Madeleine had stopped of her own accord when more time became necessary to concentrate on her academic subjects, prior to securing a university place. Madeleine had no regrets, only a lasting fascination for the sport.

At lunchtime, which was a coffee and a sandwich at a cafe close to the Town Hall, she was reading through her notes for the afternoon session with a Polish family preparing to move to a council house, when her mobile rang. It was Aniela.

Since the end of the school year the previous week, with obligatory sports days and concerts in both Emily's schools, Emily was at home doted on abundantly by Aniela and Bronek. Every night after supper Emily gave a performance of the Krakowiak dance, fully kitted out in her colourful costume. Madeleine worried about the overuse of Aniela's beautiful handiwork, but Aniela had laughed it off.

'I've made it for Emily. It's my great pleasure that it's making her so happy. She won't be dancing like that when she is twelve. Let her enjoy it for as long as she can.'

Karishma had also drawn attention at Emily's Polish School concert. They had taken her with them, as promised, and in her iridescent gold and green and blue sari she looked like a little princess. Every night Emily flicked through the photos of that day on Madeleine's tablet and pointed out the boys and the girls she knew.

Presently, Aniela spoke on Madeleine's mobile.

'Magda, nothing to worry about, but just to let you know that Emily's not that well. It's her tonsils again. I've given her Calpol, she's asleep on the settee, there's no need for you to rush home. It's just so that you know.'

This had been a recurring problem through the winter months. The doctor had advised that, if Emily could withstand these attacks for another year or so, there would be no need for the removal of her tonsils, which could prove beneficial for her in the long run.

Madeleine's spirits sank. She felt Emily's pain instantly, just as another thought rushed through her mind. Tomorrow. What about tomorrow? Everything was already arranged so she could spend a day in London with James. She felt crushing defeat. Fate had decided for her.

'Babcha,' she said without hesitation, 'I'll come home as soon as my boss finds a replacement for my appointment this afternoon.'

\*

She found Emily asleep on the settee covered with a soft blanket, and Rabbit tucked tightly underneath her chin. She was flushed, her skin dry-hot and her eyelids flickering in a fitful dream.

'Thank you, Babcha.' She gave Aniela a hug. 'Feel free to do your own things. I'll sit with Emily now.'

Aniela hovered over her uncertainly, her expression worried, her hands wrung across her stomach.

'Of all the times!' She gave a deep sigh. 'It had to be this weekend!'

'No time is ever good for this,' Madeleine said, stroking Emily's hand.

'And what about tomorrow?' Aniela's voice was heavy with disappointment.

Madeleine's eyes filled up.

'It wasn't meant to be. I can't go. I'll ring James.'

Aniela placed her restraining hand on Madeleine's shoulder.

'Don't do anything yet. You know how small children are. Dying one minute and bouncing the next. Emily could recover yet by the evening. You could still go. And you wouldn't be leaving her on her own. We'll be here.' She gave Madeleine an encouraging nod.

But Madeleine shook her head.

'I know, Babcha, and I'm really grateful. But my conscience wouldn't give me any peace. I'd be thinking about Emily all day. And it wouldn't be fair on you. No, I'll ring James. It may give him time yet to find somebody else in my place.' It hurt saying these words.

But first, Madeleine made a compress with a face cloth soaked in cold water and placed it over Emily's forehead. Emily stirred, gave a puppy cry and fell back into a feverish sleep. While Aniela returned to her housework chores, Madeleine waited until Emily looked settled before she braced herself to ring James. Her stomach churned when she dialled his number. She heard clicks before his answer machine came on. It was such a relief not to have to speak to him directly. She spoke fast.

'James, it's about tomorrow. Emily's gone down with tonsillitis. I can't leave her. I can't tell you how sorry I am. I could cry.'

It was true. She felt inconsolable.

He rang back ten minutes later.

'Sorry, Madeleine, I was out of the office for a few minutes. Please don't worry about tomorrow. It is what it is. Things happen all the time. We must look to plan B. On the scale of probabilities, our fulfilled plans still win over our failed ones.'

Madeleine could not believe his words. He was so calm, so philosophical!

'So, you're not cross?'

'How could I be cross about something that is entirely out of your control?'

'Are you very disappointed?'

'Only for your sake, Madeleine. I wanted you to enjoy a special day. But there will be others.'

'But nothing like this, again.'

'Who knows?' He kept up this optimism and she worried about the tickets.

'You've spent a fortune on the tickets,' she said.

'Nothing to fret about. I've got colleagues who'll snap them up.'

Her heart was a tangle of emotions: disappointment and sadness at their failed plan but stronger than that was her deepening love for him. His kindness melted away all her pretence of putting on a brave face. She cried. She heard his concerned voice.

225

'Madeleine, are you all right?'

She swallowed hard and steadied her voice.

'You're very understanding, James. Thank you.'

There was a pause before he spoke with renewed energy.

'Madeleine, I'll come home to Leicester tomorrow. Will it be convenient to visit you? I wouldn't wish to cause any disruption to your grandparents' day.'

Her brain needed a moment to understand his words, then her heart leapt. If only he knew of Aniela's secret love for him!

'James, they'll be delighted!'

He rang off and she cried again. With heart-swelling relief and happiness. His solution was so simple!

Emily woke up and moaned in pain. It was time for another dose of Calpol. To Madeleine's relief she did not resist swallowing the syrup and before long, as Madeleine nursed her cuddled up on her lap, Emily fell asleep, her breathing audible in her swollen throat. Holding her close, feeling her softness, inhaling her baby-soap smell gave Madeleine great comfort. She could not imagine loving another child as much. How did mothers manage to spread their love equally between several children?

She settled Emily against a soft, large pillow, covered her up and tucked Rabbit against her chest. She then tiptoed into the kitchen to tell Aniela of James's proposed visit the next day. Aniela was preparing vegetables for a stew and Bronek, who had been out earlier, was sitting at the table reading *The Telegraph*, folded back several times to diminish its size for easier handling. He looked up as Madeleine sat down beside him.

'Poor little mite,' he commented about Emily. 'Why do children have to suffer so much before they grow up?'

'Nothing in this life is easy.' Aniela quoted her own often-repeated saying as she peeled the potatoes. 'You wouldn't have survived Stalin's paradise, Bronek, if your childhood illnesses hadn't toughened you up.'

'God forbid that Emily should ever be tested like that!' He rolled his eyes. He said to Madeleine, 'And what a pity about tomorrow!'

'That's just it, Grandpa. Not everything is ruined.' She looked at Aniela. 'I spoke to James. He was so understanding about everything. He said he'd come over tomorrow, that is, if you don't mind. We can watch it all on television instead.'

Aniela's cheeks went pink and her curls bounced about her face as she left her vegetables, leaned over Bronek and hugged him around his shoulders. He looked up surprised then looked confused when Aniela said to him, 'We won't be gooseberries, will we?'

'What gooseberries?'

Aniela sat down beside him with barely concealed excitement shining in her eyes.

'Bronek, we shall go out tomorrow afternoon.'

'Why? And where do we have to go?'

She gave a long sigh, heavy with tried patience, 'Bronek, I'll ring Alina Barska and suggest to them a picnic in Abbey Park. Then we can go somewhere nice for tea and cake. And that, my dear Magda' – she turned to her, her voice almost squealing – 'will give you time with James all afternoon.'

Her childlike joy at this idea of hers touched Magda unexpectedly and deepened her affection for Aniela and Bronek. God, she owed them so much and her debt to them increased by the day. When would she be able to repay them?

'Babcha, there is really no need to do any of that,' she said with feeling. 'Stay at home and talk to James. We can watch the gymnastics together.'

Aniela shook her head and smiled with a knowing look but then Bronek surprised them both.

'I've got a better idea! We'll wait for James to arrive. It would be impolite to disappear before he comes. We'll say hello and chat for a few minutes, then Aniela and I will go to the allotment.' He turned to her. 'Another brick has become loose. But don't despair. I've got everything prepared to mend it.'

'Oh, Bronek!' Aniela stood up and went back to her vegetables while talking over her shoulder. 'Get someone to help you pull it down! No amount of ivy will hold it together if the whole lot decides to come down. Someone could get hurt, or even worse…' The unthinkable was too horrific to put into words.

'Aniela, you're exaggerating! It's just a small job and it will take me five minutes. Come with me and be my boss!' He winked mischievously at Madeleine. 'The fresh air will do you good. Bring your magazines and your knitting with you. I like to have company.'

Aniela did not argue. There were moments, Madeleine knew, when one forgot the importance of that wall to Bronek. Behind its screen he felt safe on his allotment, hidden from the prying stares of his imagined spies.

'You don't have to go,' Madeleine said, 'not because of James.'

'I need to,' Bronek said.

'The sooner the better,' Aniela agreed.

Madeleine got up and went to check Emily. Her cheeks were flushed and she was hot, but her breathing sounded less laboured in her sleep. Madeleine looked for the slightest sign of improvement, but she knew from experience that full recovery could not be hurried before running its full course. Their trip to Poland was a fortnight away. That gave Emily time to be well enough to travel and, in the scheme of things, that was more important than Madeleine's trip to London, she told herself to lighten her disappointment.

*

It felt surreal, sitting opposite James in the front room of her grandparents' house. The bright sunlight was partly screened by the half-drawn curtain. Every time Madeleine's eyes were drawn to James, he was there, real and smiling, not just a remnant from her night-time dream.

It looked like an ordinary domestic scene, replicated in hundreds of houses, a family sitting together to watch the Olympics on television. For the moment Emily was asleep on the settee between them, the Calpol medication doing its job in reducing her temperature, making her more comfortable and settled after a restless night. The pain, any pain, and the temperature always seemed worse during the night hours.

Madeleine was finding it hard to concentrate exclusively on the women's gymnastics, though the floor routines were being performed with breathtaking skills. Her eyes were automatically checking Emily every few minutes, taking in her flushed cheeks. She listened for a change in Emily's breathing forced through her swollen throat. For her own relief, she stroked gently her daughter's small hand.

Aniela and Bronek were out. They had stopped, as planned, only long enough to see James arrive, and were surprised and charmed by his gifts of luxury chocolates and biscuits. He looked embarrassed by their thanks and shrugged good-naturedly.

'I heard that that you run a tea-house for all and sundry. Something for your pantry.'

'Who told you that?' Aniela challenged with unconcealed pleasure.

'That would be telling,' he teased. She liked that too.

This was the man, Madeleine smiled to herself, whom she had considered once too serious and too preoccupied with practicalities.

And now she was very much aware of his presence, as she was watching the performing gymnasts on television. It was as if she had developed a sixth sense that could pick up his every move, his every expression, even anticipate his comments before he made them.

'She's amazing!' James said, his eyes focussed on Gabby Douglas's floor routine. Indeed, the American girl's jumps and splits and back-bends and triple rolls in the air transformed her into a gravity-defying bird.

'I could do that once!' Madeleine exclaimed, letting go of her reserve in her excitement. 'And that! And that!' Then, catching James's gaze, she felt self-conscious. 'Sorry to brag like that! I almost envy her! It's like being on the floor with her and going through all those fantastic paces!'

James looked pleased.

'Brag some more, Madeleine. I want to hear all about it! I can't imagine the effort required to reach this level!'

She nodded.

'Total dedication. At the expense of other things in your life. Not many people can do it. My uncle in Poland' – surprisingly the word 'uncle' did not stick in her throat – 'he was a sports coach. He was very keen for me to go into gymnastics seriously. I also did a lot of swimming. Not competitively. Just for the exercise. But when I fell off the bar and made a mess of my face, my Aunt Emilia put a stop to it. She was not against sport, of course, only against excessive sport that could affect my growth. Luckily for me no bones were broken, only my face looked like an abstract painting in all shades of black and blue for about a fortnight.'

James gave her another searching glance and shook his head.

'I can't imagine that. Was your uncle disappointed when you gave up gymnastics?'

'I think he was. I think he saw in me a budding Olympian. Only his imagination.' Madeleine laughed it off. 'Most young girls dream of being famous. That ambition passed, thank goodness, once I was forced to apply myself seriously to my academic studies. I still swam and I enjoyed doing floor exercises, but in moderation.'

James looked her over thoughtfully and it was a pleasant sensation being the centre of his attention.

'Do you have the time now to do any sport at all?' he asked, his fingers, with their clean, square fingernails playing with the stem of his glass. It reflected the sunlight momentarily. Madeleine had prepared a fruity, alcohol-free punch and a plate of nibbles. He had not touched any yet, just sipped his drink, as if for something to do. She answered his question.

'My sport these days is to take Emily swimming, or to go for a bike ride with her on the Aylestone Meadows.'

He smiled.

'Join the club. Josh and I cycle whenever we can find free time together. Fancy coming with us?'

'With pleasure.' This came spontaneously. Too late to retract it. He gave her a long and considered look but just then there was an eruption of applause for Beth Tweddle, the British girl.

'Wonderful!' Madeleine exclaimed. 'She should get a gold!'

'They all should,' James agreed with conviction. 'Some sort of a prize in recognition of all their efforts.'

The men's athletics came on and Madeleine turned the volume down, saying, 'That's my fix for the day, James. Please, watch anything you like.'

James placed down his glass on the coffee table, picked up a stool and moving it close to Madeleine sat down beside her. Emily was still fast asleep on the settee, Rabbit tucked under her chin. Madeleine felt James's closeness, his warmth, his direct gaze, which was like a physical touch that made her spine tingle.

'Madeleine.' His breath, sweet from the fruit drink, brushed the side of her face. 'You must know that the only reason I wanted you to come to London was to be able to spend some time with you. Just you and me. Together.' He paused. 'I'm not a poet. My words are simple. I want to tell you how much I love you, Madeleine. I'm obsessed with you. You're on my mind every minute of every day. But you know that, don't you?'

His words rooted her to the spot. Then panic struck her into action.

'James...' She wanted to stop him, she wanted to explain, everything, but no other word passed her lips, for he cupped her face in his warm hands and began to kiss her. It felt like flower petals falling all over her. Exquisite pleasure spread through her body. She did not want this to stop, but the presence of her sleeping child pulled her back from succumbing further. Gently she freed herself from James's embrace and whispered, 'Follow me.'

# CHAPTER 26

She led him to the back room, her study, Bronek's library, which faced the back garden and was now cast in the afternoon shadow. Its dusky atmosphere had a feel of discreet conspiracy, as if to assist them in what they were about to do. A sixties' G-Plan settee stood against one wall, its angular contours softened with cushions and rugs. James pulled Madeleine to him and held her close, so close she could hardly breathe. He covered her face with kisses, and her neck down to the little hollow between her collar bones. She did not want it to end. She had never imagined that what she had been denying herself all those years could ever be possible again. She kissed him back and pressed her body against his, avid for every inch of contact. She experienced a surge of desire that ran like a hot stream the length of her body. She feared she would swoon if they continued in this insatiable manner.

'James…' she whispered, but he kissed her quiet and enunciated each word between more kisses.

'Shh… time… to… just… be…'

They remained thus, holding each other tight, savouring each other with kisses. No words were necessary. What Madeleine was experiencing was poles apart from what had been forced on her that time; she was no longer afraid of a man's touch, when that man was James. She was only afraid of his rejection, when he knew the truth.

James recovered first. He loosened his embrace and led Madeleine to the settee, where they sat down facing each other, his brilliant blue eyes full of wonder as if he'd just come across a unique discovery.

'Madeleine,' he said, 'can you honestly tell me now that you don't love me? Not even a little?'

'James…' she breathed deeply, 'I do. Love you. You can't imagine… but for us to go on, I'd have to tell you about my past. And that will change everything. I couldn't bear it if you loved me less. I'd be destroyed if you rejected me. I just want to hang onto this moment for a bit longer, before the inevitable happens.'

He took both her hands in his and held them firmly.

'Madeleine, we can extend this moment into our future. We can make our future with thousands of moments like this one.' He pulled her gently against his chest. 'I love you. Trust me. Just tell me. I've tried to imagine all kinds of things that appear to hold you back. And I can't think of any one thing that would make me love you less.'

She looked up at him, aware of the warmth of his flesh beneath his cotton shirt. He would never be able to imagine or to understand her feeling of shame and degradation at having been so defiled.

'What sort of things did you imagine?'

He shrugged.

'Go on, tell me.' Her voice was harsher than she had intended and she slipped out of his embrace to face him full on.

'Don't do this, Madeleine. I love you. I want you to trust me.'

It hurt her to see hurt in his face, but a bitter streak came suddenly to the fore and she did not control her words.

'Do you think I've done something criminal in my past? Or left my partner and cut him off from seeing his child? Or been involved in some unsavoury activity? Been an escort girl, perhaps?'

James placed his hand gently over her mouth, stifling her words.

'Don't do this, Madeleine. I've told you, I love you as you are. Let go of your past. We all have a past. We're supposed to learn from it and not make mistakes in the future. But of course, it never works like that, does it? Each new situation is different and we only learn our lessons after the event.' He smiled, removed his hand and kissed her on the lips.

He was so good, so kind, she did not deserve him. Tears sprung to her eyes.

'I don't deserve you,' she said.

'Nonsense!' He pulled her close and kissed her again.

She said, 'Tell me about your past.' She remembered well that image of a distressed young man in the gazebo all those years ago, when she had been so distressed herself, when rebuilding her shattered world had seemed like an impossible task. Would he ever tell her about that time in his life?

James released her from his embrace, ran his fingers through his hair, rather roughly, and stared outside through the glazed door, beyond which patches of sunlight sparkled amongst the shadows. He stood up and moved towards it, so that when he turned to face Madeleine he became a silhouette, his features blurred.

'I loved… a girl once…' He spoke haltingly. 'I believed she loved me too… I made plans for us, I had our future sorted out… and I was overjoyed…'

Emily's hoarse voice called out from the front room.

'Mama! Where are you?'

'Coming!' The response was immediate. Madeleine stood up. 'I'm so sorry, James. Give me five minutes. I want to hear everything!' She was torn between her child and the man she loved, but he stepped forward, his face coming into light.

'Of course you must go to Emily.' He followed her.

Emily had raised herself up on her elbow against the pillow.

'Mama, I'm so thirsty!' She showed no surprise at seeing James. Madeleine picked her up and sat her on her lap, hugging her to her chest, feeling her warmth, but no longer that feverish heat on her skin. She placed her palm against Emily's forehead.

'I think your fever's gone,' she said with relief. 'I'll get you a drink, and you can look after James. All right?'

Emily nodded gravely and James pulled up his stool close to the settee, after Madeleine had made Emily comfortable against the pillows.

When she returned with their drinks, a juice drink for Emily and two glasses of punch for themselves, James was explaining to Emily the vault tasks that the British men's team were performing.

'I wish I could fly like that,' Emily commented in her thickened voice, her eyes avidly fixed on the double twists and gravity-defying transference from one height to the next.

'You could do that, when you practise long enough,' Madeleine said, placing the tray on the coffee table. 'Please, help yourself, James. And the nibbles,' she invited as she sat beside Emily with the fruit drink. Emily took a sip and cried out in pain. Her eyes filled up profusely; the tears rolled down her cheeks.

'Mama, it hurts… '

'I know, my love. Sip just a little at a time. It will get better soon.'

Emily nodded and tried again. She took small gulps, her eyes watering each time, but she continued.

'See what you'd be taking on?' Madeleine's remark was pointed at James.

He shrugged and made a 'so what?' face and spoke to Emily.

'You are very brave, Emily. Just like a warrior princess!'

Emily sat up straight, pulled her shoulders up and took another sip. Tears spilled down her cheeks.

'I'm not crying,' she assured him hoarsely. 'It's my throat making my eyes squeeze out all that water!'

'Of course, Emily. We know that,' James assured her, 'You're doing really well. Considering how nasty those tonsils are. This is a real test

233

for a warrior princess. She never gives in, no matter how hard it is. And you've just proved to me that you come from a line of very brave warrior princesses.'

'Did you know that, Mama?' Emily's tear-filled eyes looked to her for confirmation. Madeleine nodded, loving James all the more, wondering if he had learnt his story-telling skills while looking after Josh, when he himself had only been a young boy.

'Emily,' she said, 'inside your mind you can be anyone you choose to be. It can be your very own secret. But anyone else who is a secret prince or a secret princess will guess straight away that you are one of them just by seeing your kind and brave deeds.'

Emily thought for a moment.

'So, am I a real princess?'

James replied sagely. 'I have no doubt that you are, but we must keep it a secret, just between the three of us, so that the magic can work.'

Emily considered his words over a series of short sips.

'Can I just tell Babcha and Grandpa?'

'Only them. Nobody else must know. You never know what spies may be listening.'

Emily livened up.

'That's just what Grandpa says. All the time!'

'Great minds think alike.' James spoke softly, placing his finger against his lips. Then he spoke aloud. 'Look Emily, look! That boy on the bar! Wouldn't you like to have a go when you get better?'

'Can I, Mama?' Emily finished her drink and wiped her watering eyes with the cuff of her dressing gown.

'We'll start planning all kinds of exciting things, Emily, when you get better,' Madeleine promised.

She sat back with her drink, feeling all tension drain from her. It was a good feeling, after everything that had happened, that had taken her by surprise, while Emily was sleeping. Now it felt strangely normal, James sitting with them, entertaining them both with a running commentary on the televised action at the Olympic Arena, with funny little asides and anecdotes he'd read about the sports personalities.

She wandered what it was he was about to tell her about his past when they got interrupted. She'd have to ask him at an opportune moment before he left.

Madeleine did not keep checking the time, wishing the afternoon to stretch into the evening, but, when Emily began to show signs of tiredness, her eyes closing and her head lolling, James said, 'It's time for me to go.'

Madeleine's heart sank.

'Another minute,' she stopped him. She lay Emily flat against the pillow and tucked Rabbit with her underneath the blanket.

James got up but she placed her hand on his arm.

'Don't go yet, James. You've started telling me... then we got interrupted. I'm sorry about that. I'd really like to know... everything.'

He looked at the clock on the mantelpiece.

'It can wait, Madeleine. It's all in the past now. It's of no importance anymore.' He looked serious for a moment as he appraised her in that intimate manner of his that made her knees go weak. 'Your grandparents will be back soon. They'll not want to find me still hanging around.' She took a breath to protest, but he continued. 'Madeleine, you need a rest too. But listen, if there's a chance that Emily improves by tomorrow, would you come to the cinema with me in the afternoon? Just text me. I don't have to be back in London till any time late evening.'

He had a knack of surprising her. It took a moment to absorb his words, and all the while his calm blue eyes mesmerised her and turned her brain to mush.

'Well... yes... I'd like that,' then, with sudden certainty, 'James, that would be lovely! All fingers crossed for Emily to get better!' She did not wish to be perceived as prying, but could not help asking, 'And what will you be doing tonight?'

He smiled.

'I'll go home now and spend some time with my mother and Josh.'

'Didn't they mind you coming here, when you're home for such a short time?'

'No,' he chuckled, 'they did not mind at all. It rather felt like a conspiracy to dispatch me in your direction.'

'Really?' She was surprised how good it made her feel that his family approved of her.

'Yes, really.' James chuckled again. 'You've cast a spell on them, just as you have on me. And on my friends Mark and Julie. I'm seeing them tonight for a drink in town.'

'Are you?' A sinking sensation of jealousy. She made herself smile. 'Give them my best. Enjoy a good evening.' Another forced smile over a sick feeling.

She went ahead to the front door, but before she unlocked it his arms were around her and his lips on hers, moving deftly, reawakening a thousand sensations. She was left breathless and shaky when he let her go.

'I wish I could take you with me,' he said.

She believed him, but would he still repeat those words when she told him the whole truth about herself?

*

The next day was Sunday, and after Aniela and Bronek had returned from church and the pre-prepared lunch was cooked and enjoyed at leisure, Madeleine got herself ready to go out with James. Emily's fever was gone, her throat was still sore but enough improved to swallow creamed potatoes and chocolate mousse. She had made herself comfortable on the settee with her array of soft toys, cushions and rugs. The television ran on soundlessly. This was Bronek's defence against too much noise, as in any case, he declared, he could make up his own mind as to the individual athletes' abilities and their chances of winning gold or silver.

Aniela could not stop referring to James's visit the previous day, and, though Madeleine had answered all Aniela's questions truthfully, she remained reticent about some aspects of their time spent together. Aniela had decided immediately that, of course, Madeleine must go to the cinema with James.

'Emily's so much better today,' she said. 'She will not miss you for a couple of hours.'

Only, it would not be just a couple of hours, Madeleine thought, but she did not argue, grateful to Aniela, grateful to the fate. Despite the niggling thoughts about the approaching, inevitable confession, she was buoyed along with happiness and thoughts of the precious moments she had spent with James the previous day. It all seemed like a fairy tale, but their story had just begun, and she had so much to look forward to. Except for one thing. She banished that thought from her mind.

James was waiting for her at the Phoenix Theatre cafe and she saw him get up from the table and wave to her the moment she walked through the door. As she approached him she wondered, should she embrace him, kiss him publicly, or not? She did not want to cause him embarrassment, but neither did she want to appear unfeeling. He solved her problem by giving her a bear hug and kissing her on the cheek.

He pulled out a chair for her saying, 'Thanks for texting me this morning.' And, when they both sat down facing each other over the table, he grasped her hands and added, 'You've made me so happy, Madeleine.'

'I'm very happy too,' she said honestly, 'just being with you. And all this...' she looked around, 'this is a real treat for me.'

'OK.' He let go of her hands, gently, reluctantly. 'What will you have to drink?'

'Just coffee would be lovely.' She felt no hunger, no thirst, just an inflated sensation as if a bubble inside her was ready to burst. With happiness.

She watched him as he queued at the bar. The place was buzzing. Now and again outbursts of laughter would break through the general hubbub, making heads turn. This was how it had been all those Sundays in all the years that Madeleine had spent taking Emily to a playground, or going with Bronek to his allotment, or helping Aniela to entertain her friends. This had been here for a long time: she remembered 'The Phoenix' being transferred from Brown Street to this newly built venue, the place for people to meet, to enjoy a drink, a meal, a show, a film, a concert, this had been here and she had missed it all. She could not blame anyone but herself. She had allowed one bad incident in her past to rule the rest of her life, while precious time was passing. James had been right: she had to let go of her past. If only there were some easy way of doing it.

She longed to tell him everything, to get the burden off her chest. And she would do it, she promised herself, as soon as the right moment presented itself. But when it did, would she be able to recognise it? She had been rehearsing a speech in her head, so that she'd be prepared, as she had been taught to be in her Girl Guide days.

When James returned with their coffees and sat down beside her, she asked, 'What film are we seeing?'

He grinned, a touch sheepishly.

'I had no idea what was on when I asked you to come with me yesterday, Madeleine. I just wanted another chance to spend some time with you. As it happens, they're showing some vintage American films. It's like a mini festival.'

She smiled back and took a sip of coffee.

'Silent? Charlie Chaplin?' Not that she would have minded. She would have sat through an obscure film noire as long as she had James beside her.

He laughed.

'No, nothing like that. A modern 1950s. Cinemascope and colour and sound and all-improved special effects. I think we may even enjoy it.'

'What's the title?'

'*An Affair to Remember*. Cary Grant and Deborah Kerr.'

'Deborah Kerr?' Madeleine's interest perked up. 'If it's the same actress who played Lygia in *Quo Vadis*? then I have seen her before. It was already a vintage film when I was ten and my auntie took me to see it. It was dubbed, naturally, for the Polish audience, and, though it was not a hundred per cent true to Sienkiewicz's novel, it had some great special effects. I can still picture vividly Rome burning as Nero sang to his lyre.'

'Who was that author again?' James asked.

'Henryk Sienkiewicz.' She was glad to tell him something he did not know. 'The most liked and respected of Polish writers at the turn of the century. Last century. His trilogy, three historical novels, were once compulsory reading for every child at school.'

'Amazing! With you, Madeleine, I learn something new every minute!'

She liked his mood and in the same vein she suggested, 'Then perhaps I could tutor you in Polish?'

He laughed at that, a genuine, amused laugh.

'Climb Everest, Madeleine. Far easier.'

'Just five new words a day. By the end of the year you'll be an expert Polonist.'

'How about just three words a day? Starting with – I… love… you…'
She laughed.

'Dead easy. Just two words needed to express that. Kocham Cie. Ko-Ham Che.'

'Ko-Ham Che.' He staccatoed each syllable, then repeated the words, slowly holding her gaze. The general hubbub around them seemed to fade into a distant background.

'Kocham Cie tez,' she told him. An outburst of laughter at an adjoining table cut into their moment but did not diminish the rapport between them. James placed his hand over hers and held it so, even as he took a sip of coffee and reverted back to their previous discussion about the film.

'I saw Cary Grant in a Hitchcock thriller. That was vintage too. Brilliant! I was only a youngster, but I dreamed of adventures like his. I wanted to be as clever and as brave as he was and solve mysteries and chase the baddies and give them the comeuppance they deserved!' He chuckled at himself.

'Fascinating, isn't it?' Madeleine remarked, 'That even children understand what's right and what's wrong and need to see justice being done. Nothing is more satisfying than to see all the loose ends tied up at the end of a film or a book.'

'Did you want to be a detective too? Or an avenging angel?' he teased light-heartedly.

'Many times!' If only he knew. 'I was like most growing girls dreaming of fame. I dreamed of being a famous film star.'

'What stopped you?'

'Are you teasing? I grew up.'

When Dominik had come into her life, everything else had become insignificant except completing her studies and settling for a future with him. Madeleine lowered her gaze in case James could read her mind. She withdrew her hand gently to pick up her cup and finish her coffee. She said, 'I've always loved going to the cinema. The theatre, the ballet. I still do sometimes with Aniela. She loves seeing musicals at De Montfort Hall or the Curve.'

James finished his coffee and again cupped Madeleine's hand in both of his. Such a simple gesture, so deliciously intimate.

'We can do that, Madeleine. As often as you wish.'

'OK. We will.' She wanted to believe that. She pushed away the fear of having to tell him. Not today. She would not think about that today.

They sat in the back row, with the flickering light of the entertaining adverts animating their faces in the dark. They often looked at each other and smiled. James's hand rested warmly over hers on the arm-rest. It was bliss, simply being. Was this what was meant by 'living in the moment'? She wanted this moment to last.

The film started. To Madeleine's surprise, apart from the obvious fashions of the time, there was no feeling of this being an old film. The characters were convincingly played by Kerr and Grant, and the plot, with all its twists and turns, kept one's attention gripped throughout. It was an intense story of wasted time, years in fact, because the heroine, who had been injured in an accident, had turned away from the man she loved, rather than burden him with her crippled, imperfect self. The ending was a happy one with a message that true love conquers everything.

When the lights came on, people began to leave but James remained seated.

'No rush, is there?' he said. 'Did you enjoy that?' She smiled back at him.

'James, if I had a suspicious nature' – which she did – 'I'd think you had planned it all along, to make sure I saw this film. But I'm almost convinced that this was pure coincidence. How very strange!'

'Yes, it is! Very strange!' he agreed. He was serious. He added, 'Don't discard the message too lightly.' He gave her hand a pat and got up. She got up too, to follow the last few people in their row.

In the foyer, freed from the exiting crowd, James stopped.

'I don't want this afternoon to end yet, Madeleine. Will they be expecting you at home soon?'

Madeleine shook her head. Aniela was keen for her to spend as much time with James as she wished.

'But,' she explained, 'it wouldn't be fair on Emily or Aniela if I stayed out too long.'

'Could you spare me another hour or so?' James raised his eyebrow and his begging-dog expression could not have been more persuasive.

'And a little bit more.' She gave a light laugh.

Neither of them was hungry enough for a meal. They found a cosy little place in The Lanes and opted for pancakes. James chose basic lemon and sugar sprinkling and Madeleine had a berry filling served with whipped cream.

They were sitting in a quiet corner where it was possible to talk without being overheard. They indulged in small talk at first, but over coffee James's expression became serious.

'Madeleine, I find it very hard to live in this constant uncertainty. It's taken over my life. I find it hard to concentrate on my work. Please tell me at least, that all this' – he spread his hands, his elegant hands, between them – 'that today and all our previous encounters have not been for nothing. You're going to Poland soon...'

'Only for five days,' she said, but he carried on.

'Please leave me with the hope that when you come back we can move on. Together?' His eyes were soft with pleading, making her feel wretched. She wanted the same things. If only that obstacle could be erased from her life, as if it had never existed.

'James.' When she said his name, he clasped her hand again, as if he could not have enough of touching her. 'I never thought, I never imagined, that I'd be able to find someone like you. And now that I have, I'm so afraid of losing you.'

'But why?' He shook his head in disbelief. 'That would never happen. Not because of me.'

'Then can you wait a little longer, for my confession.' She made a face at the word. 'Till I come back from Poland? That way, I shall feel sure for a little longer that you'll still be waiting for me.'

His smile was one of relief. He lifted her hand to his lips. A tickle of shivers ran down her spine.

'You funny girl, of course I'll be waiting for you.' He kissed her hand again and let it rest on the table. 'Now, to the nitty gritty.' He looked at her full of purpose. 'How are you getting to the airport? If you've got nothing arranged yet, let me take you and Emily. And I shall be waiting for you, of course, when you get back. Will you be happy with that?'

Happy? Again, he surprised her.

'James, there's no need to do that. It's too much, disrupting your work, travelling there and back...'

'Is it Luton? What time is your flight?'

'Quarter past six in the morning. But...'

'That's perfect! I'll be here the night before, pick you up, drop you off at the airport and be at my desk before nine. And when you return on Sunday, that won't be a problem at all. Agreed?'

If there were literally such a thing as sweeping someone off their feet, then James was a master at that. The more she loved him, the more her fear grew of losing him.

# CHAPTER 27

E-mails from Natalia came daily. It was now just a matter of days before their long-awaited reunion. Madeleine lived the joy of seeing her friend again every time she thought about her, and that was countless times each day, despite her constant preoccupation with James. Would Natalia find her changed? What would she think of Emily?

Her father had Skyped to wish her a good visit to Poland after all the years abroad.

'Will you visit Zden? His brother and the family?' he asked, by the way.

'I can't do that, Tato.' Madeleine was emphatic. This abhorrent thought alone made her bile rise.

The grainy image of her father looked sad.

'He's family, Magda. He was Emilia's husband. She was so good to you. Always. Even for her sake alone, you should make the effort. He may be over his drinking problem now. It's worth checking. He'd be overjoyed, I'm sure, to see you and Emily. He'd have a grandchild that he could consider his own.'

Madeleine shuddered at the thought.

'Tato, believe me, if I could, I'd do it. But I really can't. He terrified me. I never want to go back to that time or that place again.'

Her father looked sadder.

'I'm so sorry, Magda. It's all my fault. I wasn't there for you when you were growing up. I should have insisted that you stayed with me here, when you came over that first time.'

'No, Tato. You must not, absolutely not, blame yourself. It was my choice, and I was grateful to you that you did not try to change my mind. I was very happy with Aunt Emilia and with my friends and with all the familiar things around me. I couldn't imagine living anywhere else. No one could have foreseen Aunt Emilia's illness or Zden's reaction to it. I have dealt with it in my own way by leaving him. I'm here now, perfectly safe and happy, and I don't want to see him again.'

Her father remained quiet.

'Trust me, Tato, please. This is the best way.'

Madeleine was ready and packed a few days before her departure, being a strong believer in not leaving anything to chance or to the last minute. She had slipped in between her folded and packed clothes little gifts for people she might meet; for Natalia and Szymon she had bought an Aynsley china tea-set with a delicate motif of field flowers. Tea-drinking being a national Polish pastime, she was already anticipating Natalia's delight at this genuine English-made gift.

There was no let-up at work. Two cases had been particularly upsetting: a young girl of twelve had gone missing and after five days the search for her was still continuing. Her parents' tortured faces haunted Madeleine every night, and that desperate look in their eyes when they hung on to her every translated word from the police statements. Another case involved the death of a young Pole killed in a road accident. His wife had just given birth to their first child, a little boy. How was one to come to terms with such cruelties of fate? After assisting the young woman through all the formalities, Madeleine had sat in the car and cried.

'Magda,' Aniela had reasoned with her, when she off-loaded her angst at home, 'think about the surgeons, performing all kinds of complicated operations. They'd be no good if they stood over their patients and cried. Of course it's not fair to have a heart problem or lung cancer. But they are there to do their best to lessen the problem. And that's what you have done. You have assisted all these unfortunate people the best way you could. And even in all their suffering they will remember that.'

Aniela had her own problems with Bronek, specifically with his forgetfulness. Looking for his keys and his mobile phone was a daily routine. He could not remember to leave them in the same spot every night to be found in that spot in the morning. He would sometimes forget where he had parked his car in town and would have to come home on the bus – if he'd remembered to have some change on him or walk from town to fetch Madeleine to help him with his detective work of locating his car.

At one time, he went to fetch Aniela from the dentist because he had heard her making an appointment over the phone. The appointment was for another day, and that particular day Aniela had been left waiting in town for him with Emily, until Madeleine got her message and came to the rescue.

One evening after dinner, Bronek's friend Edek Barski arrived unexpectedly, with everyone still sitting around the table. Aniela invited him to join them, made tea, offered him cake and all the while he kept looking at the clock, pointing at his watch, sending Bronek a sign, which Bronek appeared to be totally unaware of.

Finally, Edek Barski said, 'Are we still going tonight?'

'Going where?' Bronek and Aniela asked at the same time.

'To check your wall. Remember?' Edek Barski gave an embarrassed smile.

Aniela looked accusingly at Bronek.

'What's this you have arranged?'

His face brightened up.

'Of course! Edek, it's just as well that you've remembered! Let's go!'

Edek Barski shifted in his chair as if eager to go, but Aniela, who was standing between Bronek and him, pressed his shoulders down, saying, 'Don't let Bronek terrorise you. Finish your tea and cake, take as long as you wish, while Bronek tells me about your plan for tonight.' She sat down beside him.

'There's nothing much to tell,' Bronek replied in a sensible manner, his eyebrows raised innocently. 'Another brick has fallen out and needs fixing. Apart from anything else, it's just such a pleasant walk up there on an evening like this.'

One could not argue with that, but when they were gone, and everything had been cleared away, and Aniela and Madeleine sat at the garden table to watch Emily invent an ever more complicated game of hopscotch, Aniela confessed, 'He worries me. What shall we do when this gets worse? And this fixation with the wall. I have nightmares imagining it falling on someone. I shudder just thinking about it.'

'Babcha.' Madeleine stroked Aniela's shoulder. 'Please don't worry on your own. You've got me to help you. We'll tackle it together, whatever happens. As for the wall, let him do what he feels he has to do. If it brings him peace in his mind, knowing he is well screened off from the public footpath, then let it be. Luckily the wall is nowhere near where people could be walking. You'd have to squeeze in right between it and the oak tree. I can't imagine anyone doing that. Perhaps a fox. But animals can look after themselves.'

She looked into Aniela's face willing her to relax. Aniela's eyes were red-rimmed.

'I can't believe how this has happened, Magda. He was always so dynamic, so on the ball, planning, organising, looking after everyone, the leader of our pack, when only a young boy in Russia. Because of him, our group has always remained together...'

'And you still are, Babcha. Edek wouldn't have come if he did not enjoy Grandpa's company. They've got so much to talk about. Just as you are accepting of all the changes in them over the years, so are they with yours. I don't think they will love you any less just because Grandpa has become a little forgetful.'

Aniela nodded, a little uncertainly, but managed to raise a smile.

'Perhaps you're right, Magda, perhaps I do worry too much.'

Emily stopped her hopscotch, ran up to Aniela and threw her arms around her waist.

'Babcha, you will always have us. I shall never leave you! And I'll help to look after Grandpa. I can make him toast and juice every morning!'

*

'Look Mama! Domeczki!'

'They only look like toy houses because we are so high up!'

Emily had the window seat. Madeleine leaned over and watched as the aircraft prepared to land. She could barely contain her excitement. In less than half an hour, she'd be hugging Natalia. She had spoken to her the previous evening.

'I can't wait!' Natalia's voice had squeaked like a little girl's. 'We'll have two whole days together! I've arranged it so that we'll be left alone. Just the two of us! And Emily! But on Thursday and Friday, Magda, we'll spend time with Szymon and our two families. They'll all be wanting to see you, and there will be a hundred and one last minute things to do.'

Natalia had sounded exactly the same as Madeleine remembered her from seven years ago. It felt as if they had parted only the previous day. Madeleine was grateful to Natalia for not pressing her to talk about Emily's mysterious father, before they could talk openly face to face. She felt apprehensive; she could not help that, as she wondered what Natalia's reaction to the awful truth was going to be. But if she survived that, then perhaps it would make it easier to tell James when she got back.

Dear James. The moment she opened her eyes each morning, he was there with her, in her heart, in her thoughts, awakening every cell in her body with love for him. There was a time when she had lost all hope of being capable to feel such love again. Each day she loved him all the more. He'd missed half the night's sleep to take her and Emily to the airport and had shrugged off her reservations good-naturedly.

'That's what couples do.'

'So, we're a couple now?' she teased as the waited in the departure queue.

'Unless you want someone else to pick you up on Sunday?' he teased back and kissed her cheek. He picked up Emily and gave her a hug. 'You'll have a super time. But don't forget to come back.' Emily laughed and hugged him back.

'I won't forget in five days,' she assured him, spreading out her fingers to demonstrate. 'But you mustn't be sad, James, because I shall bring you back a chocolate cupcake.'

'How did you ever guess that was my favourite?' They watched him waving until their queue took them behind a screen for the passport check.

And now Madeleine was missing him already. Emily patted her hand with excitement.

'Mama! It's like going down a bumpy slide!' Her eyes picked up the brightness off the plane's window.

'It's the wind, Emily. Blowing us like a kite. Another minute and we'll be down on the ground.'

She closed her eyes and leaned her head against the back rest. She thought of Dominik. In recent weeks, despite her growing love for James, she had thought frequently of Dominik. He had been her obsession for so many years, her emotional crutch, her excuse for keeping other men at bay. She owed him a lot. It felt like a betrayal, loving another man. Her greatest regret was that she'd never be able to explain, to make him feel better, to convince him that what she had done was in his best interest too. She comforted herself with the thought that he had found the perfect girl who loved him and who had borne their child for him. She could have been that girl. Everything could have been so different. But then she would never have met James. And now she could not imagine her life without him.

Uncle Zden. He had haunted her mind frequently in recent weeks as her trip to Poland got nearer. Even after all the years, her stomach clenched at the merest thought of him. She had mentioned this to Aniela.

'My dear Magda.' Aniela's no-nonsense stance had been like a protective cloak around Madeleine. 'You've got absolutely nothing to fear. You won't be on your own at any time. But even if you were to come face to face with him, believe me, his shock would be greater than yours. Can you imagine the fear he's had to live with all those years? You've always had the upper hand, remember that. He doesn't know if you're likely to report him yet. Imagine his torment. Every day and every night. And he knows it's never going to end.'

Madeleine could not care less about his problems, but her own fear of seeing him never diminished. In her dreams she still cultivated thoughts of revenge, but she knew that was only a fantasy, for she could never have carried out a violent act against him. She could only hope that one day fate would do it for her.

The plane touched the ground with a bump that made Emily cry out with excitement. Madeleine stretched her arm out against Emily's chest till the speed slowed down to taxiing.

'We're here, Emily. A few more minutes and we'll see Auntie Natalia.'

Natalia, in a white top and white jeans, stood out against the line of waiting people on the other side of the barrier in the arrivals hall. She looked no different from the girl Madeleine remembered so vividly from seven years ago: blonde, curly hair worn long and tied back into a ponytail, sparkling blue eyes and a generous smile showing off her perfect teeth. With a crowd milling around them, and oblivious to it all, they hugged for a long moment before standing back at arm's length to appraise each other before hugging again. Emily watched with fascination, clutching Rabbit to her chest.

Natalia bent down and presented her with a carrier bag. She spoke to her in Polish.

'Dla ciebie, Emilia, zobacz. For you, Emily, look inside. Your mama has been telling me all about you and what a good girl you are!'

'Dziekuje. Thank you,' Emily answered in Polish, her self-conscious expression evident of her pleasure. 'Mama, when can I open it?'

'As soon as we're in the car, darling.'

Natalia gave her a hug.

Madeleine pulled her suitcase and held Emily's hand. Natalia picked up the hand luggage and led them to the car park in a flurry of talk about the journey, about Madeleine's preparations, about Natalia's one hundred things to do before the wedding, and all the while their talk punctuated by Madeleine's 'I can't believe this is happening!'

'Nor can I!' Natalia squealed and they both laughed and Emily studied them with perplexed seriousness.

Once everything was placed in the boot and they were settled in Natalia's car, a sleek white Kia Picanto, Madeleine fell quiet, overwhelmed with the familiarity of the landscape as they drove out of the airport. It felt so Polish, so natural in rich greenery, in the vastness of the surrounding woodland, in the gaps offering glimpses of distant cornfields and copses of sky-touching poplars and those delicate, swaying branches of the weeping willows, throwing shade over the ponds and the streams. Even the sky looked a richer, deeper blue than the paler English sky, that Madeleine had got accustomed to. All those sights pulled at her heart, overwhelming her with memories of her childhood.

Emily's voice brought her back to the present.

'Mama, when can I look inside the bag?' She was strapped in the back seat with the bag on her lap. Natalia was quicker to reply.

'Now, Emily. It's all yours!'

Madeleine watched Emily in the mirror as she plunged her hand inside the bag and her preoccupied expression melted in a smile. She brought out an object wrapped in tissue paper. In a flash, the paper was off to reveal a doll with beautiful yellow hair and glass-blue eyes and dressed in the Krakow regional costume.

'Mama! Look! She's got a dress like mine!' Emily laughed with excitement.

'So,' Natalia said, looking at Emily in the mirror, 'are you a little Krakowianka too?'

'Sometimes.' Emily nodded, adding, 'Sometimes we have concerts in the Polish School and sometimes I dance and sometimes I sing. And I get dressed up just like this.'

'That's wonderful!' Natalia praised her. 'And where did your Mama get your costume for you?'

'Babcha made it,' Emily said simply.

Madeleine felt compelled to add, 'Aniela's an absolute maestro with the needle. She spent hours sewing on all the sequins and the beads and the appliquéd flowers. My own little input was pathetic. Just as well she did not rely on me.'

'And Babcha has knitted this cardigan for Rabbit,' Emily added, making the rabbit kiss the new doll. Then she cuddled them both.

''We'll send your Babcha some lovely photos from the wedding,' Natalia promised.

'And one of Karolinka.'

'Who?' Madeleine turned around.

'My new doll, Mama!' Emily laughed, amused by Madeleine's slowness.

They entered the peripheral district of Krakow from the west and continued through Kryspinow and Debniki towards the south of the city, where Natalia lived. Just catching a glimpse of the Wawel Castle on the top of the far-away hill gave Madeleine a stab of longing and nostalgia. She would never have left this place out of her own choice.

'You are so lucky, Natalia,' she remarked. 'How I envy you!'

Natalia gave her a sideways glance.

'You can always come back.'

She could not, never while Zden was still alive and capable of stalking her.

At the cross-section with one of the main routes into the city, Natalia came off onto a dual carriageway, which was flanked with a parallel-running tram line on one side and on the other with rows of high raised blocks of flats. She turned into one of the side streets and stopped in a communal car park at the foot of one of the blocks.

'Here we are!' she laughed happily and unstrapped herself, eager to get to the boot first. Madeleine followed her and looked around.

In her childhood, the ground between the tower blocks was just derelict wasteland. She was impressed now with the flowering shrubs and the neat concrete surface designated for cars. Natalia pointed out eagerly her and Szymon's flat.

'It's the one right at the top with all those geraniums on the balcony.'

Madeleine looked up, shading her eyes against the glare of the sun. 'It's so lovely! You must be so happy living here!'

'We've been very lucky,' Natalia said. 'Szymon bought it off his elderly relative, who was getting too old for all the floors. Even the lift became a problem for him. The price was very reasonable. And it's bliss to have a place of our own.' Madeleine remembered Natalia's family flat, where their parents slept in one room, her two brothers the other, and when she stayed over at Natalia's they'd sleep together on the settee that pulled out to transform into a makeshift bed. 'Come,' Natalia said, 'let me take you inside.'

The ride up the lift to the topmost twelfth floor was a much-enjoyed adventure for Emily. They stepped out onto a long corridor with a number of doors, everything painted white and reflecting the light from the two windows, one at each end.

'I can't believe how much more improved these places are!' Madeleine said. 'Do you remember all those dark poky corridors when we were kids? With monsters waiting to pounce on us around every corner?' She laughed.

'Monsters?' Emily looked alarmed. 'Did they try to catch you?'

'They did.' Natalia smiled. 'But we were always faster than them. They never caught us once! Don't worry, Emily, there are no monsters now. They are long gone!' She unlocked the door to her flat and showed them in.

The flat consisted of a small entrance hall with an equally small kitchen ahead. To one side there was a living room, perhaps four metres by four, with a balcony, and on the other side the same area divided between a bedroom and a bathroom. Madeleine had never thought much of such miniature spaces as a child; most people lived in similar flats, but now, having got used to a house with two floors and several rooms, she wondered how Natalia managed in such a minuscule nest. An illusion of space had been created with white decor throughout and matching light furniture.

'I love it!' she exclaimed, looking into each room in turn.

'Szymon and I are very happy here,' Natalia said with pride. 'Come, settle yourself in our bedroom.'

'And where will you sleep?'

'No problem. The settee doubles up as a bed. No surprise there. Remember those days?'

'What about Szymon? Will he be happy with that?'

Natalia gave a short, amused laugh.

'He won't be sleeping here this week. He'll be at his parent's house. As the custom demands of a well-behaved couple.'

While Madeleine unpacked and hung her clothes in the slim free-standing wardrobe, and Emily lined their shoes neatly against the wall, Natalia prepared a breakfast of cold meats and cheeses and deliciously smelling fresh bread.

'What would you like to do, Magda?' she asked, once they were seated around the kitchen table and tucking into their food. Even Emily enjoyed her toasted bread with butter and strawberry jam. 'It's still only half past ten. We've got the whole day ahead of us.' Her face lit up at the thought.

'D'you know…' Madeleine's eyes rolled with pleasure at the taste of bread. 'If we sat here all day just talking, I wouldn't wish for anything else. Seriously though' – she took another chunky bite – 'I'd like Emily to have a little nap first. She hardly slept at all last night. Too excited, weren't you?' She brushed her daughter's cheek with the back of her hand. Emily's expression fell.

'But Mama. I'm not tired at all. Can we go to the park to play?'

'We'll do that,' Natalia promised. 'We've got a play area nearby. It'll still be there after you've had your rest, Emily. Don't worry about that. Finish your breakfast first.'

Madeleine and Natalia talked non-stop, reminiscing, remembering people they had known in the past and, when they finished eating and had drunk enough coffee to keep them awake for a week, Madeleine waited for Emily to finish her fruity yogurt and her clear weak tea with honey, before coaxing her to take a rest.

'Emily, by the time we've finished tidying up, you'll have had your little nap and be ready to go out to play. Shall we do that?'

Emily looked unconvinced.

'You won't go without me?'

Madeleine hugged her, breathing in that much-loved scent of rose talcum powder and clean hair.

'We'd never do that. We'll wait here till you wake up. We've still got a long day ahead of us and an evening meal in town. You don't want to be falling asleep at the table when we're all still eating our meal. You'll need bags of energy to stay awake late tonight.' This last sentence with a promise of a late night seemed to do the trick.

'All right,' she agreed, 'but only for five minutes.' She spread out her fingers as was her habit.

Madeleine settled Emily in Natalia's bed, together with Rabbit and Karolinka, and before long Emily was asleep.

Back in the kitchen, where Natalia was tidying up, Madeleine gave her a spontaneous sisterly hug.

'I'll check on Emily when we've finished here, and then we can have a good uninterrupted natter.'

Later, with a fresh coffee, they sat down in the living room close to the open balcony. Natalia placed a portable radio at the entrance with soft classical music acting as a sound barrier.

'Better this way,' she explained. 'The balcony partitions are made of painted hardboard. Hardly soundproof.' She sat down facing Madeleine, took a sip, placed the mug down on the circular glass coffee table and looked up, her gaze intense, questioning.

'Magda,' she said, 'you've no idea how awful, how utterly dreadful it was, that day when you disappeared so suddenly with hardly any explanation. I was in shock. I was bereft. It was like someone had died in the family.' A tear gathered in the corner of her eye. 'I worried in case it was something I had done and wasn't even aware of it that made you run away.'

Madeleine was overcome with emotion. Chopin's 'Raindrop Étude' floating from the radio intensified her grief. She placed her hand over her mouth and left it there, allowing her tears to fall freely. When she was able to speak, she said emphatically, 'No, Natalia, absolutely not! It was nothing that you or any of my friends had done. It broke my heart too to be forced to act this way. But I had no choice. I had to make plans fast. I had to escape as far as possible!' The terror of that night came back and froze her words. She screwed her eyes shut. In the silence that followed, she felt Natalia's hand on her shoulder.

'Dear God, Madeleine, what happened? You're scaring me!'

Madeleine opened her eyes and took a deep breath. She was shaking.

'Before I tell you, Natalia, you must believe me, I swear to you, I did nothing, absolutely nothing to provoke him to do it. He just did it!'

'Did what, Magda? Who?'

Another deep breath.

'Uncle Zden raped me. The same night that Aunt Emilia died.'

Natalia stared and remained staring for a long time. The noise of the traffic on the dual carriageway below sounded a million miles away. Then she got up and knelt beside Madeleine and held her close until all the shaking stopped.

A long time later, after Madeleine had recounted the most traumatic episode in her life and answered all of Natalia's questions, after they both had cried and commiserated with each other on the loss of that special time in their teens, Madeleine told her about James. This subject lifted their moods and led on to discuss Natalia's wedding preparations.

'I love happy talk,' Madeleine said with feeling and hugged Natalia yet again. 'Tell me about your family and friends who are coming to your wedding. Tell me about Dominik. You said in your e-mail that you've invited him and his wife too. I so much want to see him. But I'm dreading it too. I've hurt him a lot, and I was not able to explain. That was so awful! And when he sees Emily, he'll put two and two together, come to the wrong conclusion and hate me even more!'

Natalia thought for a moment. There was a pleasant buzzing sound of a bee hovering over the geraniums on the balcony.

'You don't owe anyone any explanations, Magda. You did nothing wrong.'

'But he wasn't just anyone. And I shall never be able to atone for the hurt I caused him.'

'He never said a thing. Not to anyone.' Natalia spoke soothingly. This made Madeleine feel worse. 'Not even to Szymon. But then he met Agata pretty soon afterwards. She is a lovely girl. Much approved by his parents. Don't worry about him. He's found his happiness. They've got a baby boy. I think you'll find him in a generous mood.'

Madeleine was not convinced. She said, 'Natalia, I'll never have the chance to tell him. Will you? Will you tell him for me?' Natalia looked hesitant as she held Madeleine's gaze. Madeleine repeated, 'Please, Natalia, please. There's no one else I could ask. I've lived with this guilt for so long. This would mean so much to me, knowing that he did not blame me anymore.'

'All right,' Natalia said, a small smile loosening her pursed lips, 'I shall make him swear his Hippocratic oath to keep your secret.'

Madeleine sighed with relief. A peacock butterfly flew in and settled on the net curtain. The perfect symmetry of the concentric circles and the colours on its wings made Madeleine catch her breath for a moment.

'I believe Dominik will keep my secret.' She trusted him. Then hesitantly she asked, 'Natalia, have you ever come across my Uncle Zden? Since that time?'

'Only once. Years ago. Not close enough to speak to. He looked ill. Terribly thin and very pale. Not a patch on the good-looking and confident man he was before. Why? Would you like to give him a good kicking? The bastard! Count me in. And my vigilante team. Does that surprise you? Good. It'll surprise him even more!' Natalia's comical determination raised a smile but could not suppress Madeleine's long and tired sigh.

'I've dreamed of that a thousand times, Natalia. In my mind I wished the worst kind of punishment for him. But that only happens in films, doesn't it? In reality, justice can take a lifetime to arrive, if it ever comes at all.'

'You could take him to court.'

Madeleine shuddered.

'And let it all come out? No, Natalia, that would be my worst nightmare. I want to leave him and my past behind me. I want to move on with James. If only I found a way of telling him. I feel so... unclean. Imperfect. I feel he deserves better than me.'

'Nonsense!' Natalia sat up with renewed energy. 'Do you believe he's never slept with anyone? At thirty? With his looks? Ask him, Magda. There shouldn't be any secrets between you.'

Madeleine was not so naive as to think that James had always been celibate, but the very thought of him being intimate with someone else made something sickly curl inside her. She concentrated her mind on the Brahms sonata floating from the radio. She said, 'He began telling me once about a girl he had loved. We got interrupted. He never finished telling me. I only got the impression that she had left him suddenly. Not unlike me doing the same to Dominik.' She made a disgusted face at herself.

'Ask him, Magda, ask him to tell you about his past. He may surprise you. Any decent man would love you for yourself, and not despise you for someone else's crime.'

'That's just what my Babcha Aniela said!'

'A very wise woman. And you're an angel. A saint. To have borne all that with such brave determination. If you don't believe me, ask Father Gabriel.'

'Who?'

'He's the university chaplain. He's the one we've asked to marry us. A people's priest. You can tell him anything.'

'How would that help?' But just hearing Natalia's words gave Madeleine a sudden lift.

'Give it a try. I'll ring him now.' Natalia got up.

'No, please… not just yet. I need to think.' Madeleine wrung her hands and bit her lip.

'Please let me ring him.' Natalia spoke softly. 'I promise, you won't be disappointed. He has a knack of saying the right things at the right time. It may be just something to make you see things more clearly, or to point you in the right direction, but you'll come away feeling much better. It's worth a try, isn't it?'

Madeleine did not argue, just watched Natalia pick up the receiver and dial a number.

'Father Gabriel?' She smiled into the receiver. 'Could you spare five minutes? Any time this week. Before the wedding?' She listened, then laughed. 'No, I haven't changed my mind. Today? This afternoon? Great! Fifteen-thirty? Perfect! A million thanks!' She looked at Madeleine. 'There! All fixed. I'll come with you and mind Emily. There's a children's play area on the Planty Walk.'

'You're an angel!' Madeleine gave her a hug. 'I'll just check on Emily.'

Emily was still fast asleep. Madeleine returned to Natalia, who wanted to know more about James. Madeleine could have talked all day about him. A twittering of sparrows, perched on the balcony's handrail, made her look at them and smile.

'If only life could be as simple as theirs,' she said. 'All I dream of is to be free of all that baggage and be able to move on with James.'

Natalia cast a surreptitious glance towards the open door, beyond which Emily was sleeping in the bedroom, and lowered her voice,

'Have you thought what to tell Emily when the right time comes?'

'Only a thousand times. I've no idea how to tell her and what to say. But the strangest thing is,' Madeleine leaned closer to her friend, 'in my mind there is not the tiniest connection between my child and *him*. She is all mine.'

# CHAPTER 28

'Before you go out to play.' Father Gabriel crouched down to Emily's level. 'I've got something here for you.' She let go of Natalia's hand and eagerly accepted the crumpled lump of tissues from his hand.

They were standing in the middle of his study, a dark wood-panelled room, with bright sunlight framed by a tall arched window, giving the room a warm comfortable feeling. His desk was made of sturdy solid oak and the surrounding walls were lined with shelves, some a touch sagging under the weight of books. There was a vague smell of tobacco and of a recent squirt of lemon freshener.

With Rabbit tucked under her arm, Emily unwrapped the tissue to reveal a flat glass angel. The pink glass of his dress was patterned with trapped air bubbles, his tresses were transparent amber and his face and raised arms were milky white. A plastic thread was attached to the loop on his back.

'You can hang him over your bed,' Father Gabriel said, getting up. 'He'll always be there looking after you. Your very own guardian angel.' Madeleine liked his kind voice and his fatherly expression.

'Thank you,' Emily said, examining the gift. 'And I'll look after him,' she promised.

'I'm sure he'll feel absolutely safe with you,' Father Gabriel replied seriously.

'It's so kind of you,' Madeleine added her thanks. He turned his attention to her. He was in his mid-fifties, at a guess, with his thick greying hair cut like a brush. His trust-inspiring face was criss-crossed with lines of concern for his flock.

'You must visit our workshop,' he said, 'before you go back. Most of our kids come from deprived homes. We encourage them to get involved in creative work. Painting, ceramics, woodwork, handiwork crafts, glass and so on. They never fail to surprise us with their talents. It's very rewarding. I have retired teachers helping us. Whatever we sell in our workshop goes back into our kitty to improve the place.'

'I'm impressed!' Madeleine said with feeling. 'Are there many in your class?'

'About twenty on average. Getting the girls to come back regularly is a problem. They are cheap labour in the rural areas. There's still much poverty in the villages.' He checked his watch. 'Shall we make a start?'

Natalia had already explained the reason for their visit on arrival. Now she took Emily's hand, saying, 'Time for us to go out to play.'

'What about you, Mama?' Emily looked up.

'I'll come too,' Madeleine assured her. 'Once I've had a chat with Father Gabriel.'

'What about?'

'Lots of things. Even about your first communion next year.'

'When I'm seven?' Emily's face lit up at once.

'Shall we leave Mama to sort out those things?' Natalia suggested. Emily agreed, clasped Natalia's hand and went out with her.

Father Gabriel invited Madeleine to sit down at his desk, facing him. Light from the window fell on his head and transformed his hair into a halo. Madeleine noticed that with a touch of amusement, despite her nervous feeling.

His tone was gentle when he spoke. 'I gather you have a problem, Magda. I'll do my best to help you. Even if we don't find an immediate solution, just talking it over with another person may help you to see things more clearly. I can promise you one thing: the power to change things lies entirely within you. It is all about belief and self-confidence.'

She nodded, thinking, if only it were that simple. She had prepared her speech beforehand and told Father Gabriel briefly about her life with Aunt Emilia and Uncle Zden, about that dreadful night and her escape to England and about her new life with her kind relatives, Aniela and Bronek.

She concluded, saying, 'I've met a good man. I love him. I feel he deserves better than me. I cannot bear the thought of his rejection, once I tell him the truth.'

Father Gabriel had listened with his gaze fixed on his clasped hands before him. Now, as he looked up his eyes picked up the brightness from the shaft of light falling across his desk. He looked animated and full of purpose.

'Magda, what you have just told me is a story of a brave girl, who has picked herself up from the most dreadful blow, who has had another human being thrust upon her, who has accepted that unplanned, unexpected duty and has carried it out to her best ability, who has worked hard and has studied hard to make a decent life for herself and her child. You are a heroine, Magda. You were a victim for only a fraction of all that time, but all your achievements since then should make you proud of yourself and anyone who knows you.'

Madeleine was stunned. It took a moment to absorb his words. She had never viewed herself from any other angle, except from within the experience that had brought her so much pain and shame. Could it be that other people viewed her like Father Gabriel? Did James?

'But...' She needed to put the record straight. 'But, Father, I didn't do it on my own. My grandparents deserve most of the praise.'

He raised his thick eyebrows and gave her a comically stiff smile, dismissing her argument.

'Magda, just think, without your goodwill and determination, they would have been helpless. Stop beating yourself up. You've got absolutely nothing to be ashamed of. But so much to be proud of. You are the victor in this whole situation. Hold your head up high. And when you look in the mirror every morning tell yourself that. It's called affirmation. Tell yourself that enough times and you'll be surprised at how that will affect your image of yourself and build up your confidence.'

She gave him a quizzical look. It all sounded like hocus pocus.

'You don't believe me, I know.' He sat back and relaxed his shoulders. 'I can only suggest. The rest is up to you.' He paused. 'Would it help to see him punished? To see justice done? Your uncle committed a crime. You could still report him. Your child's DNA and his would easily wrap up your case.'

She took a sharp intake of breath and raised her hand.

'No, Father, never! Everyone would get to know. I want to protect Emily.'

He gave her a thoughtful look.

'He deserves to be punished. This is how men like him get away.'

'I know. But the alternative is too dreadful to contemplate. Resurrecting all that horror and pain. Resurrecting the shame of it. I've buried it all, Father. I couldn't bear to have to confront any of it again!' She shook her head.

Father Gabriel nodded thoughtfully before saying, 'He could do this to someone else again... '

'He could...' Reluctantly Madeleine agreed. 'I hope with all my might that his victim would be much braver than I am and report him.' She added after a pause, 'I may be totally wrong, but I think that what he did then, he would never repeat again. He was totally out of his mind with drink and grief at the time. Up until then he had been a good uncle to me. It hurts me to say this in his favour, but that is the truth.'

Father Gabriel's expression was stern as he held her gaze, but his tone surprised her with its note of tenderness.

'You're noble to defend him.'

'I'm not!' she refuted vehemently: 'I would never defend him. But I cannot tell lies. He was not always that evil man that I hate so much now!'

Father Gabriel gave her another considered look, but his expression softened when he spoke.

'Magda, we'll leave this subject at that. But if you ever change your mind...' He did not have to spell out his meaning. 'Count on me to give you support. Now, before you leave, I wish to send you home with this simple message: promise me to give yourself a moment each day, when you stop in front of the mirror and say something positive about yourself. To start you off here are a few descriptions: courageous, hardworking, successful, generous... you get the drift.' He sat up and leaned forward across the desk. 'Take it from me, you are an asset to anyone lucky enough to be acquainted with you. A trophy for the person you love. There's no room for fear and distrust in your relationship. Promise me, Magda, to think positively about yourself every day.'

She was dazzled, she had to admit, by the images his vocabulary conjured up.

'I promise,' she said, still unconvinced how any of his advice could help her overcome her problems. 'Thank you for your time. I'm very grateful.'

He got up and accompanied her to the door.

'Good luck, Magda. Trust yourself. You can do it!'

In the vestibule on the way out, she stopped at the mirror and looked at herself. It was a full-length mirror framed inside a garland of flowers carved in dark wood. Following Father Gabriel's instructions, she made her lips smile, her cheeks lift, her dark eyes widen in the shadow of their thick eyelashes. The pale lemon linen jacket and the matching cropped trousers suited her tanned complexion. This was what James saw when they were together. Did he think she was special and an enviable asset for him? He must have done. He had told her of his feelings enough times.

Just thinking that made her feel better about herself, but how was this going to help overcome her fear when the time came to confess everything?

*

It was the second morning of Madeleine's visit. She and Natalia and Emily were finishing breakfast in Natalia's minuscule kitchen, the lace curtain flapping gently at the open window.

'Natalia, a million thanks! I really appreciate it. I can't imagine that visiting the cemetery was on your list of 'to do' things three days before your wedding.'

'Nothing to it, Magda! I'm still your chauffeur all day today! We'll make the most of it!' Natalia smiled generously.

'What's in the cemetery?' Emily stopped eating her toast, holding it close to her mouth.

'Lots of statues and tombstones and flowers to remember all the people who have gone to Heaven,' Madeleine explained. 'There is a cross on a tombstone to remember your grandma Marta, who was my very own mama, and my grandma Kasia, and my auntie Emilia. We'll take them some flowers and tell them that we love them and that we shall never forget them. That will be a nice thing to do, won't it?'

Emily nodded as she continued to finish her toast and lick her sticky fingers.

'Do I remember them?' she asked.

'No, Emily. Sadly, they all died before you were born. But their photographs are in the stone. You'll see for yourself what lovely ladies they were.'

Emily appeared satisfied. She had an accommodating nature and had enjoyed all the activities of the previous day. They had visited the dragon's cave, where the legendary dragon made of metal breathed out fire intermittently, much to her excitement; they had taken a boat ride on the Vistula; they had fed the pigeons in the old market square; they had visited all the play areas along the Planty Walk and all the while Emily had skipped ahead of them, as if pumped with some magical energy.

In the evening before seven, Natalia had driven them to the hospital to pick up Szymon. He came off his duty at the Accident and Emergency department smelling of disinfectant, though he no longer wore his white overall but a smart grey cotton jacket over a white shirt. He looked just the same as Madeleine remembered him, boyish with an ever-ready smile, his long limbs a touch gangly, his blond hair untamed. He gave Madeleine a long, strong hug, then picked up Emily and twirled her round to her squeals of delight, where they had come to meet him in the open car park.

They ate their evening meal in a little place just off the main square, where the prices were ridiculously low and Madeleine insisted on treating them. Szymon announced that this was an affront to his masculinity, but in the end was forced to capitulate to the force of three women. He entertained them with hospital humour and anecdotes about some outstanding characters amongst his work colleagues. Emily had Rabbit for company, but towards the end of the evening she placed her soft toy on the table before her and rested her head on his wool-filled body.

After the meal, they dropped off Szymon at his parents' house but did not go in. Szymon had an early start in the morning and Madeleine admitted to a total collapse of her energy; she had been up most of the previous night before a very long day.

However, before settling down for the night beside Emily in Natalia's cosy bed, she had remembered Father Gabriel's instructions to her. She could not bring herself to lavish all those superlatives upon herself (frankly she'd feel like a fool talking to her image in the mirror) but there was one thought that appealed to her. She liked that idea of calling herself the victor. She'd never again be the victim. Never. That thought alone made her feel stronger and more confident.

That was the first thought in her mind on waking up this morning. Even as she got up, she felt a fresh buoyant energy in her every movement, and a fresh optimism colour her future bright.

When the breakfast was over, and things had been tidied away, and the tiny kitchen was left pristine, they took a lift to the ground floor and walked to Natalia's parked car.

*

There was a heady scent of linden and maple trees in the cemetery. The bleach-white tombstones shone blinding-bright in the morning sun, and the flowers adorning them were like sparkling jewels piled at their feet. Madeleine had never forgotten the beauty of Polish cemeteries, nor the competitive spirit of each family to make their grave outstanding.

She and Natalia, with Emily between them holding their hands, walked down the central path that was intermittently shaded by laurel and yew trees. They carried two bouquets of fresh roses, golden, touched with red around the petals, and two ceramic vases, heavy enough to withstand the wind.

Mist rose from the ground and hovered in delicate wisps over the tufts of wildflowers that had found home in the gaps between the graves. Madeleine had walked this route a hundred times with her Aunt Emilia to her mother's and her grandmother's graves. Now Aunt Emilia was sharing this resting place with them.

It was a pleasant surprise to find the grave well kept, scrubbed clean and bedecked with fresh flowers, three large bouquets of white and pink chrysanthemums in heavy stone vases.

'Someone comes here regularly,' Natalia remarked.

'Uncle Zden, no doubt.' Madeleine looked over her shoulder nervously.

'Not necessarily. It could be a family friend,' Natalia suggested, looking around nevertheless. 'Don't worry, Magda, we're very early. This won't take long. We'll be gone before anyone else comes.'

Madeleine knelt down at the end of the flat white stone and lifted Emily on top of it.

'Look, Emily.' She pointed at the vertical stone cross within which were inlaid three glass-protected portraits. 'This is your great-grandma, this is your grandma and my own mama, and this is my auntie Emilia.'

The three photographs, a sepia and two black-and-white ones, showed the women in their twenties, young girls with expressive brown eyes and abundant hair styled in the fashions of their time: Grandma's tidy curls around her face and her two daughters' sleek long hair falling to their shoulders. The inscriptions underneath their portraits gave dates of their life-spans; Katarzyna Slomska 1935–2003; Marta Zielinska 1965–1991; Emilia Dopska 1963–2005. Such short lives, even her grandmother's by today's standards. But then Aniela, Katarzyna's sister, was already seventy-five and still going strong. Madeleine comforted herself with that thought. And on her father's side there were aunts and uncles still alive in their late eighties. She could only hope she had inherited their genes.

After explaining to Emily the relationship of the three women to her, Madeleine suggested they fetch the water for the bouquets they had brought with them. There was a tap nearby and a wooden stand with six hooks and six watering cans hanging from them. While they fetched the water, Natalia dusted the stone and wiped it with a damp cloth. When their roses had been arranged in place, they made a splash of gold colour against the pastels of the chrysanthemums already there.

'This would make them happy. All three of them,' Madeleine said, feeling pleased and touched that she'd had this chance to visit the resting place of the three women so dear to her.

'Mama, who is that man?' Emily tugged at her hand. Uncle Zden, was Madeleine's frightened reaction. She and Natalia turned around. The cemetery was deserted except for one person walking down the central path, some distance from them. He was tall and very thin and stooping, his grey hair catching patches of sunlight from the gaps between the trees. Not Zden. Madeleine breathed with relief. Some bereft poor soul seeking comfort from his loved one's grave.

'No one,' she said to Emily, and began to gather all the cleaning utensils into the plastic bag, held open for her by Natalia.

'He's coming this way, Mama.'

Madeleine straightened herself with Natalia beside her. Her heart dropped then beat like a hammer.

'It's him! It's him!' Her voice was strangled. She was rooted to the spot as she watched him coming towards them, along the narrow footpath between the graves, his head drooped forward, his gaze on the ground. He only stopped when their presence registered in the periphery of his vision. He lifted his head. There was a look of puzzlement in his eyes. They widened with surprise, then even more with shock.

'Magda? Is that really you?'

She was paralysed. It was like being encased in metal skin. He made a step towards her then stopped and rubbed his eyes with the back of his hand. His once-handsome face had the look of scrunched-up parchment, unsuccessfully patted flat. His eyes, once shiny slate, were sunken, the light in them dim. His white-grey hair looked like animal pelt ruffled in all directions. He was only fifty-five but barely recognisable as her Uncle Zden, the one-time good-looking, energetic and tireless coach of an athletics team.

Madeleine stood still, aware of Natalia's arm around her waist and Emily's closeness against her thigh.

'Mama?' Her daughter's plaintive, unspoken question pulled her out of her trance and at that very moment Father Gabriel's words came to her, like shooting stars, just when she needed them most. I'm a victor here, the victor! I'm not going to be afraid! She suppressed her tremor with her clenched hands.

'I've got nothing to say to you,' she said, the calm in her voice masking her fear. 'Please let me pass.'

There was a begging, hurt expression in his eyes. He looked at Natalia.

'Please let me have a minute on my own with Magda.'

'No!' Madeleine's vehement outburst surprised herself. 'I don't want to speak to you. I don't want to look at you. I'm going!'

She turned abruptly to go the opposite, longer way, but he stretched out his arm as if to stop her.

'Wait, Magda, I beg you! Just hear me out. I need to explain. I want to make amends. Please grant me this wish!'

She looked back and saw his speculative gaze studying Emily. She was struck with a fury she could barely control. So exhilarating! She spoke through her teeth. It was an effort not to shout.

'You can't ever make amends for what you've done. Leave me alone and never come near me again!'

He presented a sad and pitiful figure. She had the upper hand here. She truly was the victor. It was infinitely satisfying. She need not be afraid of him anymore.

Grasping Emily's hand firmly, she said to Natalia, 'Let's go.'

They turned their backs on him and began to walk away.

'I won't give up, Magda!' he called after them. 'You don't understand! I need to speak to you! You can't run away from me. I know where to find you!' But as they carried on walking away from him, he called out one more time, 'And whose is this child with you?'

The old frisson of fear was back but only for a moment. There was nothing he could do to her, nothing, the pathetic broken man, whose only weapons were threats. Mere words, nothing else. With Natalia beside her and Emily clutching her hand, she carried on walking between the graves until they reached the tarmac path that encircled the cemetery. Natalia was first to breathe out a huge sigh of relief.

'Magda, you were amazing!'

Madeleine shook her head, feeling wrung out.

'I wish I were. I was very angry then very satisfied at being so mean to him! Such a pathetic victory!'

'No, he's the one who's pathetic! And good riddance to him!'

Emily tugged at her hand. She had been very quiet all along, holding on tensely.

'Mama, who is that man? Why are you so cross with him?'

The truth. Make it simple.

'I knew him a long time ago, Emily. He wasn't nice to me. He upset me very much. I don't want to be friends with him when we have lots of good friends who love us. We don't need him.' Madeleine bent down and hugged her daughter. 'He won't bother us again. Don't worry about him anymore.'

She suppressed a prick of guilt. There was the right time for everything, she told herself, but now was not the right time to burden her child with things she would not understand.

# CHAPTER 29

The Church of St Anne was the perfect venue for Natalia and Szymon's wedding. It was a richly ornate baroque building with giddy-high columns, exquisitely sculpted saints and angels, snow-white marble, lavish gold accentuating the halos and the beams of heavenly light radiating from the central altar, crystal chandeliers that scattered a thousand star-lights onto the main nave. It made one think of icing on the wedding cake, of flamboyant wedding dresses, of lace and veils, of pearls and diamonds. Madeleine could only dream of a matching setting in England at her own wedding, if that were to happen at all.

She was sitting with Emily at the end of a pew closest to the central nave, to give Emily a good view of the bride when she arrived, and of the subsequent unfolding ceremony at the altar. Emily was looking like a delicate peony in her pink organdie dress with the multi-layered skirt, and a matching organdie ribbon woven into her plait. For herself, Madeleine had chosen a simple outfit that she could wear again of a silky-cotton dress and jacket in pearl grey, and deeper grey suede high heels with a handbag to match. Adorning her neck were two rows of pearls. Understated, perhaps, but she preferred to blend in with the crowd.

As the wedding guests arrived in a continuous stream and filled up the pews, she could not help a feeling of nervousness at the thought of seeing Dominik. She could not imagine his first reaction at the unexpected sight of her and had practised all kinds of opening lines to soften their first encounter. She found the organ music that vibrated through the domed space above and around her soothing and comforting. All the favourites that she loved and could have listened to for hours: Gounod's Ave Maria, Bellini's Casta Diva, Verdi's Slave Chorus, Mozart, Chopin – the melodies followed each other seamlessly, as she gave into thinking about James, and looking forward to seeing him the next day. The few days with Natalia had flown in a whirlwind.

She had accompanied Natalia in all the pre-wedding checking and rechecking, seeing people engaged to ensure that everything was successfully synchronised on the big day; they visited both families, and on the night before the wedding they had met the early arrivals at their hotel for cocktails and a whistle-stop chat. Last night, she had helped Natalia to transport to her parents' apartment the wedding dress and all the paraphernalia required to transform Natalia into a princess. And today, while Emily had been looked after by Natalia's cousin with children of similar age to Emily's, Madeleine and another cousin Alicya had spent most of the day getting Natalia ready for three o'clock. Natalia's mother, a kind and gentle woman, had kept them going with discreet suggestions, home-baked cake and countless cups of tea. Madeleine loved her, and remembered many occasions from her childhood when she had wished that Natalia's mother was her mother too.

Natalia's father had escaped to one of the sons for the morning, but when he arrived home in the afternoon, all wedding-smart with a pink and white carnation buttonhole, Natalia was ready. Her curly, unruly hair had been swept up into an elegant arrangement on top of her head and held in place with a multitude of hair-grips and a tin of hair-spray. Over that was pinned a floaty gossamer veil edged with the finest lace roses. Her satin wedding dress was slim in style, with long sleeves and pointy cuffs, and the stand-up collar allowed a glimpse of the gold chain around her neck. The impossibly high heels added height to the already model-like image.

'You look fantastic!' Her father greeted her with a kiss on her cheek.

'You don't look bad yourself,' Natalia replied, giving him a hug, then standing back stiffly to preserve her perfect image.

It was time to go. Cousin Alicya's husband was waiting for her and Madeleine in the car, and, just as they were driving off, the ribbon-decked wedding car arrived.

'Mama.' Emily lifted her face to whisper into Madeleine's ear. She pointed her finger at the ceiling from which a group of sculpted cherubs appeared to dance playfully in a ring. 'Why haven't they got any clothes on? Isn't that rude?' Madeleine stroked her head lovingly.

'No, my sweetheart, it's not rude, because they are only little babies. And babies are sweet whatever they do.'

Emily nodded thoughtfully then asked, 'Am I rude looking at their willies?'

'No, Emily, you can look at anything you like in the church. This is God's house. And everything that God has made is good.'

'Even the willies?'

'Of course. Without them the boys would simply burst with all the water and tea and juice drinks inside them.'

Emily nodded, apparently satisfied with the answer. Madeleine looked up and saw him.

Dominik. Everything stopped. All she could hear was the thudding of her heart.

He walked past her, unaware, his wife by his side, his baby son held up against his shoulder. He looked just the same as the image she had carried in her mind for the past seven years: honey-coloured skin, regular handsome features, dark blond hair swept back neatly off his face. His wife was half a head shorter, and, from what Madeleine saw of her profile, a very attractive girl with a milky complexion and an abundance of dark hair twisted deftly into a knot at the nape of her neck. A touch of plumpness, possibly post-natal, appeared to add to her eye-catching, feminine looks. A niggle of envy. Madeleine suppressed it but could not push away the thought of how different life could have been for her.

Then all her thoughts drowned in the rousing opening of Mendelssohn's Wedding March, as Natalia was led to the altar by her father. They were followed by four couples, Szymon's friends arm in arm with Natalia's four bridesmaids. Awaiting them at the altar was Szymon and his best man.

After the wedding ceremony and the nuptial Mass, when Father Gabriel sent them out with his blessing to the joyous alleluias of Beethoven's Fifth, a happy murmur permeated the congregation. Following the bride and groom, the guests began to vacate the pews, their faces smiling, their subdued voices unable to contain the bubbling jubilation.

Madeleine's attention was riveted on Dominik. She watched him leave his pew with his wife behind him, their child asleep against his shoulder. Her heart beat fast as he approached. He was looking ahead, then appeared to have spotted someone he knew at the end of her row. He nodded and smiled, then as his eyes travelled along the row, his gaze met hers. For a split-second, surprise registered in his eyes, his step wavered, but the people behind him made it impossible for him to stop.

He'd seen her. He'd be prepared when she followed him out of the church. That was a relief of a kind.

Outside, holding Emily's hand she stayed close to Natalia's cousin, as a crowd gathered around the newlyweds to congratulate them. The cousin's husband and another relative were attempting to direct everyone towards the Planty Green, a stone's throw away across the road.

Madeleine walked with Alicya, glad for the moment to be lost in the crowd among all the excitement. The mellow August sun brought out the colours of the women's outfits and the elegance of the men's suits, and they all formed a picturesque background to the bridal group, together with the variety of surrounding shrubs and trees, their hues deepened rich over the summer months.

As people were being called out to pose with the bride and groom for the photographs, and Emily ran up to her newly acquainted playmates of the past few days, Madeleine remained with Alicya in the shade of a copper beech. No effort at conversation was necessary when Alicya was around; she did all the talking. Madeleine had a job keeping up with the speed of her delivery, and with the energy of her constantly mobile expressive hands.

Alicya suddenly stopped, her gaze focussed on Madeleine's left shoulder. Madeleine turned around. A strange tremor ran the length of her body. Dominik was right beside her.

'Magda, this is such a surprise!' His features fell into a wide smile. She was overcome with relief. She was aware of Alicya's discreet withdrawal and her parting words, 'Excuse me, I think they need me over there.'

For a while neither of them spoke, unable to avert their eyes from each other. Dominik spoke first.

'I've imagined this moment a thousand times, yet I never imagined it like this.'

Madeleine looked around. People stood in groups engaged in animated talk. There was no reason for anyone to think that their encounter was anything other than a meeting of old friends.

'And your wife? Does she know? I don't want to upset her.'

'Don't worry,' he said. 'I told her about us, a very long time ago. As for today, you're just an old friend from our student days. Post-mortems of today can wait till tomorrow. No doubt the talk about this wedding will go on for days. She'll be joining us shortly. She's just gone to change our little Kasper in the car.'

Dominik's gaze appraised her slowly, making her self-conscious.

'You look lovely, Magda. Correction: you look more beautiful than I've remembered you all those years in my thoughts.'

'Don't say that, please,' Madeleine said nervously, expecting his wife to return any moment. 'I don't deserve any praise. I don't deserve your forgiveness. But…' She gave him a pleading look. 'If you could find it in your heart…'

He had that soft understanding look in his amber eyes that she remembered so well. He said, 'It would make it easier for me to let go of the hurt if I could understand what made you run away from me.'

She winced inwardly.

'I didn't run from you, Dominik, I swear. I was ill. I had a mental breakdown. I couldn't foist that burden on you. You deserved better.'

He shook his head in disbelief.

'Why didn't you trust me? I could have helped you. Isn't that what couples do? Support each other in good and bad times?' Madeleine couldn't tell him that, even if he had found it in himself to do this, his parents would have made his life a misery, for supporting a girl pregnant with another man's child. He turned his head and looked across to where Emily was playing with other girls, their bright frilly dresses as light as candy floss. 'I guess that's your little girl? She looks like you,' he said.

'Yes, that's Emily.' And anticipating his train of thought she added, 'Emily is six.' It was excruciating waiting for his reaction.

There was no malice in his tone when he said, 'It didn't take you long to console yourself. After me. Had there been me?'

This was worse than his anger would have been; she would have matched it with her own. Instead, his words spoken so calmly made her feel utterly miserable, made her feel desperate to make amends. He deserved the truth. She owed him that. It was time to tell him, but not today. Today was for celebrations, for joy.

She said, 'Dominik, I was afraid you'd reach that conclusion. And who can blame you? But I promise you, it is not what you think. You'd never guess the truth. But Natalia will tell you. I've asked her to do it for me. It won't change the past, but perhaps it'll make you think better of me.' She gave him another pleading look. 'I'm so happy for you. A beautiful wife and a baby boy. So much to be grateful for. And look, here they are.'

Agata joined them holding Kasper against her shoulder. He moved his tiny legs as if attempting to climb up further and made little puppy noises. Dominik took him off her eagerly and cradled him in the crook of his arm. There was a wet patch on the shoulder of Agata's smart navy dress. She smiled warmly and shook Madeleine's hand.

'So pleased to meet you. I gather you and Dominik know each other from your student days. What's it like in England? Are you staying there for good?'

Too many unresolved issues to answer this question simply. But there was one person who had the power to sway Madeleine's decision in favour of her adopted country. A warm feeling swept over her just thinking about James. She smiled.

'I'm happily settled there for the time being, but who knows what the future holds? I have missed Krakow. I had no idea how much until this visit.'

'Then you mustn't leave it so long before you visit again.' Agata sounded sincere.

There was a photo-call for everyone to gather around the newlyweds.

'Shall we go?' Dominik suggested, stroking his baby's tiny arm. 'Magda, we'll catch up later, at the reception.'

'Of course we will,' Agata added, with a smile that said, any friend of Dominik's is a friend of mine.

It was a fabulous reception in a country hotel outside Krakow. The wedding convoy of a long line of cars, headed by a horse-drawn carriage with Natalia and Szymon sitting high on it, cut through the golden fields of corn, through the sun-dappled shadows in the woodlands and out into the open land, where a beautiful country house, once the property of aristocrats hounded out of their country by invading Germans, stood gleaming white in its renovated splendour, protectively surrounded by mature oaks, chestnut trees and conifers.

All protocol and traditions were followed, speeches made and the lavish meal consumed at leisure amidst much animated talk to the background strains of Strauss and Liszt. Madeleine had been placed with Alicya and her husband, Tomasz, on one side, and on the other she had an entertaining single man, Bartek. He was an architect, amusingly flamboyant with his anecdotes and equally flamboyant in looks: a sweep of long auburn hair falling below his ears, a bright orange silk handkerchief spilling out of his breast pocket to match his tie against the lightest grey of his suit.

'Matching outfits,' he commented, stretching his arm alongside Madeleine's, making her laugh with the ridiculous comparison. She looked out for Emily, who appeared happy and well entertained on a table for children, minded by two teenage girls. After they'd eaten, the girls led the children outside to a play area in the gardens at the back of the house.

Now and again, Madeleine would catch Dominik's glance across the room. He smiled each time. That made her feel good, relieved. Did he ever think of what may have been? She desperately wanted him to be happy, to ease her own conscience. He'd been blessed with a lovely wife, a beautiful child, a steady career ahead. She did not want the slightest shadow from the past to mar the good things in his life. Did she have regrets? It could have been her instead of Agata, sitting there beside him now. She could have enjoyed a secure and normal life with her own people in her home city that she had loved so much. She hated Zden for what he had done. She could never forgive him. And yet... it had been that upheaval that had led her to meet James. Now she could not imagine her life without him.

Her mobile vibrated in her handbag. She excused herself and went to the Ladies' Retreat Room, a grand name on a grand door, an entrance suited more to a ballroom than a bathroom. Here the walls were lined with gilded mirrors, the washbasins equipped with golden taps, and on the shiny marble floor stood tall carved wooden containers providing the once-only use of white hand terry towels.

Madeleine took out her mobile and read James's message. He had kept in touch several times a day, each day, with short texts:

*Enjoy every minute. See you tomorrow.*

Dear James. She was overcome with love for him. If thoughts could travel, then she had sent him a thousand messages in the whirlwind tempo of the last few days.

She tapped the letters on her mobile and texted him:

*Much to tell. Can't wait to see you.*

Back in the main room, couples were dancing on the parquet floor. A waltz, quaint and delightful, was enticing older people as well as the younger self-made experts, eager to match the professionals of the Polish *Strictly*. Bartek asked Madeleine to dance even before she sat down. He was an excellent dancer and led her dexterously in step with him, despite her somewhat rusty feeling after years of abstention from this social pastime. The waltz was followed by a tango. He made her giggle with his theatrical intensity and passion, and she was still laughing when the music stopped, and he led her to their seats.

'I've not had so much fun for a long time,' she told him honestly, fanning her face with a menu card.

'This is just the beginning,' he told her with mock gravity. 'By the end of the evening, we shall be the World Dance Champions!'

'By the end of the evening,' she said sobering from her fit of giggles, 'I shall have to be gone. I've got a young daughter and an early flight to catch tomorrow.' She checked her watch. 'In fact, I better go and see what she's up to.'

She excused herself, crossed the dance floor and walked down the wide corridor, its rich green velour walls decorated with paintings and crystal wall-lights. She followed the sound of the children's voices singing and stopped at an open double door. Inside the high-ceilinged room with pale lemon walls and ornate white cornices, children were playing a ring game, supervised by two older girls. A little boy in the middle was just in the throes of indecision as to which child to choose to be his dancing playmate, while the other children stuck out their chests and pointed at themselves while he was making up his mind.

Emily saw Madeleine and detached herself from the ring.

'Mama!' she ran up to her, 'I don't want to go yet!' She gave her a hug round the waist, which Madeleine returned.

'All right, ten more minutes and then we must go. It's a very early start tomorrow.' It was now half past nine, well after Emily's bedtime.

'Ten minutes and another ten, please, Mama,' Emily begged her eyes huge with anticipation.

Madeleine laughed.

'Go, enjoy yourself. I'll be back when it's time.'

She stopped in the corridor to admire a painting of a young girl standing at an open window, the light touching the side of her face, the rest of her in shadow against the light outdoors.

'Beautiful, isn't she?' Dominik was beside her. Madeleine had not heard him come up. But now she breathed in his presence, his pleasant clean scent, and even a touch of that antiseptic smell she remembered clinging to him when he was a student doctor. His smiling eyes appraised her. 'I saw you get up. I wanted to see you before you left.' He gave her a slow, hesitant look, as if preparing to say something intimate. 'Magda, I missed you dreadfully that time. You can't imagine how much. I wish you'd tell me what really happened.'

She took a deep breath and looked nervously down the corridor.

'What about your wife?'

'Don't worry. I told her where to find me after she's seen to our little Kasper upstairs. We've booked a room with a nanny.'

'And she doesn't mind you talking to me?'

'Magda, why would she? It's all in the past now.' He shook his head gently, smiling at her. 'Just tell me. And I shall never bother you again.'

She held his gaze for a second, still feeling for him, feeling for his pain.

'I've asked Natalia to tell you. I missed you too, Dominik. Missed you more than you could imagine. I missed you so much I wanted to die!'

This seemed to jolt him.

'Really?'

All those years I missed you, all those long years, she thought.

'Then why didn't you get in touch with me? Why, Magda, why?' His voice was a touch shaky with emotion.

'Because...' She smiled sadly. 'The truth would have caused you even more pain than not knowing. Believe me. You'll understand everything when Natalia tells you. But now is not the time for such revelations. It's such a happy day. Natalia and Szymon's special day. Let's leave it this way.'

271

He kept looking at her, unconvinced, dissatisfied.

'Dominik,' she said briskly, buoyed suddenly by the thought of Father Gabriel's advice, 'it's all in the past now. We can't change the past, but we can try to steer our future towards good things. And your future looks good to me. I'm very happy for you, Dominik, believe me. And I'm so pleased that we've had this chance to catch up. It's very important to me that we part on good terms.'

He still said nothing, just kept looking at her, those soft amber eyes of his screening his thoughts. The odd person passing by them would have just registered a couple discussing the painting on the wall.

'When you've spoken to Natalia,' Madeleine said, 'you can decide then if you still want to get in touch with me. She's got my e-mail address.'

Dominik appeared to regain composure and replied decidedly, his hand accenting his words.

'Of course I want to keep in touch with you, Magda. Now that we've regained contact, it would upset me again to lose it.' He paused then asked quickly, 'Are you with anyone?'

Should she tell him about James? Her future still looked uncertain. She said, 'I've been too busy rebuilding my life. Working, bringing up Emily.'

'Without her father?' He raised an eyebrow.

'Natalia will explain.'

'So… you're on your own? Still?'

'With my grandparents. They've been my rock for the past seven years.'

Something like compassion, or perhaps relief, passed across his features, and then unexpectedly he hugged her to his chest. She was overwhelmed with the joy of being so close to him, inhaling his warmth, his scent. It was comforting, like, she imagined, being safe in a brotherly embrace. Gently, he let go of her and stood back.

'I'm just so glad I've found you.'

'Then we're friends?' she asked.

'I very much hope so. Agata would like to see you before you leave.'

'I want to see her too,' Madeleine said with feeling. 'Perhaps in the future our meetings will not be so spaced out?'

'The distance is no deterrent these days,' he said, and those words held a promise for her. The feeling inside her was as light as a soaring bird. She suddenly thought that Zden would never enjoy that feeling, because she had the power to withhold it from him. It was mean, she knew, compared to Dominik's forgiving nature, but there were some things that were unforgiveable.

She looked at her watch.

'I must go, Dominik. To find Natalia and Szymon and say my goodbyes.'

They were busy going around the banquet room talking to their guests. Madeleine waited, until Natalia, freed of her veil now and wearing her elegant wedding dress like an evening attire, looked up at her and freed herself from a group of very jolly merry-making friends.

'Natalia, incredibly, it is time for me to go,' Madeleine said with regret. 'I need you all to myself. Just for two minutes.'

Natalia gave her a hug.

'Let's go outside.'

It was still light outside, with the soft dusk bringing out the fragrance of flowers, of the climbing roses over wrought iron structures and of the sun-dried grass. There were small groups of people sitting at garden tables, talking, drinking, their faces catching the glow from the fairy lights strung out above them.

Natalia found a quiet spot in a sheltered corner.

'Magda.' She hugged her friend again. 'I cannot thank you enough for the past few days. Only four months ago I never imagined this being possible.'

'Nor me.' Madeleinė returned the hug and stood back from Natalia, overwhelmed with a deep sisterly feeling. 'I've seen Dominik. I've had a chat with him. It was good to see him again. I've not explained anything. I couldn't, Natalia. But he deserves to know. Will you do it for me?'

'I've promised and I'll do it,' Natalia said soothingly. 'Leave it with me and don't worry about it anymore.' She leaned over and hugged Madeleine again. 'Go back to your James and let me know the date of your wedding!'

Madeleine laughed softly. 'I pray, Natalia, that you're the prophet of good things!'

They went together indoors to find Emily. She was still walking around in a circle, singing with other children. On seeing Madeleine, she detached herself and ran into Madeleine's arms, who picked her up and felt her child's tiredness.

'You've been such a good girl all week,' Natalia praised her, stroking Emily's hair, 'Let's find Uncle Szymon to say goodbye.'

Szymon came out with them to the waiting taxi at the front of the hotel, hugged Emily and helped to strap her in the child's seat. He turned to Madeleine and opened his arms wide to give her a long and strong brotherly hug.

'Thank you for making the effort to come,' he said warmly. 'It has meant a lot to us both. When Natalia is happy, then so am I.' He gave his wife a mischievous grin. Then he added, 'Magda, we'll make tea in your pot every night and think about you!'

'Far too precious to be used every day!' Natalia protested.

'It's meant to be used every day,' Madeleine laughed. 'Bone china! For the best-tasting tea in the world! And I'll be thinking of you, every time your present adorns my arm!' She stretched out her arm to make the point. The bracelet around her wrist was a chain of silver daisies with mother-of-pearl centres. 'Even in this light they shine with rainbow colours!'

Natalia glanced at the taxi with its engine running, and, ever practical, she reassured Madeleine of the next morning's arrangements.

'Will you be all right at the flat on your own tonight? When Alicya comes to take you to the airport in the morning, she'll double-check everything, so you don't have to worry.'

'I'll be perfectly all right. A hundred thanks for everything. Send me a card from Sopot. If you find some spare time!' Madeleine hugged her friend again before getting in the taxi beside Emily.

# CHAPTER 30

The sight of James made her tingle, as if all the cells in her body sang. He was standing on the other side of the barrier with the waiting crowd, some waving and coming forward to meet their newly arrived. He looked relaxed, his long firm legs slightly apart, his arms folded loosely on his chest, a barely noticeable smile lifting his lips. The look he gave her with those piercing blue eyes, exclusively for her, made her pulse race.

Emily saw him too and with a sudden sprint left Madeleine behind, baggage and all, and ran towards James's open arms.

'I've got you a present!' she cried as he lifted her up and hugged her to his chest.

'I've got one for you too!' He laughed, placing her down and waving a small brown paper bag in front of her. Emily skipped and looked inside the bag.

'A chocolate cupcake!' she exclaimed.

Observing it all as she approached, Madeleine marvelled at the little things that brought so much joy. She dropped her luggage on the ground and threw her arms around James. It felt so ultimately good and safe in his strong embrace, breathing in his very presence, feeling the energy rippling through his body. She could not bear the thought of losing all this once he knew everything about her.

'Did you miss me?' he asked jokingly but she recognised the intensity behind his words.

'How could I not?' She leaned her head back to look into his face. 'You were in my thoughts every minute of every day.' And it was not an exaggeration.

'Really?' There was a note of happiness in that question.

'Yes, James, really. I was wishing all the time that you had been there with me.'

He hugged her again and she shivered with delight at his warm breath on her neck. People were milling round them, but it felt as if they had been soft-focussed into the background, out of reach. Emily tugged at her jacket.

'Mama, when can I eat the cake?'

'You'll have to wait till we find somewhere to sit.' A vision of chocolate crumbs and smudges and sticky fingers was too much to contemplate.

Emily's face puckered but James stepped in.

'How about if we go for a drink now? Half an hour either way won't make much difference to Aniela and Bronek, will it?'

Madeleine checked her watch.

'They'll be attending the midday Mass now. It'll be a little while before they're home. All right.' She smiled down at Emily. 'You win!'

They found a table in the cafeteria, and while James was fetching their two coffees and a fruit drink for Emily, Madeleine settled Emily close to the table, so that all crumbs would fall straight onto the open serviette before her.

'Mama, can I give James my present now?' Emily was eager, her mouth sticky and chocolate-brown after the first bite. There was no reason to postpone Emily's gratification. Besides, Madeleine was touched by her child's obvious attachment to James. She unzipped the side pocket of the hand luggage.

'Here you are, Emily.' She passed her a small slim package wrapped in blue paper. 'But you mustn't tell James what it is before he's had the chance to open it.'

Emily nodded, her eyes shining like two full moons. She took another bite of the creamy cake and smudged her chin. Madeleine wiped it as James approached. He chuckled, placing the tray with their drinks on the table.

'So glad you're enjoying my present already, Emily.'

'And here's yours!' Emily exclaimed, shivering with anticipation. He sat down, put their drinks in front of them, picked up the small package and gave Emily a very mysterious look. She giggled, her whole demeanour hurrying him on.

'I wonder what this could be?'

Emily opened her mouth.

'Shh…' Madeleine stopped her, unable to control her own laughter.

Slowly, James took off the first layer of tissue paper, then the next, while Emily wriggled with impatience. Finally, the present was out of its long slim box. It was a black-and-silver pen with Krakow's coat of arms engraved on its side.

'Do you like it?' Emily asked and clapped her hands.

'It's beautiful! Truly elegant! It shows your excellent taste!' James replied gravely. Emily's expression became worried.

'But I didn't choose it all by myself. Mama helped me. And she has another present for you too.'

'Shh… Emily.' Madeleine stroked her head. 'It's another surprise, only it won't be if you tell. Now be a good girl and eat your yummy cake. The sooner you finish, the sooner we get off. Babcha and Grandpa will be waiting.'

They drank the coffee in companionable silence for a minute or two, watching Emily, sending each other glances full of unspoken thoughts. Madeleine never tired of looking at James, absorbing his image with that dark hair falling over his forehead and behind his ears, his clear blue eyes, thoughtful, unhurried, his mouth, his firm jaw, his altogether good-looking appearance.

'Leicester felt empty with you two gone,' he said.

'Empty?' Emily was baffled. 'But there are hundreds of people in Leicester!'

'Three hundred thousand or there about,' he said and stroked her head. 'But it's like what you feel when your mama is gone all day, even when you have Karishma to play with.'

She stopped eating and studied him seriously.

'I thought… that grown-up people don't miss their mums.'

'They miss the people they love,' he said. He placed his warm hand over Madeleine's on the table and held it there.

'Did you have a good week?' she asked, very much aware of the contact of their hands.

'No more than usual. Yours must have been far more exciting, I bet. I want to hear all about it!'

'I don't know if the car journey will be long enough to tell you everything,' she laughed.

'Then we shall continue afterwards.' He smiled, and gave her a teasing look.

Not surprisingly, after a long day followed by a short night that had deprived Emily of sleep, she fell asleep at the back of the car minutes after they left the airport. For the briefest moment, James took his hand off the steering wheel and gave Madeleine's hand a gentle squeeze. Something ignited inside her. With a shock she recognised how much she desired him. She gave a short, light laugh to cover up her reaction.

When he touched her hand again, she held onto it briefly, then reluctantly let it go.

'I love you, James. I missed you so much. I thought I'd die if for some reason I'd never be able to see you again.'

'You mean that?' He spoke softly, not taking his eyes off the motorway. He was silent for a while, as if bracing himself to tell her something. 'Madeleine, I've got a proposition for tonight. Please, don't say no.'

'Tonight?' Already she worried how this would look if she left Emily with her grandparents the moment she was back. 'It depends on what you have in mind... '

He gave her a quick sideways glance.

'Don't worry. I've already arranged it with Aniela.'

'You did?' Wonders never ceased. 'So what have you got planned for tonight?'

James cleared his throat.

'Josh is away cycling with his friend Matt. Mother is on duty tonight. I'll be alone in the house. But not if you care to join me.' His gaze stayed firmly on the road while she had a sensation like a thousand butterflies settling all over her skin. She swallowed hard.

'And Aniela knows all this?' This was incredible.

James laughed a happy, hearty laugh.

'I didn't go into details. I only asked if it would be a problem if you went out with me tonight. Being as it's Sunday night and I've got to be in London tomorrow. She said that was not a problem at all.'

Dear, kind Aniela. She loved her. A strange swooning sensation affected her limbs at the thought of being alone with James. Graphic, delicious images filled her mind. She blanked them out so she could think clearly. She became aware of James talking to her.

'That's settled then, Madeleine. Now tell me about your trip.'

*

'Magda, just go! Don't keep James waiting!' Aniela could not contain her impatience. She stood in the hallway, her arms folded, her expression full of purpose as her eyes followed Madeleine, who wandered distractedly from room to room, checking things for the next day, checking that Emily was ready for bed and settled. Emily, in her pink pyjamas, was sitting in the front room with Bronek, who was reading to her from James's special edition of *Winnie the Pooh*. Emily knew all the chapters by heart and watched Bronek's lips as he read, prompting him hurriedly when he paused to take a breath.

Aniela hooked her arm around Madeleine's, and gently steered her towards the front door.

'Emily will be fine. Besides, I hope she's missed us as much as we have missed you both.'

Madeleine gave Aniela a strong heartfelt squeeze.

'I assure you, Babcha,' she said, 'that Emily never stopped talking about you. Everything she did or saw she was going to tell you about it.' A rosy glow appeared on Aniela's cheeks and her white curls bounced about her face.

'There you are, then. No need for you to rush back. Emily and us have lots to talk about.'

It felt good to be sent out with Aniela's blessing. Madeleine had been busy all afternoon unpacking and washing and getting things ready for the week. She checked herself in the hall mirror and was pleased: her white dress intensified her appearance of freshness, and her washed hair formed a fluffy bob around her face. Her handbag weighed heavy with the special present for James. For Aniela, she had brought back a white damask tablecloth and for Bronek his favourite Polish vodka.

She hugged Aniela and went out. The evening sun was casting long shadows across the street. Her Ka was parked further up the road. Out of habit she looked up and down the street, her eyes straining to penetrate the dark areas. Silly, really. What was she doing! Zden was no longer a threat to her. Had he had the cheek to come over, he would have done that years ago. He was history. Scrunched-up paper thrown in the bin.

She recalled Father Gabriel's words. They made her feel good about herself. She'd do everything to live up to that image he had presented of her, the astonishing opposite of her previous low self-esteem. She'd make James proud of her. With that in mind, she quickened her pace.

James opened the door even before her finger lifted off the bell-button. As always, he was immaculately dressed, casual, but everything crisp, clean, elegant. She could have eaten off him. She could have licked his skin.

His piercing blue eyes stayed on her.

'You look more beautiful every time I see you,' he said. She felt herself colouring. She had never considered herself a beauty.

'No need to flatter me, James,' she smiled shyly. 'I know my limitations. Only too well.'

'I love your limitations, if that's what you want to call them.' He smiled, pulled her inside, closed the door, embraced her, covered her mouth with his and held her so tight, she felt at one with him, his palpable energy igniting fires within her body.

'Are we to start with desserts?' he teased her, releasing her from his embrace, yet holding on to her hand as he led her through to the dining area. The table was set for two with an inviting spread of cold meats and salads.

'Did you do all this yourself?' she asked.

He laughed.

'My good friend M&S. But I can cook too, I assure you, Madeleine. Promise!' He made a Scouts' honour sign. 'This time I did not want to chance stinking the house out if my cooking went wrong.' He laughed at himself. 'What can I get you to drink?'

She had just brushed her teeth. She wanted her mouth to stay fresh. 'Just a soft drink, thanks.'

The back garden beyond the French window, beyond the wisteria-shaded patio, had patches of bright green, where the lowering sun had filtered through the trees. The border around the long garden was crowded with thick shrubs of hydrangeas, acers in all shades of green, and clumps of multi-coloured dahlias.

'Beautiful!' Madeleine commented looking through the glass door. 'Your mum's work?'

'Mainly,' James said, coming back with a sparkling lemonade for her and a glass of red for himself. 'She has help. It would be too much for her on her own. Even with Josh's sporadic attempts.' He smiled, took a sip and placed his glass on the table. 'Are you hungry? Ready to eat?'

'Not just yet.' Madeleine felt no hunger at all. She felt herself brimming with anticipation. She placed her glass down and brought out from her handbag her present for James. She placed it in his palm and he made it appear as if his arm was about to drop off.

'Goodness! It's a wonder the plane had the power to take off with this on board!' He laughed, a genuine happy laugh. Madeleine watched him unwrap the layers of tissue to reveal the intricately cut crystal paperweight. James lifted it to the sunlight, where it was transformed to a globe of rainbow colours.

'Utterly stunning!' He placed it on the windowsill and stood back to admire it. When he looked at Madeleine, there was a special look in his eyes, nostalgic and a touch emotional, she guessed. 'This has brought back such a strong memory, Madeleine.'

'All good, I hope. I'd never want to upset you.'

'All good.' He came close to her, drew her to him and spoke, looking out onto the beautiful evening outside. 'I was walking in the fields with my father one day. I was perhaps eight at the time. We were caught in torrential rain. We ran to the nearest tree for shelter. The shower was over within minutes, but we were soaked through. Father laughed it off, saying, what was a drop of rain for hardened explorers? He said, every adventure was a discovery. And true enough, there it was, a perfect rainbow above us. I wanted to run to the bottom of the field to catch the end of it.

But my father explained that it was not possible. The rainbow was not a tangible object but just a refraction of light in the raindrops. I was so disappointed, I almost cried. I think it was the combination of wet clothes, and feeling hungry, and wanting to go home. But then he said something else, something that has stayed with me since that day. He said that some people believe that the rainbow is a sign from Heaven that our loved ones, those who have died, are happy. What do you think, Madeleine?'

He turned his gaze at her, and she loved the look in his eyes that seemed to reflect everything she wanted to tell him.

'I love this story,' she said, 'and I believe what your father said is true. When I look at the stars at night, I feel a connection with the people I loved, those who aren't with me anymore. Their eyes have seen what I see now, and it's almost like touching them through the stars.'

He hugged her at that and smiled.

'Do you know, I have felt that too. So many times. When I was far away and lonely.'

'You need never be lonely, James. You've got me.' If you still want me, she thought, after I tell you about my shocking past.

He kissed her and turned her round towards the table, laden with food.

'How about something to eat?'

'Perhaps later? I don't feel hungry at all. But please, don't let me stop you.'

He placed a finger on her lips and began to talk fast, as if fearing to lose his train of thought if he stopped.

'Madeleine, I won't beat about the bush. I like to talk straight. I've been dreaming for weeks of a moment like this, to be alone with you. Just you and me. Like this. And more.' His mouth was upon hers, exploring, tasting, caressing, while her legs wobbled, giving under her weight. He held her up, tighter to his chest. 'I won't press if it's too soon, if you're not ready yet...'

She was giddy with wanting him. For the moment she was free of all fear, free of all bad memories that had tormented her all those years. She'd tell him, she'd tell him everything. Another day.

'I'm ready, James. I want you too...' She returned his kiss, her belly on fire. No more words were necessary. He clasped her hand and led her out of the room towards the wide staircase. It was unreal following him to the upper floor. She had been to this house so many times, but never to the private rooms of his family.

His bedroom was spacious, overlooking the back garden. It was coolly pale, dove-grey with a deep-pile carpet, and a large, freshly made-up bed, the iron-creases intact. They fell spontaneously onto the bed and did what came naturally. Madeleine shocked herself with the intensity of her desire and with the discovery of her instinctive knowledge about things she had only ever imagined before. It was as if only they existed in their own universe. Nothing else mattered.

Later, when they remained in each other's arms, flesh against flesh, their warmth and their breath and their scents blending, Madeleine whispered, 'Shall we just stay here like this forever and ever?'

He let go of her gently and propped himself on his elbow. He had a fantastic body. Michelangelo's David came to mind. It gave her the shivers of exquisite pleasure to run her fingers down his back and over his buttocks. He stroked her hair away from her brow and traced her face with his fingertips, his clear blue eyes smiling down at her.

'I'd say we make an excellent team, don't you think?'

'And that without any practice.' It was true for her. She had never had consenting sex with anyone else before. With Dominik it had never reached that stage, and with Zden it had been a travesty. You'd never believe me, she wanted to say, that this was my first time. Instead she said, 'It feels like a dream. But I won't pinch myself. In case I wake up.'

His smile turned into a serious expression.

'Madeleine, I'd hate to compete with someone from your past.'

This came as a total surprise. Her self-assured James. Her near-to-perfect James. Worried? About some imagined lover from her past?

She raised herself on her elbow and gently pushed him flat on his back. She lay on top of him, her breasts pressing against his chest, her pelvis against his, his manhood nestling between her thighs.

'My dearest James.' She kissed him all over his face. 'Please trust me. I assure you, when I tell you everything about my past, you may not like me, but you'll never worry about competing with another man. Believe me, there is no other man on this earth as important to me as you are. Not one!'

His features softened, and he pulled her to him and held her close with all his might, and she revelled in his strength and in that most delicious fusion of their bodies.

'Then why can't you tell me about it now?' he asked.

'Because…' She kissed him in the crook of his neck. 'Today has been so very special for me. Today is about us. Just us. I don't want to bring back the ghosts of my past tonight. But I promise, cross my heart, next weekend, when we meet I'll tell you everything.' By then, her mind reasoned, perhaps his longing and desire and his love for her would withstand the shock of her revelation. She turned her mind to the present. 'James,' she asked teasingly, 'are we hungry enough now to demolish your elegant feast?'

Slowly, reluctantly he released her.

'I suppose we'd better give it a go. Or mother will be very surprised to find it all intact at the back of the fridge tomorrow morning.'

'Mind if I take a shower first?'

'By all means, Madeleine. Mind if I join you?'

# CHAPTER 31

'Walking on air' was a cliché that fitted her perfectly, Madeleine thought. Each morning she bounced out of the house to drive to work to deal with a variety of cases, some sad, some harrowing, some with happy endings in which she played the role of only a bilingual parrot, translating verbatim what she had been instructed to say. And yet, without her input into a meaningful communication between the two sides, things would have been left unresolved. At the end of each day, even on occasions when she had to interpret for criminals, she had come away with a feeling of having done her best. The bouncy, 'on air' feeling came from another source. James texted her at least three times a day, and after nine at night, when Emily was in bed and Aniela and Bronek were engrossed in their Polish serial, she and James would talk on the phone for ages. He had suggested taking her and Emily to the east coast at the weekend. She could not wait.

On Thursday morning, she left at eight-thirty. There was a meeting arranged at the hospital in the orthodontics department. A boy of nine was in need of reconstructive surgery after a road accident. Poor lad. She could well imagine his parents' anguish.

In the strong morning light, the street was patterned with long lines of shadows falling from the plane trees. The weather looked settled, ideal for Aniela and Bronek's plans to take Emily out to a popular animal farm, with the added attractions of a play area and a miniature train.

Madeleine never stopped thinking how lucky she was with two such kind people to support her and give Emily the experience of family life. She could never leave them; she owed them so much. That was another issue she needed to discuss with James, if after her revelation he did not walk away. The very thought made her stomach feel queasy.

She reached her Ka, clicked the door open and was just about to get in when a figure stepped out from behind the tree. She jumped back with fright and then froze.

'Magda!' Zden stretched out his hand, his fingers bony, the skin dry and grey. 'Don't be scared. I just want to talk. I want to put things right. Grant me five minutes, that's all I ask.'

Indeed, his pathetic appearance of an emaciated man should not have struck fear, but she was gripped with revulsion; the old terror was back and all her instincts cried out to make a quick escape. Her hand sought to keep the door open, as she slid across the side of the car in readiness to slip in.

'When I saw you last week' – he spoke feverishly – 'at the cemetery in Krakow, I was seized with such a strong need to see you again that I could not rest till I arranged a flight. I'm staying at the Ibis in the centre, by the station.'

Madeleine shook her head and began to slip inside the car door, but he grabbed the edge and held it rigid.

'Wait! Just tell me one thing. Is your child my daughter?'

At that, Madeleine pushed the door at him with all her strength. He let go of it to retain his balance. She slid in, slammed the door and pressed the central lock. Breathing fast as if she had run a mile, she forced herself to concentrate. Switch on the engine, check the mirror, accelerate. She shot out of her parking space like a rocket, even as Zden banged on the window.

She drove frantically along the familiar streets, finding the lights excruciatingly slow, when all her instincts pushed at her to get away from him as fast as possible. When she had made it to the hospital car park and switched off the engine, she took long and deep breaths to calm herself. Her imagination ran wild, assailing her mind with frightening scenarios. Good God! Why now? After all the years! When her life was about to take a promising turn for the future? She ungripped her hands from the steering wheel but could not stop them shaking. She needed a strong black coffee. She checked her watch. Another twenty minutes. She had time.

She found an isolated corner in the hospital cafeteria and poured some cold water into the scalding coffee, so she could take a few gulps at once. Long, deep breaths. Her hands steadied around the cup. She must warn Aniela, but she did not want to panic her. Would Zden have the nerve or the cheek to approach her grandparents? Perhaps not, but she could not take that risk.

She dialled Aniela's mobile. Aniela was surprised.

'Forgotten something?'

'Babcha, listen. I've not got very much time. I'll explain everything tonight. And can you keep this conversation to yourself for the moment. I'm scared of Grandpa's reaction if he knew.'

'Knew what?'

'I saw Zden in our street.'

'What!' Aniela stifled her exclamation adding quickly, 'Go on…'

'Just be wary, Babcha. And don't leave Emily anywhere on her own.'

Aniela was quiet for the briefest second, then her practical nature came through.

'Magda, I assure you, you've got absolutely nothing to worry about. There's only one of him and two of us, if he were to approach us. Bronek can still be a fearsome force when necessary. Trust me. Emily will be absolutely safe with us. We won't leave her alone even for a moment.'

Madeleine believed her and a weight lifted off her chest, but the euphoria that had been carrying her all week was gone. Madeleine felt limp and empty.

Her mobile pinged in her handbag. She took it out and read the message. It was from James:

*Just to say hello. Can't wait till tomorrow. Love you.*

Dearest James. What now? Could Zden destroy what she and James had only just so tentatively built together? Would James's love be tested to the limits? Would it survive? The old anxiety was back.

Of one thing she was unshakeably sure: her love for James would remain unchanged. She texted him back:

*Love you too. For ever.*

Arriving back home at the end of the afternoon, Madeleine was much relieved to find a space behind Bronek's Volvo, right outside their front door. She got out of her car in haste, looked around swiftly and dashed indoors.

'Hello!' she called from the door, 'I'm back!'

She looked in the front room: Emily was playing with her toys on the carpet and Bronek was following a quiz on the television, as always, prompting answers and getting annoyed with the contestants for being too slow.

'Hello there!' He waved to Madeleine. Emily jumped up, ran to her and gave her a hug around the waist. Madeleine picked her up and held her close, overwhelmed with love and relief.

'Had a good day?' She held her voice steady, putting Emily down.

'Mama, I fed a little pig today. And I stroked a sheep. And I saw baby rabbits, all fluffy like snowballs. And I found an egg in a chicken coop and we bought it and brought it home and you can cook it. And then we went on the swings and roundabouts!'

'Goodness! How did you find the energy to do all that?'

'And then…' Emily giggled with excitement, 'we had a picnic and then we went to Grandpa's allotment.'

Bronek detached his gaze from the television screen and added, 'They're forecasting a gale tomorrow, would you believe it? I can't quite imagine it myself, at this time of the year, but no harm in checking. Only my little forest of sweetcorn, really. The badgers ruined them last year. But I've tied netting all round them to stop them breaking in the wind.'

'And I made a garden with dandelions and pebbles.' Emily continued with her list of achievements.

'That's wonderful,' Madeleine praised her, immensely grateful that nothing had spoilt the day. 'I better go and help Babcha in the kitchen.'

No help was needed. Aniela had it all under control and nicely cooking: chicken and potatoes roasting in the oven and a medley of vegetables steaming on the cooker. She wiped the worktop clean and rinsed and wrung the dishcloth, before pulling the door close.

'Any news?' Her voice was low, discreet.

Madeleine gave her a hug.

'Nothing. But he knows where we live. We can't drop our guard for a moment, Babcha.'

She described the morning's incident as she made three teas and a fruit drink for Emily, and Aniela's eyes were huge with shock and indignation. She returned to her after taking Bronek's and Emily's drinks through to the front room.

'Babcha,' she whispered, pulling the door shut behind her, 'it's as if my nightmare has begun all over again. What shall we do if he becomes a nuisance?'

'We won't let him, Magda, I assure you. We'll call the police!' Aniela's voice was low but emphatic.

'No, Babcha, no! I don't want to involve anyone else. All that explaining! I can't bear the thought!'

Aniela took a sip of tea and gave her curls a shake of indignation.

'Magda, trust me! I won't allow him to pester you. I'll come out to the car with you tomorrow morning. He won't dare! He'll have me to reckon with!'

Madeleine could not help the tiniest tickle of amusement, despite the seriousness of their discussion.

'Babcha, forgive me, but won't it be a little like David and Goliath?'

Aniela gave a secret smile and touched her nose.

'Maybe. But not when I call Bronek. Only if I must. He'll kill him, of course, so I won't involve him unless I absolutely must. I don't want the police arresting the wrong man. Don't worry, Magda. I know how to handle Zden. There is still such a thing in our culture as respect for old people.'

This was true. The patriarchs and the matriarchs were given due respect in most Polish families, and outside the home in public places the elderly were treated with respect on account of their wisdom gleaned from their life's experiences.

Madeleine nodded.

'That's assuming his brain is functioning normally,' she said.

Later in the evening, when Emily was asleep and Madeleine was checking her e-mails in the backroom, James rang. As always, his voice gave her a thrill, but it did not quell her fear.

'Had a good day?' His polite tone masked a bubbling energy, which she wished she could share.

'The usual,' she replied with forced lightness. 'A young boy at the hospital, a drink and drive man at the police station, and an abandoned mother with three children at the Housing Department. What about you?'

'Meetings, and more meetings,' he sighed. 'Tomorrow will be busy. Everyone works to deadlines on Fridays. But I hope to get away by four and arrive at your door around seven?'

'That sounds good,' she said, feeling something drop inside her.

'Madeleine.' He paused briefly, and then added with a lift in his voice, 'Shall we go somewhere nice for a meal tomorrow night and talk about us, about our future?'

'Funny… I had the same idea,' she said, wishing for some miracle to wipe out her problem for good.

*

The forecast gale had hit in the early hours. There were thudding noises all over the house, as if it were a boat being buffeted by a stormy sea. Madeleine got up from the table and kissed Emily and Bronek goodbye. They were finishing their breakfast, Bronek his of bacon and eggs, and Emily munching her toast with peanut butter and discussing the merits and the attraction of frogs over toads. Emily's favourite was definitely the frog, when still tiny with the fresh green colour, but Bronek pointed out, 'I have toads on my allotment. They do a wonderful job of clearing the slugs and beetles and flies. There are two, no doubt a couple, and they are like my pets.'

Aniela got up and followed Madeleine to the front door.

'I've got only one appointment this morning,' Madeleine said. 'I should be back by one.'

'Don't rush back,' Aniela said. 'We shall most probably take Emily out somewhere nice.' And, seeing anxiety in Madeleine's eyes, she added, 'We won't let her out of our sight for a second. I promise.'

As Madeleine opened the door, an almighty gust of wind blew against them. Nevertheless, Aniela came outside and stood at the gate, looking up and down the street, her hair doing a wild dance. The crowns of the maple trees were hissing like an angry sea and the sky was a turbulent mass of racing purple-grey clouds. Madeleine held her collar tight against her throat and ran to her Ka, squinting her eyes, checking there was no one about. There was not.

The moment she unlocked the car and was about to get in, a figure jumped up from behind Bronek's Volvo, where he must have been squatting unseen. She screamed. She was aware of Aniela leaving her post and running up to her.

'What do you want?' Aniela shouted at Zden, shaking her fist. She positioned herself between Madeleine and him. 'I guess who you are. Haven't you done enough? Leave her in peace! Do the decent thing for once! Go away and never come back!' Her words were blown like leaves on the wind. With the wild tangle of hair around her face, her long skirt and cardigan flapping around her, she cut out a formidable, almost a biblical figure, despite her small stature.

Astonishingly, he backed away. For a moment he looked stumped. Aniela squared her shoulders and looked hard at him, and Madeleine prayed frantically, Please God, don't let Bronek hear this and come out; don't let Emily see any of this. The whining wind was her ally, muffling the noises in the street.

Zden lifted up his hands as if in surrender and strained to speak over the roar of the wind.

'I just want a minute or two with Magda. There are things which I've got to discuss with her.'

By now, Madeleine had recovered enough from the shock to shout at him over Aniela's shoulder.

'There's nothing to discuss. Just go! I never want to see you again!' She was shaking.

He leaned forward raising his voice, 'Then tell me just one thing. Is your child my daughter? Because if she is, I've got a father's right to see her!'

Madeleine felt sick. A car passed by, but no one driving in this wild weather concentrating on the road would have guessed the drama unfolding on the pavement. Zden straightened himself to his full height, his expression threateningly victorious. Madeleine wanted to kill him. In a flash, she understood the essence of a crime of passion.

Aniela snorted like a raging bull and stamped her foot with fury.

'You despicable, shameless creature!' she exploded. 'Go! Go this minute! Wynos sie! Or I'll call the police!'

He sniggered.

'Really? And what will you tell them? That you're keeping a father away from his child? A DNA test would soon resolve this little conundrum.'

He was bluffing, for he knew nothing for sure, yet Madeleine felt a darkness descend upon her. It was like spiralling down a bottomless abyss. Dear God! Was there never going to be an end to this nightmare? It was like the end of the world for her, the sky boiling over with black clouds and the trees screaming in the gale. Then Aniela's words reached her. She was shouting to Zden, 'All right! Go ahead! I'll notify the police too. In Poland. I'll write to your parish priest. Then everyone will know what you did to Magda. The same day your wife died. How debauched is that?'

Aniela was bluffing too, but his smirk stiffened.

'And risk Magda's reputation?'

'You'd be risking much more than just your reputation. Have you thought about ending up in jail?'

They eyed each other for a long moment, neither giving way, their clothes tugged and blown, as if pulling them apart. Then Zden made a step back.

'I'm not giving up!' His face was twisted with anger as he jabbed the air with his finger in front of his nose. 'I'll be around for as long as it takes! We can do this amicably or... in a different way! The choice is yours!' With that he turned away from them and began to walk off, his long coat flapping about him like a black sail.

Magda exhaled but hardly with relief. She threw her arms around Aniela and held her close.

'Babcha, you were magnificent!'

Aniela returned the hug saying, 'Go now, Magda, go! Or you'll be late for work. And you must trust me. Absolutely. I give you my word that Emily will not be out of our sight for a second!'

The first thing Madeleine rushed to do after arriving in court was to fix her ruffled hair in the cloakroom and check her appearance. She then made a beeline to the cafeteria. She needed badly a fix of strong black coffee. The strongest. Slowly, as the hot liquid warmed her stomach, her shaking calmed down, but her mind could not blank out the sound of Zden's threatening words. DNA. His child. His rights. Do it amicably. Or else! The words whirled in her mind like the leaves outside in the gale. She must stop this, she told herself firmly, clasping her hands so hard the knuckles stood out white underneath the skin. Father Gabriel. Aniela. They were the people to think of, to smooth her frayed nerves. Look at Aniela, so small in stature, but so strong in mind. She must try to be more like her.

Madeleine checked her watch. It was time to find the court usher and be guided to where her services were required. With a strong, deliberate effort she cleared her mind, ready to do her best as an interpreter for the people relying on her skill.

It was a very sad case of a friendship destroyed by a series of worsening circumstances. Bartek and Oleg had been friends since their school days. They had come over from Poland to better their lot. They worked all hours in a distribution plant. Oleg became seriously homesick, depressed, turned to drink, incurred debts. Bartek then lent him a substantial sum to get him out of this mess, but when he asked for the constantly delayed first instalment of repayment, Oleg drunkenly attacked him with a bottle, wounding him seriously in the neck. It was only the prompt arrival of the paramedics that had saved Bartek from death.

They were both in court; Oleg, broken-looking in the dock, and Bartek, recovered now after weeks in hospital, sitting in the gallery with another friend. The barrister's mitigation speech could only clarify the circumstances surrounding the case, but it could not save Oleg from a prison sentence for grievous bodily harm, which could have resulted in manslaughter, the judge pointed out in all seriousness. Bartek was visibly upset when his friend Oleg was sent down.

The court rose at twelve-thirty. Madeleine was free for the rest of the day. The moment her mind pushed aside her morning's work, all her previous anxieties were back. She felt an uncontrollable need to rush home with all possible speed.

Outside, the gale had moved on, but the residue wind was still strong, rushing and thinning the clouds, exposing glimpses of blue. Madeleine ran to her car as fast as her high heels would allow her and then drove home with the utmost speed possible in the build-up of the Friday traffic. She only slowed down on turning into her street, but that was to scan every doorway and every tree that could give Zden his desired hiding spot. The street was deserted, except for a few parked cars. Bronek's Volvo was absent from his usual parking slot.

She stopped and jumped out of her Ka, straight into the force of the wind. She sprinted to the door and wrestled with the key, which refused to work instantly. Once inside, she slammed the door and leaned against it momentarily to catch her breath before sprinting down the corridor, looking in every room and shouting, 'Babcha! Grandpa! Emily!' though it was obvious they were not there. This should have reassured her, but panic gripped her. She needed to find them, to be with them, to be assured that Emily was safe.

She staggered back towards the front door, dialling Aniela's mobile. It was switched off. She dialled Bronek's and heard it ringing, but he was not picking it up. He did not always hear it. Her nerves were so taut, she feared something would snap inside her. Just then she noticed a white envelope at the foot of the door that she had missed before. She picked it up. One word on it: Magda. She recognised the handwriting. With her heart thumping at her throat she tore the envelope open. Zden wrote:

*Magda,*

*I just want to talk. I followed Aniela and Bronek to the allotment yesterday. They did not see me, but I heard them calling your daughter 'Emily'. Is this after my Emilia? From my hiding place, I took pictures of them. Especially Emily. I'm convinced she's mine. We must talk. You know where to find me. Ask for me at the reception desk.*

*See you tonight. Z.*

Madeleine's eyes scanned the note again and again, with a feeling of doom ballooning inside her chest, as if she were about to suffocate. She ran back to the kitchen, grabbed a glass, filled it with water from the tap and gulped it all down. She sat down with a thud and pressed her palms against the sides of her face. She must think! She must not give into despair. Panic won't solve anything. Slowly now. Where could they be? The town? Their friends? A play-park? She needed to start somewhere to remain sane. The allotment was Grandpa's favourite place and the closest point to start her search. She'd go there first, even though it was unlikely she'd find them there in this wild weather. But once she'd checked, she'd know for certain.

On leisure days, she and Emily always used the footpath that ran at the back of the houses, where once there had been a railway line. But today was quicker by car. Madeleine had the presence of mind to change her high heels to flat pumps, before jumping behind the steering wheel. She tackled the Friday congestion with simmering impatience, crying out in frustration at the snail's pace of stop and go, but once she was off the main road she whizzed down to the end of a long row of terraced houses, where one of the entrances to the allotments was tucked away. She left the car in the street and ran towards the gate, usually kept shut but this day unusually left wide open. It was only after she had run past the partly screening shrubs, and the dip with the cross-paths came into view, that she saw that something extraordinary was happening.

292

# CHAPTER 32

Madeleine's eyes skimmed the scene frantically, her brain trying to make sense, guessing, concluding with a pang of horror. Not Emily! Please God, let it not be Emily!

A police car and a fire engine stood at an angle to the path close to Bronek's allotment, and at his gate there was an ambulance with its back door wide open. Bronek was struggling with holding back the gate steady against gusts of wind, his white hair pulled up in all directions.

His allotment was unrecognisable, its entire space taken up by the fallen oak, which like a sprawling giant splayed its far-reaching branches sideways and upwards. Underneath its heaviest section was a flattened mound of broken-up breeze blocks, tangled with ivy and sods of earth. Two firemen were cutting through the thickest sections of the trunk, while two others were working fast, removing bricks and debris from the mound. Two paramedics, a tall man and a thickset woman, stood by in readiness with a stretcher held upright between them.

A policewoman was helping her male colleague to cordon off Bronek's allotment with a white-and-blue tape, something of a challenge to control in the tugging wind.

A small group of onlookers, Bronek's gardening colleagues, stood a discreet distance away and watched.

All this took a split of a second for Madeleine's brain to register and process. She ran down the incline of the path to the dip, past the parked vehicles, and up the path to Bronek, where he stood at the gate, looking distracted and lost. She grabbed his arm and shouted over the noise of the wind and the chainsaw.

'Emily! Where's Emily!?'

In slow motion, he drew his eyes away from the firemen working on the broken tree and the rubble underneath it and looked at Madeleine as if she were a stranger. Then, as recognition dawned in his gaze, he threw his arm around Madeleine's shoulders and drew her close to him as if to protect her.

'Emily is safe,' he said. 'She's with Aniela. At Barski's.' He leaned his head close to hers to make himself heard better. 'At long last people will believe me now. There was a spy behind that wall, after all!'

Madeleine heard first what she wanted to hear: Emily was safe. A burst of lightness filled her. Then Bronek's other words reached her consciousness.

'What do you mean, Grandpa? What spy?'

'Look for yourself! The KGB man! No one believed me, I know! Now I'll show them! I had been right all along!'

Madeleine strained her eyes and with mounting dread watched as the firemen released a body from underneath the loosened mound of bricks and broken wood, all that remained of Bronek's doggedly repaired screen over the years.

'Grandpa, who is this man? Did you find him? How did you know he was there?' Magda shouted against the wind. Bronek squinted his eyes and shouted back,

'I didn't know he was there. Just as well I checked. But I always do. Check every time. I never trust the bastards. They always send someone along to spy on me!' He paused for breath. 'The whole place was already a mess when I got here. As if a bomb had hit it. When I saw the rubble, I ran straight to it! I had a feeling. And I was right. I found a hand poking out. I touched it. It felt dead. I called the ambulance and the police straight away and got down to removing the bricks.'

Bronek could be amazing at times, despite his chronic distractedness. They watched as the paramedics approached the body that had been laid on the ground by the firemen. They performed all the necessary tests to check for signs of life, then they covered it up with a white sheet. One of the police officers, the young woman, walked over to them by the gate and asked, 'Would you mind coming over with me and just having a look at him? We need to identify him.'

Bronek grasped Madeleine's hand and held it tight as they approached the spot of the accident. Madeleine held her breath and watched the paramedic uncover the dead person's face. It bore no resemblance to anyone she knew underneath the layer of congealed blood and soil and brick dust, and his hair resembling a helmet made of cement.

'I've never seen this man here before,' Bronek stated truthfully, 'but then, that was the whole point, wasn't it? To spy on me undetected.'

'Sorry?' The policewoman shot Bronek a questioning glance, then seemed to decide to stick to the point. 'You state that you have never seen this man before?'

'That's correct.'

Madeleine was about to confirm the same, when she saw it. The man's hand. It lay inert and uncovered by his side. She recognised it at once, as one would recognise any feature of a member of a close-knit family. The shock of her discovery rendered her speechless, her lips parted in readiness to speak, while a current of thoughts passed through her mind like lightning. Was this real? Was this possible? It was. An indisputable fact. Right before her eyes. She need never be afraid of *him* again! Ever!

'I think I know this man,' she said, immediately regretting her premature honesty. She should have waited until she had had time to process in her brain this extraordinary incident.

'You do?' The policewoman's eyebrows shot up with interest. 'Would you be able to identify him officially?'

'I'll do my best.' Madeleine's thoughts raced. 'I'll be more certain when his face gets cleaned up.'

Bronek eyed her with bafflement.

'But you can't know him, Magda! He's a Russian spy!' Some of his words got lost in the wind, but the woman constable gave him a puzzled look. She turned to Madeleine.

'It's impossible to talk here in this howling wind,' she said, 'but could you come to the station? Your statement would be most helpful to us.'

They had no idea how helpful and they would never know. Madeleine would tell them only the minimum necessary truth.

'Of course,' she said. 'When would you like me to come?'

'There's no immediate hurry.' The policewoman spoke above the noise of the wind, 'It'll take the rest of the day to go through all the official procedures. Tomorrow morning will do. Ask for me at the main police station. Constable Laura Bright. And could I have your contact number, please?'

Madeleine gave PC Laura Bright her business card.

'You'll find all my details here,' she said. 'I'm an interpreter for the Polish community.'

Then she and Bronek stood back and watched the paramedics carry Zden's covered body on the stretcher to the ambulance. Madeleine's mind noted their every movement, heard every noise despite the wind, doors banging shut, the engine starting, the ambulance moving up the path to the wide-open gate and disappearing beyond the houses down the street.

It all felt surreal, as if she was watching herself and all the drama around her from above. One incessant thought kept throbbing in her mind throughout: Zden was gone! Really gone. He would never be a threat to her again!

295

PC Laura Bright came back to them after some consultation with her colleague.

'I'm afraid, Mr Sokolski,' she informed him, 'that your allotment is now a scene of an accident, and therefore will be closed off to everyone except the forensic team. We shall notify you when our investigations are complete.'

Bronek ran his fingers through his tousled hair. He looked resigned.

'I can't see that there's anything left now worth harvesting.'

His miniature forest of sweetcorn lay flattened underneath the thick oak branches. The broken potato plants did not matter so much, as there were fully grown potatoes in the soil that could be dug up later, but the lettuces and the carrots had been all pressed into the ground. His beautiful dahlias and delphiniums were a mess of torn stalks and crushed flower heads. Above this devastation rose a tall, sharp-pointed obelisk, where before there had been a crown of branches covered thickly with leaves.

'I'll come back another day,' he said to the policewoman. 'We'll go now. Let you get on with your job.'

Madeleine was relieved to get away. As she and Bronek began to walk down the incline, Gina, an Italian fellow-gardener and an acquaintance of Bronek's, detached herself from the small gathering of the onlookers, and waddled up to them. A hip problem, no doubt, Madeleine observed, but that had not stopped her from growing her beloved marrows, courgettes and peppers in all their glorious colours.

'Bronek! Please wait!' Her raven-black hair growing from inch-long white roots flew all over her face. She held it back with her hand. 'Who that man?'

'I've no idea.' Bronek shrugged. 'Never seen him in my life!'

Madeleine could only guess that Zden had hidden himself between the breeze-block wall and the outside hedge with the hope of spying on Emily. Her pictures would be found on his camera. This thought came to her with a sickly feeling. She'd be questioned about the significance of that. Dear God! When would this nightmare end? Only a few minutes ago she had believed she had been freed of him, for good. And now this! She became aware of Bronek still talking to Gina.

'I'm baffled! Shocked! It was horrible finding him there!'

'What the police say?'

'They'll have to find his relatives, I suppose. Inform them. And after that... it'll be for them to sort things out.'

At the mention of his relatives, Madeleine felt another wave of nausea. She must hold herself together. Nothing more was going to happen now, not in the next few hours, not until James's arrival. She had the afternoon to discuss things with Aniela.

'Shall we go to fetch Babcha and Emily?' she said to Bronek, when he bade Gina farewell. 'Let's meet at home first, then go in one car together.'

Amazingly, as they walked down to their respective cars, Bronek did not question her on how she knew the dead man. She could only hope that he presumed it was rather through her work than through his imagined spy activity. She had every intention of telling him the truth, once her mind had processed the whole incident with all its implications. She noticed suddenly that the wind had dropped.

\*

At the Barskis' house, Madeleine helped Emily to gather all her artist's paraphernalia off the kitchen table and tidy up, as she listened to her excited talk about a long walk in Abbey Park with Babcha and Mrs Barska, and how the wind nearly flew her like a kite, and how the long-haired rabbits in the pet corner had their hair blown all over their faces and could not see what they were eating. Madeleine kept fuelling Emily's talk with lots of questions, aware all the while of Bronek's account of the accident to Aniela and their friends in the front room, away from Emily. She had asked Bronek to keep this news to the adults only.

Back home, after their delayed lunch of sandwiches with tea, Bronek took Emily out into the back garden. She was eager to help him with tidying up the borders. The late afternoon turned out surprisingly sunny and warm, the sky totally cleared of all cloud. While Bronek weeded, Emily's task was to fill her little bucket with wood chippings from a large sack and scatter them underneath the flowers. She did this with unrestrained enthusiasm.

Left alone in the kitchen with Aniela, Madeleine was able, at last, to give her the full and clarifying account of the earlier dramatic incident. She showed her Zden's note. Aniela, for once, was lost for words. Now and again, as she listened, she would shake her head and exclaim, 'Incredible! Shocking! Who would have thought it? Serves him right!' and such like. Eventually, after their third cup of tea, Aniela relaxed her rigid back, dropped her stiff shoulders and even smiled a little, as if secretly, only to herself.

'Magda, I never lost hope all those years. I prayed he'd get his comeuppance, or at least never come back into your life. And it happened. The very thing I was praying for. Though I never prayed for him to die! I swear!' Her earnest round eyes stared straight at Madeleine. 'Someone up there must be looking after you.' She smiled and asked, 'How do you feel now?'

Madeleine's expression was thoughtful as she drank slowly from her cup. She felt exhausted, drained.

'I had imagined this moment countless times, Babcha. Jumping for joy. Feeling totally free and light and deliriously happy, rid of that burden that I had been carrying for years. I wanted revenge. I wanted him to suffer. I imagined all kinds of tortures for him, but never a death like this. Now I've got what I wanted, I don't feel any happier, just relieved, I suppose. I just prayed that as time went on, our paths would never cross, and that eventually I'd outlive him. What's happened today has left me truly shaken. It's not a death I'd wish on anyone.'

'Oh, come on, Magda!' Aniela's mouth curled with satisfaction. 'He got what he deserved. I wouldn't be surprised if it were your three guardian angels up there' – she pointed sky-wards – 'that have ganged up on him. I could just imagine them blowing at that tree until it broke and fell on him.'

The very whimsical image of that brought a smile to Madeleine's lips, the first smile of the day.

'Babcha, it's a lovely thought. And who knows? Perhaps they did. I think it was just a freak accident. A chain of events, culminating with the oak breaking in two. Who would have thought it? And all the while Grandpa had been fretting about his wall. It could have stood there another twenty years, if it hadn't been for the gale and the tree falling on top of it. And Zden! Wrong place, wrong time. What a price to pay for stalking and spying!'

She went quiet and Aniela stroked her arm, as she often did with Emily. Madeleine spoke after a while, giving out an audible, deep sigh.

'And it's not over yet, Babcha. I've still got to tell James. I've still got to go to the police station. I'm dreading both.'

Aniela took Madeleine's hand in both hers and gave it a loving squeeze.

'Magda, listen! Stop torturing yourself. This is really over. Tell James the whole truth. Tell the policewoman the whole truth. Zden's not here anymore to bend your truth to his advantage. You've got nothing more to fear. Keep reminding yourself of that!'

But fear tugged at Madeleine's nerves for the rest of the afternoon, as she watched the minutes ticking away towards James's arrival.

# CHAPTER 33

In the car, before James switched on the engine, Madeleine touched his arm.

'James, can we go somewhere quiet? I've got so much to tell you.' It was hard keeping her voice sounding normal.

'I hope you have,' he responded jovially, and she was aware of his energy, of his excitement bursting to get out. But then he looked at her and his expression clouded. 'You've not changed your mind, have you? Since last weekend?'

'No, James,' she denied vigorously, 'I haven't!' But you may, she thought, when you've heard my story. She said, 'Something awful happened today. But you need to hear it all in one go.'

'All right,' he said amicably, 'I'm all ears!'

'Tell me about your week first.'

He drove and talked and told her anecdotes about colleagues from work, about clients, some difficult, some eccentric, a few surprisingly obliging.

'It's the best feeling, I tell you, when your client leaves you with a smile on his face. The majority expect you to perform miracles when it comes to saving them a few pennies. They don't want to know about rules and regulations. They expect you to approve their hare-brained schemes.'

'What do you tell them then?' Madeleine forced herself to concentrate on James's words as her mind rehearsed her own speech.

He looked at her and smiled broadly.

'We're honest with them. We tell them outright we're not interested in any shady deals.'

They stopped at a pub on the outskirts of Leicester, a picturesque thatched cottage with an extensive garden at the back. They found a table outside, at the far end, well away from the tables already occupied by noisy, family groups. Madeleine welcomed the noise, an opportune cover for what she was about to reveal to James.

'What will you have to drink?' James held back the chair for her.

'A bottle of vodka.' She gave a feeble smile. 'A glass of red would be lovely, James.'

Waiting for him to rejoin her was torture. This could be the end of their relationship before it had properly started. But she could not put this off any longer. Afterwards, the decision would be entirely his own. All she could hope for was that his love for her was strong enough to withstand the truth about her.

The low evening sun showed itself from behind the thatched roof and bathed her and the table in a warm peach glow. It was hard to believe that the city and its environment had been buffeted by a gale only a few hours before. Thousands of feet up, across the clear sky, a white line was being drawn by a north-bound aeroplane. Lucky people, Madeleine thought, wishing she could change places with them.

As James approached, she raised her eyes to him and forced a smile. He looked so happy, she was overcome with misery at what she had to say. He placed the drinks on the table, sat down and took a long, thirsty gulp of his lager. The noise on the other tables appeared to distract him for a moment, but then he leaned forward to her and said, 'Now, tell me all about it, Madeleine.'

Her heart began to hammer. Here goes.

'James, today at lunchtime a dead man was discovered on Bronek's allotment.'

'What? Who was he? What was he doing there?' Then stopping himself, he nodded. 'Go on.'

His gaze was more piercing than ever with his focussed attention.

Madeleine took a giant glug. Swallowed hard.

'It was the gale. The gale did it. That big oak tree snapped half way up and the heavy top fell on the screening wall. Smashed it to bits. He happened to be behind that wall.'

James' eyes rounded with incredulity.

'What on earth was he doing there?'

Now, the biggest jump. Off the Everest.

'James, that man was my uncle, Zdenko Dopski. I can only guess that he was hiding there to spy on Emily and my grandparents. He did that yesterday too. He said so in the letter. Here it is. I've translated it for you.' She handed him the two sheets. With held-in breath, she watched his expression change from puzzlement, to thoughtfulness, to a dawning of comprehension.

'Jesus! Is this what I think it is?' His gaze, crystal clear, crystal sharp bore into her eyes. She out-stared him, clasping her hands hard, until her fingers hurt. She lowered her voice to almost a whisper.

'James, now can you understand why it was so hard for me to tell you about it? That man... I loved as my uncle. Now I hate him as the most despicable man on earth. The night my Aunt Emilia died, he raped me, he hurt me, he rubbished me, he defiled me, he robbed me of my dignity. I felt soiled, no longer pure for the man I'd love in the future. And then I met you. You deserve better than me.'

Slowly, her hand shaking, she took another gulp of wine.

James did not speak, just kept staring at Madeleine while all energy drained from her, making her feel spineless, rubbery. A child on another table let out a yell. It sounded so comfortingly normal. Then he leaned over the table, took her hands in his and held them warmly in his grasp, not speaking a word, just looking, only his features expressing an array of emotions, as if he were struggling to control an inner raging storm. She closed her eyes, wishing to lose consciousness, so she would not have to think any more, not feel anything, so when she came round she would find herself floating in perfect calm.

'Madeleine.' James's voice made her open her eyes. His voice was subdued, shaky with emotion; she had not heard it like that before. 'Forgive me, Madeleine, for my delayed reaction, but what you've told me has been such a shock. I needed a moment to take it all in. To recover.' He remained quiet, staring at the table, at their clasped hands.

She said, 'You see now, James, what I've been so afraid of. Your changed perception of me. I'm exactly the same person I was five minutes ago. But five minutes ago you did not know about my past. And now you do, my biggest fear is that of losing you.'

He looked up sharply at her, as if waking up. He caressed her hand.

'Madeleine, no. You've got it all wrong. What I'm thinking about is all that suffering, all the trauma you've been through. I'm trying to imagine how you've picked yourself up, and struggled, and risen above all that and made such a success of your life. What I'm struggling with now is controlling my rage!' His shoulders gave a shudder. 'I'm just so angry that I did not know about it before. That I have been robbed of a chance of smashing his face to pulp!'

'James.' She spoke gently. 'This is a natural reaction, but hardly a practical one.'

He shrugged.

'Perhaps it's just as well that nature got in first and did my job for me.'

'Such an incredible coincidence! Who would have thought it? Aniela says it's God's justice.' She gave him an encouraging smile.

His face appeared to relax and there was the tiniest sparkle in his eyes when he said, 'I love Bronek's wall. I never imagined it possible to love a wall so much!'

She had to smile at that. Something lifted inside her.

'James… are we still… OK?'

He gave her hand another loving pat.

'How could you think otherwise? I love you all the more, just thinking what you've been through.'

For the first time since the morning, Madeleine felt a comforting warmth spread throughout her body.

'You've no idea, James, how terribly miserable I've been all day. And now I feel as if I could collapse with relief.' Her lip trembled. 'I need to tell you the whole story. Get it all off my chest. So you know everything about me.'

While James fetched more drinks for them, she watched people on other tables, laughing, joking, enjoying their night out. Perhaps, when all this mess with Zden was tidied up and forever behind her, she could be as carefree as the people she watched.

James came back and moved his chair right close beside her. His whole manner was caring and protective and she felt herself melting under his gaze.

'Tell me everything,' he said.

Briefly, Madeleine outlined her earlier years, her mother's death when she was four, her father's absence, her Aunt Emilia's loving foster care, her escape from Zden on the day of her aunt's death. She told James how she could not give up Emily for adoption, once she had held her newborn baby to her chest. She described her years of combining her work with studying and childcare.

'I've got much to be thankful for,' she concluded. 'I had Aniela and Bronek for support. My father too. To this day he still deposits a regular sum into my bank account, though I keep telling him there is no need to do that anymore. He says it's for Emily.'

'How often do you see him?' James asked.

'Every few days on Skype. Three years ago, I took Emily with me to see him and his family. They're grown up now. My half-brother is in his first year at university, and my half-sister is two years younger. I've always liked my stepmother. She was kind to me when I visited them for the first time.'

'Madeleine, we'll make regular visits to see them. I'd give anything to have my father back!'

Madeleine laughed, with sheer happiness. Could there be a kinder man than James?

'James, my father is OK – in small doses. You could find him overbearing with his well-meant advice.'

'I think I'll manage that!'

She described her previous week in Krakow, mentioning now the encounter with Zden at the cemetery. She told James about catching up with Dominik at Natalia's wedding.

'And now?' His expression became serious. 'Have you still got feelings for him?'

It surprised her that James still needed reassurance.

'James, it is you, you alone, who has weaned me off any emotional ties with my teenage crush. I saw Dominik. I liked him. And that's all. He is happily married. They've got a baby boy.' She touched James's hand, saying, 'So you see, last Sunday... when we were together... like that, you know... I've never been like that with anyone else before.'

He hugged her then (was that with relief?) and smiled broadly, looking into her eyes.

'I believe you, Madeleine, of course I believe you. And you must promise me to put your past behind you and never worry about it again.' He loosened his embrace and sighed. 'There's something I want to tell you too.'

'OK,' she said. 'And you needn't worry. Nothing you could tell me could cause me as much stress as holding back my secrets from you.'

He sat up and focussed his eyes on a spot in the distance.

'I loved a girl once. We were at university together. It was my first year doing work experience, trying to secure a more permanent place with an accountant's firm. Not much pay, but we managed. It was a shock to discover she was pregnant. But only at first. I wasn't too worried. I knew I could cope with a baby, having had plenty of experience with Josh.' He gave a wry smile. 'Even my mother, though not exactly ecstatic, said she would help.' James paused and took a hurried sip. 'Then one day I came home to our flat after work and found a note from her. She'd had our baby aborted.'

Madeleine gasped.

'Why?'

James shrugged.

'She'd found somebody else.' Slowly he turned his gaze at her. 'What hurt the most,' he said, 'was that this baby was mine too.'

Madeleine clasped his hand, feeling deep empathy with the young man he had been at that time, feeling his loss of the woman he loved, his loss of his child, his loss of the future he had no doubt mapped out for them as a family.

'James, when did that happen?' she asked, remembering him clearly, when she had glimpsed him quite by chance, distressed and hiding in the gazebo all those years ago.

He shook his head, biting his lip.

'How could I forget? May 2005.'

She had to tell him.

'I know. I saw you then. For the first time. Though I did not know then it was you.'

He looked at her with sharp interest, his momentary bared distress retracting.

'When? How?'

She told him how she had taken refuge at the far end of Mrs Demska's garden and quite by chance witnessed his grief through a gap in the hedge.

He nodded, admitting, 'I was at my lowest then.'

'Me too. Wondering how I was going to recover and move on.' She paused, 'But tell me James, what did you do after that?'

James was quiet for a moment, gathering his thoughts. The noisy families had gone. Young people were forming Friday night groups around the tables, catching up amidst convivial merriment. Colourful fairy lights strung around the fence came to life for their night-time duty, as soft dusk began to fall. James turned his attention back to Madeleine.

'I plunged myself into work and just slaved all hours. It was mad, reclusive, but in the long run it stood me in good stead. Secured me my career. My private life was barren. I had no energy left for anything else after work. I came home some weekends. Caught up with my friends, Mark and Julie. Spent some holiday time cycling with Josh or going to Cornwall with mother. And then Josh became ill. It shook me seeing mother so worried. I made myself come home more often and involve myself more with their lives. And then, one day...' He paused, and a smile crept to his lips, as he added with a touch of deliberate drama, 'I met you, Madeleine. I knew straight away that you were the one I had been waiting for all my life!'

This made her laugh, lifting her mood.

'You're joking, James! How could you possibly know?'

'I just did!' He leaned forward and kissed her on the lips, a light, pleasant, reassuring kiss. 'Shall we go inside and order something to eat?'

She was still not hungry, but she imagined James was after his long day.

'There's just one more thing,' she said. 'I've got to go to the police station tomorrow, to give my full statement. I've no idea how economical I should be with the truth.'

He cupped protectively both her hands in his.

'I'll come with you, Madeleine. Tell them everything. You've got nothing to fear. I'll be there with you throughout.'

A blissful calm descended on her.

They got up, collected their glasses and made their way between the tables towards the restaurant.

# CHAPTER 34

## One Year Later – August 2013

It is late afternoon on a warm August day. The air is heavy with the scents of jasmine, honeysuckle and cut grass. The faint buzzing of insects adds to the soporific feeling in the air. Madeleine shifts to a more comfortable position in her lounger on the terrace and lifts her eyes from her book. Such a luxury to catch up with the reading that she never had time for before. She is discovering new authors who leave her thirsting for more.

She looks down the expanse of the lawn, at the end of which there is an orchard with apple, pear and plum trees, Aniela's haven. The gate to the orchard can be seen at the side of a magnificent chestnut tree with wide-reaching sturdy branches, the lowest ones forming a rigid base for the tree house. It is from there that the squeals of delight testify to Emily and Karishma's fun.

It is hard to imagine now, Madeleine ponders, that the dramatic events a year ago took place on a day in August, with a freak gale causing so much destruction in the county. Vivid memories keep coming back, yet not quite so often these days, with other, more pleasant and imminent matters to think about.

She still shivers at the remembered fear before her visit to the police station. It was James's presence that kept her together and had supported her courage to tell PC Bright the whole story of her connection with Zden. Madeleine sensed the policewoman's sympathy in the calm, unhurried manner in which she conducted the questioning, as if to avoid adding to her anguish and stress. A few days later, a short report had appeared in the local paper stating that a Polish national, Zdenko Dopski, had lost his life in a freak accident, caused by the gale. His death was not being treated as suspicious by the police.

Just when Madeleine was beginning to get used to her new life free of the ever-present shadow of fear, Zden's brother rang her from Poland. He informed her that Zden's body had been flown over and that his funeral had been arranged for the next day. Was there any chance of her coming over? This was surely a sick joke, no doubt his wife's malicious idea. Shaking with indignation, Madeleine expressed her regret at so little notice. Short of hiring a private jet, she'd said, there was no chance of her making it on time.

'Perhaps you should,' Zden's brother replied, 'as he's left you half of his estate! And only a half to my children. His own flesh and blood! No prizes for guessing what hold you've had over him!'

Madeleine slammed the phone down and then screamed, 'I never want anything of his! I never want to see any of his family again!'

Aniela, who had been present during this telephone conversation, calmed her down with soothing noises, as one would a child, after which she struck her usual practical, no-nonsense pose and reminded Madeleine of the unavoidable fact that Emily was entitled to certain things.

'He didn't know that but you do, Magda. This was his way of easing his conscience. You don't have to touch a penny of what he's left you. But there's no reason why Emily shouldn't have it. Open an account for her. That way his money never needs to pass through your hands. Think about that carefully.'

Madeleine did and had to agree reluctantly that Aniela had a point. It took a year of Polish bureaucracy to complete all formalities, and a few days ago Emily's bank account fattened up a size or two.

'Stop agonising,' James replied to her fretting, 'It's rightfully Emily's. She'll thank you for it one day.'

'Will she?'

'We'll cross that bridge when we come to it.' And the confident way he'd said it had appeased her concerns. For now. Not just for now, James assured her, but for as long as he was with her. And that would be forever.

Presently Madeleine becomes aware of a lively movement and excited voices around the base of the chestnut tree. Emily and Karishma have climbed down the rope ladder and are running to her across the lawn, all bouncy pigtails and swinging arms, their colourful T-shirts and dungarees shimmering brightly in the sun. Ever since the move, Karishma has been Emily's regular sleep-over guest. They run up the steps of the terrace and stop breathless in front of her, their shadows screening her eyes from the sun.

'Mama!' Emily breathes fast, her two front adult teeth comical in her child's mouth. 'Mama, can we go round to Babcha's now?'

Madeleine checks her watch.

'It's nearly tea-time, Emily. Babcha will be busy in the kitchen now. Look in their garden first. Grandpa will be pleased to see you if he's still there. But don't be long. Our meal is almost ready now. Daddy will be home soon.'

She watches them skip off, chirping like excited birds. They skirt around the flower border at the side of the main house, then follow the stepping-stone path to the cottage.

Daddy. That had been James's idea, as had been this house with the annexed cottage and their no-fuss wedding.

A week after the dramatic events last summer, James had invited Madeleine to London. Her only reservation was leaving Emily yet again in her grandparents' care and abusing their kindness, but this argument was immediately quashed by Aniela's rigid decision in the matter.

'You're going. Full stop. Do any of us look unhappy or abandoned at the prospect of your absence for a couple of days? No! You owe it to James, poor man. Always having to endure gooseberries around him!'

This was true. The much-desired privacy was unachievable between their two houses in Leicester. With members of both their families ever present, the only time together that they could have was in public places like the cinema or a pub. A room in a hotel was tempting, but Madeleine cast this thought aside, feeling cheapened by the very idea. Somehow, a stay in James's own flat felt like the right thing to do. She took a train to London on that Friday evening and was met by James at St Pancras.

His flat in Putney was an open-plan room with only the bedroom with its ensuite bathroom separated from the rest by a door. It was half-open when she arrived and Madeleine glimpsed a double-bed with pristine white linen, the ironing folds still sharp, the walls and the carpet in palest cream.

'I love it here!' Madeleine's admiration was spontaneous. The flat was bright and airy, all items placed tidily in their designated places: books, magazines, a portable radio, a few decorative pieces, a silver tankard, a wooden sculpture of a kingfisher, a slim grey-and-mauve marbled glass vase and the crystal paperweight she had brought James from Poland. The white walls were a perfect background for watercolours of birds and Cornwall landscapes cleverly grouped for best effect. 'You've thought of everything! Was this all your own idea?'

He laughed, amused, taking her weekend bag into the bedroom. There was just one photograph on the top of the bookcase. Madeleine came closer. It was of James's family, when Josh looked about three, James a lanky teenager, Jean laughing, her much longer and darker hair blown away from her face and her husband, Madeleine guessed, the boys' father, a tall, slim man with curly hair like Josh's, a wide grin and his arm around Jean's shoulders. The background was of a seashore and green-topped cliffs in the distance.

'I guess this was Cornwall?' Madeleine said, as James came closer.

'Yes. The last holiday we spent together.' And, as if anticipating Madeleine's apologetic reaction, he added quickly, 'It's all right, Madeleine! It doesn't make me sad; it's my favourite photo. Make yourself at home.' He indicated the sofa that faced the television, but she moved with him towards the kitchen area, where part of the worktop jutted out to form a small dining table. It was already set for two and an open bottle of red wine was airing.

'I think this will be just right,' James said, pouring her and himself a glass each. He switched on the oven and joined her on the settee. 'Been slaving over it all day!' His smile was mischievous, his sparkling eyes full of fun. 'Good old M&S! Will be ready in a tick!'

It was surreal sitting with James alone on the sofa, sipping wine, with no one getting in the way, with all the recent dramas pushed to the back of her mind, as a carefree weekend stretched ahead of her. Anticipation bubbled like champagne inside her.

'I feel like a child on Christmas Eve,' she said candidly, and he laughed, his genuine happy laugh. He put his glass down, took hers out of her hand and placed it next to his, then he kissed her on the lips, hugging her close and hard as if making sure to never let her go. She loved the taste and the clean scent of him; she loved the feel of his body against hers; she loved the moment; she did not want it to end.

They stopped kissing at some point to get their breaths back. His gaze travelled all over her with undisguised tenderness.

'I've got so much to tell you, Madeleine. I've got so many plans. I hope you'll like them!'

'I can't wait!' She echoed his mood.

'We'll eat first. I want you to feel good and comfortable and be easily persuaded by my propositions. Tell me about your week while our meal is cooking.'

They chatted easily about the everyday things from their past week, against some soft music that James had switched on his CD player. When the cooker's timer pinged, James invited Madeleine to sit at the table, and insisted serving all by himself, stressing that this was her night off from all her chores and duties.

His choice of food was excellent: beef in red wine, new potatoes with a mixture of baby vegetables. The delicious tiramisu finished off the meal perfectly. James pushed his empty bowl aside, rested his hands on the table and sat up straight, his features alive with what he was about to say.

'Madeleine, tomorrow...' He paused, his expression reflecting the torrent of thoughts in his mind. 'Tomorrow... I have plans for tomorrow, but only if you agree to my question first...'

'Go on…' she said slowly. If only he knew that just looking at him and being so close to him was happiness enough for her.

He clasped her hand in both his.

'Madeleine, will you marry me?' His eyes were as earnest and direct as always, with a hint of pleading and hope. She did not blink, just stared back, her mind processing the words she'd just heard. Then her eyes moistened.

'I think I'm going to cry.'

'Don't cry, Madeleine, just say yes.' He picked up her hand and pressed it to his lips, still looking at her, waiting for her answer.

'Of course it's a yes, James. Nothing could make me happier. But… I'm so nervous. It's all happening so quickly…'

He shook his head.

'What's the point of waiting? You over there in Leicester, me over here. No place of our own. So, I've been thinking. Let's start with tomorrow. Let's go into town and choose an engagement ring. Then we'll start looking for a house.' Her lips parted simply with astonishment, but he, forestalling an interruption, continued hastily. 'I think Market Harborough would be a good place for us. You'd still be close to Leicester and I could commute. It's only an hour by train. What do you think?'

She was overwhelmed, but one thought jumped out immediately: what about Aniela and Bronek? She could never leave them after everything they had done for her and Emily.

As if guessing her thoughts, James's face softened in a slow, knowing smile.

'Don't worry about Aniela and Bronek. I'll be looking for a property with an annexe. They can stay with us as often and as long as they wish to.'

She shook her head in disbelief.

'James… you are so…' There did not seem enough superlatives to describe him.

'Practical?' he prompted.

'It's a wonderful idea, but will Bronek and Aniela agree?'

'Try them. It will be like their second home. They can come and go as they please and stay as long as they want. It will be like a preparation for the time when they need support. Hopefully, it may never happen, but if it does it won't be such a big wrench for either of them.'

Madeleine was overcome with wonder at James's forward thinking, and above all with deep gratitude.

'James.' She shook her head slowly. 'You've thought of everything. How can I ever…?'

'Just marry me, Madeleine,' he interrupted with a laugh. She was fired with enthusiasm.

'James, I've got savings too. We'll look for a house big enough for your mum and Josh to stay with us whenever they want.'

'Of course we will.' He sounded happy and amused. 'We'll work it out between us.'

'There's just one more thing.' Her mind was like a ping-pong ball. 'What will Janusz and Beata think? I wouldn't want them to think that I've high-jacked their parents permanently, after living with them for seven years.'

Beata and Janusz visited regularly a few weekends every year, Janusz taking leave from his hospital in Dublin and Beata flying over from the British Forces base near Bielefeld in Germany. Their kindness, almost parental, had surprised Madeleine when they saw her for the first time, and she would have forgiven them for resenting her unexpected arrival in their elderly parents' lives. Their concern for her and equally their pride in her achievements had remained unwavering over the years, which always baffled Madeleine, yet not without a feeling of gratitude and a sense of belonging. Whenever she needed reassurance, she would raise this point with Aniela.

'Magda,' Aniela would tell her in her practical, matter-of-fact way, 'I know my children well. Even though they don't say so openly, I know they worry about us getting older, and, with them living abroad, they wouldn't be able to come straight away if anything happened to either of us. Your presence here gives them peace of mind. But, apart from that, I believe they are genuinely very fond of you. They only have to think about their own children finding themselves in your situation, and you've shown them such determination. How could they possibly resent you in any way?'

James thought the same.

'If they'd had any objections to your living with their parents, they'd have said so at the very beginning. I guess they were rather relieved that you were here to keep an eye on things. At the same time, there is no reason why Aniela and Bronek should not decide things for themselves. When we find a suitable house, they can view it with us and then make up their own minds. We can do the same with Janusz and Beata when they visit next time.'

Madeleine clasped James's hand in both of hers and brushed it against her cheek.

'James, I can't believe how kind you are to me.'

Gently, he pulled her hand back to him and kissed it.

'It's simple. I love you.' He smiled. 'Let's start looking for a house straight away. Let's get married and move in. Be together, at long last. In one place.'

'That's exactly what I want too, James. It's just… I can't believe my luck. I could never imagine being so happy. And I'm so afraid that something will go wrong and all this will be snatched from me.'

He got up, came to her side of the table and opened his arms to her. She stood up too and leaned into his embrace. It felt comforting and totally safe pressed against him.

'Madeleine.' He spoke into the side of her face, his breath warm against her skin. 'You've had enough adversities to last you a life time. It's time now to turn over a new leaf and start enjoying your life. Don't worry in advance about what may happen, because it may not and all your worrying will have been for nothing. And when things sometimes do go wrong, isn't it better to be left with memories of all the good things that you've had, than regrets that you've not made the most of good opportunities?' He leaned his head back to look at her. She nodded.

'You'll have to teach me, James, to stop being such a worry-guts.'

'With pleasure!' he assured her, smiling, then more seriously he added, 'There's one more thing. I'd love to adopt Emily.'

*

And so, all the 'to do' matters in James's plan were ticked off as they were completed. A suitable property was found on the outskirts of Market Harborough within two months: a solidly built Edwardian house, double-fronted, with gables and bay windows, spacious high-ceilinged rooms, surrounded by ample grounds, but, most importantly, with an adjoining small cottage separated from the main house by a stepping-stone footpath. This had been tastefully modernised and on inspecting it Aniela had pronounced it perfect for her diminishing energies in housework.

They had feared Bronek's opposition to their plan (he was sentimentally attached to all his old things and routines and resented changes), but he surprised them all. After the 'accident' had demolished the greater part of his allotment, he had lost all enthusiasm for it. He had returned to it only once more, accompanied by Aniela and Madeleine, but only to collect his gardening tools and belongings. Even though he appeared to understand that it had been Zden and not a Russian spy who was killed in the freak accident, he said he no longer felt safe there, without the wall to protect him from prying eyes.

To everyone's relief, on being taken to his proposed holiday home annexed to Madeleine and James's property, he saw the potential straight away of transforming the strip of land closest to the cottage into a vegetable plot and a flower garden. Trimming the hedges that

311

surrounded the entire property, mowing the lawn and pruning the fruit trees in the orchard were just the kind of jobs, he had declared, that would keep him active and healthy until he was a hundred. He had been impatient in the winter months to put his plans into action, and, as soon as the air and the earth warmed up, his and Aniela's stays at the cottage became ever longer.

Presently, Madeleine screens her eyes from the sun, looks up from her book and across to the far end of the garden: everything around her, the cut lawn, the colourful borders, the trimmed hedges, the orchard spilling out with the fruit trees testifies to Bronek's enthusiasm and dedicated regular care. Her chest swells with happiness for him. The allotment disaster, which, for a while, appeared to crush him, is now a less frequently mentioned subject, as he revells in his newly created vegetable plot, and his beautiful flower garden that produces different varieties each month. He loves taking the Barskis and the Demskis round and showing off. They visits more frequently now, since Aniela and Bronek's stay in the cottage has become almost permanent over the summer months.

Janusz and Beata had been over in October and then in March again, in addition to being guests at the wedding. Before their October visit, Madeleine had worried about their possible reaction to her idea of holding on to their parents after her move to her own house. To her great relief, they were enchanted with her idea of a holiday cottage for Bronek and Aniela, but rather surprised at Madeleine's wish to make this arrangement a permanent thing.

'Madeleine,' Beata had said, when they had a moment on their own. 'There's no need for you and James to do any of this. Our parents are our responsibility, and we'll make sure they get every assistance from us, when they are no longer capable of leading independent lives.'

'I know all that,' Madeleine assured her, 'and please believe me, Beata, with me it's not for a moment a question of duty or responsibility: I'm doing this because I really want to. Apart from my Aunt Emilia, they were the kindest people in my life. I love them like my very own grandparents. Emily would be bereft to be separated from them.'

Beata was thoughtful, then her features softened and she gave Madeleine a warm, motherly hug.

'Bless you, Magda. You're a treasure. But remember, any problem at any time, and you must let us know. You must never struggle on your own. We are their children. We love them and we would never wish to neglect any support that we owe them.'

Madeleine and James were married on the Saturday before Christmas. It was a no-fuss wedding at the Polish Church, with only the families and close friends attending. James wore a dark suit and Madeleine a chiffon dress with a matching silk jacket in dusty pink. Mark was naturally his best man and Julie was asked to stand in for Natalia, who was unable to visit them until the following Easter together with Szymon.

Madeleine's father and his wife, Adela, flew over for a few days, much to Madeleine's delight and secret apprehension as to whether he'd be able to keep all his remarks to himself. He proved to be a super-generous guest, showering Aniela and Bronek with a mountain of gifts. On meeting James for the first time, he shook his hand with macho vigour and expressed his approval of Madeleine's choice with unabashed superiority of a master assessing his apprentice. Madeleine squirmed, but James laughed heartily and promised to cherish her father's words of wisdom. After that first cringeworthy encounter, they all got on well for the rest of their stay, especially with her father's wife, Adela, who was gentle in speech and gentle in manner.

Beata came over for a long weekend in the company of her handsome husband, Sebastian, and their two sons, both following in their father's footsteps into the military career, Tim an engineer in electronics and Jeremy a vet. A little older than Madeleine, they had reminded her of her colleagues she had left behind at home, when she had met them for the first time. They had accompanied their mother on one of her regular visits to Aniela and Bronek, and at first Madeleine was nervous and wary of them. She was wary of all men at that time, bar one. She trusted only Bronek. But, before long, Tim and Jeremy disarmed her with their irrepressible good humour, constant ribbing of each other and surprising gentleness towards her. Beata must have primed them well, Madeleine guessed. After that, whenever the boys accompanied their parents, it was a time enjoyed by everyone, not least by herself in her quiet manner.

Janusz's girls too, Elle and Sophie, had shown her much natural goodwill right from the beginning, in their own individual ways. A few years older than Madeleine, they were already working when she had materialised out of the blue in their grandparents' lives. Elle was the PA to the managing director of a pharmaceutical company. Tall and slim, immaculately groomed, fastidiously tidy, she was horrified at Madeleine's struggle to juggle time between childcare, studying and a part-time job. She was a compulsive organiser, and often disappointed when Madeleine was unable to follow her well-meant advice. Sophie was fun to have around. Smaller and freckled with a mop of red hair, she could have looked like one of the children she taught at a primary school. The times when the family were over for a visit from Dublin, she would organise the others to baby-sit, while she dragged Madeleine out to the cinema or just for a train journey to Nottingham or Birmingham. And though reluctant each time, Madeleine had to agree that a few hours out in Sophie's carefree company made her feel like herself again. They all came to Madeleine and James' wedding, Janusz, Elle and Sophie, and their beautiful mother, Angela, of the Titian hair and Irish blue eyes.

Madeleine did not know any of James's relatives, but, as expected, they proved to be genteel, elegantly mannered and beautifully spoken: Jean's sister and her husband from York, their three married children with their spouses, James's father's two brothers and their wives, and their married children. Madeleine had assured them all, when she met them at the hotel the night before, that she would make it her resolution in the New Year to invite them all individually in turn, so she could get to know them better.

They had all sat together in church with Jean and Josh, who were accompanied by their best friends on Madeleine's insistence, so they would not feel outnumbered by the Polish contingent.

The Barskis and the Demskis sat in the front row at the church with Aniela and Bronek, and Emily dressed in her new red coat and a red beret with a pom-pom.

The Polish priest spoke warmly to the congregation in English, conducting parts of the wedding ceremony in Polish, when the formulated questions required only one-word answers from James: 'Tak.' James kept his expression solemn throughout, but his eyes smiled every time they met Madeleine's eyes.

She had asked the priest to say a few words of thanks on her behalf to Mrs Demska, who was instrumental in introducing Madeleine to the Hammond family. Mrs Demska coloured with pleasure and grew a few magical centimetres in stature.

Afterwards, there was a reception in a country hotel, where celebrations and music continued late into the night. Madeleine still enjoys vivid memories of her wedding day in minute detail and likes to relive the joyful encounters with each of the wedding guests.

*

Presently she hears excited prattle and Bronek's deeper voice. She looks up from her book to see the trio walking towards her, Bronek in his slightly stooping manner and the girls skipping beside him. He stops and they stop to study something on his open palm. It is a red admiral. Emily and Karishma are a picture of concentration with their raised hands and their feet on tip-toes.

The butterfly takes off and they walk onto the terrace and form a shadow around her.

'Offerings from my little nursery.' Bronek gives a self-satisfied grin and places a basket at her feet. It is filled with a variety of vegetables and balancing on top there are tomatoes, radishes, a lettuce and a cucumber.

'That's wonderful, Grandpa,' Madeleine thanks him. 'Have you got time to stop for a cup of tea?' Emily and Karishma jump up and down and Bronek looks as if he'd like to stay.

'I better not,' he says. 'I can't remember if Aniela's expecting me to do anything else. I'd better go and ask.'

Madeleine sits up.

'Grandpa, come together later on,' she invites. 'It's such a beautiful evening; we must make the most of this weather while it lasts. We'll have a drink later on, here on the terrace. Your favourite wine. Any time after eight?'

His expression brightens. From his breast pocket, he gets out his little note book and a pencil.

'I better write it down. Then I'll be sure of telling Aniela everything.' They wait until he's made a note. He looks up with a smile. 'Aniela will love it too.'

The girls wave him off, and Madeleine watches him walk away in his slow, unhurried manner.

'Mama, is there still time to play in the tree house before dinner?' Emily jumps up and down.

'Ten more minutes.' Madeleine shows her the hands on her watch.

When Emily and Karishma disappear up the chestnut tree in their playhouse, Madeleine gets up slowly, the weight of her bump making it awkward to move gracefully. She straightens herself and rubs her back before feeling the movement in her belly. They know it is a boy. She and James have already chosen names for him, their fathers' – Jonathan and Adam.

She walks indoors through the wide-open double door and across the lounge. An appetising aroma of stew permeates the hall as she approaches the kitchen. Everything is ready for the evening meal, the set table, the drinks, the salad. She only has to boil the pasta now.

She hears the crunch of the car tyres on the gravel. Through the side window she watches James arrive, switch off the engine, come out of the car. He turns, knowing she is watching him. His face breaks into a wide smile as he walks towards her.